THE FARMINGTON COMMUNITY LIBRARY
FARMINGTON HILLS BRANCH
32737 West Twelve Mile Road
Farmington Hills, MI 48334-3302

W9-BCW-527

MAR 23 2007

30036009515592

THE WILLOW FIELD

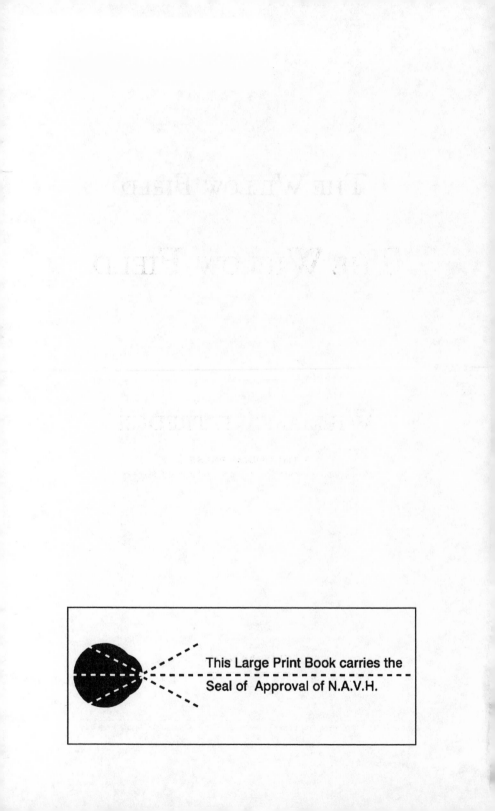

This Large Print Book carries the
Seal of Approval of N.A.V.H.

THE WILLOW FIELD

WILLIAM KITTREDGE

THORNDIKE PRESS

An imprint of Thomson Gale, a part of The Thomson Corporation

Detroit • New York • San Francisco • New Haven, Conn. • Waterville, Maine • London

Copyright © 2006 by William Kittredge.

Grateful acknowledgment is made to Wesleyan University Press for permission to reprint an excerpt from "A Blessing" from *The Branch Will Not Break* by James Wright. Copyright © 1963 by James Wright. Reprinted by permission of Wesleyan University Press, www.wesleyan.edu/wespress.

Thomson Gale is part of The Thomson Corporation.

Thomson and Star Logo and Thorndike are trademarks and Gale is a registered trademark used herein under license.

ALL RIGHTS RESERVED

This is a work of fiction. Names, characters, places, and incidents either are the product of the author's imagination or are used fictitiously. Any resemblance to actual persons, living or dead, events, or locales is entirely coincidental.

Thorndike Press® Large Print Reviewers' Choice.

The text of this Large Print edition is unabridged.

Other aspects of the book may vary from the original edition.

Set in 16 pt. Plantin.

LIBRARY OF CONGRESS CATALOGING-IN-PUBLICATION DATA

Kittredge, William.
   The willow field / by William Kittredge.
     p. cm.
   ISBN-13: 978-0-7862-9353-7 (hardcover : alk. paper)
   ISBN-10: 0-7862-9353-5 (hardcover : alk. paper)
   1. Cowboys — Fiction. 2. Ranch life — Fiction. 3. Nevada — Fiction.
  4. Montana — Fiction. 5. Large type books. I. Title.
PS3561.I87W55 2007
813'.54—dc22   2006037597

Published in 2007 by arrangement with Alfred A. Knopf, Inc.

Printed in the United States of America on permanent paper
10 9 8 7 6 5 4 3 2 1

To Annick Smith

And the eyes of two Indian ponies
Darken with kindness.
They have come gladly out of the willows
To welcome my friend and me.
We step over the barbed wire into the
   pasture
Where they have been grazing all day,
   alone.
They ripple tensely, they can hardly con-
   tain their happiness
That we have come.
They bow shyly as wet swans. They love
   each other.
There is no loneliness like theirs.
            — James Wright, *from* "A Blessing"

PROLOGUE

Under a whiter summer moon, the glaciated stone peaks in the Bitterroot Mountains looked ghostly and unreal above the meadowland valley where grizzly and elk and cougar and herds of Salish horses once roamed. But summer was gone, and those cliffs had vanished into the storm.

Eliza Benasco, a gray-eyed woman of Scottish descent, her tangle of hair white like a flag, stepped onto her stonework terrace with a porcelain mug of steaming coffee. The snow went on falling. There would be more snow, and then summers to run. She had always loved the notion of life as an undulation.

At nineteen, Eliza had married Rossie Benasco in this house, her house, a redwood structure designed in the middle style of Frank Lloyd Wright — black and white tiles on the kitchen floor, hardwood Stickney furnishings with leather cushions, and fireplaces built of worn stones gathered from Kanaka Creek, a trout stream glinting in gray light through a grove of aspen. The house had been built by her father and mother in the 1920s, when they moved west from Chicago. But they were gone to Scottish heaven. The house was hers, and had been, these decades.

Eliza had planned to educate Rossie. They would live as a secret society. But after he had slipped the wedding ring onto her finger and kissed her properly, after the festivities and the toasting, when they were alone in their bedroom, she had smiled like a crazy girl and lifted the skirts of her wedding dress to show red garters and long white thighs — and that she'd not worn underpants. "You sometimes can't expect," he had said without smiling, "what commotion you'll find." How could she not love this serious young man saying *commotion* as he touched her?

The next morning, bundled under the Navajo rug thrown over her feather comforter, Rossie had whispered for some unaccountable reason that this snuggling reminded him of hiding in thickets along the Truckee River behind the mansions on the west side of Reno, only a block or so from his mother's house. Too young for school, he'd snake through dim trails in the willows and brittle late-summer grass to watch muskrats slink along the banks of fishing holes and find matted-down nests that stank of foxes and garbage-eating raccoons, where the men his mother called hobos slept. To Eliza, this sounded unclean, and she shuddered. Not until he whispered of galloping through the meadows on sunup mornings, gathering the great Neversweat herd of work teams, did she understand that he was trying to convey to her the degree to which he now — in the house, with her family — felt safe. How could she not cherish this man who spoke of her as the find of his life?

She had been shameless. "Why don't you?" she'd whispered.

"You, Eliza," an elegant widow said, so many years after. "Rossie, chasing you, isn't that the story?" The woman smiled like a conspirator. "Your own horseman, tilting away?"

"Sort of." Eliza hesitated. "Not altogether."

■ ■ ■ ■ ■

PART ONE
THE BOY GOES OUT

■ ■ ■ ■ ■

EARLY HORSES

Horses, a junior high teacher told Rossie's class, were an ancient symbol of friendship. "Horses are the amiable creature." This was the spring Rossie became preoccupied with an incessant, secret urge to jack off that disturbed and frightened him. At his mother's kitchen table, as she weeded in her backyard garden, he sat nicking his left index finger over and over with her sharp cutlery and tried to ease his nerves by imagining the selfless companionability of old horses nuzzling at one another. It was a way to think the world was easy to live in. Training horses to ride and to pull chariots, he read in his mother's *Encyclopedia Britannica,* was vital to the power of a civilization called Assyria. "Power," his mother said, wrinkling her nose. "Imagine. Your father would say it was the freedom to ride off."

When Rossie turned fifteen — gangling and black-haired and shaving every morning at the insistence of his father — he gave up on Reno Public High School and drifted off to sit on high-board fences at the Western Pacific stockyards. He helped out with the gates as men jammed and cursed the bawling cattle until a whiskery man named Fritzy Brewster gave him a chance horseback. "Kid," he said, "a sensible boy don't work in the dirt. That's for farmers. A sensible boy stays on his horse." Up on a bay gelding Rossie jostled steers and heifers into chutes as Brewster uncapped a beer, sat on a fence, and watched.

Rossie's mother, Katrina, when she discovered he hadn't been to school since March, sat him down at the worktable in her clean, tile-floored kitchen. "What is it you most like about shit?" she asked.

Rossie went defiantly blank-eyed, and she shook her head.

"I wonder," she said, "if your father is going to let you do as you please."

Nito Benasco supervised casino gambling at the elegant new Riverside, George Wingfield's modern gambling and resort hotel on the banks of the Truckee River, just a five-minute walk north on Virginia Street from the Washoe County Court House. Women waiting out their weeks in residence before divorce paraded the hotel lobby in spangled cowgirl outfits, heading out for rides with buckaroos. Divorcées at the Riverside, Katrina said, were fools who loved dressing up in gowns, to sip at martinis and watch roulette. Women with college degrees brought books in their suitcases and were likely to stay in a house like hers, where they could be at home with other civilized creatures.

"So," Nito said, when Katrina told him about the stockyards. "What's wrong with school? A man with no education is dead in the brain."

"Algebra," Rossie said. "X equals b. They teach you to be nobody."

"You think the stockyards is somebody?"

This, Rossie knew, was a moment to be faced carefully. Nito dressed in dark suits and spent his hours standing back, watching the cards and the roll of the dice and ivory balls spinning on the wheels. He would say a quiet thing to a white-shirted dealer, then smile as he went over to the drunk at a blackjack table, or the loud fellow from Pennsylvania or Idaho who was running out of money. "We don't worry," Nito would say, "do we?" his eyes shining and his accurate hands riffling the cards as if he loved them or suspected irregularity. "Making trouble. That would be a shame.

17

We're a luxury liner, on the banks of the Truckee." This was his joke. The game never stops, not even for trouble. It's always here.

"I read books." Rossie drifted through summer evenings on his mother's screened-in veranda above the Truckee, deep in Zane Grey and the Charlie Russell book about life on the Montana frontier. He read the books the women had brought and left behind, *The Cossacks* and *Youth* by Count Leo Tolstoy and *Giants in the Earth* by a Norwegian whose name he couldn't pronounce, and *My Ántonia* by Willa Cather.

"Who kissed the girl? That's what those books are about," Nito said. "You need to know real things. That's what school is for. But you don't like school." He smiled softly, like he had discovered a cure. "You should be with experts. We'll fix you up." He made calls on the telephone, and three days later Rossie had a job as wrango boy on the Neversweat, one of the vast Nevada empire ranches, on the Horse Fork of the Humboldt River beyond Winnemucca. Nito bought Rossie a classical Hamley saddle made in Pendleton — a secondhand rig with worn bucking rolls and a high cantle — and he drove Rossie northeast across Great Basin deserts in his immaculate black Chevrolet. Clouds were massing in hammerheads above the lava-strewn Bloody Run Mountains. Sweeps of thin rain would evaporate over the alkaline playa of the Black Rock Desert before reaching the ground. Past Winnemucca, the macadam turned to graded gravel, and alkaline dust drifted behind them in a rooster tail. Nito slapped the palm of his right hand on the dark velvet seat cushion and laughed at the print it left in the white dust. "She'll clean up."

Out front of the Neversweat bunkhouse, they unloaded the Hamley saddle and a snaffle-bit bridle bought the evening before in a Virginia Street pawnshop, then Rossie's clothes and bedding: a Hudson Bay blanket, flannel sheets, a pillow without a case, denim shirts, wool socks and long-johns, and old pairs of Levi's. Rossie's shaving gear and a bar of Lava soap, two towels, and wash cloths were rolled up and strapped together inside a canvas tarp with the bedding.

Nito eyed Rossie as if estimating a distance, then shook his hand for the first time ever. "You're where you want to be," he said. "You are going to be lonely. But it cures."

Nito had come from Bilbao, Spain's largest seaport, a Basque city on the northern coast. His parents had died of influenza in

1905, when he was twenty. Nito's eyes shined whenever he told this story to the women who stayed in Katrina's house.

"My father's dream was that I should be a dealer in Biarritz, over in France with the rich. A Gypsy named Caro was teaching me cards. Caro taught me tricks. But there was no chance in Biarritz. I would be a servant. Caro told me go to America, so I sat in New York rooms and practiced cards all night and learned this language and here I am." Nito would look around to the women awaiting divorce. Loneliness, he would say, cures.

"This might be your road," he said to Rossie as twilight came over northern Nevada and the Neversweat. "But you can come home. You are always our family. Your mother and I will also be lonely."

"You think I'm going to quit?"

"This might not be the right thing. You'll know."

THE BONE-HANDLED
KNIFE

Standing beside his gear, Rossie Benasco began to see the terms of his new life as his father drove away. He was alone. In his soul he was quaking.

There was nothing to do but commence moving in. As he dropped his bedroll onto a World War I military cot in a bunkhouse room nearest to the bullpen with its barrel stove, Mattie Flynn showed herself. Got up in a shirt buttoned at the cuff and shit-heeled boots, red hair stuffed under her sweat-rimmed hat, this Mattie was not some momma's sweetheart. Freckled and wind-burned, she was a horseback girl, her long-fingered hands scabbed and callused. "You don't sleep there," she said.

"Good as any. They're all of them empty."

"They been gone eight days," she said. "That's where Francis Church sleeps. He's worked here twenty-three years and he sleeps there. You better get your junk out of

21

there. You get the last room down the hall." When he was stowed away, she told him to come and eat. "There's nobody here but me and Rudy. He's cooking. The rest of them are gone to the desert."

Old Rudy limped around and fried Rossie a patch of steak and two eggs. Mattie watched while Rossie went at the food.

"She's going to eat you alive, boy," Rudy said. "She's done telling me what to do. It's your turn."

Mattie showed him the room above the kitchen where her father, Slivers Flynn, lived when he wasn't on the desert with the cowhands. Rossie opened a clasp knife with a white bone handle, copper rivets, and a long, thin blade so often sharpened it was fragile like a razor and sharp enough to shave hair off his forearm. Mattie said it was a knife with history. Slivers had put it up to save. "That knife," she said. "It's retired. He says that knife has done its work. He packed it for eleven years."

It had been atop a chest of drawers, out where anybody could see, beside a deck of playing cards still in the cellophane. When Mattie looked away, Rossie slid it into his pocket and she was on him so quick he wondered if this was some test he'd failed. "I don't lie. He knows it," she said. "He's going to know you stole that knife. Your ass is done for around here unless you give it to me, and I put it back."

Rossie fished the knife from his pocket, and she laid it beside the playing cards.

"I knew you was going to steal it," she said. "I'd steal it if I was you. I got a secret on you. If you knew one on me we could cut our fingers and mix blood if we wanted to. But we don't. This is our first secret."

HOG ISLAND

Mattie's mother had died on a summer afternoon when she was eleven. Houseflies and yellow jackets, she told Rossie, walked the window sills in the rooms where they lived, upstairs in the whitewashed cookhouse. The pains of cancer drove her mother to fold Mattie in her bony arms and curl up in her bed and howl. "I don't remember," Mattie said. "I don't want to hear another thing about it."

Even a boy so short on experience as Rossie gave her credit for not being able to bear recalling her mother's bedsores or that howling in the afternoon. We all got to deal with dying someday, Rossie told himself. It was the thing he'd known since he was a boy studying stars in their configurations beyond the moon. Some distant day, he already knew, he would face great trouble in himself, trying to escape the thought that he was only another creature running for cover and never getting there.

Slivers and his hired hands had raised Mattie. "She's a horseback kid," Slivers would say, turning his eyes down to his hands, thumbs together like they were at war against one another, "ever since I went single." Mattie dressed like a cow-camp tramp rather than some girl, riding the greasewood deserts twenty miles out to the South Fork of the Owyhee and never showing she was tired or even thirsty. There was not much horse work she couldn't handle, nor talk she hadn't heard as she tended a branding fire or drove a feed-wagon team in the overcast light of winter. Mattie was willing to stare the devil in the eye, and Rossie dogged after her on a Roman-nosed bay named Snip as she galloped along willow-lined alleyways between sloughs. "You got a man's saddle," she said, "but you're horse-back like a schoolboy."

After the desert branding crew came back, she'd chide him at the dinner table. "Look at him eat that spinach," she'd say, that sort of thing — until one time Slivers shut her up.

"You ought to watch your mouth," he said. "Rossie is going to get tired of acting like a kid. He's going to kick your ass. I'll be thinking it's good work."

"The big old man," Mattie said, and she gathered her dish of rhubarb pie, and went to finish eating out on the side porch and away from everyone.

But then she'd ask Rossie about Reno, what it was like to try kissing girls in movie theaters, if some of the girls went for it and kissed back. Did Rossie go downtown and watch his father deal cards to the rich men? She would tilt her head, trying not to make fun of him, as if she really wanted to know what it was like.

When he was home for a visit, Rossie's mother watched him finish up a load of breakfast pancakes and fried eggs in her immaculate kitchen. "Are you just being stubborn? Your father and I thought the desert would cure you. We thought you'd come home."

"Feeling fine," he said, licking the syrup off his fork, smiling at her, lying a little, a boy sometimes sick for his mother and this talk.

"Well, then you can help me in the garden. Buckaroos help their mothers in the garden."

On a summer morning in 1933, in the shade of willows beside Hill Camp Springs,

Mattie bit at her lip, took the back of his neck in one of her strong hands, and leaned in and kissed him. Rossie didn't keep his hands to himself, and she didn't stop him. There was not a thing to it in the beginning but the fucking. They'd gone vacant-eyed and luminous. The lean, cigar-smoking woman who cooked for the haying crew took to asking Mattie about her "lovey-dovey," and though Mattie acted like she might spear the cook with her fork while the hay-hands smirked, she told Rossie she didn't care what anybody thought. "Why should we give a shit? You and me, we don't know no better. We're kids." She wanted to tell her father, the king-of-the-mountain cowman at the Neversweat, that they were in love.

A champion of the world, one of those legends, Slivers Flynn was thick in his chest and narrow-hipped, with a long spade chin, high cheekbones, and huge, quiet hands. The men who worked for him, as they put away beer by the case on the porch of the North Fork Café on Sunday afternoons, talked about Slivers and balance and how he "rode them bang-tailed horses like they was rocking chairs." He had won the 1911 saddle bronc contest in Madison Square Garden, but by 1918, home from the war in

27

France, Slivers had quit thinking about the rodeo and instead gentled horses around northern Nevada on contract. "Sweet horses," he would say, "and damned few people. That's the deal. I got out of their war in one piece but I'll run for the mountains if they try sending me again." When the summer branding started in 1921, he was put in charge of hiring and firing at the Neversweat. Nobody in their right mind would defy him and not expect consequences, but Slivers Flynn was as honest as God. Why shouldn't he be the boss?

"Love?" Slivers said when Mattie broke the news. "Who don't know that?" So the fat was in the fire. "You be careful with it. You're not playground children." He tossed Rossie a pack of rubbers from the drugstore in Winnemucca. "There's more. I bought four dozen. You use a new one, every time. You run out, you ask for more. We don't need babies. Not at this point." He told them to go fix up the slant roof at Hog Island, a one-room cabin sided with tarpaper on a lava-rock outcropping where a spring bubbled up alongside a withering orchard of apple and pear trees planted by early settlers. "You figure," Slivers said. "Water coming cold from the mountains. Miles and miles of cracks in the rock."

Hog Island was named when Watson and McGregor, a Scottish émigré landowning and livestock-raising combine, bought seven thousand acres of meadow along the Horse Fork, the core property at the Neversweat. Henry McGregor set up his hunting camp beside that cold spring. His men ranged out into the tules with rifles, shot feral hogs and dragged their carcasses into sloughs so the bones wouldn't litter the meadows, leaving the meat to coyotes and circling birds. Soon the place was known as Hog Island.

"You got the winter," Slivers said to Rossie, wiping crumbs off the table with a huge broken-fingered hand. "Nothing to do but a few colts. Give it a try. Ever'body did. There's no wages. There is not going to be, not in these times, but you're eating. That's better than some people got."

Mattie and Rossie played house at Hog Island through the winter, until it was time to go out and camp alongside the cook wagon, moving every day while driving the mother cows to their desert range. "The little woman worn to the quick this morning?" cowhands would ask, windburned lips flecked with chewed tobacco. Mattie would grin. "At least I'm not going to die horny, like you assholes."

One afternoon the joking ended. A

stocking-footed horse called Banjo charged onto a ridge populated by rattlesnakes that had emerged from their rock-pile den to bask in new spring warmth. Their buzzing agitation startled that Banjo horse sideways in a set of stumbling moves. Rossie lost his right side stirrup, hung up in the other one, and went down flailing on the rocks. He dangled there bleeding a seep of blood from his left ear, his left foot still in the stirrup and the snakes buzzing all around but none of them striking. Banjo held steady, trembling but locked in place with forelegs set like posts and looking down while Slivers Flynn got Rossie loose and out of there. If that horse had bolted, dragging Rossie across the lava, it would have been the end.

Rossie didn't come back to himself until he was laid on his bedroll inside the line shack at Lone Grave Springs. His eyes opened and he lay silent, lost like a skinned animal and paying no mind even to Mattie as she tried to feed him spoonfuls of navy bean soup before giving it up and lying there, tucked up beside him and shivering. Slivers sent a Mormon man named Brother Handel off on horseback to the ranch. At daylight, while Slivers was out catching horses for the day, Brother Handel came rattling across the desert in Sliver's black

Model T Ford and hauled Rossie and Mattie and their gear to Hog Island, where she nursed him in her rough-handed way. "Slivers said to go with you and plant a garden," Mattie said, when Rossie was into himself, "if I was going to act like a girl." She smiled at this. In a couple of weeks, Rossie was eating from a plate of scrambled eggs, not talking much but mumbling.

"Kid," Slivers told him, "you been better than lucky. You was on the edge of no-man's-land. That Banjo horse stood with them snakes buzzing all around because he saw you in trouble. Could have stampeded and drug you until you was killed before anybody stopped him. A horse can act like a woman, and forgive you damned near anything, even falling off. Nothing you ever done could have earned it. You ought to thank the goodness of horses every morning."

Three weeks after that, Slivers sent Mattie to Winnemucca with the cook to buy staple groceries for the chuck wagon, and he came over to sit on a block of stove wood in the cabin at Hog Island. "Time we got down to brass tacks," he said to Rossie. "Late May, you'll be horseback. Fit enough. But I got a different plan. I got you lined up for job going to Canada, running horses to Calgary from Eagleville. Get you out of the country."

"Out of the country?" Rossie was abruptly angry.

"Best thing that could happen. Time you left that girl alone for a while, to think her thoughts. You been sampling for free but that's at an end. Rightly so." Slivers looked up at Rossie. "You understand?"

"Guess I don't," Rossie said. "You been giving me rubbers. I thought you was happy."

Slivers shook his head. "I give you time. It's used up. You either marry her or not."

"Goddamn. Never thought of this."

"Time you did. She isn't the all-day free-lunch counter."

"Free lunch?" Rossie was abruptly angry. Fuck you Mr. Slivers Flynn, boss of the rodeo, fuck you. "What if I stay here," he said, "do my thinking, and don't take that Canada job?"

"Then you're saying you want to get on with marrying."

"I don't get no choice."

"Not around here."

"What if I'd run off with her."

"Then you'll be somewhere else. Stop and think. That girl is going to get knocked up if you keep on, and that's no good. Stay here, you'll be a married man by June. You'll be another dumb son of a bitch who don't know a thing but how to gather cows out of the brush, and you'll have a mess of red-headed kids, you and Mattie." Slivers shook his head. "You'll be feeling sorry for yourself, and fall to drinking and acting like an asshole. We've seen that one, from the beginning out to the end. It's the shits every time. You're better off seeing some world if you plan on amounting to more than nothing. If it was me, I'd be gone to Canada."

"What if I don't do any of that? Not one thing you say? What if I do as I damn please, stay right here, and keep on chasing down the road with Mattie? That's what I'm likely to be doing."

"Mattie is the only family I'm going to have. You don't treat that girl right, I'm going to kick your ass on a daily basis. Until you see the light." Slivers stood up and stretched like he'd gotten stiff during their talk. "See if you don't think I'm right."

Over the next three nights Rossie and Mattie went on as they had, using three more rubbers. But deep in darkness he lay awake listening to Mattie in her sleep. By the second morning Rossie was thinking that Slivers was right about ending up nothing more than a cowhand with redheaded kids, a fate that seemed like walking off into quicksand. Rossie spent the third night devising a story about how he'd been broken and had healed back into a different boy, how he was owed one summer on the road, and how going away couldn't be explained better than that.

Decades later Rossie would see that night of concocting as a step toward faithlessness. But as they ate breakfast the next morning, and Rossie stared Mattie in the eye, he believed what he was saying. "It's the shits," he said, "but I'm gone, no matter what. It's just one summer."

"I got to think," she said. "I would have died if you died, and I might die if you leave forever. I got to think about that. Dying is not what anybody wants."

The next day she got her clothes and gear together, and moved back to the cookhouse, into the second-story room where her mother died. She ate at a linoleum-topped table in the cookhouse kitchen, sharing chatter with the lean woman who cooked and ignoring long looks from the hay-hands before she went off to work out her days irrigating in the vegetable garden.

Most men would have said that Canada without her was a crazy idea. Mattie had grown into a brilliant creature, tall but not fragile, with thick, red hair in a braid down her back and freckles as large as pennies head to toe. Even after Rossie announced he was leaving, she would make her way through the meadows to Hog Island on a path she'd worn along the tops of sod-and-manure dams spanning the swales and over planks bridging the head gates, while blue-winged teals cut and banked over the swamps.

Still healing, his head slow to give up aching, Rossie would sit on a three-legged stool in the sunlight, braiding riatas from eighty-foot strings of rawhide soaked in washtubs. He couldn't sell those braided ropes — nobody had any money, and anyway, cowhide came free at slaughterhouses all over Nevada. But the braiding felt like work, something he could manage.

Announced by a racket of magpies in the cottonwoods, Mattie would climb into Rossie's bed, curling her long body under his blankets, and roll her cigarettes, playing invulnerable by running her sweet mouth and blowing smoke until she commenced weeping because he was leaving.

The day of Rossie's going she wore a short, home-sewn, green dress that showed off her luminous white and freckled legs. In the palm of her right hand was the bone-handled knife she had that morning stolen from her father's room. She found Rossie constructing a pair of buckskin gloves like the ones he'd once fashioned for women in his mother's house, before Katrina said divorcée women were looking for men and not gloves. His saddle and bridles and chaps were bundled into a burlap sack beside the doorstep, alongside his bedroll in its canvas tarp. He was waiting on his ride, and on his way. The evening before, Mattie had rolled a cigarette and lit it, stared at him a long, green-eyed moment and said, "Adiós, asshole." She'd walked away into twilight across the meadows.

But here she was again, wearing her dress, on a mission to make peace.

"Pretty flowers," he said, careful he didn't smile. "You look like a ready-to-go girl yourself."

"Pretty fucking stupid. Flowers." She was holding out pale field lilies and wild pink roses. "Anyway, there they are."

Rossie kept his eyes on his stitching. "Making you some gloves." He was intent in his work, the left glove inside out while he sewed around the heel of the thumb.

"What I don't need is gloves. I've quit anything where you'd need gloves."

"You're breaking your own heart, pissing

and moaning." He turned the glove right side out and whacked it over his knee. "I never made a mistake on these gloves," he said, getting off the topic of heartbreak.

"I'm done playing boy, then. From here on I'm all girl. What I'm going to do is smile. This morning it's going to be sweet, and that will be the end of that. What I'm going to do is pick another batch of flowers and start over."

She circled out among the lilies and the wild roses on the fence lines while Rossie sat there like he didn't care what came next so long as he got on the road and trying not to look at her in that green dress.

"I thought I'd come over," she said, "and fuck you out of leaving. Now I don't want it. I'm going to the college in Reno. I'm going to learn to be something."

"Shit, just shit. You might go to Reno, but you'll never make it up the hill to that college. You don't even own a book. I never saw you try to read a book. You could be something but it's not going to be a college girl. That's one you're not going to be."

She hurled the flowers and in two running steps caught him with his hands down, landing a right-handed hook that took him off his three-legged stool. Mattie stood panting and rubbed her nose with the back of her fist. "You know what? Hope I broke your head. I don't care where you go." Her lips were tight and thin against her teeth, and her eyes were glassy as she gazed toward the blue-white sky as if like someone — maybe even she, herself — might be up there watching. She ducked her head, lifted her skirt, and dropped the dress onto the grass, leaving herself to face him in pale-green undershorts she had sewn to match the dress. Her whiteness in the light was nothing he could look at.

"What the hell are you doing? What do you think this is? You think you're acting in some movie?"

"Being a woman." Mattie folded her arms across her breasts and looked away. "Tell you what I want. Unstrap that bedroll." She met his eyes.

Fucking was a thing they'd learned to do, but never in the sunlight. Mattie lifted herself so his slide into her was the beginning they'd know. She hooked her legs over his shoulders, and as they moved he let his mind glide until she was sweaty beneath him, panting and not moving.

"I never looked up at the sky before," she said. "The whole empty sky and here we were." She got back into her green dress. "Here's the funny part. I stole something so you'll come back when you've got Canada out of your system." She showed him the pocketknife. "From Slivers."

Rossie opened the long blade and shaved a path of bare skin down his forearm. "I'll be back before the summer's out."

Mattie smiled like she was done with sorrow. "Yeah, you might. If some Indian don't kill you. But this is not something you get over. It don't work that way." Rid of him, she turned for home on her path across the meadows.

THE MADARIAGA HOTEL

Sitting on his bedroll, Rossie waited for his ride to Reno. Oscar Dodson was coming in the Packard he'd repainted a mustard color he called gold. He'd bring cold beer.

They drank it before they made Winnemucca, so Oscar bought another case of A-One, talking all the time as he did when he was drinking, shouting in the wind, not altogether drunk but acting like he wouldn't mind if he was. "You need a ride and I need to blow off the stink. Another summer to run."

By midnight they were in Reno and stalled in a tavern called Whistling in the Dark. Oscar talked about doctors and bought shots of whiskey. Newspapers called him Schoolboy when he was on his three-year run, winning saddle bronc contests from Cheyenne to Fort Worth. But for most of a year Oscar had been wearing a stainless-steel brace belted above his left knee to curve under the instep of his boot. Unable to walk much without it, he was spending his afternoons at lightweight gambling. "A dollar, something to do. You get to chasing the women. That costs money. There I am, gimping around on the dance floor, looking for a rich one."

Rossie wondered what it was like listening to announcers talk about you on the radio. Oscar lit up another Lucky Strike. "For a while I thought nothing could be so easy. But this leg don't heal."

He had made it look like a cinch. Three years older than Rossie, he had been riding rough string at the Neversweat when he won the bareback and saddle-bronc finals at the Labor Day rodeo in Winnemucca. Then he went off to make his fortune. "That boy," Slivers Flynn had said, "is as pretty on a horse as I ever saw." But now Oscar was twenty-two and crippled, nothing to show for his pretty moves but a steel brace and that high-assed automobile in the parking lot.

"When it gets down to selling the Packard," he said, eyeing Rossie, "I'm at the end of my shit, working for wages. You know what I'd do? If I was you? I'd marry that redheaded girl. I'd have Slivers looking out for me. But you're running off so I'll try it.

41

I'll marry her while you're gone if you tell me one thing: how was it?"

Rossie didn't say anything for a long moment. Kiss my ass, he thought. None of what went between Mattie and him was any of Oscar Dodson's affair. He was used goods, Rossie could see it — up to nothing but bullshit and not much but a cripple after all. "That is a sorry fucking plan," he said.

Oscar shook his head. "Didn't guess you'd like hearing about it." He pushed back his chair and went off to the bar.

"What are you going to do up there?" Rossie said. "Admire yourself in the mirror?"

"Better than looking at you."

"Crybaby heart," Rossie said when Oscar came back to the table, "where we going to sleep?"

"On the ground."

And Rossie did. He woke up with his face in the sun as leaves along the southern bank of the Truckee fluttered in the bright morning. Sometime deep in the night while Oscar was trying to bum an after-hours drink from a bartender in a back-alley joint off Virginia Street, Rossie had walked away toward his mother's house, just on the other side of the river. But ringing the doorbell at three in the morning might wake Nito, and then there'd be hell to pay. Whatever happened next Rossie didn't remember, but now, awake on the lawn in front of the Blalock Mansion only half a block from his mother's house, he was stunned and sick. He'd lost his hat.

Light shone in colors off the cut-glass windows around the front door, and Rossie tried out his morning smile. Katrina in her lavender dress and yellow apron, her graying blonde braids curled over her ears as they always were when she was at her morning work, smiled in her way. "Aren't you cute?"

This was her for damned sure, Katrina. "Not much," he said. "You got any coffee?"

"Come here." She pulled him to her and didn't let him duck away from the kiss. This was ancient, his mother, her strong hands. "What you need is water, big glasses of water. Where'd you sleep?"

"Down on some lawn."

"Jesus Christ. Are you going to be a hobo? Are you going to go down to the river and sleep with bums? One of those men could kill you and drag your body back in the bushes and steal all you've got out of your pockets. These are hard times. Some would do it. There's hundreds of them, coming on the railway, riding the tops of cattle cars, camping along the river, stealing and bumming and begging. This is not a ranch back in nowhere."

"No shit," Rossie said. It was an old line she was talking but he knew it wasn't altogether wrong-minded. A black-handed greasy fellow had come out of the willows along the Truckee one afternoon when he was a boy. "Kid," he'd said, voice rasping, "you might as well figure. There are men out here who will fuck you to death, boy like you, right from behind." The man had smiled like that was his own idea. Rossie told Katrina, and that was the end of his summer days along the river. "Lost men," she would say, going off to California. What are they going to find in California? Why don't they go to China?

"You got any coffee?" Rossie asked.

Katrina led him to her stone-floored kitchen at the back of the house, and poured him a big glass of ice water. She watched as he drank, poured coffee thick with cream and two spoons of sugar, and fed him three eggs and fried sausage. "You left that girl," she said. "You watch out. There's only so many. You can miss all the boats."

"What do you think, I should marry her and turn into a cowboy with some pregnant woman?"

"Pregnant?"

"She won't be, not by me."

"You know what you sound like? You sound like a boy trying to sound like an asshole."

Rossie lowered his head. "Lost my hat. What I wonder is how I'm going to amount to anything." He was thinking about how his mother had settled her life in this inherited house and married a Basque gambler. The ease with which she'd let him, her only boy, drift off to the Neversweat. If that wasn't coldhearted, what was?

"If you don't amount to anything?" she said. "That's not to worry about for a long time. You can break your heart on that one."

"I never knew I cared. I just started thinking about it up there braiding ropes."

Katrina stood and cleared his plate. "Your father's sleeping. Where are your things?"

"In that Packard of Oscar's."

"You hope." She studied him and shook her head. "You'll amount to something. Unless you never get over being a fool. You should learn to think. Don't get used to a woman unless you mean to settle. You'll need a place to rest. A good friend you sleep with." She turned on her big smile. "A warm heart and babies. That's in the someday."

Rossie wondered what she really meant as he drifted toward sleep in one of her feather beds in a high-ceilinged room at the back of the house. "You," she'd told him the last time he was home, "you'll be our ranch man." As if each family had a rancher, and that was the Nevada plan. She meant to tell him, he knew, something his father wouldn't, to bed his life in a woman — and in work.

An immaculate blue-striped dress shirt that belonged to his father lay folded on a chair when he awoke. So she'd been in while he slept. After making sure the door was locked, Rossie walked around naked in the room and sneaked a look through curtains to see the divorcées gathering on the slate terrace outside the kitchen for evening cocktails, laughing, midlife women in his mother's house, where his father came and went without paying them much attention. "You don't try to remember their names," Katrina would say, smiling like that was a good thing. Nito would reply that it was like living in a hotel, laughing so as to show he didn't necessarily think that was bad. These woman came on the railroad from the faraway east, and Rossie had grown up listening to their endless talk of returning to shaded streets in Cincinnati and Syracuse and Cambridge. They'd tousle his hair and rub his shoulders and tickle his ribs and go on about how he was handsome. By the time his voice changed Rossie had seen more than one woman weep because a cowboy hadn't come around to say good-bye. He'd learned to spy on them and told boys in his school a thousand jack-off stories about the divorcées. Once he'd said to his mother that these women were like cats, complaining around the kitchen and want-ing to be fed, and she'd slapped him. Then that night she'd gone up to his attic bed-room and sat on the edge of his bed. They're swell, she said. When the legalities finish they go home. They send me Christmas cards. They're interested in another try at life.

Rossie started hot water into the big lion's-claw tub and poured lavender bath salts and laughed at himself and soaked and ran more hot water until his mother was rapping on the door, calling him out for drinks. So he dried with one of her heavy, green towels and combed his hair and took his time buttoning the blue-striped shirt, because this was the first time she'd offered him a shirt that had been worn by his father. Looking in the mirror, Rossie wondered if he was his father's boy.

A horse-faced man had joined the women by the time Rossie made his way out onto the terrace.

"There he is," Katrina said. She brought him a cold drink in a tall glass. "This is my Rossie. Gin. This is his first drink with gin in his mother's house."

Rossie lifted his glass to the women and the horse-faced man, who looked away, as if not quite sure of his part in this moment.

A pale-eyed old woman rested a papery hand on Rossie's shoulder. "I suppose that we should start locking our doors from now on."

"Wouldn't that be wonderful," Katrina said. "What you should do," she said to Rossie, when he was finished with his gin and already feeling it, "is go down to the Riverside and join your father. He's expecting you for dinner. So you get out of here. But come back tonight. You come home for one more night."

The elegant new Riverside, poised beside the river on the west side of Virginia Street, was a hotel for wealthy men and divorcées. Rossie put his hands on his mother's shoulders and smiled down the way he thought a man would smile.

She shook her head. "You think you're a movie star. You want to outsmart some poor girl." She ducked away as he moved to kiss her.

"Katrina," he said. This was a joke. "I'm not Katrina," she said. "I'm your mother."

Decades later he recalled this evening to a reporter in Montana, who studied him through glasses tinted blue. "Those were the days," he told her, "although nobody thought of it that way. I was nineteen years old, had just left my first love to go on down the road. There was my drink of gin in my mother's house and a night with my father. Initiation into the rambling life and enough booze to numb the fearfulness. Two days later I was helping drive two hundred fifty-seven head of saddle horses to Calgary, a boy joining the free men."

"Fear of what?" the young woman asked.

"Bootlessness, too much of it."

"Bootlessness?"

"Freedom," Rossie said. "Sometimes there was more than you wanted. But those were the days. Or so we think."

"What do you really think?"

"I think," Rossie said, "that those were the days."

Rossie found Nito in the art deco lobby of the Riverside, watching as tuxedoed white musicians syncopated their rackety way through "Take the 'A' Train."

Nito touched Rossie on the shoulder, his firm touch. "A fine shirt. Those old fellows, they're playing new music, not worrying about a thing. We could take a lesson." This sounded like an idea his father had been thinking about and waiting to lay out.

"Hell of a shirt," Rossie said. He would fold it carefully the next morning, and tuck it into his bedroll, to travel with.

"Tonight," Nito said, "we're going to Madariaga's."

The Madariaga was a three-story brick and white-frame hotel and rooming house on the eastern fringes of downtown, which served as the unofficial headquarters for Basque culture in northern Nevada. Lifetime bachelors might live there for months when they'd had enough of herding and isolation on the deserts, talking to dogs and sheep. They'd stand ranged along the hardwood counter his father called the bar of justice and trade homeland stories about northern Spain.

This was Rossie's first trip in Madariaga's as more than a boy, as a man alongside his father. Black-haired women and their hardhanded husbands were setting down for early dinner in that big, plain room with benches and trestle tables covered with oilcloth, while the waitresses hustled ironstone platters — heaped with steaks and bowls of bean soup and iceberg lettuce salad with chopped eggs and fresh peas — to married couples with children in arms, and to grandfathers and aged women. Men in off a ranch-hand job — faces washed and hair combed while their worn shirts showed sweat stains — were talking and laughing and finishing with peach pie and coffee. Nito led Rossie on through into the back room to find two of the old herding men, in from the distances to spend a few weeks living upstairs in one of the rooms, silent and alike, perched on stools apart from one another, their eyes fixed on their dark, thickened hands, one with a double shot of rye and the other with Picon punch. The bartender, a heavy-wristed man whose bald head looked to have been polished, was reading the Reno newspaper.

Nito leaned his elbows on the counter, put his hands out before him, flexed his fingers, and brought them together to form a child's steeple. "Louis, this is my son. His name is Ross. Have you seen him before?"

The bartender folded his newspaper and smiled. "Never. Not standing up to this rail. What would he like to drink?"

51

"Do you think he's man enough for whiskey?"

"He wouldn't be here with you if he wasn't."

The pride was doing its talking, this first time with his father, in this barroom among men, where women did not often go, nor stay for long if they did. "What are those fellows doing in there? Making theories. Nothing," his mother would say. But she would seem bemused, her eyes bright, as if she knew they were doing just what she wanted them to do, holding up their end of the bargain.

"Louis," Nito said to the bartender, "do you have a package for my son?"

"First, let me shake his hand. Then I will serve him. Then I will bring his package."

So it was with a shot glass of whiskey in front of him, and a glass of beer to back it up, that Rossie confronted this surprise wrapped in plain paper.

"Tear it open," Nito said.

Woven of the finest white Panama straw, the hat was unlike any Rossie had ever seen.

"A New York hat," Nito said, "for chasing horses. Imported from Honolulu."

Rossie saw himself in the mirror behind the bar, the brim just above his nose. He met his father's eyes in the reflection. Nito was seeing him as someone to be envied.

The surprise lasted as the bar filled with Nito's friends, men from Reno who bought drinks and more drinks. Rossie had not expected that this would be anything more than dinner with his father. But a dozen tables had been set up. Men carried their drinks with them as they went to sit with their backs against the walls. Serving girls distributed white bread and bowls of the garlic soup that was said to be a stay against morning hangovers.

Nito tapped a knife against a glass. "Wearing his hat indoors, this is my son, Ross." They toasted Rossie, as they would again later when the steaks were served. "The end of his being a boy. We've all suffered. No more mother." Some men laughed, but they raised their drinks. "Now, my son." Nito lifted his hand to Rossie. "Remember that these are men you can count on all your life. That's a lesson to learn."

The lettuce salad and sizzling rib steaks and rounds of drinks came and were cleared, and musicians among the men brought harmonicas and tambourines out from behind the counter, along with a violin and a guitar. Six Basque women, wives of the musicians, came in and sang "Pretty Baby" with their arms around each other, taking elaborate sideways steps as they moved. Then they stepped into traditional dances with their husbands. The two sheep-herding men went on the floor together and cavorted with each other. Bright-eyed single women came and joined the men. A thin black-haired woman asked Rossie to dance, and as they waltzed she kissed him flat on the mouth and whispered, "Vaquero."

Nito caught his arm. Rossie was surprised at the strength in his father's fingers. "I'll take him home," Nito said to the black-haired woman. "His mother waits."

"His mother waits," Rossie bellowed in a big voice, echoing and mocking his father, making a little fun. Nito turned serious, and Rossie shrugged. This was foolish. His father was known for style with the women. Everyone knew it. Katrina knew it. Rossie was going off to be his own man, to have his own style. He would be that man of his own making if he ever came home.

Nito smiled. "You are one smart-assed baby."

Katrina fed Rossie three eggs and a slab of ham and made him drink water instead of coffee. "You'll thank me," she said, "when you're asleep and Oscar's driving."

But Rossie wasn't hungover. He was giddy

and not entirely sober. Katrina poured herself a cup of the French-blend coffee she served, and was sitting across the table as if to study him, when Oscar Dodson knocked at the kitchen door.

Shaved and slick, ironed top to bottom, Oscar was wearing Levi's creased from the laundry and a dress shirt of a reddish color Rossie had never seen, cuffs buttoned and boots shined. "Where's your gear? Lost your gear? That high-cantle saddle?" But he was grinning.

"You." Katrina pointed to Oscar. "There's the coffee, and there's the cups. You're a big boy. Get your own."

Oscar poured for himself and sat across the big, round table from Rossie. "If I was a big boy you'd bring it to me."

"But you're not. You're like him." She nodded at Rossie. "A big baby." She was smiling altogether at Oscar, flirting.

Rossie didn't enjoy watching.

"Sons of bitches," she said. "What you don't want to be, big boys, is one of those sons of bitches." She turned to Rossie. "You. Go shave and comb your hair. It's time you were leaving." She smiled at Oscar, looking entirely happy. "Me and the big boy will talk while we're waiting."

Nito was at the table when Rossie came

back. His black hair was slicked down, as immaculate as his new, white shirt and heavy, gold cuff links in the shape of tiny dice. His dark precise hands folded softly around a steaming mug. Nobody was looking right or left, nor were they talking. Something had happened.

"You know what I'll remember from last night?" Rossie said. "I'll remember wearing my father's shirt."

Nito looked up. "Do you have any money at all?"

"Fifty-three dollars." Rossie slipped a flat little fold of greenbacks from his hip pocket and lay it open for his father.

"If I gave you a hundred, would you make me a promise? No whorehouses? Not a nickel for whorehouses?"

Rossie shrugged, like maybe this was a joke. "That's a tough one. But sure."

"I'll give you fifty." Nito fanned out five unfolded ten-dollar bills and eyed them for a moment. Then he fanned out five more crisp tens. "Fifty more for the whores."

Oscar drummed the table with his fingers and gave a whistle. "Mr. Benasco," he said. "How about poor Oscar? The crippled fellow doing the driving?"

Nito stood and looked down on them.

"What you are, poor Oscar, is shit out of luck."

"Whores?" Katrina asked. "What about this house, where you live?" This didn't seem entirely to be a joke.

Nito pulled a snakeskin wallet from his hip pocket and took from it a perfectly new hundred. He smoothed a single fold from the bill and dropped it onto the tabletop. "For the house."

"What about the woman?" Katrina was not smiling.

Nito gazed down at them with what looked to be fondness. "The woman, the boy, the house. They have all my cash. Now I must go earn more. My son, stay with the horses. Leave the women alone, or you'll come home broke. Or broken."

"Pretty advice," Oscar said. "I can tell you that."

So they were all smiling when Nito had one more thing to say. "That girl." He looked directly to Rossie. "She'll keep until winter."

"Mattie Flynn. She has a name." Katrina was not smiling and this was no joke at all.

Nito ducked his head and grimaced, and was out the kitchen door. Trouble had been edged around but not missed altogether.

Katrina lifted her porcelain cup, and

snapped it down. The handle broke and coffee splashed onto her hand. "Mattie, that's her stupid name."

"Good thing that cup was empty," Oscar said, pushing back from the table.

Katrina smiled to Rossie. "I'll send you letters," she said, "to General Delivery, in Calgary. I'll tell you everything."

EAGLEVILLE, CALIFORNIA

They passed whorehouses along the truckee — rows of one-room cribs where women lived under cottonwood and Lombardy poplar — and white-painted gazebos on vast lawns, made for outdoor cooking, drinking, and afternoon dancing. Neither of them said a thing until they were on the road into the Paiute reservation town of Nixon, where the river — or what was left after most of the flow was diverted into canals for the Federal Irrigation District in the deserts near Fallon — drizzled into Pyramid Lake. Rossie fell into recalling Katrina's stories of the ranch her father had owned on Fifty Mile Creek, south of Carson City. The Paiutes there, she said, lived in a tin-roofed house in sagebrush alongside the meadows. The last of them, a man named Sam Juniper, too old to care for himself after the women died and the children left, came to this reservation. The tin-roofed house and

59

the willow ramada at Fifty Mile Creek had been burned. She told of playing war with the Indian kids on her father's horses, "galloping after one another like movie actors." When she was sixteen she fell in love with one of the boys, Truman Juniper, who had a basketball scholarship to the University of Nevada. But the summer before his freshman year, while he was pitching hay to horses, his eye was stabbed out with a pitchfork — pure accident, but the end of basketball — and he went off to hang around this town, Nixon. Katrina offered no sense that she'd grieved over him. It was pointless to imagine his mother married to an Indian, but Rossie wondered if that Truman Juniper, the man his mother loved when she was a girl, was at this moment in one of these rundown houses alongside Pyramid Lake. "It's a cockeyed story," he said, after telling it to Oscar.

"Sure as hell is," Oscar said. "They found bones of three-toed horses along about here."

Pyramid Lake, a thirty-mile trough between the desert mountains, was what remained of an inland sea called Lake Lahontan, glassy water which had been drying up for thousands of years under a white sky, leaving pyramid-shaped stacks of minerals, called tufa, fifty feet above the water.

"More toes than a cow," Rossie said.

"We could get you a homestead," Oscar said. "You could hunt three-toed horses and help out down in Nixon, in the Indian store. You and old Mattie."

They traveled across an elevation of brush-covered dunes into the dry valley known as Winnemucca Lake, then over the swell dividing the Limbo Range from the San Emido Mountains, black in the far distance with lava and thickets of gin-smelling juniper. Dust ghosted up behind as they fell to greasewood flatlands toward the playa of the Black Rock Desert.

"There's nobody out toward the Smoke Creek Desert but for one ranch," Oscar said, and he went on about a place called Shoshone Meadows at the mouth of "a little toy canyon" where year-round cold water bubbled up from a field of massive basalt boulders and fell through a lava-rock rift where no one, not even old-timers, would ever go because of rattlesnakes, not even to fish for the landlocked cutthroat trout that had been there since the beginning of time. "We should have bought beer but I thought we'd hold out until we hit the Jersey Lily." Oscar twisted his head like he was stretching his neck. "It was a piss-poor idea." He commenced tapping his fingers on the steering wheel to some internal music, and whistled.

Rossie's hangover was settling in. What was the Jersey Lily? "Oscar, how about if you shut up with the whistling?"

"You'll be whistling soon enough. We're coming up on Malinda. She'll cure your shit."

A wagon road fell from the sagebrush hills to the west, and a Model T touring car, back end cut off and rebuilt into a hardwood utility box, was waiting at the intersection. Rossie mistook the woman leaning against the Model T for a man. "Malinda Harrison," Oscar said. "She lives out at Shoshone Meadows. Malinda says she has to travel."

When they coasted up, this Malinda Harrison had her white hat in her hand, a ranch woman with money, if snake-hide boots and silver conches on her belt meant anything. Her black hair was cut short, waved in a way that revealed a precise line of white scalp.

"This is Malinda. She's on a runoff," Oscar said.

"Time number two hundred," she said, smiling at Rossie in a quick, ironic way, as if they were already friends. Her tone was soft, a drawl, but also impatient, Rossie thought, the voice of a woman who could get bored and turn mean. "My husband don't care what I'm doing so long as I'm not doing it to him. I'll tell him I was down to Reno, gambling. He won't give a shit."

Rossie tried his pretty-boy smile on her. "I'd give a shit."

"This here is Rossie Benasco," Oscar said. "He's going off to be a man."

"Let's hope it works." Malinda bit at her lower lip with those good, big teeth. "You're Nito Benasco's boy?"

"You know him?"

"Yeah, I did. We don't know each other any more."

With her canvas-covered suitcase strapped down on the rear of the Packard, Malinda rode between Oscar and Rossie. The dust of their going was strung out for miles across the sagebrush flats as Malinda told her story. She wasn't married to anybody named Harrison, but to Bobby Cahill, a laconic man known for his rudeness with fools and his soft hands and patience as he trained roping horses. Cahill horses were renowned in Nevada for being quicker off the mark and smarter than ordinary. Them Bobby Cahill fellows, it was said, can do algebra.

"I kept my girlhood name. You start marrying these boys and pretty soon you got six names. Who are you going to be then?" Malinda dropped a hand onto Rossie's knee, and gave him a big cockeyed smile.

Rossie wondered how fuck-minded she meant to be with this feeling his knee.

"Bobby talks to horses in his sleep. He keeps Morgan studs for strength and those long-legged mares for travel. I tell him I'm one of the long-legged mares, built for travel. We live a hundred miles from anybody in country so fine it can lead you to crying. I get tired of the cooking for nobody but me and him. Bobby is out with his mares and those colts, so I'm feeling sorry for myself. This traveling gets me over it. I'd be total cured if we was drinking a beer." All the while she was acting like her hand wasn't there on Rossie's knee.

"Gerlach," Oscar said. They were speeding beside a cinder-bed rail line up from Reno that serviced the salt mines. In the distance Rossie could see a loaf of black basalt amid heat waves. Before it, Gerlach was no trees, no grass, and low buildings with whitewash stripped by the Nevada winds to bare boards except for those that had been tinned-over.

"Nothing to do around here but wear out your life," Malinda said.

The Jersey Lily was a line of shacks towed

together with doorways cut between. A lot of the off-duty wearing out took place here.

"Strange as the moon in there." Oscar parked the Packard in front. "You keep it quiet," he said to Rossie. "There might be a man in here who'd love to beat the dogshit out of a kid like you just because you never had to live in Gerlach. You got a ride and a meal ticket and he don't. What they got is mining for salt."

"You're with Bobby Cahill's woman," Malinda said. "So don't worry about nothing. Nobody fucks with Bobby Cahill's woman. That would be a way to get your ass handed to you on a platter." Malinda stated this as a matter of fact, her hand on Rossie's arm, eyes burning slate gray. Rossie felt her fingernails.

The interior was like a cavern, each surface beaten as if with clubs, a battered maze with a bar running in haphazard angles along the wall and out of sight into other rooms. Windows, crusted with salty yellow filth, hummed with swamp coolers. An enormously fat man in a home-sewn, flour sack shirt came shuffling and wheezing from the far depth of the interior, mopping at his face with a towel and regarding them silently, small reddish eyes sunk in his cheeks.

"Benji," Oscar said, "where is your drinkers? You finally drive 'em all away?"

"Shit." The man's voice was high and tremulous. "You read a newspaper? We got a depression in this country. People can't be playing around. Everybody is working or getting ready to move out, the ones that are left. The playboys is gone from this town."

"Well, that's poor news," Oscar said. "No wonder I don't read newspapers. What we want is a case of Acme beer. Iced down, ready to travel." The twenty-four bottles of Acme came in a burlap sack rustling with cracked ice. Oscar departed from the depths of the Jersey Lily with the sack over his shoulder, limping on his bad leg. "Ice costs more than beer. But you got to have it."

The road continued north, winding through steep curves in Gerlach Canyon and over the top of the Buffalo hills. Beyond, they crossed an utterly dry flatland known as Duck Lake, with the Warner Mountains dim and a timbered pale blue on the western horizon. Rossie snapped off the second round of bottle caps. They were getting there, the Packard ghosting along on a two-track road.

"Right then," Oscar said, talking to what he'd been thinking about, "with old Bunky dead and blank-eyed, it got into me that I'd be staring down the sun all my life, and that

I'd better get used to it if I was going to be a man because there was no going back to being a kid."

"You don't make sense," Rossie said.

Oscar was recalling the spring he was sixteen and running wild horses up in Oregon with a man named Bunky Wilson. One morning he'd found Bunky dead in his bedroll beside Sagehen Springs. "It was his turn to cook breakfast," Oscar said. "He didn't get up, I was bitching at him, and there he was dead. Bunky and I was going to get rich with horses and he was dead. Until then I'd been a fucking squirrel-assed kid." He took a pull from his bottle of Acme, and glanced at Rossie. "Your mom said a grown man don't leave a girl he's been fucking. Only a kid would do that. She was hot on the topic. Nito got pissed off."

Rossie listened to the rumble of the Packard and kept quiet. Oscar didn't know all there was to know about anything. Finally he said, "That don't make sense either."

"What does make sense," Malinda said, "is going to Montana. The prettiest country you are ever going to see. You won't come back to Nevada, not after the Bitterroot. I'm sorry for which woman you're talking about but you won't come back for a woman."

Oscar looked across to Malinda like she was probably lying. "You been to Montana?"

"Born there. Wish I was there right this minute, in the tavern that my daddy owned on Railroad Street, by the switchyard in Missoula. My momma died before I remember seeing her, so I had the run of the bar. Grew up with switchmen and drifters and they taught me to keep my knees together. My share of that bar when daddy died came out to six thousand dollars so I shook the dust and come down to Reno the fall of 1923. Married three times — can't stop liking men — but Bobby Cahill, he's the one that counts."

"So you was a princess in the Railroad Tavern," Oscar said. "And now you're true blue to Bobby Cahill."

"You can kiss my big true-blue ass. You are a mean son of a bitch." She rubbed her dark hand on Rossie's knee. "This sweetie is going to Montana," she said, turning a hard smile on Oscar. "That's a damned shame. The wrong sweetie is leaving."

"Calgary," Rossie said. "It's Canada where I'm going."

A reef of dry thunderstorm was building over the Warner Range, lightning flaring at great distance. The road, dusty but smooth before it fell into a break in a lava-flow rim, became a jostling run of stone along the floor of a narrow canyon. The next miles were slow and jolting until the ridges opened to Surprise Valley — meadows and willows along native sloughs and rows of Lombardy poplar and cottonwood boxing white houses with their gardens and apple orchards, and their red barns and willow-thatch corrals out behind. The borrow pits were thick with tules. Fenced and graveled, the roadway was ungraded, like a washboard. Silver-black magpies and redheaded blackbirds flared up.

"Here you got it," Oscar said.

"No surprise to me," Rossie said. "I smelled it for miles. You can smell water from far off if you been enough time on the desert." The ice was melted from the burlap sack and the melt was puddled on the floorboards. Rossie pitched his Acme bottle into a culvert. His head was buzzing.

"Seventeen miles an hour," Malinda said. "You afraid you're going to shake this outfit to pieces? You ought to get it up and sailing."

"You bet I'm afraid," Oscar said. "This Packard goes down, I'm done, looking for work and afoot. This valley is nowhere to be afoot. Man ought to be happy enough in

69

Surprise Valley. But I'm not." He reached across and slapped Malinda's thigh, where her Levi's were tight.

She jumped. "Damn you! What's wrong with you?"

"Horseflies."

"*You* are the goddamned horsefly."

These had to be the horses for Calgary. Nobody would have this herd otherwise. Most were reddish bay, a few with white stockings and blazes; spotted red roans and a blue one; buckskins and three red-and-white pintos. They were nervous and thrilled by the storm over the Warner Mountains. The late afternoon was going electric with early-season lightning as the horses drifted through corridors in the willows, from one island of meadow to another. These two hundred and fifty-seven three-year-old geldings plus one bell mare were the most horses Rossie had ever seen in one field.

"Quick and spooky," Oscar said.

Eagleville was mainly the Sunrise Hotel, a two-story affair with a false front and a covered veranda on three sides. Across the road a general store, which looked to be the usual combination grocery and hardware, was tucked into a collapsing log building. Shingle-sided houses, surrounded by lilacs and tulips and hollyhocks, straggled off beyond.

Oscar parked alongside a dusty, black, two-door Model A Ford and smiled a big, fake smile. "Well, buckaroo. Here you are."

"Shit," Rossie said. He didn't move.

"What he's thinking," Malinda said to Oscar after they'd sat a long moment, "is you're kicking him out. That seems sudden."

"The whole goddamned world is sudden," Oscar said.

Rossie finished his beer and tossed the bottle under the wheels of the Model A.

"You better pick that up," Oscar said. "This is a settler town. They don't want cowhands throwing beer bottles."

Rossie fished in the wet burlap sack for another beer, jerked off the top and took a long pull.

"Besides that, you work for Clifford Dufferena, who owns that Model A Ford. For sure he won't want hired hands throwing beer bottles under it. But it's not my ass." Oscar climbed out of the Packard, swinging his braced leg before him, and gimped off into the hotel.

"Find me another beer," Malinda said. "Then get out and pick up that bottle. Or you might be fired before you start."

Rossie went through the whole act of opening the last Acme, then picked up the bottle he'd thrown and dropped it over onto the back floorboard of the Packard.

"You're acting sick, and sick won't get you no pity."

"What I'm thinking is where in hell have I sent myself?"

Oscar came out of the hotel. "It's going to rain," he announced. "Roll up my windows and get inside. You got people to meet."

Rossie claimed his new, white hat from the backseat and thought he at least looked good as anybody in Eagleville. But as soon as he stepped into the shadowy dimness of the Sunrise Hotel he realized showing up halfway drunk wasn't a hot idea.

The dusty Model A outside did indeed belong to the man who owned the horses, who would also be paying Rossie's wages. Clifford Dufferena had been a force with open-range cows and sheep on Great Basin deserts since before the trench war in France. He was known for claiming he never wanted to own an acre of property. "You got your money in land you are crippled. Got to keep money dancing, and crippled money can't dance. Animals is where the profit is. Land is fine if you need to admire the view." He lived out of the

Model A, traveling ranch to ranch and hotel to hotel, and everybody knew about him, saying he couldn't be beat trading livestock — he wouldn't cheat but you couldn't beat him. With the high-top, lace-up, leather shoes he wore both walking and horseback, he didn't look like a rancher, though he'd been trading cows and sheep and horses for fifty years. Lots of people thought he was rich even if he never lived in like a wealthy man. "Old Man Dufferena could buy a dozen ranches if he wanted them," Slivers Flynn had told Rossie. Nobody needed to wonder if this fellow could pay his bills.

Now, in the combination lobby and dining room and tavern of the hotel, Clifford Dufferena was resting on a red-and-black Indian blanket spread on a worn leather couch. His fingers were woven into a steeple before him as he studied Rossie. "Them other boys come yesterday. Horseback. You don't even got a horse. But you have a new hat. Hell of a hat." The old man smiled at his joke.

"Thought I'd be riding your horses. You got horses. That's what Slivers told me." It was a good thing, Rossie thought, that he'd had a few beers. Otherwise he'd be letting this man pick on him.

"You drunk?" Dufferena said, his teeth

huge and white and no doubt false. "But you're right. Horses go with the job. Slivers told me you were all right for a kid. And that is a hell of a new hat." Dufferena clacked those teeth and gazed up toward the ceiling. "He told me he had to get you on the road so you and his girl could calm down."

"Women," Malinda said, sticking a forefinger at Dufferena, "are the reason for things."

"What I wanted," the old man said, "was to hire Slivers Flynn. But nobody can hire Slivers Flynn. Man like that don't hire out on a horse drive to Canada. So I got Jap Hardy, he's the boss. You'll be all right if you listen to Jap Hardy." Dufferena stared into the steeple of his fingers again. "Here's the deal. Five of you on horseback and Louis Clair, the cook, in a truck. And a wrango boy, I forget his name. You horseback fellows got four horses in your string, a four-day rotation. Take care of your horses and they'll take care of you. Jap Hardy is from Red Bluff. He's done the bossing on horse drives before. Last year he took four hundred horses to the U.S. military in Grand Forks, all through Wyoming and the Rocky Mountains and across the Nebraska sand hills. He scouted our route to Calgary in a motorcar. This trip is nothing to him.

But you're a kid that don't know a thing except how to eat dinner so you listen to every word Jap Hardy says. You listen like it was the Lord speaking. You spur your horse and you jump." The old man dropped his hands and looked straight at Rossie. "The rest of the deal, for a kid like you, is one hundred dollars cash in Calgary. You'll sew your saddle in a burlap sack and ship it home with you on the railroad, traveling at my own expense, Calgary to Vancouver to San Francisco to Reno. Man who don't ride the railroad gets two horses to travel with and be his own." The old man smiled. "I want to see that hat dirty and frazzled in Calgary. I want you in the market for a new one. That's it. You go pick the horses on your string. You go down there and talk to Jap Hardy. Them other boys don't have nothing to say about these things."

"Down where?"

"Where I got them camped, at them barns this side of the creek. Where the hell did you think? You think I'm paying for horseback hands to live in a hotel?"

Built of cottonwood logs, the low-roofed barns were holdouts from the livery stable days that ended in the 1920s. Beyond the barns were the corrals, one of them round and willow-walled, with a heavy deep-set juniper post in the center.

Food and bedrolls would be transported on the cook's truck. An old-fashioned chuck wagon box was built into the tail end. The bins and drawers were already filled with roasting pans and tin plates, a scramble of knives and forks, and flour and onions and beans. There were two gray canvas tents, one to shelter the cooking and another for sleeping and only to be set up if it rained.

Two of Rossie's traveling companions, a short, dark man who was rolling a cigarette and a raw-skinned, blond fellow who looked to be Rossie's age, were lounging on rounds of sawlog set up as stools around a fire pit.

The youngster didn't look at Rossie, but the bowlegged man rolling a cigarette said, "Hell of a automobile." Then he finished his rolling and lit his smoke. "Jap Hardy," he said. "But I got nothing to do with Japan. I'm what's called a Port. My people came on the boat from Portugal though I been horseback all my life. You ever heard of Portugal?"

"In school," Rossie said.

Jap Hardy gave Rossie a tight little smile.

"So how come they call you Jap?"

"My daddy started that. No telling why. He was a shithead."

"First time you been out of Nevada?" the

76

blond kid asked. "Bet you don't know where you are. You're in California. This Surprise Valley is up in the corner of California. You ever been in California before?"

"This boy is Bill Sweet," Jap Hardy said. "You'll hear him talking all the time. If he don't shut up somebody is going to kick his ass. It might be me."

Bill Sweet was studying the distance like he hadn't said a thing.

"These horses was shod down in the Sacramento Valley," Jap Hardy said. "Those boys did it right. Otherwise you'd be looking at rasping hooves and shaping shoes — a week of aching backs, if you ask me. So I told Dufferena no horseshoeing. Except a few on the road."

"Don't have no horse to shoe," Rossie said. "The old man said I should be picking a string."

"You're the geek who don't have no horse," Jap Hardy said. "I cut one out for you. Big, good-natured, traveling fellow. Anybody can ride him. Don't want you in much of a rodeo right away. I got him in the wrango pasture. You pick the others after we get going on the road tomorrow."

"Tomorrow?"

Jap Hardy smiled that tight smile again. "Not too early. The old man is buying us dinner up in the hotel. Going to be a late start. But after that we're out at daylight. It's six or seven weeks to Calgary. There won't be much sleeping. I was three weeks figuring roads and renting fenced pasture for the nights, so there won't be no night herding, either. You want to lose horses, try night herding. We're getting there with all our horses. And we're sleeping down here alongside the barn tonight, but you can throw your bedroll anywhere out of sight from the road. You got that woman with you."

"That woman don't have anything to do with me."

"Damn shame if it's true."

"How about if I sleep up in the hotel?"

"You can sleep anywhere you want, if you can pay for it. I'm not your daddy."

This wasn't going right. "Maybe you ought to show me that horse," Rossie said. But just then two men — they looked to be in their midforties, same as Jap Hardy — came easing from the bedroll tent, one of them heavy-shouldered with a thick, graying mustache draped over his upper lip. The other, gray-faced and clean-shaven, was busy sharpening his pocketknife and didn't even look at Rossie. They must have been trying to sleep, since they were standing around in their stocking feet.

"Ahead of the horses, anyway, you ought to meet these fellows." Jap Hardy gestured toward the heavy-shouldered bowlegged man with the stained mustache over his mouth. "This here is Tarz Witzell."

Rossie had heard of Tarz Witzell, a man with a reputation. His grip, when Rossie shook his hand, was soft as a child's on the surface. Underneath, it was otherwise. There were drunkman stories about Tarz Witzell battering his way through the taverns in Elko. But then he turned crazy for horses and gave up on whiskey and women. "Cute as pie," Slivers Flynn had said about him.

The gray-faced fellow sharpening his pocketknife turned out to be Dickie Wilson, who'd been cowboss for the Flying Cross, out of Battle Mountain, before the owners sold off all their livestock and settled in to cultivate a kitchen garden and wait out the Depression. So. Even these men had been reduced to trailing horses toward Calgary.

"This is how it sets up," Jap Hardy said. "Two old hands, two kids. And me. A cook and some goddamned wrango boy."

"Tell you what. I don't hire out to play kid."

"The cook and chore boy," Jap Hardy said, "ride in the truck. You're horseback.

You roll your bed every morning and then you don't worry about nothing before dinner but what's going on horseback. Turn out to be a kid and you won't last long. Slivers told me you'd be fine soon as you settle down. I figure that's about right. I figure you'll learn."

"Show you something." Rossie pulled out the white-bone-handled knife Mattie had stolen from Slivers Flynn.

He knew this was a mistake even as he opened the thin blade. "Slivers gave me this. He said to earn it."

"That sounds like bullshit. Slivers Flynn never said anything like that. You just got a worn-out knife. Let's go see your bay horse."

Five horses were prowling the fences in the wrango pasture, flaring their nostrils and eyeing the lightning flashing across the oncoming storm. "Bay with the star on his face," Jap Hardy said, "I picked him for you. Fine, strong fellow."

"Rock, " Rossie said. "I'm going to call him Rock. Had a horse looked just like him called Banjo. But he got away from under me, and damned near knocked my brains out. I was bleeding from the ears."

"Call him whatever you want. You might be bleeding from the asshole before this is over, but that horse will stand the traveling." Then he smiled. "Hope that Banjo didn't knock your brains out. You come along in that big car like a movie actor. There's a chance you didn't have any brains to start with." Huge, single drops of rain began striking in the dust around them. "We're going to get wet. We better run for them tents."

A thin, graying man had a fire blazing through the rain in a fire pit, and coffee steaming.

"This is Louis Clair," Jap Hardy said. "He cooks. We treat him nice. He don't pick up your shit. Leave something behind and it's never going to be his fault. It's your fault and you shut up about it. Fuck with Louis and you're fucking with me."

"Drowned rat," Oscar said, eyeing Rossie. A shot glass of whiskey shimmered by his elbow.

Rossie was soaked with rain running a stream off the brim of his straw hat before he hung it carefully on a wooden peg. "Don't worry about that hat. We got rooms. One for you. Altogether they cost me nine dollars. My treat. You ought to sleep indoors one more night."

Lightning illuminated the common world

in shades and shadows. Heavy wind brought a great limb thunking down from the poplars before the storm passed and the rain settled into a steady downpour.

Rossie ducked out to the Packard, dragged his tarp-covered bedroll into the lobby, unbuckled the leather straps, and rolled it open to dig out one of the dry shirts tucked inside. In the men's room off the lobby, he ran his comb through his hair, laying it slick and damp and black along his skull. Oscar found him there and handed him a glass of whiskey and water. The Eagleville drinking was under way.

A heavy lady in a black cookhouse dress and matching apron came into the kitchen through a back door and began chopping spuds and banging on steak cuts with a tenderizing hammer. Malinda carried a ladder-backed chair onto the veranda and sat out of the rain, watching the storm. Rossie got a chair and joined her, listening to the thunder and the softening fall of rain as the rumbling diminished, until Oscar followed them. "A couple of rainfall lovers," he said.

"Beats cowhands," Malinda said. "Soothes the nerves and shows up once in a while, every six months or so."

Oscar stepped to the edge of the porch

and stood facing them. Rossie wondered if Oscar was drunk enough to step backward off the veranda. "Fucking women," Oscar said.

"You got us right," Malinda said. "We're the shits. There's too many women who won't act right. So the crybaby assholes they married go to beating on horses, who have to put up with it." Rossie wondered if this line of talk had anything to do with Bobby Cahill. But he didn't wonder for long. Pissiness was about to brew over the top in Oscar, and here it came, as Oscar tossed the remnants of his whiskey and water off into the grass.

"What I'll be doing," he said, "is any shitting thing I please. When old Rossie gets home I'll be moved in with Mattie Flynn, down the hall from Slivers. I'll be a happy boy. Rossie thinks I'm telling a joke, but he'll see." Oscar was eyeing Rossie in a glassy way. This was right to the edge of fighting talk. There was no answer to it other than fighting, or ducking your head and walking away.

Malinda glared at Oscar "What you should do, you tiresome asshole, is leave this kid alone and go fuck yourself."

Oscar drew back, and Rossie thought he might swing on her. But a thought flickered across his eyes.

"If you're worried about Bobby Cahill," Malinda said, "that's a good idea. You want to think about Bobby Cahill before you swing on me."

Rossie took a long pull on his whiskey and water, then went into the lobby of the hotel. Dufferena was limping down the stairs as Rossie hoisted his bedroll onto his shoulder. "I'll be sleeping down by the barns," Rossie said. The old man nodded like this made a lot of sense, carrying your bed off into the rain when you had a paid-up room in the hotel. Rossie went past Oscar and Malinda out on the veranda without looking at them. He thought of his hat on that peg in the lobby and felt like a fool but kept walking, out to the shelter of a cottonwood tree. The rain was down to a mist, and the wind and lightning had died. He turned to see Oscar and Malinda trailing after him, carrying drinks.

"For shit's sake," Oscar said. "We'd leave you out here sucking your thumb like a baby if you wasn't so pitiful." He was down off his high horse. "Mattie's around, and I think about her. But I'm just bullshitting. That's what it is."

"Yeah," Rossie said, "you're a beauty." He took a sip from Malinda's bourbon and water. "Goddamn it, I feel like I better drink this whole son of a bitch and a couple more if I'm going to catch up."

Tarz Witzell, up from camp, appeared wearing a yellow slicker like a seaman. Oscar snorted. "Like to see that boy get on a horse with that slicker."

"That's Tarz Witzell," Rossie said. "He can probably get on his horse."

Oscar stalked off toward the hotel. "We got to take it easy on him," Malinda said. "Oscar's crippled for good and he knows it."

"You think he'd go after Mattie?" Rossie asked, and Malinda considered a moment, like a theorist.

"He might. He might look pretty good to her. Oscar was winning saddle bronc when she was a girl. She might think he'd quit running if he liked her hot enough. Wet pussy has changed a lot of minds. She don't know what a son of a bitch he can be and maybe she wouldn't care. Oscar's not dumb. He's just looking for a place to lay his head down — and he could, working for Slivers. Who knows?"

"Mattie is not any chickenshit girl. We're talking about her like she don't have a brain of her own."

"Well, she's not here to defend herself,"

Malinda smiled. "If it was me, I'd count that girl gone and wouldn't hold no grudge against Oscar, whichever way it goes. I'd figure I left her and made my trouble. You ought to carry your bedroll back over to the hotel. This is foolishness." She took hold of his arm, and dug in her fingernails. "But you know he means to go after that girl. She may have gave up on you already. That's the point of this, him trying to tell you."

Somebody from the hotel cranked up the power plant out behind, and the dinner was served under electric lights that flickered occasionally. "Get it or I'm throwing it out," the cook announced. The meal was silent as platters of breaded steak and bowls of string beans and mashed potatoes with white milk gravy shuffled up and down the long table.

Dufferena sat at the head like a king of wisdom.

Oscar was off into a sullen drunk until, as the cook distributed three deep apple pies, he stood and held his drink up to the ceiling. "Damn," he said, "I didn't come up here for pie. I come looking for a send-off."

"You going somewhere?" Dufferena grinned like the idea of Oscar going anywhere was a joke. "You drove your ducks to a mighty poor pond. That's the big trouble with drunk all the time. You don't know what's going on. That's why these are my horses and you fellows will be hoping I show up in Canada with the wages."

"You know what you are?" Oscar said. He took a long pull on his drink and narrowed his eyes, thinking. "What in hell do you know about work? You're just a goddamned thieving old fool."

Malinda lifted a hand to hide her eyes. Rossie was staring at the precise line of scalp where her hair was parted.

Tarz Witzell cleared his throat and tapped his thick fingers on the tabletop. "What you sound like is some jackass about to get his other leg broke."

Rossie realized why Malinda was hiding her eyes. She was working to keep from laughing.

Oscar was watching her. "You'll get your deal," he said. Just what deal wasn't clear.

Malinda looked up and shook her head. "Oscar, you talk like a crazy man. You need a nap."

"He's the crazy one." Oscar didn't seem to be looking at anybody in particular.

"Oh, Christ!" Malinda scolded. "Sit down."

But Oscar wasn't having any of that. He looked up toward a corner of the ceiling, staggered into the doorjamb on his way out, slammed the door, and stomped across the veranda. Eventually they heard the Packard crank up. "Guess he's leaving," Clifford Dufferena said.

Thinking he could get Oscar headed off, Rossie was getting out of his chair when a gunshot blew through the screen door and took out one of the lights over the table, shattering glass down over them. The second shot hit the ceiling. Rossie sat back down in his chair and they stayed put, waiting to get shot.

"Me," Dufferena said, "I'm not going out there." Then it wasn't a question.

The Packard roared and spit gravel. From the veranda Rossie saw taillights growing fainter down the gravel road. In moonlight he spotted the saddle and the burlap sack of his horse gear out in the parking lot where Oscar had dumped them. The moon hung over glowing meadows and the horses moved like shadows among the dark reefs of willow.

It had been settled that Dufferena, on his way to Reno the next day, would drive Malinda to her Model T touring car. The electric plant had been shut down and the lights were out, the men had gone to the bed tent and Dufferena up to his room. Rossie and Malinda, just the two of them, sat out on the veranda in a glaze of moonlight.

"He said I was going to be in your bedroll," Malinda said, "that he could see it coming and that I was going to make you a going away present. I told him I wasn't planning anything like that, bedding down with anybody. I don't do that anymore, even if I might think it would be a hot idea." She told him about the stonework Bobby Cahill had set in place over the years at Shoshone Meadows, house walls and barn walls built of black lava, a stone-walled chicken house with chickens in the yard and roosters crowing over the sound of the little creek just outside the kitchen. "Shoshone Meadows is where you don't try to forget where you are. I mean to live there all my life, sprinkled with some running like this, so long as Bobby don't kick me out. He says horses will make him famous and he's got to do what he's doing. He thinks people will come to see his horses. But nobody would come to Shoshone Meadows unless it were his own kids and he's not going to have any kids — he tells me, *no kids* — so he's going to be alone except for me and his damned old horses." She walked to the edge of the veranda. "Tonight you got a room of your own. Lock that door so I don't get any drunk-girl ideas. I want to wake up believing I'm my own momma."

NORTH

Thirty or forty miles every day totaled up to a thousand miles to Calgary — wagon-track roads across sagebrush distances in eastern Oregon and clattering along two-lane macadam highways in the Snake River plow grounds of southern Idaho, then a long arc to the east before turning north to the grassy plains of Montana — that was the plan, so they wouldn't have to attempt driving horses through timberlands. The Chinese Wall country, where the rich men from Reno went for elk hunting in the fall, deep in the high Rockies, would loom to the west as they progressed north toward Alberta.

Out of bed before sunrise, Rossie carried his bedroll and gear down to where Louis Clair had a fire going and coffee steaming in a blue tin pot. Clifford Dufferena was hunched up over a cup, his rheumy eyes already sharp. "Thought you might sleep out the morning," he said to Rossie.

When they eventually drifted out toward the horse corral, a stocky boy in a floppy, gray hat was closing the gate on that day's saddle stock.

"Angus Jackson," Jap Hardy said. "One of them Scottish boys. He'll be with us all the way to Calgary. Scottish boys learn to work, so he'll be fine."

Angus Jackson eyed the world with no trace of expression. If Jap Hardy was making Scottish boys into dumb jokes, he wasn't having any. The crew carried bridles with snaffle — or Spanish bits or hackamore woven of rawhide, depending on which horse they'd be riding — and spoke the names of the creatures they had in mind.

Jap Hardy clearly knew which one was Whisp or Denio, Happy Hat or Tinkertoy or Lark. He not so much spun his riata as flipped it to hang and drop without fuss around the neck of one horse or another, never going for the wrong horse and never missing — a good sign that morning as a spiral of dust stirred counterclockwise by the horses lifted straight up to the pale cloudless sky. Each rider went down the rope to touch and soothe his horse for the day. They eased the saddle up, just trying it, cinched it tight and hard, checking to see if

92

this boy was humped-up and cranky, liable to crowhop and buck.

When Rossie called for Rock, Jap Hardy grinned. "Shit, kid, he's the only horse you got."

Turned into the rope, the big bay was wild-eyed, nostrils distended and snuffling, quivering but nowhere near panic, as Rossie made his way down to him. Rossie lifted the back of his left hand. "Smell it and stay nice," he commanded as he lifted the headstall, and without much fuss got his snaffle-bit bridle in place.

"Looks like Rock was broke for kids," Jap Hardy said, coiling his riata while Rossie led the bay out the corral gate.

"Broke to lead anyway," Rossie said.

"You ought to call him Rocking Horse," Jap Hardy said.

Nothing happened until the cinch was jerked up tight. Then old Rock squealed and set back on his hocks, rearing and twisting away, throwing his head, and jerking Rossie halfway off his feet. The others were watching, but nobody was saying a thing. Nothing to do but get it over with. Rossie eased his way up to the trembling horse, turned the stirrup, and got his toe into it, testing a little weight on it. Rock was steady enough, not rearing away, so Rossie swung up into the saddle, hoping he'd make it to the other stirrup before this big, old bay came unglued. But nothing. Rock was trembling and stock-still. Rossie touched him with the blunt spurs he wore for colts, and the horse stepped out and broke to a run before Rossie turned him, let him out into another run, and set him up. It was ragged, but nothing to it. He touched Rock with the spurs again. This time the charge was less avid.

"Pretty cute," Jap Hardy said. "Guess I was right. That big, old horse was broke for kids."

Rossie eased out of the saddle, waiting for some quick nonsense from Rock, but not a thing.

"You got to be a lucky son of a bitch," Jap Hardy said. "Some fellow did a good job with that boy. That horse is aiming to please."

Dufferena had come gimping down to the corrals to watch his crew and their horses. "Most of these horses come from along Cottonwood Creek, out north of Red Bluff. That's where the best of these horses come from."

At breakfast they sat on rounds of firewood, balancing in their laps platters of eggs and sausage or thick, crisp bacon, then tossing the tin plates into a dishwashing pan for

Angus Jackson. Each day was to begin with these ceremonies.

"No running, and no stampeding," Jap Hardy said. "Ease them along, let them get used to traveling. No rodeos." He was looking at Bill Sweet and Rossie as he talked.

They headed into sunrise to begin gathering, their horses' hooves thudding softly on dry-sod ground. But out among the willow-lined islands, in a slough fenced off by six strands of barbed wire, they came to trouble. The fence, meant to keep animals from floundering into quicksand, had been torn through in the night. A big, blue roan, bloodied by wire cuts but not mortally, was deep in the murky water after a night of struggling and sinking. He'd likely got into a panic while running from the lightning.

Jap Hardy was the first one there. For long moments he sat quiet on the black gelding he'd chosen that morning, folding his hands on the Spanish saddle horn before digging into his saddlebag for a pair of wire cutters, which he held out to Rossie. "Here you go, kid. Climb down and clear that barbed wire. That crazy son of a bitch just run straight-away through all that goddamned wire. There's always one crazy son of a bitch. So this is him."

The roan was belly deep. A couple of rid-

95

ers would have to lasso him by the head, turn their horses and spur them, and drag him out, watching as his neck stretched and hoping nothing inside him tore loose. Jap Hardy unstrapped a seagrass rope from the forks of his saddle and began uncoiling it, shaping a loop. Tarz Witzell took his own time, got down, tightened his cinch, then unlimbered his own seagrass, and tossed an effortless loop over the head of the blue roan. These men weren't carrying rawhide riatas, which were lovely and alive but too easy to strand and ruin when you were roping horses. Rossie was learning a thing or two. Get your hands on a seagrass rope.

"Wake up, kid," Jap Hardy said. "Get after that wire."

Rossie jerked wire loose from the wild roses that grew along the fence line, then folded it back. Jap Hardy dropped his loop on the blue roan and dallied down, and with Tarz Witzell, their horses farting and straining, dragged the roan out of the slough and onto the meadow grass. Slathered with gray mud, the roan was kicking, throwing his head, and banging it against dry, hard sod like a hammer. Rossie dodged in to crouch with a knee on the animal's muddy neck, putting all his weight there. The riders undid their dallies, Rossie jerked the ropes loose, and the roan came up wheezing and staggering. And lucky, Jap Hardy said. Though the wire cuts across his chest were seeping blood, they were shallow and didn't even need sewing up.

Tarz Witzell coiled his seagrass, strapped it on the right-hand fork of his saddle, got down, and loosened his cinch as if nothing had happened. He smiled at Rossie, teeth yellow under his stained mustache. "Damned old horses. They got brains about as big as a pea."

As the sun warmed, mist lifted from standing water in the sloughs, and morning light shone through in rainbows. The horses streamed single-file across the meadows and gathered into a herd that could be counted out through a pole gate onto the fenced country road — two hundred and fifty-seven three-year-old geldings broke to ride, four private horses belonging to the other men, and the red-and-white-pinto bell mare for the lot to follow. The Model A Ford truck driven by Louis Clair was already loaded and gone down the road. "They'll have the cook tent set up north of Vya," Jap Hardy had said. "Up toward Massacre Lake." This was a short day, twenty miles, a shakedown day.

Tarz Witzell and Dickie Wilson went off

ahead to keep the leaders in check. While Rossie and Bill Sweet hazed the herd through the gate at a gentle trot, Clifford Dufferena and Jap Hardy set up alongside and counted out one final time. The bloodied blue roan was in the middle of the pack, moving without a limp.

After a dozen-odd miles they passed the little Surprise Valley town of Cedarville, where they turned west toward Nevada, rounding a landlocked lake with a reach of white alkaline borderlands before stringing out along a dusty, unfenced road through gray hills. Midafternoon, after a day of eating pale dust, they turned the herd to graze through the night in a brushy pasture along the east side of the flat called Massacre Lake. By sundown they were bedded into a dry camp.

Rossie woke deep in the night feeling sick with emptiness and lay there listening to the men in the tent snuffling and muttering as they slept. "Your own daddy," he told himself, then recollected Mattie touching her tongue to her teeth. Oscar was probably on his way to the Neversweat, intent on getting after her. Dust rose behind the Packard in Rossie's imagination, and he wondered if Mattie was already changed from the girl she had been to someone who might welcome Oscar. And why not? There it was, he thought, the why-for of this sadness, not a thing to it but the way he was thinking. Nothing to be done but breathe and eventually drift into sleep.

The next day Jap Hardy caught Rossie another big, strong fellow, this time a horse Rossie had picked, stone black with white stocking feet. Rossie named him Blackie, and when he bucked under the saddle in a halfhearted way, Rossie rode him out with ease and was pleased to see the others paying no particular attention as they went to breakfast.

Bill Sweet, the other youngster, smirked. "You been a bronc rider?"

"You bet your ass," Rossie lied.

This day was a steady twelve-hour traipse, the pace slow and easy. Dickie Wilson stayed in the lead, followed by the bell mare, while Rossie and Bill Sweet brought along the trailers. A long day of backland roads across Nevada and into the Oregon deserts followed, past sage-covered ridges with dark mahogany brush up where snows collected in winter drifts and not a house or a traveler or any other person until they reached Thousand Springs, where they found the Model A and their tents set up alongside a fenced but abandoned homestead field.

Mallard drakes flew up as the horse herd jostled through a brokendown gateway to the water, the birds circling and then returning to the tiny weave of desert swamp.

Jap Hardy dug out his fencing pliers and sent Rossie and Bill Sweet to ride the fence and patch it. "One horse in the wire and your asses are mud."

But the rusted fence was mostly up. They'd cantered half a turn around the field's perimeter before stopping the first time to hammer in a few staples. Bill Sweet pushed back his hat. "You don't say shit, do you? That how they teach you in Reno?" Scabby with sunburn, he was trying to be his own man.

In later years Rossie would recall that Thousand Springs was the exact place where they started being friends. "Bill Sweet asked about girls like he'd never seen one up close, so I told him I'd never seen one bare-assed, which was a lie, and he said at least I had better sense than to bullshit him. After that we were onto one another, both of us liars, no trouble."

When they got back to the cook tent, the food was boiled beef — which Louis Clair had rustled up on a visit to the old IXL Ranch over in Guano Valley — along with mashed spuds and milk gravy, canned peas, and canned peaches for dessert. There were cases of peas and peaches in the truck.

"In nineteen twenty-nine," Tarz Witzell said, as he cleaned his dinner plate, "we camped right here with the MC. I waded into that swamp to wash off. Come out, my legs was covered with bleeding leeches." He examined the cigarette he was rolling, wheezing as heavy-bellied men will, and went on about wintering at the MC buckaroo camp in a hayfield valley maybe fifty miles to the west when that ranch was selling its mother cows in order to send money to widows back east in Philadelphia. Their husbands had bought shares in establishments like the MC during rich times earlier in the 1920s.

"Only money them old ladies had left coming to them," Dickie Wilson said. "Otherwise they're goners. That's what you hear."

"What you kids need to know," Tarz Witzell said, eyeing Rossie as he talked, "is the horses across this country, one ranch to another. You need to know them every one, one by one, by name and by disposition. Over at Rock Springs in the buttes, I quit the Seven-T over a horse they called Horace. Ernie Whitehead was the Seven-T cowboss. He took my Horace horse for himself. I had to quit, no choice. Horses is it."

Rossie knew the 7T had gone entirely out of business. Ernie Whitehead was dead of poisoning from whorehouse trouble in Elko.

The next afternoon they went out across Catlow Valley, a fifty-mile swale where homesteaders, who'd come to the west in response to railroad promotions in the years before the First World War, had settled and plowed up 160-acre plots, and planted rye and failed. The valley was bare, no sign of the eleven post-office towns that had once been there, nor of any of the saw-lumber houses. Just rusting barbed wire snarled around fields going back to brush. Jap Hardy led them miles to the west along the flanks of the Beatys Butte in order to stay out of the wire.

Camped beside a spring in a draw called East Road Gulch, Louis Clair killed three rattlesnakes as he set up the cook tent. He smiled for the first time Rossie had seen as he laid the snakes out on the table where he did his cutting and bread making. "You boys be careful," he said to Rossie. "You might find snakes in your bed."

"You going to cook them sons a bitches?" Tarz Witzell asked.

"I could. You want snake, I can cook snake. I've tasted snake. Sort of like rubber." But he just cut off the rows of rattles, stowed them in the drawer with the knives and forks, and tossed the thick, limber bodies off into the brush.

The ten-thousand-foot fault block of Steens Mountain, under snow in late April, glowed off east in the twilight. Dickie Wilson cleared his throat and told them about riding a bicycle a couple of hundred miles on desert roads north from Elko to hunt work as wrango for the Whitehorse Ranch, beyond the Steens, when he was sixteen. The Whitehorse cowhands told him German dogs came off the mountain at night — Donner und Blitzen, phantom dogs — and he had stayed awake listening for noises when they were all of them sleeping. "If them wasn't the damndest fellows," Dickie Wilson said.

Toward the foot of the Steens, they passed Blitzen, the last remnant of a town left in Catlow, comprised of collapsing shiplap houses and a store with a wall slumping in on itself. Three women and a man with braided red hair came out to see them pass. "They think we're going someplace," Tarz Witzell said.

Bill Sweet was hanging behind Witzell, as he liked to do, listening. "Compared to here, shit, we're going to heaven."

They led the pinto bell mare through a

gate into meadows at Roaring Springs, a ranch belonging to the same Scottish land combine that owned the Neversweat. The cows had been sold off, with nobody there except for the man who'd overseen the selling, an old-time cowboss turned into a whiskery fellow in a food-stained shirt who kept the fences mended. They camped beside the Roaring Springs bunkhouse, where Jap Hardy had lived in years past.

Tarz Witzell stood on the porch and began stripping out of his shirt. "Me," he said, "I'm taking one of them baths."

Buck naked and pale, they gimped and tromped through skunk cabbage alongside the bunkhouse and splashed into snow-cold spring water bubbling into a sand-bottomed pool, where they soaped themselves and plunged their heads again and again before clambering out to dry off by the cast-iron stove Louis Clare had fired up in the bunkhouse bullpen.

Into his dusty road clothes again, Jap Hardy favored Bill Sweet with a slap on the shoulder. "By God, kid. You got it right. This here is heaven. Damned sight colder and cleaner than Blitzen. I always figured heaven was cold and clean."

"Could be," Tarz Witzell said, "that it's really slick and pink."

After loafing over breakfast the next morning, they went a dozen miles along the foothills of the mountain before cresting a lava ridge to sit looking down on the wide swampland valley and home fields of the old P Ranch. The valley was intricately cut by creek waters flowing from the Steens through a canyon that was three thousand feet deep, one of five such formations eroded into the mountain.

"Cut into the rock by glaciers," Tarz Witzell said. "Gospel truth. That's what schoolteachers say. If you believe them schoolteachers."

Peter French had set up the P Ranch in 1872 after driving cattle into the country from California, Jap Hardy explained. He reined in and sat looking. "There she is. French and his vaqueros, trailing cows all the way from Red Bluff. They didn't know this valley was here, and there it was, empty for the taking."

"French was twenty-three," Tarz Witzell said. "You young fellows better get a hurry on."

Jap Hardy shook his head. "This whole country, it was dead empty. Now the federal government is buying the swamp for a bird refuge. That's what they say. Hard to think about. Birds."

"They was Indians," Bill Sweet said in his know-it-all way. "They was always Indians. A lot of years before that Pete French. But French, he probably run them off."

The horses streamed past the Frenchglen Hotel, framed by Lombardy poplar and just like the one in Eagleville from its looks, and out a fenced lane to a small field where the main P Ranch house had burned down to nothing but chimneys in a grassy lot.

"No money for hotels," Jap Hardy said, once they had done with the evening meal. "But there's a dollar or two for beer. There is not going to be any women for you boys, but we ain't lost a horse and that's worth something. So we'll spend Dufferena's money on beer. You fellows think you could drink a beer?"

Louis Clair claimed he didn't drink and that he was honor bound to be sure the Scottish wrango boy didn't either. "Promised his daddy."

"I could drink a dozen," Bill Sweet said. "I'll drink yours."

"Two beers," Jap Hardy said. "Two or three."

The gray-eyed woman running the hotel studied them, then nodded. "I got a case and a half. That's it." She snapped caps off the bottles, handed them out, then stayed in her kitchen while they drank the first round.

There was a ring on her finger but no sign of any husband. "Kinda shy, that woman," Tarz Witzell said. "Don't blame her."

But when it was time for a second round she opened one for herself and came into the lobby where they were sitting quietly, nobody saying a thing.

"Where you headed?" she asked.

"Calgary," Rossie said. But she wasn't asking him, didn't even look at him.

"Who owns them horses?" she asked Jap Hardy.

"Man named Dufferena, out of Reno. They're California horses, going to the Mounties in Canada."

"Rich man's horses. Why would the Mounties be buying California horses?"

"Don't know about that. But they're mine until we get there."

"You ought to make off with them, sell the outfit, and split the money. Teach them rich bastards a lesson."

Jap Hardy shook his head. "You hear that kind of talk. That mining camp talk about stealing the prize. But who in hell would buy that many horses?"

"You chickenshit to try it?"

"Why don't you be our ringleader?" Tarz Witzell cut in, laughing at his joke.

107

"I'd do it," the woman said, and she didn't smile at all. "Show them bastards a little justice."

"Don't put no money on justice," Tarz Witzell said, laughing again.

"You laugh at me one more time, and this beer drinking is over."

"Aw, hell. We was just getting started."

"Yeah. To hell with it." She raised her bottle. "Here we are. I'll drink to you boys. You brought the horses."

"You got any playing cards?" Jap Hardy asked.

"There," she said. "That's a idea."

So they sat playing hands of pinochle until the beer was gone. As they went out into the darkness to their horses, the woman stood on the lighted porch. "You boys," she said, and closed the door.

By noon the next day they'd crossed a boggy narrows in the Donner und Blitzen Swamp, and beyond to the east side they approached a round barn with a conical roof that looked stranded like a ship left over from an old story, isolated as it was on a knoll among the sage hills. They herded the horses into a fence corner and held them quiet.

"You young fellows," Jap Hardy said, "this you ought to see. There was corrals and a cookhouse. But they been torn down, so all we got left is this barn." He sat on an orangey-red gelding, eyeing Rossie and Bill Sweet like one of them might have some dumb-shit thing to say. "Been here four times. This makes five."

"You take them boys in there," Tarz Witzell said. "Dickie and me will keep these horses herded."

Double-wide doors in the board-and-batten wall creaked as they were pulled back to reveal a circular track and inside that a mortared stone wall eight or so feet high and, in the exact center of the interior corral, a juniper post, burnished by ropes — from years of men snubbing horses — supported a conical roof where the rafters came together at the apex like spokes in a wheel. Noontime light drifted in through a circle of ports in a high, octagonal cupola and lay over the reddish interior woods like dust.

"You think of Pete French building that stone wall as a fort against Indians, and those Mexican boys from California chewing their snoose and gentling horses all winter," Jap Hardy said. "French took care that his hands was out of the winter. He was alone and afoot if they left him."

Rossie ran his fingertips down the center post.

"If you wanted a church," Jap Hardy said, "this would be it. French hated all them barbed-wire boys. Fucking settlers. One of them shot him. Ruined the country."

All through the rest of his life Rossie would tell the story of Peter French and the Mexican vaqueros and their kingdom ranch in that faraway valley and the round barn French had built so his men could work with their horses in the wintertime, out of the weather.

Sweeping past high desert settlements like Princeton and Juntura and Vale, overnighting at willowy springs, the men caught their horses before sunup and were rolled in their blankets not long after darkness settled around the cook fire. Rossie listened to the others snoring and muttering in their sleep and thought about how it must have been for Indians through all the years outside in the dark and hearing others sleep hour after hour in the night.

They held up traffic at a long, sway-bellied suspension bridge over the Snake River into Idaho. As the horses clattered across the macadam a woman wearing a white straw boater came from a motor car, green dress flapping in the breeze, and set up a tripod for photography.

Jap Hardy spurred his black horse and trotted up, somehow amused. "Pilgrim," he said. "You're going to cause me a stampede."

The woman smiled, eyes vividly and handsomely alight. "Isn't that the idea? Aren't you cowboys? You sound like a cowboy right out of the movies. If you could move off a little ways and take off your hat, I'd photograph you."

"One thing about cowboys." Jap Hardy looked to be happy as he could be. "They don't take off their hats."

"Fair enough," she said.

Jap Hardy touched his spurs to his horse, rode off, and sat while the woman focused her camera.

"You ought to be famous," she said, as she noted his name. "When this photograph is exhibited you might be famous in Berlin. Germans adore cowboys."

"My pleasure," Jap Hardy said, as the last of the herd moved off the highway bridge. Then he did take off his hat and tipped it to her. "My people are Portuguese. None of them had much use for Germans. But you could put a notice in the newspaper if I ever get famous in Portugal."

"I will," the woman said. "In the Boise newspaper."

"The Reno paper would be a better idea."

The woman nodded. "You're a sweet man."

That evening they turned the pinto bell mare and the herd into another fenced pasture and camped under apple trees. The green knobs of fruit were just beginning to show.

"Berlin," Jap Hardy said. "You think she knows anything about Berlin?"

"What's Berlin?" Tarz Witzell said.

"She said I was a sweetheart."

"That's what they claim." Tarz Witzell rolled his eyes like a comic. "She said you was a cowboy. We ain't no fucking cowboys. What we are is buckaroos. All we ever been."

Off by the massive Snake River, as it flowed in a surging oxbow around a cottonwood grove, men in uniforms were playing baseball on a dusty field with automobiles parked around it. Other men leaned against fenders, spitting snoose and swigging at unlabeled bottles of home-brewed beer while women chopped kindling, built fires, and tucked their Dutch ovens among the coals. Raggedy children ran in routes, kicking cans and tagging one another and old motorcars kept rolling in through the twilight. "Fucking Okies," Jap Hardy said.

"My people are Okies," Bill Sweet said. "Along with Arkie in their blood."

"Stands to reason. You act like a Okie Arkie cross."

"Wonder if those people ever seen bucka-roo dancing?"

Jap Hardy shook his head. "You got to try it, don't you?"

"Me and him," Bill Sweet said. "Me and old Rossie. We're going down there and visit them girls."

"You keep your dancing to yourself," Jap Hardy said. "There's hay-hand boys down there who will kick your ass into the river. They won't let you out. You'll be swimming for it."

"That mean we can go?"

"Shit, kid, you're five hundred miles from home, you can try anything you can think of. But don't get up sick and afraid to saddle your horse in the morning."

So there they went, Bill Sweet leading the way and Rossie following behind and feel-ing chickenshit because he'd hesitated.

"Nobody knows it," Bill Sweet said, "but I can swim like a duck."

A man with a beard and gray-white braids was tuning a fiddle at fireside, and more people were coming in wagons and beat-up flatbed trucks. A heavy woman with long hair frothed around her head set up a circle of camp stools by a fire. Her features were painted red, her forehead dotted with blue. She dealt a deck of outsize playing cards onto a yellow blanket. "The fool," she said, holding up a card. "He's here, so we're all right. There's no sweetness in things without the fool."

"She sees you coming," Rossie said to Bill Sweet.

"One other thing she'll see," Bill Sweet said. "She'll see me going." He wasn't smiling. "The Gypsies have took over around here. This is no place for us."

"What the hell?"

"That's right." Bill Sweet had a hand on Rossie's sleeve, pulling at him. "They's hell all right. Thieving and hellish."

"Thought you was going to be dancing."

"They'll be dancing on our ass."

"What if you had a drink of whiskey?" Rossie dug into his front pocket for the coins and roll of dollars he carried. "What if I bought you one drink of whiskey?"

"Where from?"

"That greasy fellow."

Buying whiskey was easy. Rossie passed a quarter to a tall bedraggled-looking man with taped-up boots who in turn produced a flat flask from his hip pocket. Rossie took a burning swallow and passed the flask.

"Wonder if we don't get disease," Bill Sweet said as they walked away.

"Yeah. The dancing pussy disease."

"You think that's going to happen? These is families. These little girls not going to be fucking with horseback boys."

"Buckaroos," Rossie corrected him. "You see that girl over there?" They edged up alongside one of the fires, where a cluster of people were watching a toothless man tune a banjo. Rossie nodded toward a black-haired, dish-faced girl on the far side of the fire, who was showing pregnant inside her lavender dress. "That girl has been fucking around. She's going to be a momma."

"I think she's smiling at me," Bill Sweet said. "She's already ruined herself and don't give a shit."

"Thought you was worried about Gypsies."

"I'm done with that. The whiskey helped."

"You're going to be done with your ass if you think she's smiling at you. These people seen your kind before. They'll eat you for dinner."

But Bill Sweet had turned away. Three boys had come up beside him, two of them stocky fellows of eleven or twelve and a third, bright-eyed and gawky, maybe fourteen or fifteen. They were wearing shit-crusted hand-me-down lace-up farmer boots and brownish home-sewn shirts with sleeves turned up at the cuffs. "You looking for something?" the tallest one asked.

"Girls," Bill Sweet said.

The tall boy showed greenish teeth. "Sister Sue. You got any money?"

"You talking about charging?" Bill Sweet swallowed before plunging on. "You talking money for fucking your sister?"

"I don't talk about free. Neither does Sister Sue."

"What kind of money?"

But the black-haired, pregnant girl had come around the fire, and she was smiling at Rossie, her eyes bright and clean as her teeth. "These asswipes bothering you?" she asked, without a glance at the boys.

"Five dollars," the tall one said. "For the both of you."

"Jamsie!" The girl spoke sharply in the direction of the toothless man, who had given up tuning his banjo to regard them with small eyes lost in wrinkles. The boys, when Rossie turned back, were gone, that fast. The girl was smiling again. "My momma should have drowned them dick-heads at birth," she said. It seemed an extreme thing for a pregnant girl to say, even when softened by her slow southern inflection.

"Do you down-home sweeties all talk that way?" Bill Sweet asked.

"First," she said, "I'm not some slice of pie. I call myself a woman."

"A woman and a growing half," Rossie said.

She nodded seriously, like this idea pleased her. "That half is the baby boy. He's entirely sure a boy."

"What's his name?"

"William. William Amos."

"After Amos and Andy?"

"That's mean," she said. "But I can take it. I like a little smart-ass in my men."

"So I'm one of your men?"

"Could happen. Where you from? Can't be from Idaho. Nobody with enough brains to be smart-assed ever came from Idaho. We found that out."

"Who's we?" Bill Sweet asked.

The girl nodded at the toothless man with his banjo. "Me and Jamsie and them. We come all the way from Arkansas, but there's no work."

"Where's your momma?"

"They're gone to Oregon. Momma and daddy are picking fruit out of trees around Corvallis. Jamsie is too old, and them boys are plain worthless, and I got knocked up. Now we're waiting for them to come back in the fall with money. I should have gone with them."

"You think they'll come back? Sometimes people don't."

"Yeah. Nobody knows about money, but they'll be back. My momma is a saint and my daddy is a good man."

"What accounts for them boys?"

"They'll grow up." She bit her upper lip and studied Rossie. "You can see there's no husband for this baby. And here you are, looking for girls. And here I am looking for a dollar."

"We got about six dollars," Bill Sweet said. "Between us."

"Well, bullshit," Rossie said. "I don't do bargaining for pussy." He pulled out the two dollars he had folded into his hip pocket and held them to her. "For you," he said. "For nothing but your sweetness."

"There was never no hope of you getting any pregnant pussy, anyway." She took the dollars, looking happy. "Those your horses that come through?"

"Not mine. We're running 'em to Calgary."

"Cowboys," she said, her eyes on the ground, smiling something of a secret angry smile. "You fuckers. Let's dance. I like dancing. You got to dance with me. That'll show those assholes." She flapped the dollars in her hand against her other palm and showed them to Jamsie, who lifted the banjo over his head in a gesture of thanks. "Slow," the girl said. "One dance for the cowboy."

For a long four or five minutes Jamsie picked out the chords of a song Rossie knew as "The Cowboy's Lament" while the girl got Rossie's arms around her and led him through a series of shuffling turns, kicking up puffs of dust as they went.

When the old man gave up his playing, she stepped out of Rossie's arms and curtsied. "Thank you, brave gentleman." She smiled, then ran like he might be following.

"How come you give her that money?" Bill Sweet asked, eyeing Rossie like he'd gone borderline crazy.

Rossie smiled. "The goodness of my heart."

"So you and me are pals. Since you gave away your money." Bill Sweet bought another couple of swallows of whiskey and the darkness settled. Swimmers were splashing in the river, and the music was awake with strumming, fiddle picking, voices from around the various fires singing out and replying, and a man counting one and two,

three, four, and quick-time music com-
mencing.

"Sure makes you feel like fucking," Bill
Sweet said.

"What do you know about fucking? Nothing, is my guess."

"You better get on with your dancing.
She's waiting for you."

"Dancing. We got horses in the morning.
You could have danced. You was just chickenshit."

"Yeah. Anyhow this place is running with
Gypsies."

"Where's the difference?"

"Them Gypsies is spooks."

"They's not any such things as spooks.
It's all in your head."

Bill Sweet studied Rossie for a quiet moment. "There's plenty you don't know nothing about."

That night Rossie wondered if an inclination toward just riding away was a sign of
cowardice even if it was common sense. In
the beginning of his dream Mattie was on
the meadow, and though he wanted to keep
his hands away from the secret silent jacking off, he couldn't.

Rossie called for a red-and-white, bald-
faced pinto named Pinky. First there was

Rock, the bay with a white star on his forehead. Next was Blackie, and third, asking for trouble, Rossie had picked a smooth-gaited traveling horse and named him Banjo. Now he was going to saddle this pinto, his Pinky horse. It had all come out perfect. He felt nothing of his old confusions about what to do. He was clear in his head and sure-handed and at ease. The sun rose and shadows from the cottonwoods by the river leaped off toward the west. So this is it, he thought. Here it is.

At sunup they were traveling between the fences along graded roads linking up white houses and row-crop fields and orchards. The horses were quick and nervous but followed their pinto bell mare.

"Tractor farmers," Dickie Wilson said, gazing out over the fields. "If they're not a sorry breed, what is?"

Jap Hardy rode off to Boise and came back with news. They had been planning on a night with the horse herd secured away in a fenced field and a trip to the bars, but it was not going to happen. "That town is in trouble," he said. "Three or four hundred men on the streets, going through on the railroad and camping by the river, bumming, boozing, and stealing. No-account, out-of-work assholes from Portland and

Seattle, coming home from Washington, D.C., and talking revolution. Useless bastards, looking for handouts. They say they would have burned down the Capitol building and the White House, but General MacArthur got the army out, and ready to shoot. They say the federal government is coming apart. I say let her go. Nobody would miss the son of a bitch."

"Don't think they'd bother me while I was having a drink," Tarz Witzell said. "They'd be bumming on you," Jap Hardy said. "You'd run out of patience, I've seen it. Some of them are carrying pistols. Bad trouble. We are not going in there. We're running horses. They got troubles we don't need."

Dickie Wilson set down his coffee. "Them boys spend all the day milling and stirring. What do you think? Do they like it?"

Over the next week they swung a long arc along the unfenced edges of the Idaho plains where the irrigated farmlands dried into pasturelands. To the north lay an impassable eighty-mile moonscape of lava flats and volcanic craters, beyond which they could see faint snowy mountains in long north-south reefs. After they crossed a low grassland pass, Jap Hardy told them they were in Montana. "Pretty country from here on," he said. "She's grass all the way to Calgary."

Upstream along the Dearborn River, the Rockies Front Range looming to the west, the herd flowed over a grassland bench and down to the Teton River. At the end of the long day, Jap Hardy counted the bell mare and the two hundred and fifty-seven Dufferena geldings and the private horses into a pasture and set of corrals called the French Field. They were upstream on the Teton from the settlers' town of Choteau.

"How come it's called the French Field?" Bill Sweet asked. Jap Hardy studied him like a problem.

"It's owned by a fellow named French. What'd you think, there might be French girls around here? Hope you boys don't like milk shakes. They got a milk shake store, girls, and a movie house. But you're not going to see 'em." He had counted seventeen head which had thrown at least one shoe. "We're not showing up in Calgary with lame horses. We'll stay here tomorrow to nail on shoes."

Using the portable forge hauled all this way in the bed-wagon truck, they rasped hooves and shaped horseshoes to fit, nailing them in place.

Once the blacksmith's fire was out and the little anvil tucked away, Bill Sweet brought up the idea of testing the new horses. "I'm going to try out that old Hammerhead, the squealing blue roan son. I'd like to show him something."

"You'll be kicking and squealing," Jap Hardy said. "But you ought to put on your spurs. It might shut you up."

"Or I might ride him right down."

"We'll hear about you in Madison Square Garden," Tarz Witzell said. "We'll think about how we knew Bill Sweet when he was just a kid."

Rossie kept quiet, not wanting to bust his head. He was beginning to think that rodeo was bullshit and wondered if that labeled him an all-the-way coward. Later he felt guilty, like he'd known what would happen and should have warned Bill Sweet. But who guessed luck could run so quickly haphazard?

Corralled, the blue roan stood quiet as Bill Sweet got a toe in the stirrup and tested his weight there. He swung aboard and speared the big gelding with his sharp Spanish spurs. It was, as Jap Hardy said later on, a kid's trick. The roan settled on his haunches, then charged, not bucking so much as escaping, across the corral and directly into the pole fence, where he recoiled backward and fell. That quick, Bill Sweet was underneath on the dusty ground as the roan scrambled to his feet and stepped for no reason other than bad luck with his whole weight on Sweet's left shin. Rossie heard the snapping bone, the cracking.

"That son of a bitch is broke off." Already Bill Sweet looked green in the face.

"It's not off, but she's broke," Jap Hardy said, taking his knife to Bill's Sweet's trousers as he howled. White bone and blood showed through the flesh.

"You are going to do some crying," Tarz Witzell said. "But we are taking that one to town."

They splinted the leg with rawhide thongs and willow sticks and eased Bill Sweet into the Model A truck.

"You're coming with me," Jap Hardy said to Rossie. "You can sit on that boy if he starts thrashing."

Rossie found himself holding Bill Sweet's hand.

"Tell you a sad thing," Sweet said. "You are what family I got. Right here. You're it. If this ain't the shits-for-luck."

"The complete shits." Rossie looked away.

"There's never no justice to it," Jap Hardy

said. They reached the hospital in Choteau by late afternoon. The doctor was a bright-eyed fellow who'd been out fishing on the Teton River and was still in hip boots when he came into the operating room. "You boys clear out of here," he said.

Rossie and Jap Hardy walked the leafy streets of the town, passing elaborate white-painted houses where roses bloomed in the yards.

"Pissant shame, but they is nothing we can do about it," Jap Hardy said. "You get used to it. In these farmer towns people think they can't break their leg. They think they're getting away with something."

"What you going to do about him?"

"He can't travel. I'm going to pay the doctor and give the kid fifty bucks. He can get the rest of what he's got coming from Dufferena. If he had any sense he'd stay here, find a girl, and live in one of these houses. Best luck ever struck him. For us, it's open prairies from here to Calgary, so we can go shorthanded."

"He said we was family."

"Then he's got worse luck than a broken leg. Anyway, he said you was, not me."

"What if I broke mine?"

"Same thing. Except I'd have to hire somebody."

Bill Sweet was white-faced and passed out with drugs in a hospital room when Jap Hardy scribbled a note that read: "Here's fifty. You'll get the rest from Dufferena. Left your gear and your horse with the fellow who owns the French Field. Good luck."

So now, Rossie thought, you know. You got no excuses for trusting to luck.

CANADA

Coming north through Montana, they rode rolling grassy hills within sight of Browning, the headquarters town for the Blackfeet Reservation, where unpainted houses lined the dusty streets. "Nothing like Choteau," Jap Hardy said. "Them Indians are living at the bottom of a well."

They rested the horses alongside the windy shores of Duck Lake, just short of the Canadian border. Off west the peaks in Glacier National Park gleamed under remnant snow, and hummingbirds hovered over the white and yellow prairie flowers.

"We're going into Canada with rested animals," Jap Hardy said. "Dufferena wants these horses first-rate plush when they're delivered."

The crossing into Canada took place the next afternoon on a back road with no one to notice, about a hundred and twenty miles from Calgary. "Boy, this your first foreign country?" Tarz Witzell asked.

Rossie hadn't thought about it. He was listening more and more to the creaking of his saddle. The clarity of air over the mountains looked touchable.

"Me, too," Tarz Witzell said.

Half a dozen miles upstream from the haze of home-fire smoke that hung over Calgary, they camped at a place called Liskie House, a ranch leased out by the Royal Canadian Mounted Police on the willow-lined banks of the Bow River. Alexander Beets, a string-bean of a man who managed property for the province of Alberta, came to greet them on a black-flecked gray that showed Appaloosa blood. He and Jap Hardy counted the same two hundred and fifty-seven horses into one last fenced field.

"Son of a bitch," Tarz said, "if we isn't been good boys? Got here with the entirety of them."

Clifford Dufferena wasn't due off the train from Vancouver until the second day of June. They had three days. Louis Clair and Angus Jackson set up planks on sawhorses for a table, a fire pit lined with stones, and rounds of log for stools. They ate in the twilight with the lights of the Liskie house showing through the trees.

"Been so long at traveling I forget what it would be like indoors, sitting there with a woman waiting table," Dickie Wilson said.

Tarz Witzell eyed him. "Don't worry. We get to one of those whorehouses, you'll remember."

Jap Hardy came back from a look-around with the news that just a mile or so down-river, toward the smokes of Calgary, there was a cluster of buffalo-hide tepees huddled beside log buildings roofed with mossy shakes. "Nobody told me about an Indian camp."

"Them Indians don't got it left in them to steal horses," Tarz Witzell said. "Down there at the Klamath Marsh, at Bear Flat, they was eating dogs. Snow three foot deep and dogs was hung up and skinned behind the store. If you offered to buy food, they cut off a frozen shank of dog and cooked it. We don't got any dogs. There won't be no trouble." He smiled, showing teeth like this was a fine irony. Jap Hardy shook his head. "These Blackfeet are another kind. They got more stomach. This is their home country. They see us like we was magpies."

"I knew an old white woman, made her living cooking bootleg whiskey at Bear Flat. She said the plains people was ruined, acting like they was wolves. Wind and snow,

130

that's what they got left out on the plains, she said. It's gone, anything they would want."

"Shit, Hutterite farmers are making a living out there. Raising turkeys and pigs and every other goddamned thing." Jap Hardy was smiling like he had won a debate.

"Hutterites is crazy. They gone crazy on religion."

"Crazy enough to work hard."

"That's no accounting. You and me are proof of that. Running down the road like we was warhorse buckaroos. She's over, that show."

"Not everywhere, You know where I'd try? Australia and South America. You can stay right where you grew up but I always figured that's a dumb-fuck thing to do when there was new country."

"We could," Tarz Witzell said.

"What's that?"

"We could take that train to San Francisco and go boating off to Australia." Tarz Witzell smiled at this first-rate joke.

Jap Hardy looked at him like he'd never heard such idiocy before.

"I'd do it," Tarz Witzell said.

"What we're going do is draw straws and see who gets night-herding shifts. We deliver these horses and then we can think about

Australia. Hold up a bank in California and run for the South Seas."

In the end they all put in their shifts. Rossie saddled a horse in moonlight and patrolled in circles around the pasture, waiting for sunup. This was a waste of time — there wasn't going to be no horse stealing — but it set him thinking of Bill Sweet down in Choteau, in some boardinghouse room, probably watching out the window for morning, trying to guess how long it would be before he could get horseback again.

Come morning, his pinto horse turned loose to roll in the dust, Rossie was cradling a cup of coffee by the cook fire when a rider on a shaggy, white mare approached over the prairie. Pushing back a sweat-stained hat, the rider turned out to be a hawk-faced girl in a pale blouse and baggy, black trousers. Rossie took her for Indian until he saw her gray eyes.

She spoke in a clipped way, from astride her horse. "I have come to appeal for breakfast, on the hope you have bacon. I can pay for breakfast if you have bacon. Thick and crisp-fried." She lifted her chin at Rossie.

"Thought you was an Indian," he said.

She studied him. "You're the one who

might be. From your coloring."

"Guess I should get a haircut. What I am is half-Basque. From Spain, but nobody calls us Spaniards. My grandfather was a dockhand in Spain. My father is a cardsharp in Reno."

"European." She considered this. "You look like a cardsharp."

Rossie had dug out his white-handled knife and was peeling away wisps of thumbnail. Why, he didn't know.

"The Blackfoot tribe and I, we're outlaws," she said. "We know abandonment."

"Abandonment," Rossie said. "Do you think about saying that stuff before you say it?"

Her smile hardened, though she looked reluctantly amused. "Aren't you an asshole." It was not a question.

Jap Hardy stepped in front of Rossie, one hand up, palm open. "You got to forgive this boy. Been on the trail and lost his manners. Get down and we'll give you bacon." He gave Rossie a sideways look, like this was joke between men. "We got a cook to fry it up. That's his job."

The girl swung off the shaggy mare. She was almost as tall as Rossie, holding out the bridle reins in her big hands. "If you were going to be a gentleman, you'd do something with my horse. Her name is Sky."

"Will she stand?"

"She will."

"So you could just drop the reins any-where, and she'd stand like a cow horse. Something you could do yourself if I wasn't busy being a gentleman."

"Of course, but will you do it for me?"

"Sure will." Rossie took the bridle reins and led the mare off to the Model A truck, dropping the reins over the front bumper. "There she stands."

"Thank you." She smiled with what seemed to be no trace of irony.

"Louis," Jap Hardy said. "We got com-pany. Break out the bacon, and you could mix up some pancakes. You've got plenty of time. We ain't doing nothing but entertain-ing this lady."

Louis Clair produced a slab of bacon and Angus Jackson bit at his tongue as he labored to slice it evenly.

"My name is Eliza Stevenson," the girl said to him. "Tell me yours."

"Angus."

"And you?" She smiled at Louis as he mixed the pancake batter.

"My people," Louis Clair said, "under-stand that food is a sacrament."

Tarz Witzell was eyeing Louis like he

thought the cook had gone crazy. "You saying a sacrament? What about women? Be a big thing for me if women was a church. That way I'd have spent my life dreaming about church."

"Angus," she said. "You must be Scottish."

"My mother come from the Hebrides Islands," the boy said. "When she was a baby child."

"What of your father?"

The boy stopped sawing at the side of bacon, swallowing before he spoke. "Nobody knows. Not even my mother, according to what she claims."

"Tragic. Do you feel your life is tragic?"

"Lady, I'm supposed to be cutting bacon. My last name is Jackson and my mother says she just made that up."

"My father," she said, "is related to Robert Louis Stevenson. The Stevensons are a Scottish family you may know about. That's what my father claims. But I don't believe him."

"Why's that?" Rossie asked.

Eliza Stevenson smiled faintly, then raised her eyebrows. "He's unreliable — spoiled and unreliable."

Bacon and pancakes and a dozen eggs sizzled on a griddle over the fire. The table

135

with sawhorse legs was set with butter and canned syrup while Louis Clair filled each tin plate.

"Here we are with bacon, breakfasting," Eliza Stevenson said. "Isn't this a holiday."

"I'm happy you come," Tarz Witzell said, dropping his slick tin plate in the washbasin where hot water was steaming on the grill. "We don't eat this fine every morning."

"It's not a easy thing to cook over an open fire," Louis Clare said.

"By God, no," Jap Hardy said. "We're damned proud of you, Louis. Ask anybody."

Tarz Witzell turned toward Eliza Stevenson. "So, you might settle me a mystery. What are you doing here on these plains? Who's looking after you when Louis isn't cooking?"

"Nobody looks after me. No one but me." It didn't seem to be a subject she intended to pursue. "All of you should come to my gathering. It's on Sunday."

"Too bad," Jap Hardy said. "We'll be on the train out of Calgary."

"Some church thing?" Rossie said.

"It's a party with friends. My friends are Blood Indians. You look like an Indian, so you'd be comfortable. A going-away party." She broke into a phrase of song, her voice high, light and clear. *"Fare thee well, little darling."* She smiled. "I'm going home to the Bitterroot Valley because I'm three months with child and the father has run off to the warrior life. And my own father tells me he's dying of a cancer, my second reason for going home."

"That cancer's a hell of a thing," Tarz Witzell said.

"I'm taking the Canadian Pacific Railroad to Vancouver," she said, "and a train to Seattle, and then Missoula. I'm going to my father's house in the Bitterroot Valley, where my father and mother will look after me, don't mistake it, and my child."

"What sort of a cancer?" Jap Hardy asked.

"In his groin, where he sits, a slow cancer. It doesn't pain him yet, but he says it inevitably kills. The doctor tells him that and he won't have it cut out." She looked up and her gray eyes were dry and still.

"My daddy had that damned old agony," Tarz Witzell said. "Sat on a feather pillow at the end."

"And I'll be a pregnant woman on the train," she said.

"Woman?" Rossie scoffed. "You're a girl."

"Whatever we are," she said. "Sweethearts. We could be, in another world. That's a wonderful idea." She batted her gray eyes, not morose at all but at sport with her flirting.

Clifford Dufferena arrived in a rented, red-painted buggy drawn by Standard-bred geldings.

"Pretty team," Jap Hardy said. "Never seen them kind of horses broke to harness before."

"Pretty enough to suit us," Dufferena said. But his attention was on the horses drifting among the willows along the Bow River. They had to be counted through one more gate and the deal was done. He stood with Alexander Beets beside him and the two of them counted the animals.

"Good enough," Alexander Beets said.

Dufferena produced a fan of paycheck envelopes and a bottle of Irish whiskey. He pulled the cork, tossed it into the brush, then sat with the bottle beside him. "I got a bank in Calgary that'll cash these checks." He tossed them the pay envelopes, each marked with a name. "I got another envelope for the boy that hurt himself. He sent a letter to General Delivery in Calgary, begging for his pay. He's doing chores for a deer-hunting camp headquartered in a Montana town called Charlo. Three pages of his scribbling but no hint of where to send the check."

"I could find him," Louis Clair offered, "if I'm driving the truck to Reno."

"That truck is sold to a man in Calgary. You ought to be happy on the railroad. You'll be eating in the dining car."

"I been thinking about them rock mountains," Rossie said. "I might never get back to this country. That Malinda, down in Eagleville, she told me the Bitterroot Valley was a dandy for horses. I'm thinking I should ride down there before I go off for home."

"There's extra horses," Dufferena said. "I promised these boys I'd buy the ones they brought to Eagleville for twenty-five dollars cash, now, in a minute. Three extra private horses. You can take two, and that would leave one more I can sell to the Mounties. Then I don't got to pay your way on the railroad. You carry this paycheck to that boy if you find him. That would be a fair deal all around."

"What if I got his check cashed and kept his money?"

"Then you'd be known far and wide around Nevada as a cheap-shit thief."

"What if I didn't care?"

"Then you would be a cheap-shit thief, and nobody would want to deal with you another time."

"I'd want that Rock horse, and the pinto called Pinky."

"Square deal," Dufferena said, and it was done.

"Wondering about square, how much in dollars do you realize from us running them horses for you, and you selling them?" Dickie Wilson asked.

"That's for me to know." Dufferena began pouring Irish whiskey into tin cups Louis Clair had set out before him.

"Me," he said, licking his lips in an old-man way, "I am thirty-five hundred dollars to the good. And you fellows did the work."

"We ought to have two bottles of that whiskey for that," Jap Hardy said. Dufferena offered his false-toothed smile. "I got three more in my bedroll."

GHOSTS

Morning rose across the prairies with surging winds and spitting rain. Louis Clair and Angus were up and wearing slickers before sunrise, working around the fire, coffee already made. Jap Hardy stood with a steaming cup, his back to the fire, while Rossie pulled on his boots and went out to stand beside him.

"Miserable son of a bitch," Jap Hardy said. "Always is, if the outfit breaks up. Rained the day they auctioned the Seven-T horses in North Warner. September and it damned near snowed. Never seen it to fail." Then he eyed Rossie. "You been good help. We'll see you in Nevada, around them buckaroo camps."

Rossie heard Jap Hardy calling him a man.

By midmorning Dufferena was gone with Jap Hardy in his buggy, tug chains rattling behind the Standard-bred geldings. Tarz Witzell and Dickie Wilson rode in the

Model A truck loaded with their bedrolls and saddles in gunny sacks for the last stretch to the railroad in Calgary.

That quick, Rossie was on his own. The Rock horse was loaded with his gear and roped down on a packsaddle bummed off Alexander Beets, and there was nobody he owed any answers. He would cash his one-hundred-dollar paycheck in Calgary, then move on to Montana with greenbacks in his possession. He didn't know a soul within a thousand miles but for Bill Sweet in Charlo in the Flathead Valley, if he was still there. And that gray-eyed girl.

The rain drizzled and quit, but the cold wind went on singing of isolations as the cook fire burned down to coals. Rossie considered building it up and watching as it burned down again, and building it up another time, stalling with his mind on that Stevenson girl. Beside the dying fire, Rossie flinched at the thought of Alexander Beets coming along to find him jacking off — at how that would look — as finally the wind fell away altogether.

The night before, working to fathom what to do next, Rossie had decided to be simple and smart with work and his money, and maybe he would just naturally turn out like Nito, able to deal with a slippery new deck of cards every time. But this was at the end of boyhood, and he was playing without plans. He'd drifted off to dream of slipperiness and fucking with Mattie, and he'd awakened with his mind on Eliza Stevenson.

Now, with the fire burned to embers, Rossie got up horseback and headed out onto the lane that ran up and down above the Bow River. From the low hills, soon enough, he could see down into a camp clustered among the riverbank willows just as Jap Hardy had described it — tepees scattered around shake-roofed cabins built of rotting cottonwood logs, surrounded by a straggling garden. Nothing moved until a pack of yellowish dogs came out barking. The horses were used to this and held their own, giving the mutts little attention as Rossie climbed off Pinky, scaled a flat rock into the midst of the hounds, and hollered, "Shit eaters!" The dogs shut down the racket and came slinking toward him, sniffing and wagging, as if they might be fed. Hounds at his heels, horses tethered, Rossie made his way toward the houses.

A tiny, ancient woman in buckskins appeared, her face seemed collapsed though she was smiling. "Nevada," she said, her tone high and lilting, as if she were singing.

"Son of a bitch."

A sharp-featured young Indian man wearing metal-rimmed eyeglasses came out from the building that was sending smoke into the cold sky. His shirt was striped red, white, and blue, and his long, tight, black braids, interwoven with red and white ribbons, dangled yellow feathers from their ends.

"Nevada," the old woman said again in that singing voice.

"Ross Benasco?" The young man in the lurid shirt closed the door behind him, as to hiding whatever was in there, and held up his left hand, palm out.

"You got me," Rossie said.

"Not for long," the man said. "For tonight, you got us. If you come inside, we'll open a beer, then take care of your horses." He spoke precisely, as if trained to speak, and Rossie wondered if he actually was an Indian.

"How'd you know my name?"

"Eliza," the old woman said, her smile so insistent Rossie wondered if her mind was haywire. Her hands, folded together before her, were swollen and gnarled. Rossie saw that her hair had once been blond, that her eyes were gray. She clearly was not an Indian. "You meet everyone," she said.

144

"Eliza said you were half-Basque. That was enough to make you welcome with Eliza."

"How's that?"

"She is inclined that way," the man said. "She and I are the strangers here. She's the white girl who showed up with Charlie Cooper. I've been to schools in British Columbia and in Missoula, the college."

"Hell of a thing for an Indian," Rossie said, thinking here's an Indian with eyeglasses, he's been to college and says words like *inclined*.

"Indeed," the man said. "Two years. My degree will be in forestry, the care of forests. I owe it to Eliza's father, my employer. Part of my work involves looking after her."

"What's the other part of your work?"

"Pity," the man said, and that seemed to finish the topic. "I should introduce myself. My name is Leonard Three Boy. There's a joke in there, but I don't know what it is. The names the whites put on Indians were usually jokes. This woman is Barbara. She used to be British, or that's what she tells us. Isn't that true?" he said to the woman.

"True as you'll ever know." Her smile didn't waver.

On the porch, Rossie had thought he was alone with the old woman and Leonard Three Boy, but the room inside, when they entered, was thronging. There were no young people, no sign of children, nothing but old faces. A dozen, four at each of three tables, sat silent, playing dominoes. Others were intent at card games. Two men, boots beside them, slept on folded blankets along the back wall. A cluster of women — the grandmothers, Rossie thought — had claimed a circle of broken-down chairs. With hair braided in tight-to-the-skull styles, they were got up in shawls in patterns of red and blue and yellow.

"Here we are," Leonard Three Boy said. "Raise your right hand. Smile and say hello."

Some nodded, but most looked away to their cards and dominoes.

"They disdain you," Leonard Three Boy said. "But they will be polite until they know you. Then we'll see."

"What they got against me?"

Leonard Three Boy smiled. "Fifty years on dole food."

A battered sink with a pitcher pump was set in a counter lined with wooden cases of home-brewed beer. A cast-iron cookstove and a stack of split firewood took up the far wall.

"One rule is no whiskey," Leonard said. "Nothing but beer. Which would be illegal if this was a reserve. Hope you can drink it warm." He opened a dark bottle. "Warm is what we got."

"If this isn't some reservation what is it?" Rossie asked. "You got rules? Like a school?"

"This is nowhere. Mormon missionaries abandoned these buildings. The blond daughter died and they left. They said missionaries would return but it's been seven years. Even the Mormons have forgotten us. So we treat the place like it's ours." The abandoned Mormon school, onetime classrooms and dormitories where the teachers had lived, now made up the shelters that the Indians occupied.

"These people wait in a web of dreams, as if the old days might return. They're waiting like spiders. The galloping and war — that they remember like it was a dream. They live a mystic life, full of stories about guardian animals and spirits that are as real as anything. The sun and earth are alive, and spirits from dreams will care for them if they live right. But they are actually as alone in the world as anyone, as deep into their need for assurances. It doesn't matter how they live. The dreamers are dead. The survivors are helpless. Their world died, and they don't know how much it had to do with you. They don't hate you yet. But they will if you act like someone who might have killed the world. So you be careful."

"You believe any of that?" Rossie asked. "You're not talking like a man who believes it."

"I was born in it, but I don't believe it. Mormon schooling took with me. I was the smart one, and I went to British Columbia and trained to translate for Franz Boas, in case he ever came to the Rockies. It was a mistake. I wanted to believe in dreams but Boas taught me to believe in facts and theories. Then Eliza's father, Bernard, found me and sent me to the university in Missoula, saying he'd pay for me to look after these people and I could be a hero. All he wanted was someone to look after Eliza. I think of myself as her guardian animal, but an animal who is on his way through university. I'm an educated savage, pimping for whites. I could be going dumb though. I think about coming back here." He smiled like he was sharing a joke. "You're looking for Eliza. She's sleeping. There's too much sleeping. But Eliza has her reasons. Tonight we'll be awake."

Rossie and Leonard Three Boy went outside again through the main room, the old people paying them no attention. The dogs followed them as they led Pinky and Rock to the barn, where Rossie unsaddled, pulled the pack off Rock, brushed the horses and left them in empty stalls.

"It must be that you trust us," Leonard Three Boy said, "or else you're a damned fool. Blood Indians are famous for stealing horses, and you're leaving yours for the taking."

"You call yourself Bloods?"

"In truth, I'm Salish, from the Flathead. But these are the Bloods. In Canada the Blackfoot are called Bloods."

"Could be I'm a fool, then."

"No stealing tonight. That would be like picking cherries. There'll be plenty of horses this evening. Young men bring their women, and the women bring their children. They come here to sing with the old men who care for the medicine bundles."

Later, they sat sipping their beer on the edge of the veranda of the main house, dangling their legs, while the dogs lay in the dirt at their feet.

Leonard Three Boy stretched his arms over his head. "Where you could go is to Eliza's tepee, the one with the magpie feathers. A girl with feathers, wishing she was Indian. She thinks being Indian would make her life significant. I'm wishing I was rich.

Don't want to be white, but rich would be elegant." Leonard spoke long words slowly, parsing out their syllables in parts. "I earned my feathers. I was born in a tepee."

When Rossie called Eliza's name, she ducked out from under a dirty orange blanket over her doorway. Her black hair was tied up in a braid, and she looked scrubbed in a long-sleeved bluish dress that hung to her ankles. She seemed to be happy that he was there even if she would not meet his eyes. "You came," she said.

Rossie saw that her feet, when she sat across from him on the layered blankets, were bare and callused.

"Tell me," she said. "This is what girls want to know. Why did you come?"

Rossie shrugged as if it wasn't anything he'd had to ponder over. "A party is a party. And you're a handsome outfit."

"Even pregnant with another man's child?"

"How'd you get so pregnant?"

"There's only so much pregnant. One way or the other is how it works." She turned her smile away from him. "Charlie Cooper, he's the one. We came to live with his people but Charlie went batshit — that's what his mother says, batshit, meaning crazed but not crazy. He went down to Montana to

150

hold up a bank, but he never got to the bank. Instead he met Chevrolet White Tribe, who wanted to be a warrior, and together they beat a farmer almost utterly to death outside a bar in Great Falls."

"Chevrolet White Tribe," Rossie said. "That's some name!"

"A pink-eyed idiot. He ruined my life." She studied her long hands. "My father told me to stay away from Charlie, that he would be famous for his anger and nothing else. But my father was wrong. Charlie will be famous for my child. They gave him seven years. But he'll do something else. Prison forever is Charlie's fate." This sounded like words she had polished.

"You should cut off a finger," Rossie said. "Isn't that what they do? Or shave your head."

"You should talk like a grown-up," she scoffed. "Charlie was meant to be a warrior but the Blood Reserve doesn't have any use for that kind any more. He's also half-French, so his heart can break. Seeing the old men die drove him broken. His mother, on the other hand, is like me."

Charlie Cooper's mother had grown up in a family from the south of France that raised vegetables for Paris. Every night they loaded boxes onto the train, and the next morning their vegetables were sold in a market in Paris, Les Halles. Then her French father heard about free land in Alberta.

"She was like me," Eliza said. "She ran off with a Blood warrior. Nowadays, Charlie lives in a sad room where the door is closed. I don't hear Charlie's voice any more. I'm looking for a sensible fellow."

"That would be me," Rossie muttered. "I'm sensible to the point of chickenshit."

"I knew I was pregnant," she said, ignoring him, "by early March. It would have happened about Valentine's Day. That's what my mother said. Since I wouldn't come home, my father sent Leonard to look after me, saying I needed looking after before I made an entire whore of myself."

"People make whores of themselves," Rossie said. "It gets them where they got to go. That's what it seems."

"Sometimes they fall off the world for a while. Leonard tells me to find a new man. My father says I'm ruined for serious men."

"Leonard says you want to think you're an Indian," Rossie said.

"Not an Indian." She turned her gaze. "Like an Indian. It must be plain that I love no one but warriors, and I don't want to believe you're chickenshit. Why not think we're an Indian? It beats dying of boredom, watching horseflies swarm in the Bitterroot. My father says that's nonsense. He asked me if I wanted to be a defeated, starving creature. He says not anybody gets anywhere stealing from the rich, that you need to *be* rich. But he's down there in the Bitterroot dying of his cancer, stewing in his juices. Because of me, he sends money each month in the mail to a woman here I call Auntie Red. She manages the spending. He believes in charity, but not too much. What I believe in is give everything away. But that's ridiculous. It's suicidal, my father says . . ."

"You want a straight answer, as to what I'm doing here?" Rossie went on without waiting for her to reply. "I'm chasing your ass."

"A lost girl, that's what I am." She looked up, clear-eyed. "I'm glad you came. A girl likes to know she's admired. But there are things to do. I'll come for you."

She left him to lie back on her blankets, wondering where he'd got himself as he kicked off his boots, curled up, and tucked his left arm under his head. The blankets stank faintly but warmly of her, and he slept even though he wasn't tired. In his dream a woman carried green branches thick with yellow flowers as she crossed a meadow. Lost in sleep, he knew this was his brain talking, making excuses and saying good-bye.

When Eliza woke him it was evening. She tied a beaded belt around her waist. "Simple," she said. "That's the thing if you're showing." And she was, the curve of her belly faintly distended.

Children populated the old schoolhouse yard, some batting a ball made of twine wrapped tightly around rags, while others played kick-the-can. Down by the horse barn, wood smoke rose from an antique buffalo-hide tepee, huge and mended with stitched patches. The blue trim around its base bore yellow circles that represented moons in the night; paintings of long-bodied otters undulated above them, each following the next, forever. The crown was a night sky, painted black with yellow stars.

Eliza, with Leonard following, led Rossie inside the tepee to confront old men in grease-slicked, beaded buckskins, eagle feathers dangling from their braided hair. A bundle wrapped in buffalo and elk skin lay before them, and a fire burned on a platform of sand inside a circle of river stones, smoke drifting upward.

"Those are the chiefs," Eliza whispered.

"No one expects you to do anything but nod. They don't want anything to do with you but they want you to acknowledge that you see them." One of the chiefs was named Gone to the Wolves, and Eliza said she called the other one Bright Red. "That's not his name. It's what I call him. Bright Red representing pride." Eliza gestured to a heavy, broad-faced woman. "His daughter, Auntie Red — also my honorific name — is the one who manages the money. Nobody will tell me their real names. Leonard says I'm a joke and jokes don't get to know your name."

The crowded interior of the tepee quieted as Rossie and Eliza approached the old men, who fell into whispering and signs and looked beyond Rossie and Eliza as if they were invisible. One of the old chiefs finally grinned and spoke in a quick, soft way.

"They're saying you're a ghost," Leonard Three Boy said. "A phantom. But they didn't say phantom."

"They say they should kill you but won't because the women like you. It's a joke," Leonard Three Boy explained. "They know they can't kill you so they say you're a spook and a joke, but they don't laugh."

Eliza seated Rossie by the back wall and sat herself directly before the chiefs on a ragged buffalo-skin robe, with Leonard beside her. The ancient man Eliza called Bright Red lifted a coal from the fire with a forked willow stick and set it on a twist of sweet grass. He and Gone to the Wolves scrubbed their hands together as if washing them in smoke, and chanted. As the group joined in like a chorus, a carved, reddish stone pipe was lighted and passed from the chiefs to the men and the oldest women and eventually even to Rossie. The women lifted their left hands, and the old chief chanted again, then spoke in harsh but articulate English.

"For you, Eliza, I say this. The earth will give you food. Prayers rise for you along with this smoke."

The others repeated this as Eliza stood, stepped across to Rossie, and held out her hand. "Now they open the bundle. We'll wait outside."

The soft beating of drums and rattles, the blowing of whistles, and the singing went on while Rossie and Eliza sat on the veranda and the sun went down.

"What they do when I'm there never makes much sense to me," Eliza said. "Leonard tells me their true rituals and intentions are none of my business. I call it praying. But they won't do it with me there, and I don't know what they think beyond sadness."

Auntie Red came to stand before Rossie with hands clasped before her. "We are poor," she said in immaculate British tones. "Do you have money? I am not above seeking money. Eliza will tell you that I am responsible." She lifted her chin and looked away. "Five dollars?"

Rossie fished out his thin wallet, and handed over four folded dollar bills. "That'll have to do," he said. "Where'd you learn your English?"

The woman smiled, then turned away. "She did school with the Mormons in Cardston," Eliza said. "They stole her from her family. But it took. She writes a beautiful hand and keeps immaculate books. Your four dollars will be precisely recorded."

"There's a first for me, giving up money. Don't think I like it."

Eliza cocked her head sideways. "My father says it's an acquired taste."

When the twilight had settled and the ceremonies were finished, the people came to the cookhouse. Women with babies sat on benches at tables covered with worn, white oilcloth that showed faint, floral patterns. Lean men in cowhand boots or moccasins and ragged shirts stood with their

157

arms folded. The cases of beer, thus far untouched, sat on a table. Old women struggled from their chairs, came to Eliza, and patted and stroked her stomach. "This boy," one said, "can he keep it happy?" At this they cut their eyes toward Rossie, lifted their hands, and waved their fingers, laughing. Eliza did a two-step shuffle, girl on the run, and they laughed again.

"If them women don't know ghosts," Rossie said, "who does?" But he'd lost her.

Eliza was looking past him. Two young Blackfeet men had come in from the veranda, each with a washbasin heaped with steaks. "Yearling elk," she said.

Women ladled cold soup into blue tin bowls, which older girls then distributed along the tables, while other women tended the fire in the cookstove. Another came from a back room with cast-iron frying pans.

"So this," Eliza said, "is my going-away-forever party." She was trying to look ironic but not bringing it off. Rossie thought she looked about to cry.

A woman with her hair bound into a graying knot brought pitchers of creamy milk from a burlap-covered cooler. She began filling tumblers for other women to place at the tables. Tin plates were set out in piles, and forks and a handful of knives were aligned with the bowls of cold soup. Children came in from their games, the little ones hanging on the skirts of their mothers, who lighted kerosene lanterns and hung them from nails above the table, casting shadows across the board walls.

Eliza led Rossie to a table and sat him beside an old man who had his elbows on his knees and was staring at the toes of his ankle-high shoes, leather cracked at the seams but immaculately polished. "This is William But Not. You'll be all right with William. He's our genius."

Rossie wondered what he was doing hiding in a corner — if there was some chance he'd not be all right. How could this man with woolen underwear bagged around the tops of his shoes be a genius? Wings of black hair along with some strands of gray hung around the man's face. His hands, gripping the edge of the table, were so huge and lean that brownish-white bone shone through his skin.

He tipped his head and studied Rossie. "Dusty son of a bitch," William But Not said. "Lovelock. Dusty son of a bitch. Nevada, time for a beer."

He gestured imperiously to a young woman. "Beer," he said, "for this Nevada, and for me." The woman brought the beer, and after one long swallow from his bottle, William But Not settled back to staring at his shoes, holding the bottle between his knees in those huge hands. "Dusty son of a bitch in Nevada." The whites of his eyes were yellowish, their pupils dark and intense. Abruptly, as if a decision had been made, he began a story. "My father went down there to Walker Lake, to Wovoka, after the massacre. Wovoka wouldn't come out of the house. His wife said the messiah was tired and we should go away."

"Massacre?" Rossie had only the vaguest notion what this man, who was studying him intently, was talking about. Wovoka had been a ranch hand on the Walker Lake Reserve, south of Carson City. He'd told the tribes they wouldn't be touched by gunfire if they wore "ghost shirts" — Rossie had learned that much in a Nevada history class in high school — and that the Indians, wearing their ghost shirts, had been slaughtered by bullets. But he had no idea which massacre this old man was talking about.

"With the Gatling gun," William But Not said, his voice soft.

Rossie nodded like it all made sense.

William But Not sighed as if giving up on Rossie, and went back to studying his shoes.

Leonard Three Boy was standing with

three cowhands, their thumbs hooked into belts with silver buckles. As Eliza went to join them, one of the men uncapped a pint of booze. When Leonard shook his head and put his right hand on the open bottle the man smiled a hard smile but tucked the pint into his hip pocket. Leonard Three Boy took off his eyeglasses and studied them for smudges, looked to Eliza, and followed the men out the door.

William But Not looked up at Rossie. "Eat," he said. "I got nothing to say."

Eliza came from across the room. "Eat," she said, too. The cold soup was faintly bluish and sweet. "Service berries. Gathered yesterday."

Lard sizzled in the frying pans when the sliced potatoes were dumped in to be crisped and salted, and an aroma of frying meat rose, warm and heavy.

The old woman named Barbara, who claimed to be British, jerked at Rossie's sleeve. "Nevada," she said, "it's okay." Her wattle chins shook as she laughed, her joke playing out perfectly. "It's okay!"

Rossie wondered if this was craziness.

A cadaverous man with hair hanging in threads from under a high-crowned, black cowman's hat cut his steak, thrust chunks into his gap-toothed mouth, and chewed with great deliberation. Rossie met the man's eyes, then quickly cut his glance away to the side of the room where the broken, taped-up windows reflected the lights but were otherwise gone entirely dark.

As he made his way to the stack of plates, and to join the line for a steak and spuds, Eliza came up abruptly beside him, her breast firm against his arm. "Give me that plate," she said, and she stepped in front of him.

Rossie put his hands on her hips, and she didn't move away but leaned back against him as if there was nothing on her mind but fried potatoes and steak.

"What do you think?" she said, once they'd reached the far end of the long table where Gone to the Wolves and Bright Red had settled over their own steaks.

"I think you've got me so hard up I could cry," Rossie said.

Gone to the Wolves looked up at Rossie, eyes glinting. "Me too," he said, then turned back to whisper to Bright Red.

"If I were a Blood woman," Eliza said, "they wouldn't laugh. They wouldn't want to see you with me. But what we do doesn't matter. They expect anything from us. So let's eat." She speared a choice steak. "For you, backstrap." This wild meat was richer than beef, not fatty but tender. After the steaks, she put a hand on Rossie's shoulder and whispered, "Outside."

The young men had their pint of whiskey uncapped in lantern light flickering from the windows. A heavy-bellied fellow with a wispy beard passed the pint to Rossie. "You don't need nothing more than a shot of this."

Rossie sipped the hot whiskey.

"Don't mistake it," Leonard Three Boy said. "This isn't the old life. That other life wasn't anything we can imagine."

After they'd gone to her tent, Eliza told Rossie to unroll his bed outside her door. "You sleep out here. I sleep in there. People should see that. Besides, I don't hump up for men who don't love me."

Inside his blankets, Rossie heard people drift down from the schoolhouse to their tepees. When the lights were shut down, he slept, and then he was awake under starlight. She was crouching above him, looking up into the moonlight and then down at him.

"Did you hear it?" she whispered. "The howling?" She touched his bare shoulder and kept her hand there. "I think it was in my dream. I'm coming in with you."

There had never been any woman, any fucking, but Mattie. Rossie wondered what to do until she was inside under his blanket.

"Hold me," she said, and Rossie moved to do what she said, and put his arm over her.

Then she had his hard cock in her fingers and was stroking so softly. Her cool thighs, flesh so full and swelling, were clamped tight together as he kissed her, tongue in her mouth until her legs eased apart. He lowered his lips to her nipples, and rubbed the dampness of her pussy until her knees lifted and he eased over her. He took her hand and put it on his cock again so she could help him into her, where she was wet and slick, and she did it.

Weight on his elbows, Rossie slipped in, and she raised her thighs over his shoulders to enclose him. He moved without a sense of anything but good fortune and then he was driving at her with no thought of anything at all but coming off into her. They fell away, gasping, and he was after her again. She lifted herself, gasped, and locked her legs around him.

Come daylight, Rossie woke and saw her eyes were closed. But he couldn't leave her alone and touched her breasts and kissed her and he was surprised as she opened herself under him again. He kissed her eyelids, and she was muttering without saying anything he could make sense of, and then her eyes opened and they were looking into each other as he slid into her another time. He rocked slowly in her until she closed her eyes and bit at her tongue and clasped at him, drawing him in deeper as he came, and thrusting up against him, raking at his back with her fingernails. Her interior was tense and then soft. As she stroked his back with her fingertips, Rossie let his head fall into the hollow of her shoulder and neck, her hair all around him.

"Everybody knows," she whispered. "See how easy it is. I was frightened and alone, and I couldn't stay away. You see how easy I can be. You could come with me. We could be it, entirely it."

"Entirely it," he whispered. "That's me."

"Don't be too proud of yourself. This was a way of telling everybody goodbye." Her expression was almost amused. "Aren't I," she said, "a pissant? Adiós to Charlie."

Even though she was playing it like a joke, and it was clear she wasn't altogether easy, Rossie knew that "come with me" talk was an actual offer.

"I'll pay your way on the railroad," she said. "You could work for my father."

"You're scared shitless, that's the truth." He thought of this as a sympathetic thing to say.

"What would shitless be?" she asked, trying a severe look. "You befoul everything you say."

"Befoul? Anyway, your father doesn't want a horseback bum in his house. Bet on it. I got these horses to take care of. Your father would think I was some boy who chased his daughter for a living."

She was abruptly angry. "You might as well fuck me for a living. Why not, for a while? Then you could learn another trick." She folded the blankets back, and got to her feet, angry and naked, luminous and pale in the morning. "What I want is for us to just shut up. You could stay with me. My showing baby doesn't mean you couldn't." Her eyes softened. "If you vanished," she said, "I would be abashed." She smiled, girlish. "Abashed," she said again.

Rossie thought it was a fine act, and he was happy with her, that she liked him this much.

"I don't know," he told her. "Your daddy might say I was after a sugar tit. It would be hard to blame him. Slivers Flynn run me off. He was the boss in Nevada. He said I'd been overfucking his daughter. Another mousetrap is what you get with me."

Eliza wasn't having any. "The overfucker," she said, and her gaze was ferocious. "Remember, a pregnant woman can't be much overfucked."

He tried another tune. "I could work for your father. What's he pay?"

"Privilege. You get to bang away on his ruined daughter." She started to duck under the blanket that hung over the door to her tent, then turned back. "I didn't come into your bed just to get at you and get you to come after me. I enjoyed it. What I like most is the fucking, if you can't tell. I'm a victim of my love for fucking and I'll say things like that, the truth. What you better do is think this over. You better get out of here."

"Right now?" Rossie asked.

"The fucking is over for now." With that she was gone into her tepee. With the saddle on Pinky, his pack roped down on Rock, Rossie rode off toward Calgary, wondering in what ways this was different from Mattie, because it sure as hell was.

■ ■ ■ ■

PART TWO
HE FINDS GOOD
FORTUNE

■ ■ ■ ■

WILDERNESS

With the horses put up in a livery stable on the outskirts of Calgary and his gear stowed in a padlocked room, Rossie took a yellow Chevrolet taxicab to the bank where Clifford Dufferena did business. He claimed his one hundred in five-dollar U.S. bills, counting the little wad twice and tucking it into a wallet he'd bought for ten cents. At the post office he found one letter in general delivery — though his mother had promised more — composed of nine sentences typed on her fine stationery. He read it there in the post office, wadded it into a ball, threw it into the trash, fished it out, spread it flat to read again, refolded it, and tucked it into his new wallet with the hundred dollars.

Mattie, his mother wrote, had taken up with Oscar Dodson, which she hoped was only a temporary thing. And she, Katrina, was going to divorce his father. She was "broken-hearted but firm about it. We always made it up in bed but I've had enough of his chasing and you haven't been home for a long time. Another sad woman in my house for sad women. No need to worry about Nito. I've changed the locks but he'll survive."

So would he, Rossie thought. But he was shaking in his innards, his heart was jittering, and he felt like his scaffoldings were coming apart and might leave him to fall down onto the floor in the Calgary Post Office. A plain, Hutterite woman was staring at him, and Rossie wondered if he had said things, and so went on with motions that he hoped looked sensible. Breathing deep, he rode another taxicab back to the livery stable, wanting to be horseback and not stuck in thoughts about Nito and his mother, "making it up in bed." *Humped up,* as Eliza had said. He wanted to see his mother watering plants in her quiet house, and Nito's hands riffling the cards.

"What would you think," he asked a big-whiskered man at the livery stable, "if your mother kicked your father out?" He tried to make this sound like it was leading toward a joke.

"I'd think your daddy was goddamned lucky," the man said, and he spat his snoose. "You drunk?"

"They got a telephone office around here?" Rossie asked.

The man turned abruptly solicitous. "You going to call your momma?" he said.

"Yeah, I'm going to give it a shot."

"Might be a good idea. You're looking like you might cry. Don't want no crying."

So Rossie took the walk to the west-side Calgary offices of the Alberta Telephone Exchange, leaned his elbows on the counter, and eyed the short-haired blond woman seated at her elaborate switchboard.

"I got to call Reno," he said.

"That's international," she said. "Cost you a fortune. Five, six dollars."

"You plug it through. I got the money."

"You rich?"

"Rich enough for this one."

"You know the number?"

"In Reno, when I call in town, it's four longs and four shorts."

The young woman shook her head, trying to look exasperated. "What's the people's names?"

"Benasco, same as me."

"You calling home?"

"Sure am."

"That's sweet. You sit in one of those chairs and look at the newspaper while I do my magic. We'll call Reno. I never did it

173

before. I called Seattle, but never Reno."

It must have taken her a quarter of an hour, plugging and replugging, and talking to other operators, but then she got through.

"Got your party."

And she was right. Simple as that, Katrina was calling his name, sounding far away, but it was her with no doubt. "Rossie," she was calling.

"How you doing?" he shouted.

"Did you get my letter? Then you know how I'm doing."

"Where's Nito?"

"Who knows? Who cares? Where are you?"

"Alberta. Calgary, Alberta."

"Are you all right? Are you coming home? Why else are you calling?"

"Just wanted to hear you talking."

"You come home," she said. "You just make it home. Don't cook up any stories for yourself. The only story you need is right here."

"I'm fine. What the hell are you talking about?"

"I know you," she said, "and I hear your voice. Like me, you get scared and tell yourself some story about who you are, about how you'll go to sea in a sailboat. Don't do that. Keep telling yourself that you're having a fine time and going home.

You do that and one day you'll be home."

"What it is, I met a girl."

"There'll be one more and one more."

"I'll hang tough. I'll see you Labor Day."

"You be here. I love you," she said, and she hung up. Without warning, her voice was gone.

The young blond woman in the telephone office was smiling. "Does she love you?"

"Like a blanket," Rossie said.

Sure enough, he felt better just from hearing his mother's voice. But his feeling better was troubled and perplexed by what Katrina had said, by what he kept hearing her say: "Like me, you get scared."

And he had been. Too scared to think. Katrina had been telling him to remember that the world was no different than it always was, and that all he needed to do was find a sure route home. Walking back to the livery stable he thought over his options. He could have rode home on the Canadian Pacific but now the train was gone on its route west along the valley of the Bow River — the main doorway through the Rockies, as Dufferena had told him. And he was looking for a doorway, all right. So that would be his route: up the Bow, through the Rockies, south to Montana, then to Reno. Simple enough, it was a plan, he had figured it out. Saddle on Pinky, pack on old Rock, keep moving and he'd be home for Labor Day.

By evening he'd made camp upstream on the Bow and suppered on creek water and cold biscuits and bacon. Late in the night, and again as the sky lightened toward morning, he was awakened by trains racketing along south of the river.

On the third day he reached the trails leading through the foothills of the Rockies into wilderness where streams cascaded from hanging ice fields and over great cliffs and evaporated into spray, wisping down into timber, then gathering again and running over gravel fields into the Bow River. As squirrels ran to their hideaways, Rossie studied rock slabs worn slick by glaciers and lavishly purple flowers that grew in the shadows. The summits and bluish skies beyond left him dizzy and utterly muddled — better suited to eyeing the squirrels.

When twilight came, he'd been watching the ground and not seen beyond himself to notice that the day was ending. Through the wilderness afternoon he rode tucked into his fright like a child, listening to the creaking of saddle leather and the horses huffing, letting them pick their way. "Baby boy," he'd scolded himself. But the mutter of his voice hadn't carried much in the way of comfort. This night, on a sodded embankment with the forest at his back, Rossie ate the last of the cold, crisp bacon and stale bread, then built a fire before drifting to sleep still fully dressed. Later, in darkness softened by glowing coals, he woke to another train, its roaring far off and growing until searchlights swept past and steel wheels hammered at the tracks. Kicking off his boots, he got into his bed, but didn't doze again until first light, after another train had passed.

The next day he reached a clearing, where midmorning sunlight cut through yellow pines to lay in patterns on the mown grass just ahead. Rossie heard a man curse and a woman call out, hooting laughter. "Nice one." He had, he discovered, emerged onto a meadowland golf course, fairways with old-growth evergreens between them and artificial mounds cut into orange-yellow sand traps. Flags blew in a breeze across the greens and limber-legged elk grazed while golfers in neckties played through.

The summer he was fourteen, Rossie had earned spending money caddying at the City Park Golf Course in Reno, sweating under leather bags of sticks that belonged to bankers and automobile dealers who wanted him on the job every morning as if they owned him. He'd carry double, and they'd tip him two bits. It was work to hate.

Startled for an instant to find this unexpected spectacle in the Rockies, he kept on crossing the fairways. Men and women in their foursomes waved, and the elk snorted at his horses but never stampeded or charged. What astonished him most was the green-roofed Banff Springs Hotel, a vast château built above the river by the Canadian Pacific Railroad Company, nine stories skyward and elegant against the glaciated mountains and snowfields, like nothing in Reno.

Having clattered across rocky shallows to swim his horses through the current of the Bow River, Rossie rode to the little town a mile or so downhill from the hotel. He put his horses up in a livery stable and paid to roll out his bed on a cot in a bare room upstairs. There he was, lodged in a distant place in the mountains, where he knew no one, and had nothing to do but keep moving. He lay back on his bedroll. Fright is no door to anywhere, he thought, gathering himself to walk down the street to a barber shop for a soaking bath and a haircut and shave — the first time a stranger had shaved him. He trimmed his fingernails with the

178

knife Mattie stole from Slivers and changed into the blue striped shirt his father had given him.

Back at the stable, he found the milk-white heavy woman who'd rented him the room. "Where would you go," he asked, "if you wanted to see the sights alongside the high and mighty?"

"Up to the hotel, to the big bar looking out on the golf course. You order a cocktail and sit there like you owned the world." She folded her soft arms across her chest and smiled like a light had gone on inside her. "You might take me along," she said.

Rossie saw that she wasn't much older than he was, only fat and tired out. "Tomorrow," he said, and she sighed.

"You damned fellows," she said.

Rossie cleaned his straw hat best he could and caught a free ride on a topless, red, German-made bus transporting tourists to the hotel. An Asian woman in a stiff embroidered dress sat beside him and poked a finger at his hat, and spoke a question in her strange language.

"Buckaroo," Rossie said. He wasn't the real grown-up item but he said it anyway and smiled.

Lined up on a stonework balustrade in front of the hotel, a trio of big-bellied men in greenish leather shorts handed out flyers advertising steam baths and evening hay-rides. Strangers thronged on all sides, paying him no attention, some wandering the raked gravel walkways across the lawns to the river, where a bridge would lead them toward the abrupt mountains. A suntanned, balding man in a gray tweed suit snipped the end from a cigar and lighted it, taking ceremonial puffs.

"Where could you buy that smoke?" Rossie asked. The man stared at him. "Smoke shop," he said in a British way. He gestured toward granite steps leading up to intricately carved double doors into the hotel.

"*Anybody* go on in?" Rossie asked. "I mean you don't need to be living there to go on in, or do you?"

The man smiled. "Suppose you can come and go as you please. It's a commercial establishment, so you can do any thing you need to do, at least for a cigar, don't you think? Or would you like one from me? A gift?"

But Rossie hadn't thought of wanting a cigar. "No, sir. I want to sit in a bar beside a window, looking to the mountains, and order a gin martini." He had been thinking about his father, what Nito would order: a martini, up, in one of those conical glasses, with onions on a skewer.

"Early in the day for that one," the man said, "but then, why should the hour matter? There's just your place up the stairs past the shops."

A boy in a bellman's getup, about Rossie's age, smiled without irony and held the door. "Sir," he said, "welcome to Banff Springs."

Well, Rossie thought, yes sir.

A narrow staircase rose just beyond a shop crowded with woolens. It opened onto a lobby with parquet flooring, where the profile of a bull elk had been pieced together from intricately sawn hardwoods of various shades. Beyond, wide doors opened into the tavern, all polished woods and brass fixtures. Huge windows looked out to the river and the slab-faced mountains.

Rossie stood at the bar with his hands on the brass rail and eyed the barkeep, a thick-fingered, dark man with heavy jowls and a formal, red bartender's coat — one of those men who shave twice a day.

"You tell me," Rossie said, "can I sit at those tables by the window?"

"Sir, you can sit anywhere you choose."

"A martini," Rossie said. "British gin, up, with onions."

The barkeep nodded. "Sir, I'll send it to you."

"I'll just stand here and watch you shake it. You should know this is the first time I was ever of age to order my own martini. Twenty-one years old." Rossie wondered if the barman knew he was lying, and if the man cared.

"This would be your birthday?" the bartender asked.

"Four days ago. Took me that long to find a bar where they made martinis."

"Then this will be on the establishment, and it will be a double. You watch carefully. You'll never get to do this again, not for the first time."

"I'll stand right here, and have the first sip."

"Fine," the barman said, shaking the ice and gin in a quick-wristed way. The silver shaker, embossed with intertwined flowers, was coated with frost. "Go easy, it's a double."

So Rossie took the first cold, bitter sip, and looked up to find himself in the mirror behind the bar, dressed in a good shirt and an expensive hat. Why not?

"I'll send it to your table," the bartender said. "We don't allow patrons to carry their drinks around."

From a table placed dead center on the wide windows, Rossie watched a gray-faced woman approach with his martini in hand. Dark pockets of sad flesh sagged under her eyes — she was old enough to know his mother.

"It's your birthday?" she asked.

"Not exactly, but close."

She studied him. "You're not twenty-one. But nobody cares about that around here. You be careful with that drink. Martinis are like bombs, and that's a double."

"Tell you what," Rossie said. "I've had bad news, and I'm trying to look on the bright side." The woman waited for him to finish his story.

"My mother kicked my father out of the house. That was in Reno, Nevada. So I'm alone here in Alberta."

"There are people all around you," the woman said. "That's the bright side. Everywhere you go." Then she rolled her eyes and turned away. She'd heard enough of this story, or stories like it.

Balancing the long-stemmed glass perfectly between his right thumb and forefinger, he took a second sip, which went down slicker than the first, and rested the glass on a freshly laundered, white cloth napkin. A mountaintop snowfield glittered back at him in the afternoon light.

Abruptly, none of what he'd learned from

his mother seemed like bad news. This was the gin kicking in, he knew, but suddenly Rossie imagined Katrina and Nito here with him, drinking their own double martinis, eyeing each other and laughing, and then he imagined them touching at each other and going into a room with a bed and not looking back — something he had never allowed himself to think about in his mother's house, listening as one of the divorcées in the guest rooms moaned and protested her loneliness in the dark hours.

When Rossie's martini was empty, the bartender shook another one while continuing to talk with a tall man hovered over the bar, his yellow suspenders stretched over a red flannel shirt. The woman who'd brought his first drink carried this one over, along with a tall glass of ice water.

"One more of those," she said, gesturing at the martini, "should be enough for you." She gestured toward the tall man with yellow suspenders. "Compliments of Mr. Bob Waters."

Bob Waters was already on his way to Rossie's table, carrying a pint glass of what looked to be black beer. A long-jawed man, his baldness seemed to accentuate his high-domed head. "You're the fellow on the pinto horse," he said, after sitting down across from Rossie. "You rode the golf course, right over the edge of the fifth green. I was watching. Your pack animal went to shitting there, so I'm buying you a drink. Where you coming from?"

"Nevada."

"Where you going?"

"Montana."

"You got any idea what's out between here and there?"

"Timber."

Bob Waters shook his head. "Yeah, out there in the timber there is going to be cold rivers and grizzly bears hunting you. That's what I tell my hunters. What rifle you carrying?"

"What kind of hunters?" Rossie asked.

"Rich men from California and France, for the main part. Helpless men looking to kill sheep and a bear. Those men pay me for the parts they can't do for themselves. And they got rifles, every one of them, otherwise I don't take them. Big rifle, you got some protection."

Rossie shrugged. "I don't carry no rifle."

"You know anything about dying the hard way? Crippled by a bear, can't move, wolverines and porcupines about to eat your asshole out?"

"I seen plenty of shit."

"Sure. Bet you have, kid like you."

So Rossie told a story he made up as he went along, about a sister with freckles who had died of bad cancer. Rossie was imagining Mattie's mother, and though he knew the gin had a lot to do with it, he thought this lying was funny as he talked. "I got so sad-assed and lonely," he said, "that I thought about smiling all the time, to persuade people into liking me, but to hell with the smiling. I'm my own man from here on in."

Bob Waters reared back in his chair, rubbing a hand over his shining baldness. "You got me smiling," he said. "You're some talker. You drunk already?"

"Two drinks. I could have one more martini. You got rich hunters, so these isn't hard times where you're concerned?"

"Not much. People got their ways. Men who stayed out of the stock market, who own railroads and Kansas City livestock yards. They got money locked down, and pay in advance or don't go. I don't take fat men or cripples but men who stay sober and hunt and come back year after year. So now *I* got my money locked down. That's what I know about the Great Depression."

The third martini came, and soon it was empty.

"You better drink that ice water," the man said.

"Forgot your name," Rossie said.

"Bob Waters. Like in ice water."

So Rossie took a long draw on the ice water as Bob Waters pushed back from the table.

"I watched you coming across the golf course," he said, "and I thought, there is a fellow who knows how to sit a horse. That fellow could help me. I know every man in town, and the good ones are gone looking for work in Vancouver or Victoria. None of the rest is worth hiring — too much time pimping for railroad tourists. So I talked to your girlfriend at the stable, fat Linda, and tracked you down."

"You mean a job?"

"A week or so, helping me set my hunter's camp over in the Kootenay, same direction you're going. Three dollars a day and what you can eat."

"Couldn't do it," Rossie said, trying to think and talk carefully, past the gin. "I'm hurrying in my traveling — need to find a fellow named Bill Sweet in a town called Charlo, and after that I got to hunt up a girl who is pregnant." The part about hunting up the girl felt like a discovery, but it was what he'd been intending all along.

"You'll travel easier with me, and you'll see the backcountry," Bob Waters said. "Otherwise you'll be traveling down that Kootenay Highway with automobiles and macadam, the mountains way off as you're nursing sore-footed horses." He smiled a big-toothed smile and rubbed his bald head. "You think about it, or don't. But I can't let you go out there with no rifle. Tell you a deal, though. Tomorrow, if you're sobered up, you go see a man named Bignell Robinson, rifle maker's shop west of town. He'll sell you a good Model 54 Winchester .30-06 in a canvas scabbard for twenty-eight dollars American. He'll sight it in for you and include a box of shells as part of the price. It's a hell of a good price. You tell him you talked to me, Bob Waters. Better yet, I'll write it down. Bignell Robinson. You don't look like you're going to remember too much tomorrow."

He scribbled the name on a page in a little notepad he carried and reached over to tuck the paper into Rossie's shirt pocket.

Rossie was abruptly, drunkenly furious. "Bullshit. All I got is ninety-four dollars. I don't want no twenty-eight-dollar gun."

"You don't?"

"I never had a rifle. I can't afford no fucking rifle."

'It's not going to be like you lost the money. You can sell it once you get where you're going. Besides, you might want to kill something to eat. No grocery stores or cafés out there."

"What I think," Rossie said, "is fuck rifles."

"Then you are thinking like one ignorant, drunk son of a bitch. You are likely to die ugly."

Rossie started to come out of his chair. Hell, he decided, was going to commence. But it didn't.

Rossie woke up hours later, feeling no pain but in his hungover head. He was still dressed and booted on his bed in the room above the livery stable, the horses snuffling below. After he'd staggered across the room and slurped acidic water from the sink tap, it came in on him that he hadn't a single memory of getting to this bed from the big hotel barroom on the hill. But nobody had hit him and his money was still folded in his wallet. At daybreak he counted the bills to be sure, and found he'd drunk those martinis without spending a dime. Then he encountered the note tucked into his shirt pocket: *Bignell Robinson — man with rifles.*

Rossie bought himself bacon and eggs in the café beside the livery stable. Bob Waters was right, he thought. A man without a rifle was likely a damned fool — what he most of all didn't want to be.

When Rossie found him and stated his case, Bignell Robinson bridged his long, precise fingers before his mouth before lowering them to speak. "You're the cowboy. Heard you took a dive."

"Damned if I know," Rossie said.

"Heard you swung on Bobby Waters. Lucky thing you went down before you hit him."

"How's that?"

"You just passed out, went down untouched. Bobby would of beat the dogshit out of you, and them hotel police would of thrown you out on the lawn, and then some bird would of robbed you. Bobby Waters took the trouble to bed you down. Took him an hour or so to get rid of you, with everybody laughing at him."

"People know my business?"

"Small little town, and we know Bobby Waters. He was over to see me for breakfast. Least you didn't puke in the bar. Bobby would of left you there if you was all-over puke."

"Must think I was a damned fool."

"Ever'body is," Bignell Robinson said. "Now, how about a rifle? I'll sell you a rifle that isn't no fool. But let me tell you one more thing first. You find Bobby Waters tonight — he'll be having supper at the café right there by the livery stable — and you tell him you want that work he offered. You travel a week or so with him, into Kootenay country, and you won't be stumbling around in those wilds for a month. You'll come out the other end alive. There's men around here who got most of what they know from Bobby Waters. And this day and age, work is work and money is money — that's my guess. Let's start fitting a rifle to your shoulder."

Bob Waters didn't smile or shake his head or bother with any other nonsense when Rossie found him that evening in the café. "I got a Model 54 Winchester rifle," Rossie said. "I'm looking for work."

Bob Waters stuck out his hand to shake on the deal. "Sit down," he said. "We'll have some dinner. Tomorrow we'll load the packs, and be out of town the next day before sunup."

They'd spend three or four days heading for meadows high in the mountains along Verdant Creek, where they'd set tents and rebuild corrals for the fall season.

Two days later, with the sun coming up over the mountain, they set out on the road west of Banff. Bob Waters was trailing eight loaded packhorses, and Rossie eight more, counting one of his own. A dozen miles up the Bow River, they turned south into a cedar grove along Redearth Creek, a canyon cut deep into a steep, stony maze. Rossie listened to the horses snorting as their iron-shod hooves struck the rocks, the only breaks in the quiet. The trail came down off a bench onto a stony beach and a crossing — thirty yards of swift, twisting water.

"Snow water," Bob Waters said. "Belly deep, anyway, and cold as you want, rolling stones on the bottom. One horse goes down and you can lose the outfit, horses scattered halfway back to town, while you can end up afoot, water in your boots, walking out like a half-drowned greenhorn. We'll set a tow rope." He shook out a seagrass rope and tied it to the halter on his lead packhorse. "Once I get across," he said, "I'll start towing them from the other side. You give that lead horse a kick in the ass and they'll come." He eased into water over his stirrups, lifting his feet to stay dry. "They'll get the idea," he shouted.

On the other side Bob Waters dallied down and the string of loaded horses followed, stumbling and floundering their way across. Then they did the deal with Rossie's string.

"No trick," Bob Waters said. "We're over, bone dry, no water in our boots."

They ate cold beefsteak sandwiches at noon, then camped before twilight. As Rossie unloaded the pack animals one by one, feeding them each a bait of grain as he tethered them, Bob Waters baked two big spuds and two thick-cut pork chops, then poured the pork grease over a mess of greens he'd gathered along the creek.

"Out here, you learn these plants," he said. "There's every damned thing to eat out here in the summertime."

"What do you call them?"

"Watercress. This pepper woman here spices up the meat, plus it's good for your system. Learned that from an Indian up at Jasper when I was a boy."

After Rossie had scrubbed the tin plates in the creek, Bob Waters sent him to hang a burlap sack with their meat from a tree limb off about a hundred yards to avert the bears. Then Bob Waters poured them each three inches of whiskey in enameled cups and settled by the fire with his bedroll at his back. The twilight sky was lurid with incandescent clouds.

"I was never given to singing about fresh

country," he said. "But she's a better place than town. Unless you're horny. And then your martini drinkers love a town."

"Shit," Rossie muttered, and got busy unrolling his bed.

The next morning they turned up Pharaoh Creek, south between stone mountains where banks of icy snow endured into midsummer. The crossings were low water and easy. By noon they reached timberline between barren rock cliffs near the Continental Divide at Redearth Pass. A wisp of waterfall fell from a cirque above them and trickled beneath the mosses. The evergreens were wind-stunted to stand only waist high.

"There's a little tarn up there," Bob Waters said. "This time of summer you might hike up and look down on grizzly. They like to play in them high-country potholes of water and eat the ice. You'd want to take your rifle with you."

"Think I'll pass," Rossie said.

Bob Waters nodded. "We got no business up there. Your wild bear don't want a thing to do with us. We ought to stay down here in the sun and warm our brains. This is the best we're going to get." Bob Waters was all at once very serious. "You get older," he said, "you sometimes think this is the equal of pussy."

"Did you ever pray to pussy?" Rossie asked.

But Bob Waters wasn't having any jokes. "Son of a bitch," he said, "if that isn't some kid idea." He stared at Rossie a long moment and let it drop as he started unwrapping their beefsteak sandwiches. "This is it for the meat we brought. Tomorrow we got to butcher a venison."

The afternoon trail worked down through steep switchbacks. Even where the footing was solid, the talus slope fell off to a cliff over breathtaking emptiness, the creek meandering far below. Eternity beckoned if your horse went crazy. When they had worked their way down to the creek, they moved through groves of aspen into a meadow fenced with toppling jack-pine poles. Bob Waters had been setting his hunting camp there for eleven years.

"Camp wintered fine," he said. "She'll be pristine with a week or so of work. In August we'll come up here for the grizzlies that gather on the berries, fattening up for winter. We set up on the ridges and catch them grizzly below us, kill three or four, depending on how many hunters. I got help to pack out the hides and heads right after they're killed. Then in the fall we go off north of Jasper for the sheep and come back here when that gets too bitter. Load up trash, whiskey bottles and cans, and get the last of them boys out of here before Christmas." Bob Waters smiled. "Never seen you shoot that rifle. You ever kill anything with a rifle?"

"Nothing big," Rossie said. The true answer was no, nothing at all.

"You go down the creek three or four miles. That way the bears feeding on guts don't get used to coming up around the camp. If you tether your horse and walk softly and set up with the wind at your back, the deer will come to water right out front of you. Don't kill nothing but a buck. The does are still trailing fawns so you leave those alone. When I hear shooting, I'll be along for the gutting and cutting, and then we'll hang it. You break in that rifle and I'll be along. Or we got no meat for supper."

Moving soft-footed was a childhood trick Rossie had mostly lost, but he could sit quiet. He leaned his back against an aspen, with grasses from the previous summer tucked up around him and a breeze moving past from across a swale of meadow. A muley doe and spotted twin fawns eventually appeared, ears twitching as they moved among the aspen like shadows within shadows, skirting the edge of the meadow. For a little while Rossie watched without thought of shooting, before placing a cartridge in the firing chamber and switching the safety off. The first little buck, he'd kill it.

But the buck wasn't little. A four-point with horns in velvet, he eased along the meadow's edge, taking care that his new-grown rack didn't touch so much as a branch, and came out straightaway in front of Rossie without sign that he saw anything unusual. Slowly lifting the Model 54, Rossie centered the sights and breathed as Bignell Robinson had instructed him and pulled the trigger just as the buck turned back to see him before collapsing, instantly dead. Only as the silence echoed did Rossie know he'd shot.

The slug had penetrated the head just below the left ear, the entry hole neat and precise. One horn, soft in the velvet, had cracked when the animal fell and now hung obscenely. Rossie touched the back of the head where the slug had exited, leaving a sharp bloody cup of bone. With the blade of his white-handled knife he sliced the jugular. Blood flowed hot around his wrist, and he recalled a cowhand at the Neversweat who drank a household cup of blood each time they butchered. That unshaven old man would grin at Rossie, blood drying and caking on his lips. "Keeps your pecker blooming," he'd say.

Bob Waters came along on horseback, equipped with skinning and butcher knives, a short axe, lengths of cotton rope, and canvas meat sacks. "Hell of a shot," he said. "He's your animal. You get the heart and liver. Go after him."

"Tell you something, you better do it. I never cut up a deer."

"Same as butcher cows," Bob Waters said, then turned to opening the belly, slicing around the penis and the testicles. "Don't want any piss in our dinner." He opened the abdominal cavity and eased his arms in elbow deep. A steaming tangle of intestines spilled over his hands as he dragged them out on the grass. Then he split the breast bone and propped it open with a stick to reach in for the dark-red liver and the heart. Running another stick inside the tendons at the knees, he hung the carcass, got quickly through the skinning, disconnected the head, and split the long backbone with a few precise strokes of his hatchet. Together they loaded the quartered carcass into stained meat sacks, leaving behind the hide and head and the intestines. "For bears and big cats and varmints," Bob Waters said. "Everybody gets to eat. One of the cats might be calling tonight. Sounds like a woman."

The bulk of the meat was wrapped in cheesecloth to keep flies away and hung from ropes thrown over high limbs down-slope a couple hundred yards from the camp. They cooked tenderloins and the liver on sharp willow sticks over the open fire, and later, sipping a cup of whiskey, Rossie tried to talk about the deer looking at him and then away, "like he didn't want to see me."

"Indians up to Jasper used to talk about animals walking out to be shot, making themselves into gifts," Bob Waters said. "It don't hurt to think about it that way. Sometimes it's like the animal is done want-ing to be alive. Damned spooky, but it's real."

"In this country it feels like I never grew up."

"Damned right, in this country you are a boy who don't know anything. But you'll grow out of that sooner than you'll like. Don't get in any hurry." The fire snapped and Bob Waters stoked it. "What's this pregnant woman?"

"Well, I like her plenty, but it's another fellow's baby," Rossie said.

"So what do you care whose baby it is?

Just be careful you don't end up without a steady woman. You go to bed with the same woman for months and you get used to the smell and sleep like a child, like you remember sleeping when you was little and smelling your mother."

"You got a wife like that?"

"Not any more. She blew up, started going around in taverns saying I was queer for men since I was all my time in these camps. I hit her, a damnable thing. I asked her pardon and thought it was made up. Next time I come back, she was gone on the railroad to Vancouver, taking what money we had. Never heard a word of her since."

"Queer for men?" Rossie said.

"She was too much alone is my guess. Or she wouldn't have talked such bitchery. I'm in the mountains five, six weeks at a time. Up in the snow with my hunters, she used to say. I see how she came to think what she said." Bob Waters poured himself another slug of the whiskey. "Anybody is happy with some warm thing in their bed, and getting their nuts off," he said. "I've found full-grown rich men bundled together."

Rossie was seeing beyond the fire to a childhood Sunday morning in July with his friends in downtown Reno. A pale, bald man with a line of scabs across his forehead had been drunk and singing in a deep, ruined voice, a gravelly Irish lament. What Rossie saw was the man's bluish linen suit and his long fingernails as he gestured toward the boys, who were mocking him. Smiling like a cat, the man tucked his chin, beckoned with a terrible white hand, and said, "Why don't you strike me? Would you like to do that?" The oldest boy turned away and spat. "Fuck him," he said, when they were down the block. "He's just a queer."

Rossie had felt a run of shuddering that day on the sidewalk, and he was feeling it again here with Bob Waters. He'd taken his knife out and was trimming his fingernails.

"What I dream about," Bob Waters said, speaking slowly, "is her. Black-haired woman. She was named Jerrine."

"Are you telling me queer stories?" Rossie asked.

Bob Waters studied Rossie for a long moment. "No need for that knife," he said, getting to his feet, and starting to lay his bedroll open. "So that's what I got to say about that. Except for one more thing. Nobody told you queer stories. I was telling you about my wife, and how I missed her, and you take it to be a story about how you might get fucked in the ass. You ought to be goddamned well ashamed of yourself. Do you know the word bigot? It means an ass-hole who can't see any side of things but his own. You ought to know there's nothing more sideways with two men in bed than with any other two people. Here we are in the tall timber with nothing but this fire and our rifles between us and the spooks. I'm thinking about how living out here has turned out to be my life, and I don't know why. And you worry about butt-fucking."

Rossie slipped his knife back into his pocket. There was a faint trembling in his shoulders as he turned and put his backside to the fire.

"But fuck all," Bob Waters said after a long moment. "You're just a kid. You don't understand a hell of a lot." He sat on his bedroll and started kicking off his boots. "Shit, everybody is strange as cats in the barn. Waiting to hear an owl hoot. Some hide it better than others."

"She, your wife, was she ever pregnant?" Rossie asked.

"Not that she told me. Sometimes I've wished she would've been. So there would be a kid and she'd stick around and I wouldn't be out here in this camp with nobody but you."

"That woman I'm after, she's knocked up

and all I know is there's some look about her. You wonder why a woman sticks in your head."

"I told you. Maybe it's a smell, like your momma." Bob Waters was standing in his longjohns, folding his trousers. "It can happen with horses. There's horses you can't get out of your head, even after you sold them. Got a different look around the eyes."

"What she's like," Rossie said, "is there's a field of horses, and one good one, and any damned fool can see the difference."

Bob Waters tucked his trousers into the foot of his bedroll, where they would be warm in the morning, then pulled his blankets up over him. "A cunt that fits you. That's the Spanish Curse. Your freedom is over. That's the joke. It's few men who work out a life with no woman."

The next morning they started putting the corral fences back into place. By the third afternoon they were working on tent-house frames, and by the fourth they'd unpacked the canvas tents, the cook stove, and the ice boxes, and set the tents.

"Tell you one thing," Rossie said. "This kind of sweat work is why I took up a horseback life."

"Right there, that's an ambition. The job is figuring out how to make things go your way. There's deep Christian people who say a good man lets the world go any way it wants. That's horseshit. A man with sense goes after what he wants."

"You a secret preacher?"

"What I'm preaching is sweat. All day long. I'm making the world go my way."

"Back in Banff, you going after a new woman?"

Bob Waters went on talking like Rossie hadn't spoke. "This fall it'll be coveralls and fur-lined gloves. We'll be in this country until heavy snow. That switchback trail will be nothing but ice."

"I'll be way south," Rossie said, "riding the flatlands."

"Bet you will. You're the boy hunting a woman."

"One of them quick-blooded kind."

"There are times," Bob Waters said, "when I think I could live up in this country with nothing but other men. I think men and women are too strange from one another. But it isn't true. There's no other side to life without the women, whether you love them or not. You dream about them and then maybe you find one who can stand you. It's something to keep thinking about."

Three mornings later Rossie was up on Pinky, ready to go south through the mountains toward Montana.

"Be your own fella," Bob Waters said. A balding man, hat in his hand there in the British Columbian highlands, he smiled and shook his head as if at some mystery.

Rossie slept that night in a meadow where the Verdant Creek swung south into what Bob Waters had told him was a run of wild country best avoided by a greenhorn. Deep in the dark hours there was screaming like a woman, a big cat not far off, and Rossie loaded the Model 54 and set it by his bed.

The next afternoon he made his way down a set of switchbacks off the Hawk Ridge into the valley of the Vermillion River, then over to the Kootenay Parkway. The narrow macadam rolled through timberlands into Vermillion Crossing, a settlement where food and gasoline were sold out of a log-house store. When Rossie knocked, a thin man appeared in a sleeveless undershirt and no trousers, obviously drunk, and muttered, "Can't help you a lick," before waving his hands softly and closing the door. So Rossie made his dinner on the last of the venison he'd brought and the next day got out before sunup.

For the next three days he traveled fast and hungry down trails near the roadway, which at last crossed through a rocky narrows and into a British settlement called Radium Hot Springs.

The wilderness abruptly ended. Behind a granite-wall dam men and women in bathing suits were swimming and soaking in a bright pool of steaming bluish water. Beyond were motor courts and paved streets, a café and bungalows with elaborate landscaping, and a stable with a loft above the horse stalls, where Rossie unrolled his bed and anticipated awakening in the night once again to the sounds of his horses shuffling and snorting. Through the open hay-doors the man in charge of the stable pointed to a river and to an open valley beyond. That river, the man insisted, was the Columbia, near its headwaters, flowing north before turning south into Washington and on to the Pacific.

"Could be," Rossie said. "Geography was never my main thing."

"Me neither," the man said, "but I know that much. I know a fella who floated the whole damned river in a canoe, then drowned when he tried to sail her into the Pacific. *Used* to know him. Crazy son of a bitch."

"Plenty of those."

"Kid, they's everwhere."

In the café down the block, Rossie feasted

on chicken-fried streak and biscuits and sausage gravy, and when the apple-cheeked waitress asked if he was a stranger in the country, Rossie told her he was and that he was going to Montana.

"You been up swimming in the hot pool?"

"Not me. There wasn't no water deep enough to swim in where I come from. I'd drown." He thought she liked him so he told her about working for Bob Waters, and she said everybody in the country knew Bob Waters.

"If he isn't something," she said. "Wish he would come and take me to the mountains."

"He'd like to know that. You ought to ask him. You ought to send him a letter saying you talked to me. Tell him how you'd try the mountains. He might come down here looking for you."

"You're pretty damned cute," she said. "You got cute ideas."

Rossie thought about asking her if they could get together after she was done with her working, but he didn't. Why was he so taken with that girl Eliza, feeling so goofy he'd duck his head and start eating and not grin at this girl? He'd turned into a fool who couldn't see much in his mind except for the gray complications, the distances and ferocity and decent humors in that Eliza's eyes.

By the Fourth of July, Rossie was into the Flathead Valley of Montana, riding surveyed roads through barley fields turning from green to yellow in streaks. Men hauled cured field grasses over the slanted planks of beaver slides, building stacks of meadow hay to be doled out to the herds through the winter. Moving south above the shore of Flathead Lake, a vast glassy expanse speckled with timbered islands in the noontime stillness, he passed cherry orchards on the east shore where crews comprised mostly of women and children were harvesting the fruit. In the afternoon he reached the ranchlands south of the lake, which gave way to the cliffs and peaks of the Mission Range off to the east, its shadowed ravines glittering with summertime snowfields.

By sunset he was approaching the farmers' settlement of Charlo, where someone was launching skyrockets from a hill beyond town, their sparks cascading against the darkening sky. Rossie's pinto stutter-stepped through a clamor of fireworks, barking dogs, and the rumble of a herd of boys running along the echoing plank sidewalks.

The stable manager was a stocky young

woman with luminously blue eyes and muscular suntanned arms that showed under her rolled-up sleeves. Once Rossie had put up his horses and laid out his bed up in the hayloft, he asked if she knew someone named William Sweet.

"What you want with that asshole?" she asked.

"Bill Sweet? I suppose I can figure how you'd want to call him an asshole."

"I know him pretty well," she said. "Right now he's drinking up his paycheck, and after a while he'll come over here drunk and try to get his hands on me. Wouldn't you call him an asshole?"

"I'd call him a man with good sense."

"I guess that's true," she said. "My name is Margie, and he lives at my house. You ask, they'll say he's over with Margie if he's in town. But where you'll find him is in the Blind Pig. That's why I'm giving him hell behind his back."

"The Blind Pig?"

"Used to be drinking was illegal and it was a hideout. Now it's just the tavern. I could lock these barn doors and walk you over there."

The Blind Pig was underneath the hardware store, down a narrow, unmarked flight of concrete steps that echoed with a woman's howling laughter. This was a pool hall with tiny windows high up on the far wall, and it stank of sweat and booze. Cue balls clacked and the wash of voices went abruptly silent when Rossie and the girl from the stable appeared in the doorway.

The woman who'd been laughing wore a town-lady hat decorated with fake flowers over her gray hair. She turned to Rossie like he was a wonderful discovery. "Hello, cutie."

"This fellow," Margie said, "is with me. He's my new boyfriend."

The bartender rested his hands on the bar, studying Rossie. "How long's that boyfriend shit been going on?" Huge, yellow teeth looked loose in his jaw.

"About ten minutes," Margie said.

"Then I'll buy him a drink," the bartender said.

"This here," Margie said, "is Diamond. It's the name he claims."

"All the name I can afford," the bartender said.

"Diamond is on the run from Detroit. He won't tell us what he did."

"Ran with the communists. We raised communist hell all over Detroit." The bartender gave Rossie a loose-toothed grin. "The ruling class would like to lock me up until I'm in the grave. That's it."

Bill Sweet was already stumping down from where he'd been at the end of the bar, his filthy cast thumping as he limped along. "Boyfriend, shit," he said. "This fella is no boyfriend. He never had a girl. This is a son of a bitch I've rode with. He's bringing me my paycheck from last spring. Or I hope he is."

"There you are," Rossie said, handing over the paycheck from Clifford Dufferena.

"Don't get to thinking there's going to be money in town," the bartender told Bill Sweet. "You're thinking you're going to have a ruling-class string of credit."

"Well, set us up down the line," the woman in the flowered hat shouted.

The bartender ignored her. "Going to take a week anyway to get that money. You go up to the bank in Polson and they telegraph to the bank in Reno and Reno telegraphs back to Polson and Polson takes its time about letting you know the money's waiting. Meanwhile, capitalists up and down the road are collecting interest. Banks and banks and more banks. Shit." The bartender was spitting saliva. "So I am not running you no tab. You might never come back from Polson."

"Well, I'll buy him and me and her some drinks," Rossie said.

"How about me?" the old woman hollered.

"Too bad, you're on your own."

"Well, rich boy. Fuck yourself."

"Wish I could," Rossie said, turning to the bartender. "Mr. Diamond, buy her a glass of beer on me."

"Obliged." The bartender set up the glasses.

"That's it," Rossie said to the woman. "One beer. You know what? I've learned one thing. Don't let folks buffalo you around. So you lay off of me."

The woman smiled in a way that resembled a semitoothless rat. "It'll be a goddamned pleasure."

"I'm crippled up," Bill Sweet said, after they'd sat at a table, "but I'm not one lick bitter, not so long as you are here and buying drinks."

"Margie says you keep chasing her."

"Good idea, don't you think?" Sweet said.

Rossie studied Margie. "I guess so. But I got bad news. I'm down in money, so I'm not buying many drinks."

"You're buying tonight. I got two dollars total cash."

"How much was that check?" Margie asked Bill Sweet.

"One hundred bucks."

She tilted her head at both of them. "Lucky thing is, money isn't my problem. Girls drink, they don't buy."

"Yeah," Bill Sweet said, "they sell."

Margie abruptly flushed, blue eyes electric. "What the fuck would you know?" She stood, pushed her way through the crowd and stomped out the door.

"Beautiful girl," Bill Sweet mused. "Strong as a man. You headed back to Reno and your momma?"

"Going to the Bitterroot Valley. Hunting a pregnant woman. She's knocked up by an Indian."

"You pick the dandies."

Here we sit trying to talk like men, Rossie thought.

"They don't allow no Indians in this town," Bill Sweet said. "This is the Flathead Reserve, but that don't make no difference. These people here, they don't put up with Indians."

"You know how them Bloods in Canada would answer to that? They'd say bullshit and cut your dick off. Anyway, this one is a rich woman."

"Well, you keep after her. Boy like you won't meet many rich ones."

Rossie smiled, and the room was for an instant quiet. Rossie heard a voice from the poolroom say, "Wouldn't have to cheat to beat you."

"Shit the bed," the bartender muttered in his beard. "You want to fight," he yelled, "get out in the street."

But nothing happened, talk at the bar picked up, and the pool game progressed.

"That's what you see," the bartender said, his voice calm. "Poor people want to beat up on one another because they're afraid of bankers. In Detroit we had organization, went on strikes, and we knew our enemies: industrialists and bankers, men who own steel mills. Out here they don't know shit so they just pound on each other."

Bill Sweet gestured to Rossie. "This boy, he's going down to team up with some rich people."

"Stevenson, in the Bitterroot," Rossie said. "You heard of them?"

"Writes letters to the Missoula newspaper?" Diamond said, blowing up into a passion, just short of shouting. "The shame of it is, he's educated and writes freethinking letters to the Missoula newspaper, letters they wouldn't print if he wasn't educated and rich. But he don't understand action. I know about him. You won't see him giving away his educated shit to your kind."

Rossie found himself going hostile.

"What's my kind?"

"Working, if you're lucky. Digging ditches and herding cows. Things are going to stay the way they are for boys like you, busted and thieving and poor and drunk on the weekend."

"Good idea," Bill Sweet said. "One more drink."

"Two or three," Rossie said, and Diamond laughed, and hours got away. More drinks were ordered, and Margie reappeared, touching her fingers to Bill Sweet's hat where it sat on the table.

"We ought to get out of here," she said, and Bill Sweet smiled.

"This is my poor girl," he said to Rossie. "I don't know any rich ones."

"That's how Bill Sweet pisses me off," she said. "I don't sell nothing. I haven't got no price."

Bill Sweet eyed the ceiling, then looked back at Rossie. "Tell you what. Pregnant or no, you marry that rich woman. We'll come visit."

"Getting married?" Rossie said. "Marrying a rich woman sounds like a whorehouse deal, don't it?"

Margie leaned in close to him. "You been to a whorehouse, not like a kid, but to get in some fucking?"

"Never had to."

"You sit in some little dress, trying to sell your cunt," she said. "Them whiskery old boys come in the door, and they are drunk and you're trying to think, *Come fuck me please so I can make some money,* but you're really thinking, *Get on out of here, go drown in piss.*" Margie studied Rossie with her head tilted sideways, studying to make sure there was no chance he was going to laugh. "All night long, between fucks and mopping off, you are thinking about running away. I came to Montana from Carson City as a hired-out whore in Missoula where there was good pickings. But I was the pickings, so I run away."

According to Margie, Missoula was cobbled streets, trolleys on steel rails, and hundreds of automobiles honking downtown past brick buildings — a place to be avoided by a man traveling with horses.

"I don't ever go back to Missoula nor do any whoring," she said. "So long as you aren't whoring you can do what you please. What I do is keep a list of things I'll never do, like fuck a dog or beat a baby's head on a doorjamb. A man in this town killed a baby that way last year. If I don't whore I can do any whichever things I want." Her eyes gleamed as she stood at the door, and then she was gone again.

"If she's not a beauty," Bill Sweet said.

"I'm not going down there after any rich woman with my hat in my hand," Rossie announced. But Bill Sweet was gone out the door, trailing Margie to wherever they slept.

BITTERROOT

The sky was stained with smoke from tepee burners where the timber mills outside Missoula burned their scrap. After crossing railroad tracks, Rossie came onto a camp in cottonwoods along the Clark Fork of the Columbia, which even in that dry season was a hundred shallow yards wide. Scatterings of men, some asleep on blankets, surrounded fires on the gravel bars. A few were shirtless and in the river washing or hanging laundry on bushes, while others dove from boulders into deep swirling water, most of them lean and nude and stark white in the water and afternoon sunlight, except for what looked to be three Indians.

Rossie leaned from his horse to talk to a skinny old man sipping from a tin-can cup. "Where you fellows going?"

"Went east last year," the man said. "Traveling after justice. But there isn't none. Two years ago last month that General Douglas

MacArthur brought tanks and tear gas and fixed bayonets against men like me — veterans of the Great War. We was there at the Anacostia Flats outside D.C., in an army of our own. There was white men and niggers in the same camps, women and their childrens. MacArthur scattered us like vermin. That was the ruin. This America never heard of justice. That part is over."

Rossie shook his head, uncomprehending.

"You ever read a newspaper?" the man asked. "You ought to get down off that horse and come to town. You could find a library and read up."

"Not meaning to disagree with you," Rossie said.

"Good thing. There's nothing to disagree with."

A fat, dark man playing guitar sat on a fallen cottonwood log, his music sliding and haunting over the warm shallows like nothing Rossie had heard before. The man was weeping long tears as he played. He was Hawaiian and blind, and only his music was his. "Enough to cry over," one of the men said after telling Rossie the story.

"Shit," another said. "He's earning a handout. Son of a bitch is no more blind than I am."

"Sounds pretty fucking blind," the other said.

Rossie rode off across the Clark Fork with the Hawaiian's music strumming in the distance and camped a few more miles south along the Bitterroot Valley on a ridge up away from the mosquitoes. Dreaming of Eliza, he woke thinking about the tilt of her head when she was pissed off, and her eyes narrowing. He thought, how did this come on so fast that she's what you're after?

The Bitterroot Valley was a sixty-mile river swale of ranch and farmland with creeks working down from east and west to join the shallow Bitterroot River that rose in the south and meandered north through groves of aspen and cottonwood to join the Clark's Fork of the Columbia near Missoula. On the western skyline, the stony Bitterroot Mountains hovered above open fields that in late July lay before Rossie like a promise.

He swam his horses across the river twice, then tied them to a hitch rail out front of a six-stool café in the town of Victor. Rossie was the only customer, and after serving his eggs and sausage, the tall, ruined-looking woman, who doubled as waitress and cook, lit up a Camel cigarette and asked where he was heading.

"Right here," Rossie answered.

The waitress blew a slow string of smoke from her thin nostrils. "Poor idea. People are broke around here."

"You got a job," Rossie said.

When she smiled, Rossie saw that she must have once been a considerable looker, and that she remembered. "Hope you isn't after my job," she said.

"Never know what I'm hunting. But mostly I'm hunting a man named Stevenson. Met one of his relatives."

The waitress frowned. "What you got on him? Nobody's got a thing on him."

Bernard Stevenson, Rossie learned, was a Scottish businessman from Chicago. In the past decade this Stevenson had bought up — cheap, after a decade of dried-up years — acreages of pasture where he ran dairy cows. And he owned a creamery in Florence. He'd once considered raising racehorses but gave it up when the New York money market fell apart.

The waitress lit another cigarette. "You got to hand him that. Horses are a fine thing in the morning, if you catch them running. Salish ran thousands of horses in this valley before they was cheated out, first by the smallpox then by U. S. Grant." She went on to describe Stevenson's creamery, his milk and butter and cheese in grocery stores from Butte to Spokane, and grazing lands on benches east of the valley. "He don't run stock over there. Says he's resting the elk and the mule deer, like they was overworked. But the spotlighting sons of bitches around here are out there killing and butchering under his nose. You tell me, I'm trying to guess. What do you want with Stevenson?"

"I ran across his daughter up in Canada."

"Sounds right," she said. "Looking for girls is nature. But I wouldn't go up there, not even if I was invited. Nobody has much to do with them since Eliza ran off with her war whoop. But shit, I like that girl. I might run off if the right guy came along. I'd go have fun. What would I be losing?" She began wiping down the counter, which was already immaculate, then snubbed out her Camel. "People around here can't stand the idea that it was that Charlie Cooper, halfway Indian who wouldn't cut his hair. It's trying to think about what happens at night with white women and Indians that gets people's goat. That's what you hear said."

"Where would you ask about working there?"

"At the office. But it won't do you no good. Nobody's hiring, and anyway you wouldn't want to try your life in that big house around those people."

"Where's that office?"

"Highway toward Hamilton."

Rossie found an old schoolhouse building with a sign that read Kanaka Creek Ranch, and under that, Stevenson Enterprises. But it was empty, doors locked. So he turned onto a road alongside a shallow canyon, figuring that the stream coursing through it had to be Kanaka Creek and that the Stevenson house had to be upstream. Ahead, he could hear the rattling of a steel-wheeled steam tractor and soon saw that it was towing three hitched-up wagons loaded with timothy hay, which he followed through a cottonwood grove and into an open field.

The man on the tractor parked below the hayloft of an elegant, yellow-and-red brick-work barn with dormers and a roof that supported pigeon-roost cupolas.

"Anything I could do for you?" the man shouted, approaching Rossie on foot. "You been following me. There's nobody but me. This barn is empty. It's never seen horseshit."

"Empty?" Rossie said. "That's a handsome barn for empty. What I could do is help unload your hay. That's a two-man job."

"No," the man said. "You couldn't."

"Why's that?"

"If you did, you'd be working for Stevenson — this is Stevenson's high-assed horse barn — and you isn't working here. Nobody is but me, and I don't work here. I'm just on contract for this hay."

"That's fine horse hay," Rossie said.

"Pure timothy. Stevenson is talking about boarding horses. But you isn't supposed to be here. You don't work here."

"Where's the redwood house?" The waitress in Victor had told him about the house, its lumber shipped up from the California coast on railroad cars.

"Around the corner there, four or five hundred yards. But they isn't hiring."

"You sure of that?"

"Perfect sure."

The road curved to reveal a parkland with fire-scarred yellow pine, their lowest limbs fifty or so feet off the ground, the crowns blunted by lightning strikes. On a slab-faced ridge above the creek stood an ancient barn with cottonwood log walls, and a plank-sided cookhouse attached. The logs had long since gone punky and rotten and needed tearing down, Rossie thought.

But the main house, the Stevenson house, was a hundred yards up the road on higher ground, its chimneys built of river stones and its walls of twenty-foot, straight-grained redwood planks interrupted by floor-to-roof panels of window. Rossie tied his horse to the split-rail fence and headed up across the rise of lawn, then stopped abruptly in front of a totem pole carved from cedar.

A massive, unpainted frog perched on the top while six more frogs, not so small themselves, angled headfirst down the line of the pole to the ground, where a bed of white and yellow tulips surrounded them.

Beyond, at a table surfaced with blue-and-yellow ceramic tile, sat a dark-eyed woman of middle years sipping wine from a long-stemmed glass. A pale, unshaven fellow in rubber boots stood beside her.

After a hint of surprise, the woman stood. "Lemma Stevenson," she said to Rossie. "My husband is not here. You should know he will not be home until evening."

"I wasn't looking for him," Rossie said.

This woman was barefoot, her long feet suntanned and streaked with mud. She smiled uncertainly. "This gentleman is Nelson," she said. "Nelson is Irish, from County Cork. But inexplicably he's named for the British admiral. Which is a dreadful shame. These grounds are his responsibility. We're toasting our success with marigolds. Would you like to join us in a glass of pinot gris?"

"Pleased," Rossie said. "They are men in the Oregon desert valleys from County Cork. They come and settle with their families. I would sure like a glass."

Nelson's upper lips collapsed inward as he smiled. He had no front teeth. "Cork," he said, rolling the word. "We'll pull another cork."

"Cork, indeed," the woman said. "We pull the cork, don't we Nelson?"

"Bet you do," Rossie said. "My name is Benasco. Rossie Benasco."

"That would be Basque," she said. "Nelson, would you bring out another glass for this Basque gentleman?"

"Big frogs on that pole," Rossie said.

"Aren't they?" she said. "It's a Haida pole, the rather famous All Frogs Pole, stolen from the Queen Charlotte Islands in 1911 by thieving Germans. They took it down with a crosscut saw, roped it onto the deck of a yacht, and carried it to Bavaria. An art dealer brought it to Chicago in nineteen twenty-seven. Before the economy failed. My husband bought it at auction and shipped it out here on the railroad." She studied the pale sky. "Native peoples on the edge of a stormy sea, carving their vision into wood. There's no accounting."

"Sort of a Indian daydream," Rossie said. He sat his glass on the table. "I come looking for Eliza."

"Eliza is in San Francisco. So, when you finish with your wine, you might be going. Eliza won't be back for some while."

"Well," Rossie said, "I have to thank you." On his ride back down into the valley, Rossie puzzled on whether he was altogether a fool.

The next morning, over breakfast at the café in Victor, Rossie thought about riding on out of Montana.

"Heard you went up to the Chicago house," the waitress said, leaning on the counter, lighting another Camel cigarette. "Bernard Stevenson wasn't the first fellow out of that town to settle here, you know. An entire flock of professors from the University of Chicago was tricked into buying farms in the Bitterroot, that was advertised to them as an orchard paradise. They put them Chicago houses up by the dozen, thinking they were going to pay for them with apples. But the apples failed. Too far to markets. Good lot of the houses were burned down for insurance." She ashed her cigarette. "Then Stevenson came twenty years later. His house was built on those famous designs, only bigger."

"Well, I seen that one house. She's a strange world," Rossie said.

"I got a surprise for you. I know about some work. The real thing. You'd be working for my cousin, Samuel Burton." She paused, and shook her head. "He's always been pure asshole, but he's got an outfit stacking hay for the dairies. You're lucky, it's work. You won't like him, they say it's a killer, stacking for Samuel, but it's work."

"When is this coming up?"

"It's up right now. My sister's husband fell off the stack this morning. Twisted his back. Samuel is stacking while you're eating breakfast, waiting for somebody to send a man from Hamilton. He's sweating and he don't like sweating, so you get down to Three Mile Creek, where you'll see them out in the field by the willows, stacking with a beaver slide. Be there before the fellow from Hamilton, and Samuel will hire you — strong boy like you, count on it — so he can get off that stack himself."

"What if I don't like stacking hay?"

"It's more than you got."

"What about the man from Hamilton?"

"Guess he'll be sucking hind tit. If he ever shows up."

At eleven-thirty in the morning, Samuel

Burton stopped the stacking operation for about ten minutes, climbed off the stack, and hired Rossie on the spot. "Two dollars a day, roof over your bed, and all you can eat, three meals. You can turn them horses in the pasture and wrango for us. Guess you got work gloves, don't you? You'll sure as hell need 'em. You won't like the work but you'll like the food. Good cook this year. We work fast, load a minute, hundred ton in every stack, two a day if we don't have to move the slide more than a quarter mile."

Rossie hobbled his horses in a corner of the stack yard, buttoned the neck of his shirt, and tied some short twine around the cuffs of his pants to keep out the chaff. Pitchfork in hand, he climbed the slick planks of the slanting beaver slide and floundered off into loose hay where a dusty broken-toothed Swede named Lootie was leaning on his pitchfork and sucking hard candy. "You done this?" he asked.

Rossie shook his head no. "Son of a bitch," Lootie said. "Well, stand with me a few loads. I'll do your work this morning and mine. You'll learn."

Rossie had always avoided the stacking crew at the Neversweat, but he knew the dynamics. Four men drove buck rakes, each with a team of plodding geldings that pushed half-ton loads of cured hay before them across the meadow and onto a rope-work net spread before the beaver slide. The net setters were pale, blond brothers named Leverton. They cinched the net around the load and hooked it onto the cable that ran up the slide and along the length of the stack to the rear, where a steel trigger hook linked that far end to a two-wheeled pull-up cart drawn by a four-horse team. Soon as the net setters called out, the pull-up driver, a bowlegged man named McWhorter, urged his team forward, and another buck load of hay was drawn up the beaver slide and over onto the stack. Once the load had been drawn roughly into place, the stackers shouted and the pull-up driver kicked at his trigger, releasing the hook. The taut cable rebounded with a snap and fell loose, and the pull-back boy, on a patient saddle horse, dallied the long rope attached to the net, kicked his horse, and dragged the net and trailing cable back down the beaver slide and into position. Then the pink-eyed, net-setting Leverton brothers could hop to the awkward job of laying it out for the next load of hay. A load every sixty seconds, sixty loads every hour, all day long.

What Rossie didn't understand was the actual art of stacking, building with hay, load by load. One load went left, the next to the right, and the grasses were layered into a woven, hundred-ton edifice that would be essentially watertight in the snowy winter, so as to prevent interior rot.

By midafternoon, as they were topping out, Samuel Burton had disappeared. Rossie was struggling, sweating and exhausted, floundering hip-deep in the hay but anyway getting into the rhythm, when Lootie yipped, wiped his forehead, and shouted, "Fini."

Raising his pitchfork over his head, Lootie plunged down the face of the beaver slide like a skater on slick-soled boots. Rossie, meanwhile, sat on the boards and scooted like a child, thankful that no one laughed. In the shade under the slide, Lootie pried the top off a five-gallon steel can wrapped in damp burlap and handed Rossie a tin cup. The water tasted of metal. The net setters rolled the net and hooked the pull-up cart to the front of the beaver slide, and then they were moving on, like phantoms in the brightness.

"I got to bring my horses," Rossie said.

By quitting time the beaver slide had been towed a quarter mile to the next stack yard and set up again. Rossie chomped Lootie's hard candy, recovering.

"Great life, huh?" Lootie said. "No quitting."

There was no quitting, not even with his shoulders aching and money in his pocket. Collapsing toward sleep, Rossie wondered why he was sticking around for a daydream about a girl who was pregnant and gone to San Francisco. Could be her mother had lied, and she was at this minute in an unimaginable rich-girl bed, and had wrote him off altogether. She might be the kind to write people off.

The next sunup Rossie dragged himself from his bedroll, went out to a corral to catch and saddle Pinky, and rode the meadows to wrango the work teams. Mists folded over the sloughs. Driving those big horses at a canter toward the hay camp, their hooves echoing on dry meadows, Rossie recalled the waitress — he didn't know her name — and what she'd said about the old-time Indians running horses and the pride they took in this valley. So this was it.

The crew ran their hundred tons of meadow hay over the beaver slide every day, as one week turned into two. Bunkhouse philosophizing drifted to growing up poor, dynamiting whitefish and giant trout in the river and rowing out to gather them, eating pickled fish canned in glass jars through the winter, cutting timber for fuel with nobody to guard it but the men who were doing the stealing, and going out with a spotlight to kill and butcher somebody's heifers in a far field while wives out along the road watched for headlights.

"Girls I grew up with," Virgil Leverton said, "Momma's cousins from Phillipsburg, they wouldn't be shy about shooting. Women are liable to shoot. They act like cats, they don't give a shit."

The pull-up driver, McWhorter, grunted. "One of them Alabama women is worth a dozen of you boys."

"They's mean."

"They are supposed to be mean. Otherwise they'd be letting their daughters marry some fucking net setter like you." McWhorter turned to Rossie. "They say you went over to Stevenson's house, rode right up and talked to the old lady. Heard that from the Irish gardener. Nelson. He says you talked to the old lady, said you was looking for the girl."

"Momma put me on the run," Rossie said.

"You can hate them people and steal what they got, or you can join 'em. You give up on the Stevenson girl?"

"Not altogether, or I'd be halfway home to Nevada by now."

"How come you don't go back up there?"

"Waiting for a rainy day."

"Might be a while," McWhorter said.

But six days later it came, thunder and jittering bolts of lightning over the Bitterroots in late afternoon and soft rain all night long. There was no stacking the wet hay, so the next day, with the fields steaming, dry in the hot sun, Rossie caught his pinto.

"You might come back disappointed, with a good reason to quit," McWhorter said. "Riding to Nevada has got to beat stacking in the Bitterroot."

Rossie rapped on the main door, an oversized slab of redwood with a big *S* for Stevenson carved into it. Eliza's mother answered.

"I'm here again," Rossie said, "looking for Eliza."

"There's no accounting for desire." The woman adjusted the straying bun behind her head, studying him a long moment. "What a thing for me to say. Desire. Isn't it romantic?"

Lemma stepped back into a hall floored with stone. Stained-glass windows shone in the alcoves with hardwood benches built into the redwood walls. In the rooms beyond, expanses of oak and maple flooring were inlaid into zigzag patterns.

"Bernard," she called. Then she turned back to Rossie. "What was your name?"

"Rossie Benasco."

"Yes," she said. "Bernard, it's a Basque gentleman, Mr. Benasco." She smiled at Rossie, a formal, welcoming smile. "Eliza has returned."

"Glad of that," Rossie said.

"I suppose you are. We were."

Bernard Stevenson shuffled toward them in house slippers. He was a small, quick man with reddish hair and a beard tightly trimmed and turning to gray. His blue-gray shirt looked to be made of silk. "Pleased," he said, as he shook Rossie's hand.

"This explains Eliza," Lemma said.

Bernard turned to his wife. "What does this explain?" He gave Rossie a tight little smile. "Nothing explains Eliza. Nothing in the known universe."

"A young man," Lemma said, "as we know, can explain Eliza."

"What needs explaining?" Rossie asked.

"Restlessness," she said. "Discord."

" 'In my cosmos,' " Bernard proclaimed in an elevated voice, " 'there will be no feeva of discord.' That's cosmos spelled with a capital *K,* as in capital *K* crazy and capital *K* cat. Eliza acts like a Krazy Kat. It's a perplexing thing."

"I don't even know what you're talking about," Rossie said.

Bernard stared at him before drifting into a slight smile. "You two are made for each other. Uninformed and humorless."

"Bernard, this young man is a friend of your daughter's and thus a friend of the family's," Lemma said. "He can't be left standing at the doorway while you go on with your bewildering nonsense."

"We'll find Eliza," Bernard said, "but let me show you *Krazy Kat*." Up the wide curve of main stairway, Rossie was led into a room with a tattered buffalo robe on the floor and floor-to-ceiling windows looking out over hayfields and fence lines overgrown with wild roses and beyond that over the far-off barns and cottonwoods beside the river.

"My hideout," Bernard said. "Here, I can watch the world rotate." He gestured toward a wall lined with books. "Lemma wants to call this a library but it isn't. It's for denning up and keeping an eye on things." He stroked a hand along the backs of an entire shelf of books. "These are Robert Louis Stevenson, my great-uncle. We haven't been a literary family except for Robert Louis. My people were engineers. They built Scottish lighthouses on rocks in the sea." He

236

patted the books. "First editions."

"This Robert Louis." Rossie said. "He's dead?"

"The great ones are dead. Greatness, then clerks, that's the way of families."

"You don't live like no clerk."

"It's hard to evaluate the self," Bernard said. "I've not felt like a clerk. But we came to see *Krazy Kat.*" He gestured toward a large cartoon in a silver frame, a group of hand-colored humanized animals with speech in balloons over their heads — a cat, an ostrich-like bird, a crow, and a dog, thick-bodied and badge-wearing. All of them, except for a rat picking up a brick were gazing at reddish spires in a desert.

"Tell you what," Rossie said. "I'd say that's the craziest-looking thing I ever saw."

"*Krazy Kat,*" Stevenson said, moving in close to the framed drawing. "It may be actually one of the sanest. You see what it is? Praising wildness."

Smoke rose above round-roofed houses in the cartoon desert.

"Somebody live there?" Rossie said.

"Natives," Bernard said. "Navajo."

"Must be thin going."

As he spoke, Rossie felt it: Eliza was in the doorway, the tails of a washed-out calico shirt hanging out over baggy, tan trousers.

Her sleeves were rolled up, her black hair in a tight bun. "Men in the study talking wisdom. I was at the barns." She was speaking to Rossie. "Waiting got tiresome. But now you're here."

She lifted the tails of her calico shirt, and there was her belly, the top button on her pants tied across into the buttonhole with a little string.

"Eliza," her father said, "for Christ's sake."

"Come here," she said to Rossie. "Kiss my cheek."

Rossie did. He slipped along on the slick soles of his boots as if walking on ice, leaned forward, and kissed the cheek she offered.

"Nice," she said. "Like a gentleman."

"Does he not be nice?" her father asked.

"Nicer than nice, nicer than you."

"Of course," Bernard said, grinning at his daughter. "He be as nice as pie."

"Out front!" It was the mother, Lemma, calling from partway up the stairs. "Betty is setting up for tea!"

Bernard led them down another flight of stairs, along a hallway, and through a darkish room with a huge fireplace made of river stones. Double doors led to what was called the "out front," a sunporch floored with huge black and white ceramic tiles. Plants in red Mexican pots bloomed in the corners, yellow and purple and white and red, and giant ferns reached near to the white-painted tinwork ceiling.

A woman who could have been anything from thirty-five to fifty was setting porcelain plates and saucers and cups on a sparkling, glass-topped table — the blue willow pattern, Rossie knew the pattern from his mother's house — on lilac placemats.

"This," Lemma said, "is our invaluable Betty. Betty, this is Mr. Benasco. From Nevada."

Betty turned to smile at Rossie. "So I've heard." Her grip, when she shook his hand, was carelessly strong as a man's.

"My mother would do tea for her ladies, on dishes like these, the blue willow," Rossie said once they were seated, after Betty had poured and gone off for what she called "the cakes."

"Her ladies?" Bernard said, raising his eyebrows. Lemma shot Bernard a scornful glance. "Actual prostitutes?" Bernard said.

"Divorcées," Rossie said.

"It was Nevada," Bernard said to his wife. "Prostitution is legal in Nevada, and it can be after all a form of commonality."

"Bernard," Lemma said, "prostitution is each and every time, in all cases, however jolly it may seem to you, a form of hideous

239

exploitation."

"It's not legal in Reno," Rossie protested. "People just act like it's legal. They act like anything is legal."

"Bernard," Lemma said. "There are prostitutes in Missoula. There are prostitutes in Hamilton."

Eliza's father looked away, playing an ironic moment of sadness before saying, "Women don't want to understand."

These people made a game of talking against each other, a game of trapping and releasing. "Women." Bernard directed this closing remark to Rossie, then continued. "George Herriman, he does *Krazy Kat*. I have a friend who knows him, that's how I came by the print. Herriman loves deserts and warmhearted people. We'd call it hospitality. He goes to Kayenta, a community centered on a trading post, and finds a people at one with their desires. As people can be, anywhere."

Eliza hooted. "At one with their desires?"

"Where's he live otherwise?" Rossie asked.

"Southern California. Burbank, in the City of Angels, surrounded by clamor and anxiety."

"That kind of thinking," Eliza said, parodying her father, "is clamorous and anxious." She turned to Rossie. "You should know how lonely we are. We're showing off for you."

"Where are you bound?" Bernard asked Rossie.

"Making my way. Stacking hay down the valley."

"You're living in the vicinity?"

"Yes, Daddy," Eliza said. "In the vicinity. We'll be seeing him, on occasion, for dinner. I'll go riding out with him on Sundays."

Her father frowned.

"Piss on daddy," she said, lightly, then stood and spun away. Three long twirling steps and she was gone without looking back. Betty returned with "the cakes," which were huckleberry tarts.

"Well," Lemma said, "aren't we having a moment?"

Shirt off in the heat and sweating alongside Lootie as they sealed and slopped the final loads into a canopy, Rossie was surprised when Eliza appeared on a bay horse, going by at some distance toward the line of poplars along the river.

"There's the rich girl," Lootie sang, giving Rossie a broken-toothed smile. "She's come all the way to see you."

She didn't stop, but kicked the bay horse and cantered on, waving as she went, a happy-go-lucky girl on her afternoon ride.

"She was looking at us," Lootie said.

In the cookhouse that night, all of them at a single long table, Samuel Burton at the head, Lootie brought her up again. "That rich girl," he said. "You been to that house, how's the chances with her?"

"They run me off," Rossie said.

"You should see your face when she waves," Lootie said. "Looks like your face will fall off. Thought you might fall off that stack. Thought that might be the end of you."

McWhorter was at the other end of the table, facing Samuel Burton. "Samuel," McWhorter said, "I was hoping this kid was going to run off with that girl. You'd be looking for another stacker, and you could hire my cousin Tim."

"Your cousin Tim," Burton said, "is the sorriest drunk in the Bitterroot."

McWhorter laughed. "Yeah, but he's a stout son of a bitch."

Rossie quit his eating, and looked around to them. "You seen that brickwork barn sitting there empty, never seen a horse inside?"

"It's more of them people's bullshit," Burton said. "It's a beauty of a barn except it's bullshit. But one thing. Humping on that girl, it might be a living if you didn't mind the pimping. Rich people is always a pimping deal."

"You calling me pimped?" Rossie said.

"No," Burton said. "You and me, boy, we sweat our asses off, and they don't. But they get the money and we don't."

"Those people were fine with me," Rossie said.

"Some kid. You don't know shit about shit."

"What you could do for me," Rossie said, and this was out before he could stop himself, "is go fuck yourself."

"You'll eat that, or I'm going to beat your ass."

"Outside," Lootie shouted.

The conflict on sod in front of the cookhouse was quick. Burton faced off with hands down, and Rossie caught him along the neck with a left hook. But Burton shrugged and lifted his left shoulder, dropped it and came under. Next thing, Rossie was down, nose streaming out blood, seeing double. Lootie was holding Rossie's head, and all the rest of them were inside the cookhouse, talking and finishing dinner.

"You give it up," Lootie said. "He's a famous man for hitting. Kicks like a mule."

All Rossie could recall was Burton's fist out of the twilight, then not a thing. He was passing out again. The next morning, before sunup, Rossie woke in his bed when Burton shook his shoulder.

"I got me another stacker," Burton said. He tossed a sliver of paper on the floor. "There's a paycheck. Thirty-six dollars for eighteen days. Catch your horses and get out of here before breakfast."

Rossie's head felt lopsided, aching seriously in the very early morning, as he eased his horses toward a bank so he could cash the check. Goodbye to this and head for Reno, that was the idea. The thought of breakfast made his stomach seize up, but by the time he had his horses tied at a hitching rail in front of the marble-faced bank in Hamilton, he was hungry. He pocketed his money and slipped down the block and into an empty restaurant called Staninger's.

"You serve whiskey?" he asked the bartender in the back room, who didn't even study the ruined look of Rossie's face as he served up two shots, a beer back, and a rib steak.

Then Eliza was framed in the light from the doorway. "If I'd missed you," she said, "I'd of been devastated."

"I'd buy this woman a drink," Rossie said. "You're a beauty." She touched her fingertips to his face. "What I want," she told the barkeep, "is one of those bourbons, like him. But I'm pregnant, so give me a glass of water." She turned back to Rossie. "Margaret Poore called, like you would never do. She said you were beat up, paid off, and heading for the bank in Hamilton."

"Margaret Poore?"

"She runs the café in Stevensville. She got you the job. She thinks you're a cutie. I'd have been sooner but I came horseback. A pregnant woman shouldn't be horseback, but I go slow and it's all right. I came on horseback so I could ride with you."

"How else were you going to come?"

"We have automobiles. Telephones. People do. You could have called me on the telephone. You're a goddamned mess, but it's not every day a man comes after me. You know what my mother told me? She said, 'He's not our kind. Bring him around a few times and he'll be here forever.' "

Outside in the street, where their horses were tied to the hitch rack, two bulging canvas saddlebags were draped over the flanks of Eliza's bay gelding.

"Food," she said. "I thought ahead."

"You figure we're going to need provisions?" He was hurting but nonetheless feeling smart-assed, his head buzzing from the whiskey.

"Sweet, old Hamilton," she said. "We used to go to the movies. Now I don't. Run off with Charlie Cooper and the good girls don't invite you to movies."

They rode north along the highway until Eliza turned them onto a narrow, dusty track that progressed up toward the mountains, climbing steadily in switchbacks until the valley was spread below.

"They're stacking hay down there," Eliza said. "You're not. Be happy."

After another hour, the track leveled high up on the mountain and turned toward the canyon.

"This, when we get there, it belongs to me. Me only. It's my surprise," Eliza said.

Kanaka Creek gleamed far below in the canyon. A barn and cabin, scrapped together from unpeeled logs and unpainted salvage lumber, stood utterly alone on the fractured edge of a gray basalt cliff.

"The Cliff House," Eliza said. "My father had it built for me the summer I turned ten, my birthday present. The deed was wrapped in a ribbon, beside the little cake. But I cried. I wanted a horse. So I got a colt, too, a baby mare for my own."

"Sounds like a tough life," Rossie said.

"Spoiled, ruined, and wrecked," she said.

"Our family was supposed to camp and stay overnight here. So that's what you and I are going to do." She went on about barrel racing in rodeos the summer she was fourteen. "All around the valley with Daisy. But Daisy got in the wire in the Tailfeather Field and they put her down."

"Daisy," Rossie said. "That was her name? The Tailfeather Field sour you on horses?"

"For a couple of years. But no more."

The barn reeked of pack rats, but there was timothy for the horses and a fifty-gallon steel barrel half-full of oats and lidded over with planks.

"Don't look like anybody's been here," Rossie said.

"Not since Daddy told us the news about his dying," she said. "Slowly, but dying. I told you that."

"Don't think so."

"I told you in Canada," she said. "Do you listen, or just whistle?"

"Thought I was hearing you, " Rossie said. "He don't act like he's dying."

"He will. You wait. He'll let you know."

The house was backed directly onto the cliff, its dusty windows looking over the canyon. Trails of mouseshit decorated the floor and the blankets covering the home-made furniture, chairs built of unpeeled pine, and a pine bed frame without mattress. Eliza propped open the door, sent Rossie to a trickle of water springing from the edge of the cliff, and began gathering the blankets.

"I'll sweep," she said. "You bring buckets of water and man the mop."

He went back and forth, first waiting at the spring for the galvanized bucket to fill, then sloshing down the floor and mopping before retrieving a fresh bucket for the rinse. This mountainside with this glowing woman showing pregnant was the best thing he'd found.

She came looking for him, a woman with her sleeves up, shaking blankets.

"Somebody turned down your fire," he said when he had the plank floor shining with unstreaked luster. "You don't act so jumpy."

"Now, we'll need your bedroll on the bed," she said, ignoring him, and digging food from her saddle-bags. "And since I've got us here, it would be romantic if you made the salad. The vegetables are washed. You could cut up the chicken."

"Don't think I ever made a salad. But I made plenty of peanut butter sandwiches." Rossie grinned as he got onto slicing cucumbers, tearing up leaf lettuce, chopping little onions, cutting the roots and sprouts off red and white radishes, mixing them, and pouring on the salad dressing she'd brought in a little sealed, screw-top jar.

She sat and watched. "Cooking is a serious matter," she said. "You've got to train yourself. It's not a joke. Don't give me that sheepdog grinning. Did you ever cook one meal? In your life?"

"First," Rossie said, "Burton kicks my ass. Then I got to cook."

"You want to talk like a fool," she said. "You have nice hands, but nobody can talk to hands. You know what I dream? I mean, daydream? I daydream about my father's death. He's into a garden ditch, fallen into the water, flowers and birds all around. Birds calling and the cold water's the last thing he feels and he hears birds and feels himself flying. That's it, I can talk to you about flying. I have impulses. My father claims many of them are akin to jumping out of windows."

She stood and went outside, and he watched her from the big window as he cut up the cold chicken and laid out the plates and utensils she'd washed. She was standing at the edge of the cliff, gazing down. But she was not there when he finished, not where she had been, on the edge of the cliff.

Abruptly, she was nowhere.

When he called there was no answer. Silence flooded, and Rossie was suddenly breathless, running to the cliff's edge. She was utterly gone. Then he saw she was huddled on a slippery ledge below the tiny spring, her knees under her chin, staring off.

"In the name of Christ," he said.

"That's it, in the name of Christ, acting like an asshole." She stood, casually, like an animal there on the precipice, and stretched. "I wondered if you'd come and find me."

He was recovering his breath and close to angry.

"It's three hundred and fifty-seven feet," she said, clambering up to stand beside him. "I worked it out with trigonometry. A clean fall. Just about sure to kill you on your way to heaven."

"Sounds like you been close to crazy," Rossie said.

"For a minute." She moved past him.

He found her dishing out the salad and salting her chicken, and they ate without much talk. The whiskey had worn off, and Rossie ached everywhere, so he kicked off his boots, stretched out in sunlight, wadded up the pillow from his bedroll, and slept. An aching bladder woke him in the darkness to find her quiet beside him, her hair faintly aglow in the moonlight. He pissed near the edge of the cliff and saw that the canyon was black but the valley off to the east faintly luminous here and there from what had to be kerosene lanterns burning in kitchens.

In the morning, banging around, building a fire, making coffee, she roused him without apology. Rossie watched as the coffee percolated, then sat with a cup she'd handed him. But she wouldn't look at him.

"You about to cry?" he asked.

"Not exactly, but I need to tell you, down in San Francisco I was scheduled for an abortion. Steel tools. I just walked the floor in a room in the Mark Hopkins Hotel. It was eleven stories down to the people in the Union Square, and I was frightened by tools. So I canceled. I was a fool, but here I am with my baby coming."

"You was alone?"

"That was how I wanted it. Tough girl who wasn't so tough. But listen. At the Mark Hopkins, in my daydream, I thought you could carry my baby on your shoulder. You. I didn't daydream about anybody else."

"Man with a baby on his shoulder," Rossie said. "What I thought, camped up in Canada, I thought this is it, you. I couldn't

251

think why that should be true in any long run. But here I am."

This didn't seem to be entirely what she wanted to hear. "What there is for breakfast," she said, "since you finished off the chicken, is peanut butter sandwiches and coffee."

"Some cook," he said.

"Better than you're used to lately. But I'm not your momma. You feel like walking around?"

The trail went off into scrub pine above the cliff, steadily climbing.

"Two weeks, this will be loaded with huckleberries," she said. "Black bears will come for the berries. But they don't want anything to do with people." As if she'd called it into being, they came upon a heap of scat. "Shit," she said.

"That's what it looks like?" Rossie asked. "Some monster shit himself."

"Bear shit. Stick your finger in," she said. "See if it's fresh."

"Stick your own finger in. I don't stick my finger in shit." But he did it. The scat was soft and faintly warm. He held the finger out. "You want to lick it?"

"At least it's not steaming. If it's a sow with cubs, even a black bear, we should get out of here. She could be in those trees, anywhere."

Walking back, they heard the chugging of a Model A Ford, which labored into sight as they emerged from the pines.

"More shit," Eliza said.

Bernard parked and sat with his hands on the wheel, staring ahead, then climbed out. "Have you had your fun?" he called, and he seemed to be trying to smile.

"Not enough," Eliza said.

"We've been searching for you since last twilight. Look at you. Running off into the woods. Betty finally told us that you'd planned on coming up here." There he lost momentum and looked away, conceding that these were stupid, useless things to say.

Rossie ducked his head and thought, Fuck you, goodbye.

"So," Eliza said, "here we are. You found us."

"Cohabitating," Bernard said. "Look at you."

"Look at us," she said. "Fully clothed, gone for a walk in the woods. You may have noticed that coming here was my idea." She stalked off to the edge of the cliff, no one following, and skimmed a small, flat stone into the emptiness. "I have the entire weight of myself on this," she said, "so you might as well get used to it. Which is how you've told me to live."

"The weight of yourself on what?" Bernard asked. But he was eyeing Rossie, visibly gathering himself. "Apologies for my tone," he said. "I wish you well. Eliza makes me crazy."

"We'll be riding home together," she said. "I promised him a room in the bunkhouse."

"He'll be your special guest."

"Yes," she said, "he will."

"You never promised me any place," Rossie said, after Bernard had driven away.

Eliza smiled. "One little lie," she said.

As they rode through the timberlands, a sense of aimlessness came down on Rossie. Maybe it was the natural result of getting knocked out. Or maybe this scenario was nonsense every moment, and he'd be back in Nevada by September. "The air is gone out of my tires," he said.

"My father," she answered. "The air is mostly out of *his* tires. He no doubt imagined we were up there fucking and fucking away. But we weren't. We didn't even act like we thought about fucking."

The bunkhouse was a run of rooms tacked onto the side of the old barn and home to only two men and a cook. "The cook," Eliza said, "is an old shithead named Albert. The gardener is Nelson, you met him. The cowboy is Larry. Who knows what he does?"

They left Rossie's bedroll and pack at the bunkhouse and unsaddled and turned their horses loose into the Tailfeather Field, where the animals rolled, toured the fences, and commenced grazing.

Back at the bunkhouse a bowlegged man in an undershirt came limping out from a back room.

"Larry," Eliza said, "Rossie will be living in the bunkhouse. Bernard said you would find him jobs."

"Plenty of those," Larry said, like this kind of thing was no surprise if you worked for rich people. "What kind of work?"

"Horses," Rossie answered.

"Well, that's took. I got the horse work," Larry said.

"How many they got around here?" Rossie asked.

"Nine, right this minute, a work team and seven saddle horses, counting three of mine."

"There'll be eleven with mine. Hell of a job," Rossie said. "Take an hour or so a week just keeping them grained."

Larry didn't grin back. "I'm not looking for a job," Rossie said. "I'm a boardinghouse hand. Working enough to pay my keep."

"Heard you was coming, from Nevada.

The Mister told me. The only place I ever worked in that country was the Circle Square out of Battle Mountain, up toward the South Fork of the Owyhee."

"Where I come from is the Neversweat."

"Well, then, you'll do. Throw your gear in the saddle shed there. I'll see you for dinner." He turned back again before walking away. "Slivers Flynn, he laughed like I was crazy when I told him all I knew was tying hard and fast."

Rossie nodded and grinned. "Too much Texas."

Eliza listened like they were speaking in tongues.

"Hard and fast is Texas style and crazy," Rossie told her, after this Larry had gone back to his room. "Rope a fence post and you're tied down on your saddle horn. Horse keeps going and the post stays still. You are in a wreck. Then again, I never worked anywhere but the Neversweat. I don't know any other way but California dallying."

"Now you work here."

She started to leave, then turned back. "There are dreams," she said, "where I think I'm my father and can know what he dreams. He wants to see me content and old when he's been dead for years. Other times he's a dragon. I've got to go talk to my dragons."

"Old and happy," Rossie said. "Think about that. I'll be sweeping up my room."

"Guess you will. You've got a new place to live. Have a nice dinner with the boys." After sweeping the worn flooring Rossie drifted to the barn, where harnesses hung off wooden pegs in the log walls, but nobody was there beyond the spooks left by men and horses from other times. He returned to his bed and napped until the dinner bell was clanging his aching head. Albert, the tiny cook, who claimed he was Mexican, was beating it with a steel chisel and smiling a toothless smile. "Thought I'd ring, else you thought you was going to sleep through."

Albert and Rossie and the Irish gardener named Nelson sat down to eat. The cowhand named Larry was at the head of the table, which was long enough for twenty. They had roast beef under wild mushrooms, green beans, lumpy mashed potatoes, and dark gravy spiced with very hot peppers.

"I'm eating like a pig, and it's making me sweat like a dog," Rossie said.

No one answered.

So he gathered his plate and utensils, making ready to carry them to the kitchen.

"You ought to hold on," Larry said. " 'Less you don't like pie with rhubarb and strawberries mixed."

As Rossie sat down to breakfast the next morning, Larry shooed him away. "They want you up to the big house," he said.

So Rossie made his way uphill to the kitchen door. Betty answered when he knocked.

"Breakfast," she said, "with the Mister."

Bernard Stevenson was alone at a table in the kitchen, ignoring hash browns but halfway into an omelet smothered in catsup. "Sit here," he said, gesturing in his quick way.

"What would you like?" Betty asked Rossie.

"What you're cooking. Same as him. Maybe some sausage."

"Sausage, indeed," Bernard said. "You should know I am dying. Having you here is one of Eliza's prerogatives, as the daughter of a man who took care of what money he had." He smiled faintly. "Sausage. I envy you. Betty will feed me sausage only on Sunday. She says it's to preserve my health although why anyone would bother no one knows." He dribbled more catsup on his omelet. "Despite what you may hear," he said, "I am not wealthy. In nineteen twenty-six I had the luck to take my money out of the markets and bring it to Montana. I wanted another life, so I bought in cheap on these properties. I got a last dance."

Rossie sat on that. "Makes me wonder what you and me think we're doing," he said. "If it was me, I wouldn't spend much time on a fellow in off the road. Them properties of yours don't make nothing to me."

"A remarkably Western notion. But I wonder." Bernard sat a moment poised with a forkload of omelet. "Don't mistake me. I'm not in the habit of charity."

"You think I'm a bloodsucker? Come to leech on you?"

Bernard wiped his mouth with his white linen napkin and tucked it into a silver ring. "You think I never seen people like you?" Rossie asked. "We got linens where I come from."

"You might be crazy for an idle life," Bernard said. "Betty will get you fed. She'll call me when you're finished."

"I may not be here," Betty said, standing over Bernard with a spatula in her hand. "I work in civil households. This boy has done nothing to warrant this display." She turned to Rossie. "Are you mending? This is simply hideous behavior."

"Feeling better than yesterday."

"Betty," Bernard said, "my apologies if I've offended you."

"It's this boy you owe an apology. For God's sake!"

Bernard stood. "Betty," he said, "you're never weak." He poured coffee from the pot on the stove, then sat back down facing Rossie. "Young man, none of us enjoys eating crow. But I'm in the act. Accept my apologies. Let's try to enjoy one another."

Out on the front lawn, in a luminous morning, before getting into the Buick, Bernard stood a moment surveying his properties. "At this location," he said, "with fingers of acreage reaching into three canyons, we have eleven hundred acres. Overgrazed for decades, they are now devoted to amenities — this house, a few horses. There is no income generated here."

Down the valley, after crossing a long, rickety, two-track bridge over the Bitterroot River, they came onto a narrow gravel road between irrigated fields where black-and-white Holstein dairy cows grazed, udders swaying as they moved.

"What they are, the lovely beasts, are decorations that also pay the bills. My herds and the creamery down at Florence are required to support my family. Which they do, if tightly managed. On this property there are one hundred and twenty-three animals milking fresh at the moment. The barns are nearly full, with room for just two more. I have fee-simple title to five hundred and sixty acres in these pastures, which are grazed in strict rotation. Up the valley, in the riverbank meadows near Florence, we graze another two hundred and fifty, which are milked in barns adjacent to the creamery. Those meadows also sustain the cows that are dry at the moment. Six men milk the morning shift in each set of barns, twenty cows each day, four hours a day, mostly before sunup. By noon they are finished and go home. Another crew does the evening milking."

Milking was long since over on this morning. Sloping concrete floors in the two milking barns — fifty stalls in one, seventy-five in the other — were being hosed off and swept down by men in white coveralls. Two boys were clanging five-gallon steel cans of milk one against another as they loaded a flatbed. The milk would be hauled to the creamery in Florence.

"Absolute cleanliness," Bernard said. "There's my secret. Every day I'm down here watching." He tapped his fingers on

261

the steering wheel as he drove. "What did they pay you," he asked, "for driving those horses to Calgary?"

"One hundred dollars. All you could eat. Two head of horses at the end."

Bernard grimaced. "How much when you were stacking hay?"

"Two dollars a day, board and room. Free grazing for my horses."

"In the San Joaquin Valley, it's twenty-five cents an hour for picking cotton." Bernard said. "Two dollars a day. They feed themselves. Here, we pay forty cents an hour, which averages to three dollars and fifty cents a day. They feed themselves. So we're paying reasonable wages in Montana."

"Unless you're a married man, with babies and a woman."

"The women can work."

The creamery was a set of white brick buildings that housed stainless-steel vats in cold rooms with heavy, insulated doors. It stank sweetly of milk and what Rossie estimated were the sourish odors that went with churning butter and making cheese.

"Profits," Bernard said, "lie primarily with cheeses. Milk pays the rent. Butter and cheeses pay for excess."

"Don't see those creamery women."

Bernard ignored him. "So what do you

think about going to work? Three dollars and fifty cents a day, milking in the barns. I'm offering you a job, decent work. That's what this morning is about."

"Don't think so," Rossie said. "There's not going to be any milking while I got traveling money in my pocket. There's nothing I want to know about milking cows."

"Do you expect to be traveling? In that event this morning has been a waste of our time."

The next morning at breakfast, Nelson said Rossie was to come up to the ridge behind the house. "You'd be helping with the vegetables, that's what they said."

Albert and Larry suspended their eating, and watched Rossie's response.

"Might be," Rossie said.

"Strawberries. We could begin hoeing the strawberries," Nelson said. He narrowed his eyes at Rossie. "Nobody knows what you're doing around here except for that Eliza. She told her mother you were feeling your way. I heard them shouting. Women got no mercy with one another."

"I don't do no hoeing," Rossie said.

"Fine with me."

Rossie once more considered catching his horses. Fuck these asshole idiots. He couldn't look around to Albert and Larry.

The garden, up the hill and out of sight beyond the big house, was a sunny, precisely kept irrigated acre of plantings in perfect rows with flowers in blossom around the uphill edge. Bright water flowed from the creek along clean, sod-banked ditches, diverted from one row to the other by tiny redwood head gates. Rossie had pulled off his boots and socks and gone to step barefoot into the warm, loamy soil when Betty came by, carrying a straw basket, along the sodded bank of the irrigation ditch.

"Barefoot boy," she said. "Cheeks of tan."

"Don't know what I'm doing," Rossie said. "But I didn't come here with the idea of picking strawberries and most sure not carrots. I don't hoe in gardens, not before I'm starving."

"We know what you had in mind," she said. "Nelson can hoe. But you'll like those baby carrots at dinner, braised in butter."

"Braised in butter," Rossie said. "That's me. What's there to like about hoeing?"

"Vegetables. Kale and beets and scallions, lettuce and peas and carrots and green beans just coming. All of which I've seen you eat." She hesitated. "Hoeing and whoring. Is that your problem?"

"You are a tough woman," Rossie said.

There was nothing to do but duck his head like any spoiled jackass trying to get off the hook.

After pouting through the morning, Rossie caught his pinto and rode down to Hamilton to buy a pair of heavy, horsehide gloves. The next day he took a team and wagon loaded with barbed wire and a stretcher out to mend fences around the home fields. Chopping wild roses from the fence lines along the edges of the timber — a mix of white-barked aspen, larch, and pine — he could see dust rising from roads in the valley and hear the hawks calling as they soared. Here he could work himself into a sweat or not as he pleased.

"You've invented your own work," Bernard said, a few nights later. "That's admirable. What wages do you expect?"

"Dinner," Rossie said.

"That's foolish," Bernard smiled in his brittle way. "But isn't Eliza part of the reward? Since you're part of the family now?"

He asked Rossie to take on the nightly task of cranking the Delco generator that charged glass batteries ranged along the walls of an insulated building the Stevensons called the "engine room." These kept the electric lights burning in the house. Rossie came to relish this day's-end ritual of washing up at twilight to put on a fresh shirt, cranking the Delco, then sharing the evening meal Betty served to Eliza and her parents.

"Here's to us and linen napkins," he said one night, before his first sip of the red wine.

"What do your people think of your continued presence in Montana?" Lemma asked. "When do they expect you home?"

"No way of knowing."

"You must telephone. Let them know you're with us and safe."

"Safe?" Eliza said to her mother.

Bernard smiled. "You should be a field marshal," he said to his daughter, "never neglecting an advantage."

"My people figure I'm all right," Rossie said. "They're not worrying. We don't spend much time hanging onto one another."

"Nevertheless, you should call your mother," Lemma said. "I speak from experience, as the mother of a wandering girl."

Bernard snorted.

"You can use my telephone," Eliza said.

"In your room?" Lemma was incredulous. "Do you think that's such a good idea?"

"Mother, leave it alone, it's hopeless. I'm already pregnant."

Lemma shook her head, mimicking sadness. "Eliza is afraid thus arrogant and always reassuring herself. She's afraid of besmirching herself."

"Besmirching? Mother, I'm big-bellied and besmirched. Goodbye. We're going now."

"Good Lord, wait for the meal," Lemma said.

Betty brought the bacon and spinach salad and they ate with no more talk.

Then Eliza led Rossie to her rooms, her separate apartment at the back of the house.

"You," she said to Rossie, rolling her gray eyes, "don't get them worked up."

Her rooms were right out of a hotel lobby — a leather couch under windows looking to the mountains, heavy leather chairs, hardwood floors, metal tables, lamps with silvery metallic shades, and Navajo rugs on the walls. These furnishings had been hand-picked in Chicago. Nothing girlish for this girl, as Eliza herself said.

She rang up the operator in Missoula, who rang the operator in Reno, who plugged the four longs and four shorts into the line. Katrina, when she answered, sounded as distant as she was from him.

"I'm with these people in Montana," Rossie shouted.

"Is that you? Good God! When are you

coming home?"

"Not right away. End of the summer."

"Why not right away?"

"There's a woman, I'm visiting her, she's pregnant, and I'm staying around, helping out."

"Jesus Christ! Pregnant?"

"Hell," he said, "it wasn't me."

"Well, be careful. Who is this woman?"

"She's living with her folks. They're well-off."

"What's she want with you?"

"She likes me. There's people that do."

"Well," Katrina said, "you should know that Oscar is done chasing Mattie Flynn." Then she caught her breath. "Your father is back in this house. You never know how things will turn out."

"See, everybody is doing fine."

"Is there a number? One I can call?"

"Victor, Montana. People called Stevenson. One long, one short."

"Do you have money? Enough to get you home? You call me if you don't. You call me anyway."

"Sure enough. These people have worlds of money." Then, abruptly, he hung up.

Eliza stared at him. "You hung up without saying goodbye to your mother. I wonder who you are. I do. I just realized. Tell me, what do you think you're doing?"

"Chasing you. That's what I can figure."

"Why don't you talk to your mother? You should tell your mother anything. You should tell me anything. There aren't supposed to be secrets. Otherwise we're alone. That's what my father says."

"Looks to me like you people say anything and you got nothing but secrets."

Eliza smiled. "That's our sadness that I'm trying to cure."

"Right now," Rossie said, "I'll tell you one secret. We're sitting around here next to your bedroom, and I want to get after you. That's true."

"After me?" she said.

"Well, you know what I'm talking about. But you might hammer me one."

She stood and lifted her dress. There, barelegged in lavender underpants, her white belly extended, she smiled and her gray eyes softened while Rossie touched her navel with his fingertips.

"Feel it?" she asked. "Charlie Cooper's baby. This is his baby. Feel it trembling?"

Rossie did feel the trembling. He wondered if he should be staying away but she didn't move when his fingers circled to her hips. Stroking her slowly, he listened to the quickness of her breathing.

"Dammit," she whispered, and she hooked her fingers inside her underpants to slide them down.

Rossie slid his touch to the insides of her thighs, and she rested her hands on his shoulders, then stepped out to open herself. He slipped his fingers inside, where she was entirely wet. Smiling directly into his eyes, Eliza eased herself onto his hand. As he stroked, she staggered, her knees collapsing before she stepped back, pulling away.

"Shit," she said, grinning, and gasping slightly, "this time I was going to stay true to motherhood."

Rossie got up and followed as she went off through the door into her bedroom, a gauzy place where she was already on the bed, her dress on the floor. He undid the buttons on his fly and let her take hold as he moved over her with his pants around his knees. Her legs came up around him, and she guided him in, and they were gone into fucking.

"Your mother was right," he said, after they fell apart. "We is not to be trusted."

They got out of the rest of their clothing, and Rossie slipped back into her, slowly thrusting, so that they were looking into themselves at the end.

"So," Eliza said. "The first times were

rebellion. Now it's an affirmation."

"Better than that."

She showed him to the door that opened outside behind the house onto the lawn that ran away to a grove of yellow pine. "The secret passage," she said. "You should slip away."

Rossie grinned. "I'm thinking pussy is the secret passage."

Bernard would talk about the creamery and deplore the dry weather, worrying about drought and fires in the upland timber, but his talk was often nothing Rossie understood, particularly when it careened into the vagaries of literature and philosophy. Over roast beef he complained to Lemma about trying to read Immanuel Kant, taking weeks to "recover his balance."

"What's dangerous about Kant?" she asked.

"The world is real."

Lemma lifted her hands and looked away, to indicate that she was giving up.

Rossie kept quiet. There was no making sense of it. "They talk some other language," he told Eliza.

Two days later Bernard led Rossie upstairs to his "hideout" and poured them shots of a single-malt whiskey. Sitting under *Krazy*

Kat and looking out to the Bitterroot under its summer twilight, he began explaining "our thoughts." This talk will be, he said, "informing, a way of enhancing your liberties and our future."

Rossie didn't answer. "Do you think about liberties?" Bernard said.

"Some," Rossie said. "Traveling with horses was liberties."

Bernard was smiling ironically. "Scots revere freedom and individualism, and we specialize in pride and achievement. My people battled Atlantic storms to build their lighthouses, defeating the oppressions of nature. Thus we decorate our days." He laid out a sheaf of photographs full of bearded men and lighthouses on outcroppings in dramatic seas.

Rossie could see in those men and their stonework the basis for Bernard's pride, and he thought of his father and the proud men studying their drinks at the counter in Madariaga's.

"Them Basques," he said. But Bernard wouldn't be interrupted. "The Stevensons are to me like a dream," he said. "Talk of Scottish exploits is a pleasure I don't often get. Their courage was almost unthinkable. But the lighthouses are real, invaluable, and the stories are true. My grandfather came to the Carolinas and managed crops. His son, my father, made his way to Harvard Law School — the redheaded prodigy, as they called him. He practiced in Chicago until he died in nineteen fifteen — an automobile accident — my junior year at Northwestern University. My mother also died. There are times, still, after all these years, when I speak to her, and I tell her stories. But she's dead."

Rossie looked away and thought of his own mother's voice. "In devastation," Bernard said, "I was able to relocate myself by reading in the Scottish intellectual tradition. Having inherited funds my father put by in stocks, I rode the market, importing Scottish woolens on the side. Which led to merchandising trips. The glorious Canadian Pacific, Winnipeg, the Plains, Banff and the mountains, Vancouver Island and Victoria, a most British city. But I was often idle in hotel rooms, gazing on the empty streets from high windows at three in the morning, and beginning to imagine that my personality was dissolving. You've been a traveler, in strange places, grasping at straws?"

"Calgary," Rossie said, and Bernard smiled.

"Women, they're the cure," he said. "I decided to marry Lemma, if she'd do it,

and she took me in, had me, and saved me."
He hesitated. "So tell me, is Eliza the straw
you're grasping at?"

"Wouldn't call it that," Rossie said.

"Anything that floats. That's the essence.
After Eliza was born, I determined to escape
cities and persuaded Lemma to join me on
this frontier, though she still believes that a
paradise can be found in cities. By good
fortune I'd pulled my father's funds out of
the markets long before the crash and
bought these Montana properties."

"Living with this money is kind of like cities, ain't it?"

Bernard ignored him. "My persuasions
indeed restricted both Lemma's and Eliza's
liberties. I feel guilty but it is mitigated by
the fact that I acted to ensure their futures.
My health, soon enough, will fail seriously,
and they will appreciate what I've done. My
holdings will pass to Lemma, who will manage them with the advice of her brother, a
banker in Chicago. Upon Lemma's death
whatever is left passes to Eliza. And then to
this coming child, God spare him. I stipu-
lated such progressions with my written
will."

Twilight was fading to darkness. Bernard
labored to his feet and poured two more
shots of the single malt.

"I've come to prefer the highland Scotches," he said. "I hope they pass with you. Eliza has made it clear that your feelings are important to her. As a consequence your inclinations and feelings are important to Lemma and myself. I suppose it means you've gotten to her heart. But you should understand that there will be no room in my will for anyone like you, not ever. Not financially. These properties are a locked room, open only to the ownership of Stevensons." He smiled faintly. "Eliza is a mystery, her own creature. She so often gets what she wants because she is so ruthlessly and utterly resolved to have her way with matters she considers important. She underlined this by going off with the man responsible for her pregnancy. There's steel inside that girl. It flexes and springs but does not break."

"Never thought about breaking anybody," Rossie said. "I'm not a bad man, trying to steal your girl. I run away from a redheaded beauty in Nevada to get gone on my own. Which is where I plan on staying. On my own."

"What about Eliza?"

"Eliza is all I see right now, but there is no way I'm milking cows. That's what I know." Rossie sat flexing his fingers. "My father does card tricks. He's a gambler. Follow your luck, is what he says. I was following horses, I met Eliza, and that's what I'm doing here, following my luck."

"What about your parents? If you never went back to Nevada?"

"They're fine. Me and my people are not after what you got."

"Wouldn't they miss you?"

"I might miss them. But hell, even here, I could go back and forth."

"You've been thinking about it?"

"What's that?"

"Staying."

"It crosses my mind."

"What about your mother?"

"There's trains. She could come and go on trains if she needed to visit."

"So there we are," Bernard said. "I'm progressing toward nothing but death. The question is how to live correctly at this minute, this day. How to bless and honor the days? If your drink is finished, time to crank the Delco."

Downstairs, Eliza's eyes were glowing with good humor. "You're in for it," she whispered after dinner. "The son he never had. It's sweet. Did he talk of a thing besides himself and his family and Scottish history? It's his insecurity topped off with egomania.

We forgive him, but you don't need to. Did he tell you about the lighthouse builders? There's no known connection between the Lighthouse Stevensons, as he puts it, and his field-boss grandfather in South Carolina. A lot of the time he's just talking to himself, reassuring himself. We all do it, but you should call him on it. You should talk about your family."

"Don't think I'll call him out on anything," Rossie said. "Not right away. Around here, for the time being, I'm walking with a light step." Easing his way into this strange dream of family and power was a thought that, strangely, made him feel like his own man. "Maybe *I* got Scottish blood in me,"

"What you've got in you," she whispered, "is fucker-faster blood."

After the peach ice cream Betty made in the kitchen, Bernard would crank his Victrola and lift fragile recordings from the box where he stored them. Rossie had never heard this gentle music in his life, not even in his mother's house. "Clarinets and Mozart," Lemma called it, as if Mozart might be somebody she knew. Rossie loved this music. That he did was his secret, and one more reason to stay.

But his main incentive was the continued prospect of making his way across the lawn on nights gone from starry to moonlit and letting himself in through Eliza's outside door to her rooms and her bed and then back into the bunkhouse before daylight. At lunchtime Eliza would meander slowly out on horseback, bringing a thermos of coffee and sandwiches to where Rossie was fencing in the fields with his team and wagon. They'd eat by the creek and spread a blanket and ease down into the tall grass where they went in their ways into each other another time. Eliza called all this "ceremonies and rituals." Days in the fields, fencing, and nights with Eliza, one after another.

Not long after Rossie got beyond worrying about what might come next in his life, Lemma walked out alone across a weedy, yellowing field to perch herself on the tailgate of his wagon. "I do so hope you aren't going to pick up and go," she said.

Rossie wondered how Eliza and her mother were talking when he wasn't around.

"I hear you, in the night, as you go to Eliza. She'll soon be too pregnant for such nights. Charlie Cooper, he nearly ruined our lives. Ruining yourself can be an attractive idea, but it can be outgrown, and I think Eliza has managed that. You could be the reason. Or it could simply be because she's with child. In any event, I want you to stay."

Rossie told Eliza about this encounter. She laughed. "She loves men and hinting around about fucking. She's a little hot for you, and I think she envies me. Poor Daddy. It's over for him. You watch, she'll be showing you her parts, sort of by accident but not. You wait."

"You know what I'm thinking? I'm thinking you're not such an easy girl. I don't think Mrs. Lemma is worrying about me at all. I think she's worrying about you."

"You and me," Eliza said. "She's worrying about us. And she's worrying about wishing she was in my bed."

Two or three evenings a week, Bernard read aloud from leather-bound volumes of David Hume and Adam Smith, full of marginalia in his tiny, spidery script. "In Scottish masters you see the idea of America being invented. Democracy, liberty, and capitalism. Listen to Hume, writing on capitalism. *'It rouses men from their indolence; and, presenting the gayer and more opulent part of the nation with objects of luxury which they never before dreamed of, raises in them a desire of a more splendid way of life than what their ancestors enjoyed.'*" He closed the book by way of a thought. "You and I, Rossie, are fortunate to be located where extraordinary ideas, from Europe, took root. America is the gayer and more opulent part of Hume's nation. Freedom to accumulate is creative. But accumulation can constitute fascism if it is not tempered by compassion. Hume and Adam Smith foresaw this. They argued that selfishness must be countered by a willingness to imagine the condition of others, by deep fellow feeling." Sipping his glass of Bernard's whiskey, Rossie found this making sense, and enjoyed the fact that he understood. "I'm listening," he said. "I should have stayed in school."

"Imagination is the key," Bernard said. "To Low Scots, of course, nothing is more important to them than self-interest — and that they take no shit." He smiled as if he'd tasted nastiness. "Which is a form of idiocy. Do not disturb the happiness of others. That's the first rule. The second is play. Have another Scotch to generate the illusion of meaning. Start the Delco. Anticipate dinner."

Then came an August afternoon when Bernard asked Rossie to ride with him in the Buick once more. They drove two-lane asphalt into Missoula to meet a passenger train from the east. "You should have time with men," Bernard said. They were to meet his long-time friend from Chicago, a socialist photographer named Arnold Meisner, who would spend a month or so recording the effects of poverty on life in the mountain west. "Arnold speaks a radical game," Bernard said, "but he's well paid. Don't take his egalitarian theories too seriously."

They rode the first miles in silence. "First, you can't piss," Bernard said abruptly. "When I was diagnosed, I thought my malady had been caused by too much jerking away as a young man, leading to a swollen and eventually cancerous prostate. There has to be some reason for what happens to you. My doctor says the idea of overexercising the glands is nonsense."

"Hope so," Rossie said.

Stevenson surprised him by an outburst of laughing. "Don't let Lemma hear that," he said, shaking his head. "She'd lock up her daughter. Understand me, I know you can't wear it out. I was a rabbit, or thought I was." He rubbed his jaw. "Not that I'm a threat any more. Lemma, what a girl she was, you should have seen her."

Rossie stared out the window. It was just talk.

After crossing a long bridge over the Clark

Fork River, they went banging along on the cobbled paving on Higgins Avenue between brick-and-stonework buildings. Bernard parked behind St. Patrick's Hospital. "You'll have to give me a few minutes," he said. After half an hour, during which Rossie scrupulously trimmed his fingernails with his white-handled knife, Bernard came across the lot whistling, strangely agitated. "The prostate," he said to Rossie. "First you can't urinate. Imagine the horror of a greased rubber tube draining your bladder. I'm not to that point. But inevitably the pain begins."

"What's the chances of cutting it out?"

Bernard grimaced. "There are drawbacks. The possibility of death during the cutting." He hesitated a long moment. "This is awkward . . . Union with women, after the operation, is a thing of the past. So, another loss, another death. But sweet as pie, that's how I am at the moment." He went back to whistling a quick downtown-sounding tune.

Arnold Meisner came off the Pullman sleeper wearing brown tweed with a vest and a brown fedora. A French citizen with a German name, he had learned his photography in Paris, then emigrated to Chicago after World War I. His suitcase and trunks full of cameras and lighting equipment were set off the train by a lanky black man in a Pullman porter's uniform.

Arnold introduced him. "My newfound friend and keeper, Jack Greenway, has looked after me since Chicago."

Once the luggage was fitted into the Buick, Jack Greenway stretched and looked around to the brown hills. "Sweet little town," he said. "Might be my town."

"Don't believe it," Bernard said, and he slipped him a crisp five-dollar bill. "This town would be worse than Chicago."

"Mainly joking. Black man don't want nothing to do with these towns. I know that much. I'll be riding off toward Seattle." He touched his cap in a mock salute.

"Jack," Arnold Meisner said. "You could stay in Montana a month or two and work for me."

"Can't think so," Jack Greenway said.

On the slow drive up the Bitterroot, Bernard and Arnold talked about friends who'd been fired by the University of Chicago, reduced to the soup lines, and other men killed in the strikes.

"Catastrophes," Arnold said. "And here we are in your wilderness, got away untouched."

Except, Rossie thought, for Bernard with cancer riding shotgun every trip. Still, these were men to think about, who had cut themselves off from whatever home they had in order to go after what they wanted. In that, Rossie was surprised to see, he was like them. Listening to these men was better than listening to a bunkhouse full of tired old fellows who'd spent their lives in a circle of ranch-hand jobs and mostly stared out the windows. "Must have been a long while," he said to Bernard, "since you saw anybody who understood what you're thinking."

"What is it?" Arnold asked. "What do we understand?"

"Liberties," Rossie said, proud to offer the right answer.

"Arnold and I," Bernard said, "we've been down the road." He turned to Arnold. "Of course, so has Rossie. He was all the early summer on the road, trailing horses from California to Calgary."

Arnold came up with a tiny zinc flask. "I'll drink to that. Good Scotch, a single malt from the Highlands."

Rossie felt welcomed into their conspiracy.

Near noontime, Bernard pulled off and parked in front of the elegant red-and-yellow brickwork barn.

"A fellow told me empty was the main thing about that barn," Rossie said.

"Not entirely," Bernard said. "A few weeks ago I had the loft filled with timothy hay."

"That's the fellow I talked to."

"I built this barn in a flurry, a rush of enthusiasm. The stalls have two-inch cork floors." He looked to Rossie. "We used to take the train down to the Kentucky Derby," he said. "Bloody Marys in the morning, all day long. I fell in love with the idea of blooded horses, but I didn't buy, not in that economy. Anyone could see the bubble in the market. Thus I was saved from Thoroughbreds. Ridiculous to imagine your own horse in the winner's circle at Santa Anita."

"Your own sleek beast," Arnold said.

"Cork floors," Rossie said.

Bernard smirked at them both. "We'll go to lunch. They'll be waiting."

Rossie unloaded Arnold's baggage into a back bedroom he had never seen before, then returned outside to find them all at the table on the grass beside that All Frogs totem pole. A cotton tablecloth printed with purple grapes was set with white china dishes.

"At last," Lemma said. "Betty can bring the salad. How was your morning?"

"That frog pole?" Arnold asked.

Bernard nodded. "One of my mementos."

"We talked, dreams of the Kentucky

Derby," Arnold said to Lemma once their wine was poured. "That's a French pole. I mean, the frogs." Bernard smiled.

"Betty got out a tablecloth from Provence," Lemma said, then turned to Rossie, as if he might know what she was talking about. "My degree is in French literature, nineteenth century. Stendhal was my primary man."

"Back from her year in Paris when I met her," Bernard said. "What a girl."

"I got to thank you all," Rossie said. When they turned to him, paying him particular attention, he bridged his fingers, as Old Man Dufferena had, and tried a faint smile. "I come looking for Eliza. Now you got Betty bringing me lunch."

Bernard lifted his right fist. "Well, then. Bravo!"

"Daddy," Eliza said, "you are such a condescending asshole."

That evening, after Rossie had cranked up the Delco, they dined under electric lights strung around the All Frogs Pole, feasting on trout from the river, vegetables out of the garden, wines from France.

"All natural," Betty said. "Good for what aches in you."

"But there is no absolute cure," Arnold said, lifting his wineglass. Without the brown fedora his hair was steel-gray and cropped tight to a dark skull. "A toast to the cook, and all attempts at curing."

"Betty has a healing idea," Lemma said. "Community gardens, irrigated acres, open to all, tended by all, free to all. Bernard is thinking of funding it."

"That's pretty," Arnold Meisner said.

"Just the ditching," Bernard said. "I'd pay for the ditching. Nothing more. It's possible."

Arnold mocked surprise. "What? Possible that you might back a generous impulse?"

"Not so generous," Bernard said. "Tomorrow we'll tour."

The meal finished on cheese and fruit. Bernard went off and returned with bottles of whiskey and a pitcher of chilled water, followed by Betty carrying small crystal tumblers, and Eliza with a white bowl of ice from the icehouse, chipped small. She had sewn panels into each side of her dress to accommodate the rapidly growing bulge of her pregnancy.

"Ahh," Arnold said, "the malts, the Scottish cure."

Bernard pulled a cork and tossed it into the bushes. "Take care of yourselves," he said.

Arnold did the pouring, a darkish shot in

each tumbler before he dropped ice into his own glass, swirled it, and sipped. "The old dirt. The privileged will always be with us." He eyed Bernard ironically. "Bless them. The trick lies in shaming them into sharing the wealth. In Bernard's case, at least for this evening, I think we've got it working. But, old friend Bernard, there's darkness coming at us out of Europe. All your Scottish enlightenment won't cure it."

"Then I will change the topic to good news. Rossie and I stopped at the hospital. My fine doctor says I have some time left."

"Bernard! Jesus, what talk!" But Lemma was smiling. "Jesus!" she said again.

Rossie wondered what they told each other alone in their room, if she had ever seen him pissing blood, or evidence of blood in the white bowl of the toilet.

"Lemma thought there was more to life than an endlessness of parties in Chicago." He was continuing the talk he and Rossie had begun in the morning. "I had holed up with my jazz records and the Scottish thinkers, but Lemma took me by the back of the neck and dragged me into life. And we hauled each other to Montana. My forebear, Robert Louis Stevenson, hauled his family to the South Pacific, where he died. His example was an inspiration. There are men like Arnold who have been jealous of me ever since."

Arnold smiled. "We've missed your people." He turned to Rossie. "You do understand that you've taken up with crazies."

"Wealth," Bernard said, ignoring Arnold, "is produced by acts of innovation based on careful observation. Each individual his own expert, that's the model."

This was fuel for Arnold's fire. "Rossie," he said, "are you listening? We're both of us travelers, anthropologists who hear local economies in Montana talked about so seriously we think they might be descriptions of a religion. Here we witness rural beliefs and customs."

"Not all things are relative," Bernard said. "Freedom is freedom. Truth, after all, resembles truth." He directed his gaze at Rossie. "Don't you think?"

"I don't even have much idea what anthropologists are," Rossie said. He saw fit not to mention the fact that Bernard wasn't any proven relation to Robert Louis Stevenson or his own thought that anybody's wisdom was different from everybody else's. This was what he had been coming around to thinking.

"He's a horseback man, with Nevada

ideas," Lemma said.

"Western," Arnold said. "No wonder Eliza loves you."

"Eliza defends him like a mad bear," Bernard said.

Arnold seemed to be assessing all this. "So, what do you think of being a fixture?" he asked Rossie. "What jobs do you do? Are you essential?"

"I do what I can stand."

"Courting Eliza is clearly one of your items."

Rossie sipped at the whiskey. "Anybody could stand that."

Arnold lifted his glass to Rossie. "We hope you've found the sweet cunt that fits you." In the silence that followed, he added, "That's an old Spanish curse."

"Arnold!" Lemma shrieked, smiling.

"I heard that one up in Canada."

"Do Spaniards," Eliza asked, "have something against cunt?"

"A cunt that fits you," Arnold explained, "is solace and a set of chains, the beginning and end. That's the meaning."

"Spaniards. What the fuck would some Spaniard know?" For that rush of moment Rossie had forgotten any impulse to walk softly. He spread his dark and callused hands on the table.

"What I learned, riding in the Big Beef Field down at the Neversweat when it was flooding, was don't quit. I didn't know one thing about horses or swimming and I thought I was going to drown on the old red horse that Slivers Flynn give to me. But I knew" — this talk rolled out of him — "I knew you don't quit on Slivers Flynn. Free is fine when you are, but anyway you don't ever quit." The others sat quiet. Rossie thought he'd said something they respected.

"Working for Slivers Flynn," Bernard said, "must have been an agreeable freedom."

Arnold snorted. "Forgive me. It sounds like subservience."

"How do we tell the difference between freedom and subservience?" Eliza asked. "Am I freed to have my baby or chained to what's growing inside me?" She looked away casually, then turned back, clearly furious. "Arnold," she said, "if I were a cat, you'd be my mouse. I'd play with you on the kitchen floor."

"I came west admiring Marcus Daly," Bernard said, as if nothing of note was transpiring. "He was the mining baron from Butte who raised his Derby horses in this valley. I envisioned horses supported by dairy farming."

Arnold ignored him. "Eliza, what do you

291

mean, mouse?"

She met his gaze directly. "Chickenshit little creature."

"Which is a way of saying you're spoiled and insulted?" He stood and worked his way around the table, distributing ice and pouring shots of the Scotch. "My father made a life working for a billiards club in Paris. He swept floors, my mother cooked. The men who owned the club loved my father and mother but paid them nothing. I fled to the streets where I attached myself to Eli Meisner, a photographer who taught me everything. He so much influenced my being that I took his name when I was sixteen. Then Eli began photographing merchants and restaurant owners, forgetting his art to eat. The horse-race rich and the poor don't get much opportunity to enjoy life together, and when they do subservience is always in the mix. It's everywhere, we know it, you and I. That's my point to Rossie."

"That does nothing to mitigate your condescending arrogance."

"Mitigate," Arnold said. "What absurdity requires mitigation?"

"Maybe I'm the one," Rossie said. He was lost in his anger at the frivolity of this parrying. "Maybe I'll mitigate your ass into next week. But you're an old man. So I should shut up. It's no good picking at shit like a magpie."

"There we have it," Arnold said to Bernard across the table. "We value the same things and can't talk to one another." He looked up to Eliza. "Are you bitter to a point beyond reconcile? Where's your good humor?"

"Bitter beyond reconcile?"

"Eliza, accept my apology." Arnold turned to Rossie. "I hope, young man, that you don't mitigate my ass into next week. What an idea."

They can't say one single thing straight out, Rossie thought.

"It's a game we've learned, and it doesn't occur to us that we might look ugly," Bernard said. "So permit me to do some mitigating." He strolled inside to the Victrola to put on a record.

Louis Armstrong serenaded them with "I Can't Give You Anything but Love." "At last," Lemma said. "Frivolity of the right sort."

"Music in the trees above. The universal language," Bernard said.

Eliza was on her feet, skipping along in front of Rossie, the ice in her eyes abruptly gone. "Can't you dance?"

"Waltzing songs, that's what I can do."

"Pull off those boots."

He kicked out of them and she pulled him onto his stocking feet.

"Bend your knees, you can move. I've seen you."

Fleet and spinning, she circled the table and came back, taking his hand to lead him. Rossie caught up with her, reaching for the sweaty, round-bellied, and so solidly fleshed girl of her.

As the trumpet solo to "Shine" commenced, she pulled Rossie into a spinning arc, looping through light and shadows until her sweaty hand slipped free and sent him flailing backward. Eliza and Lemma joined hands and went wheeling on, barefoot on the lawn as Rossie skidded on his ass. When he floundered to his feet Lemma reached for him with her long arms, her hands strong and dry as they circled out and back until the music flared its finale.

"There," Lemma said, panting. "Anybody can dance."

"If that's what it was," Rossie muttered as a slower, crackling recording began to play.

" 'Broke and Hungry Blues,' " Bernard said when it was finished. "Blind Lemon Jefferson, recorded in nineteen twenty-seven, in Chicago, where miracles happen every night.

The talk drifted to Chicago nightlife, the horse-race gamblers and barflies, a woman they'd called the Princess of Drift, newspaper writers, and club owners.

"People ask after you," Arnold said, then smiled at Lemma. "The both of you. They're praying to black-cat bones."

"Good of them," Bernard said, and he looked pleased as he poured shots of the whiskey, passed the ice around.

Arnold told of Lemon Jefferson, known as the Blind Homer of the South Side, going off to play a rent party on a cold night in 1929 and getting lost in an alleyway. "Drunk, but why not? Who wouldn't be? Frozen to the pavement and dead on the south side of Chicago. He had made the money to hire a chauffeur. In French, *chauffer* means 'warm keeper.' A lot of good that did him. Where were we on that night in 1929? I was uptown in some tavern." Arnold went on about men who froze in Duluth and Milwaukee and again in Chicago. "Drunk in the alley, a blind man with a guitar."

"Bardolino's?" Bernard said. "The best osso bucco in town. Wonder which of the boys would be at the joint now. But it wasn't any joint, it was an 'eatery,' that's what we called it. It was our clubhouse. Carl Sandburg and Theodore Dreiser came in together once."

Lemma turned to Rossie. "You should have heard that talk. I was a girl and sick of the dunces. These fellows were mean and foulmouthed and rabid and going to change the world."

"We were your age," Bernard said to Rossie. "We believed in causes. I volunteered at Hull House, mopping floors. Can you imagine? That's about the time I started reading the Scots."

Lemma recollected to Rossie. "Immigrants leading their children by the hands into Hull House, a settlement house, run by a woman, Jane Addams, a true saint. She fed them and gave them a place to re-gather. Here's to absolution." She moved around to pour a hard drink that tasted powerfully of apples.

We're in the Bitterroot Valley, Rossie thought, under Montana stars at a table beside a stolen totem pole. Nevada got farther and farther away.

Eliza led him off with no pretense of his going to the bunkhouse. In her bed, he dozed with his hand on her belly, feeling the moving child as she stroked his back.

"They called your card," she whispered. "A cunt that fits."

"No escaping."

"She says Daddy's terrified. But they're all terrified. And us, we aren't, are we?"

At breakfast Bernard announced "the promised tour." Arnold and Rossie piled in the Buick with him, the rancor of the night before forgotten or at least dissolved in the light. Bernard puffed a cigar and tried lecturing about the sights. "History here is simple. Looks like paradise, but there's a lot of impoverished farmers. Eighty years ago they trailed steers to Wyoming, feeding wagon trains headed for California. But transportation to markets is nowadays a killer. The woods were seriously overlogged for timbers in Marcus Daly's mines in Butte, great acreages denuded."

They traveled through irrigated lands, heading toward sage-covered hills that rose to the Sapphire Mountains. On the east side of the valley they crossed a plank bridge over a canal. "The Big Ditch," Bernard said. It had been built early in the century with horse-drawn scrapers. It flowed from Lake Como well to the south, then crossed the Bitterroot and wove north for sixty miles along the sunrise side of the valley. "Below the ditch, we have irrigation. Above it, the natural grasses were overgrazed to sage and weeds. Water percolates out through its gravel banks into spring creeks that flow back to the Bitterroot — fine trout fisheries, but no one makes a living off trout."

"This is indeed a neck of the woods," Arnold said. "You've learned your terrain."

Bernard parked on a ridge where they could see west to ordered fields, cottonwoods along the distant river, and the peaks of the Bitterroots. "Plagued with drought and falling beef prices, the men who dealt their lands to me thought I was a savior. Others attempt to survive on farms with fifteen milk cows. They starve and think I'm a demon."

"What you are, around here then," Arnold said, "is a bull of the woods."

Bernard climbed out of the Buick and stalked off through the low sage. "Six ruined sections, bought cheap. I retired these hills to let them recover. Locals hate me for it. Retiring land is seen as arrogance. It offends the idea that the world is here to use. Getting to America ought to have solved their problems. Their people suffered, and crossing to America should have earned them everything. That's what they think." He plucked wisps of grass. "They feel betrayed. Eliza believes our luck might turn if we fail to support the impoverished. I support her, in a way — financially, that is —

although her thoughts are based on mystic nonsense. We can't give away the entire farm. But we also don't want the indigent coming after us."

"A far land exploited and ruined by industrial barons," Arnold said, obviously amused. "Revived by the baron of milk cows and fecundity. What if you took us to lunch?"

Rossie remembered Nito riffling his cards as he talked about the diamond-necklace New York divorcées at the Riverside Hotel in Reno. "They come down from the moon."

Leonard Three Boy was coming in on the motor stage from Calgary to escort Arnold Meisner on a month-long photographic trip. Starting with the Salish south of Flathead Lake and ending north of the Blood Reserve in Alberta, he would serve as Arnold's paid guide and factotum before beginning his final year at the University of Montana. Bernard proposed that Rossie take the Buick to meet him at the stage stop in Hamilton.

"Can't drive," Rossie replied. "Never could."

"Can't drive, can't dance, can't cook, can't talk on the telephone," Eliza retorted, fresh from her bath and brilliant in a ballooning yellow dress. "We can take the Model A, have a lesson as we go. We'll make a man of you."

"Got to ask," Rossie said. "What's happening to those people we saw up in Canada if Leonard's down here?"

"The monies go to Auntie Red every month, as they have been."

Despite being six months pregnant, Eliza drove like a whirlwind, plunging the Model A in and out of curves between old-growth pines and groves of aspen. Only out on the straightaway, a mile or so short of the main Hamilton highway, did she pull over. "Your turn, brother."

She put Rossie through the moves in the Model A starting drill — open the gas line, twist the choke a quarter turn, lift the spark on the left full-up to retard, and drop down the gas control rod on the right. He turned the ignition key, pulled out the choke, hit the foot starter on the floor, and passed two revolutions of the engine before jerking the spark lever three-quarters down and jamming the gas rod up to idle. The first three attempts the engine caught but jerked and died. On the fourth try he got the Model A in motion, weaving between barrow pits.

"Very slowly," Eliza said. "We'll inch along or Leonard will be waiting while we get out of the ditch." She called it off after a quarter mile. Their thin tire tracks wobbled side-to-side in the dust. "It's like swimming," she said." First you can't do it, then you dream about it, and then you can. We'll try it tomorrow."

The stage had let Leonard Three Boy off outside the grocery store on the outskirts of Hamilton. Standing beside a stained canvas valise, Leonard was as he had been, wearing those perfectly clean eyeglasses with metal rims, the patriotic striped shirt, and the same yellow feathers dangling. He raised a hand in greeting while the Model A came to a dusty stop.

"You're here for the party," Eliza said, and she and Leonard studied each other.

Rossie was not included in whatever was passing between them.

"You and me," Leonard said to Eliza. "We're the party." He held out a flat package wrapped in brown paper. "I found this."

Eliza tore off the paper. "Shit," she said. "Where'd you get it?"

"From Wanda."

Eliza used both hands to hold the sepia-toned photograph, framed under cracked glass. "Goddamn," she said. "Charlie, you son of a bitch." She spun past Rossie, took three long running steps, and hurled the picture across the street to land on a curb, where the glass shattered. As Leonard crossed to retrieve the photograph, she cocked her head rigidly to one side, eyeing the sky.

"Who's this Wanda?" Rossie asked.

"His mother, the French woman," Leonard said. "She's alive in Alberta."

Eliza abruptly got herself in hand. "So's Charlie . . . He's alive. Except he's useless."

"Sounds that way," Rossie said, studying the photograph. A burnished, hawk-nosed man gazed directly back at him. "Pale-gray eyes like granite," Rossie said.

She nodded. "Half-breed eyes."

"He don't look whipped."

"He doesn't think he is. But he's demolished. Deer Lodge Prison will be his life if he's not careful."

Rossie was startled to look up and find her not at all furious as Leonard loaded his old canvas valise into the Model A.

"Rossie doesn't drive. So we had a driving lesson. No damages."

"It would be a treat if I could drive. I've almost forgotten how," Leonard said.

She gave them her cold-eyed smile. "I'll be the woman. I'll ride in the backseat."

"And pout like a baby," Leonard said.

Once they were on the road, Rossie turned

in his seat and held out the photograph to Eliza. Shards of glass clung in cracks around the frame. "This isn't a present for me."

"Yes, it is," she said. "You're exactly the one it's for."

Just before dinner that night, when Rossie and Leonard, freshly shaved, showed up, Arnold offered to mix Rossie a martini that would settle him down.

"Last time, in Canada," Rossie said, "I passed out on them things."

Arnold went on mixing. "It's easy to start spilling, and just one will undermine your best behavior. It will be a good idea."

"Tonight," Lemma said, "in honor of Arnold, Betty is serving osso bucco, veal shanks braised in wine."

"Brussels sprouts?" Bernard protested as Betty served a portion only to him.

"For what ails you," she explained.

The martinis, there'd been two of them, had quick fingers in Rossie's thoughts. "What ails me is gin. My brain is thinking anything it wants to think."

"That's how it's supposed to be," Lemma said.

"Rossie thinks *buckaroo*," Eliza said, caressing the word. "He carries a bone-handled knife, but he won't cut meat with it. Buckaroos don't."

This might have been a way of bragging him up, but Rossie understood that she was making a stranger of him. "Don't eat with your nutting tool," he said, fishing the slim-bladed item from his pocket to shave a feather of hair from his forearm. "Might cut your tongue."

"Rossie," Bernard said, "believe me, I'm sympathetic. This is distant to you, I know, but you'd better eat something."

Instructed by Arnold, Rossie fished the garlic marrow from hollow bones with a tiny fork.

"Pretty decent," he said.

"Kid," Arnold said, "stick with me. We'll be eating sunshine."

After they'd polished off Betty's peach ice cream, Bernard produced a magic lantern borrowed from the hospital in Hamilton while Lemma tacked a white bedsheet to a wall in the living room. Chairs were arranged, coffee was served, and the lights, except for a bulb on the projector, were turned out. The bedsheet was brilliantly illuminated with the image of a whiskery man sitting on a steel bridge over a great river. He was sucking a cigarette, his nose mottled by exploded capillaries, his eyes white with a webbing of cysts and interwoven tentacles.

"Bennie Loomis," Arnold said. "Last year

in Davenport. I went over there hoping to find a magazine series about Bix Beiderbecke. There was a hotel by the river. I sat out front on a bench and shared cigarettes with Bennie. But I didn't get far with Beiderbecke. That tragedy seemed utterly what it was, American sadness beyond control, a worn-out story."

But when he recounted the long story of Bix's disintegration, everybody but Rossie acted like they knew what he was talking about.

"Booze," Arnold said. "Willingness and booze. They don't mix with genius. That's the cautionary tale we know and love." Next he showed a photograph of men in New York, dozens of them along the curbs selling apples from wooden crates. "That's from nineteen twenty-nine. It was around in the newspapers." He loaded another slide. "Now, Chicago, in black and gray." Four young men stood before a garbage truck, their shirtsleeves ripped off at the shoulders to show their biceps. A street milling with men spanned the background, and metal buildings loomed over it all. "Out of work," he explained. Next, in a room with peeling wallpaper, two black women and one white one rested back on an unmade bed surrounded by seven thin-armed, indolent children. Then, a snaking line of men against a brick wall that reached beyond sight. "Waiting for soup," Arnold said.

"You see those fellows in Reno," Rossie cut in, but the picture had flicked to a suited man, hard-eyed under the brim of his fedora, smoking a cigar outside a beer joint.

"The proprietor, the boss of Whiskey Mountain," Arnold said.

"The King Bear," Bernard said.

The final photograph displayed a massive Klan gathering, men in sheets beneath dark trees. Arnold shook his head. "Enough," he said. "It's a trapeze. I take pictures and we lament and sympathize, swing on our sorrow." He smiled. "But it doesn't change a thing."

"It takes time," Leonard said.

"Ah, youth. I hope you're correct." Arnold switched off the projector. "Has anyone seen the Germans? Do you get the newsreels? Hundreds of thousands hailing Hitler."

"We never see newsreels, we wouldn't," Lemma said.

Arnold turned to Rossie. "You've made the right move. You've got yourself isolated. The Nazis will never make it this far."

"Rossie's our blue-moon boy, walking on water," Bernard said. "Every day of his life is once in a blue moon."

"Every day," Arnold said, "is once in a blue moon. But Rossie has aligned himself with people like you. The starve-to-death West will learn to hate him." He turned to Leonard. "What do you make of it?" But then he went on without giving Leonard a chance to answer. "Indians hate us. Wouldn't they? We sit on our moral mountain with our Victrola and Scotch whiskeys. The world will get us."

This was the moment Rossie would recall as he aged, in which he intuited, right or wrong, that they all but Eliza took him to be a sort of know-nothing cipher. A joke on innocence.

"Bernard," Arnold said. "Play us a sweet one. Let's forget political shit."

Bernard dropped the needle on a recording of Bix Beiderbecke and his syncopated cornet. "A sound like that of a girl saying yes," he said.

"Or the right boy," Lemma said. "A sweet, insistent boy asking, how about it?"

"Louis Armstrong split his lip in London," Arnold said. "He's in Paris. Unable to play."

Bernard crooned, imitating Armstrong's inflections. "Just another jig I know. Just a gigolo."

"I hadn't noticed that you'd been into the

martinis," Arnold said in that lean way. "You and Rossie have an affiliation."

Bernard smiled. "I'm reduced to jazz and milk cows, divorced from the world."

"Ordered joyousness," Lemma offered. "That's what we can make of our lives."

"At this vivid moment," Bernard said, "I choose to announce a trip to Chicago. Arnold will be on the windswept plains confronting verities with Leonard. We'll be at a table in the Grand Pierce Ballroom and Terrace, watching Earl Hines broadcast on NBC."

"We?" Lemma asked.

"You and I and Rossie and Eliza."

"Me?" Rossie asked.

"You're becoming part of us." Bernard spoke this as if this should be obvious.

"Don't think I bargained for Chicago."

"Don't think you've bargained for anything," Bernard said. "But I'm astonished at your reluctance. Do you imagine that I'm trying to purchase your attention?"

"Shit," Rossie said. "I thought it was the other way. You might get tired of me hanging around."

"You must see people buying their way in Reno," Bernard said. "Men and whores. Boys off the ranches with rich women." He smiled. "This is nothing like that."

"I guess it isn't," Rossie said after a long moment. "I talked to a woman up in the Flathead Valley. She said it was a good idea to keep a list of things you'd never do, and Chicago isn't on my list of things to never do."

"Have you notified Howard?" Lemma asked.

But Bernard went on talking to Rossie. "Understand," he said. "When we left Capone and Bugsy Moran were machine-gunning and beating enemies to death with baseball bats. I refused to go on living in the proximity of barbarians, but I continue to love the city. The last week of September, as baseball ends."

"We could have looked forward to it if we — and my brother — had been consulted," Lemma said. "But it's settled? The tickets are purchased?"

"We're going?" Eliza asked, clearly deferring to her mother.

"Well," Lemma said, "certainly."

Bernard eyed Rossie. "Are you coming?"

"You're giving me a tryout," Rossie said. "That's fair enough. I can pay my way. I've got a hundred and some dollars."

"That," Bernard said, "is not a problem."

"On that happy note," Lemma said, "it's settled."

"They don't know anyone in Chicago anymore," Eliza said, when Rossie had come through the darkness to her bedroom. "And there's no one in this valley but strangers and hired help. You're their luck, the man who does not mind about my baby. They're greedy. They want to take you over. But this is ours, isn't that the idea? What an idea." She lay back, knees apart, and lifted her pale thighs. "Quietly," she said, drawing quick breath as she touched at herself. "Slowly. Put it in me. This is a pregnant woman." After half an hour of resting, she said, "Put it in me again," and it was midnight when he made his way down to the bunkhouse and into his bedroll.

At daybreak he was awake, considering how running off from Mattie had been like ducking a trap, and how this life of dinner parties could be a greater predicament, or whether their talky ways ought to be admired, and wondering if holding his own with a photographer from Chicago was part of what he wanted to amount to.

Eliza, wearing her gray, sweat-stained hat, was dressed as she had been when Rossie first saw her, in baggy, black trousers and the starched, cornflower blouse stretched over her belly. She'd showed up for breakfast in the bunkhouse and wanted to ride into the jagged ridges of the Bitterroots.

She and Rossie and Leonard headed up the creek into Kanaka Canyon, which Eliza told them was named for Hawaiians who'd arrived a hundred years ago, shoveling gravel, working for gold nobody found, and freezing to death in January. She led them into a boulder-strewn headwater cirque where trickling streams drained from ice fields lasting into summer.

"Freezing and death," Leonard said. "Stories about the mountains told the Bloods how to live. But mountain stories won't help the Bloods anymore."

"Stories was never my hobby," Rossie said.

"Gods live in mountains," Leonard said, and Rossie wondered if he was serious.

"I'm going to the top," Eliza called out, starting up toward Idaho on the trace of trail that angled across a vertiginous fall of scree.

"Get used to it," Leonard said. "Climbing everything. Right now it's you."

"Talking to you is like talking to a book," Rossie said. "Everything means something else."

Leonard smiled. "Go to school with Mormons and that's what you learn. But I'm reverting to type, back to pureblood."

"You and me could go into the horse business," Rossie said. "Bernard is hot for the horses." He waited as Leonard digested this. "We could build corrals over there by his brick barn and train horses. Bernard would own them." Leonard looked skeptical. "We could do it," Rossie said. "We'd be our own hired men."

"I'm going to back to Alberta."

"I got to get beyond wages. I got to do a business. Indian fellows could come down here from Canada. We could buy shares and someday own ourselves. Otherwise, nobody is going to carry any weight. I'm learning that much."

"She could evaporate," Leonard said. "Look at her up there." Eliza was high on her trail across the jumble of scree.

"I'm asking myself," Rossie said, "am I just crazy for pussy? Or are these people something I could amount to? I'm trying to stick with her without turning into a fool who fetches and carries. Me and you, we're going the same speed."

Leonard was cleaning his eyeglasses on his shirttail. "We are not going the same speed," he said. "I'm going to graduate from the university and go back to Alberta. Why should I put my life together with you? And why are you letting them drag you to Chicago?"

"Hell," Rossie said, "I might learn something. One thing, though: I'm not going to spend my time in a Buick, beholden to a woman, driving around and checking on dairy cows."

"Beholden? Do you love her?"

"It's a voice gets in your brain. It won't get out. You get to answering when she's not around."

"That's it," Leonard said.

"Shit. How would you know?"

CHICAGO

On a bright autumn morning on the great northern platform in Missoula, a stack of suitcases behind them, they stood for photographs as Betty snapped away with her Kodak. Lemma and Bernard were elegant in their city-going suits, Bernard in tan and Lemma in lavender.

But Eliza, showing a plentitude of pregnancy, had got herself up "like a frump," according to Lemma. She'd drawn her black hair into a bun at the back of her head, worn a brown dress let out to accommodate her belly, and not a ring on her finger, nor a shawl, nor even lipstick to color her paleness.

"From here on," Eliza said, "I'm a quiet creature, soon to be a mother."

"I don't worry about you," Lemma said. "You'll be dancing."

Rossie wore his Panama hat, which Betty had steamed until it was elegant again, and slick, tan gabardine trousers with cuffs that broke at the instep on his polished boots. The pants, as well as his matching shirt with a button-down collar, were presents from "the family," bought at the Missoula Mercantile. He even had a saddle-leather valise, a gift from Bernard.

"On time, and here we are," Lemma said, as the black steam engine and string of Pullman cars came sighing and clanking in from nighttime travel over the mountains from Spokane. They were the only passengers getting on in Missoula. A black man named Mr. Horton loaded a brass-bound trunk and suitcases into a sitting room and bed chamber reserved for Lemma and Bernard, and their bags in the separate singles for Eliza and Rossie.

"Our steel railroad kingdom," Eliza said. "Closets for our clothes, hooks for our hats, fold-up sinks, a table, a toilet, and a bed that Mr. Horton will make up. We look out and watch our people at work, haying and harvesting. I'll be your princess."

At lunchtime Bernard led them on a swaying walk to the dining car for fresh Dungeness crab. They were east of the Rockies by late afternoon, and dinner was rare steaks at a table with blossoming flowers in a tall, thin-necked vase. Later, seated in a green, leatherette lounge chair in the bar car, Eliza announced that she had quit drinking until the baby was born. But she begged sips from Rossie's Ramos gin fizz while Bernard and Lemma played muttering bridge with a Norwegian couple named Rolfing, who'd gotten on the train in Livingston, Montana, after a vacation spent camping in Yellowstone National Park. "In tents?" Bernard had asked, concerned.

The Rolfings were returning to Rochester, New York, where the pale, blond husband worked as a chemist for Kodak. Chemists, he said, were like bartenders, mixing components. They had been hoping to observe the great bears before beginning a family. Thus, tragedy, should they be killed or mutilated by the creatures, would be their own and not their children's.

"We must see all of the world we can," Mrs. Rolfing said. Her first name was Inge. "Yellow bears. Imagine them coming to you."

Late in the night Eliza knocked softly on Rossie's door. "Imagine them coming to you," she whispered. "This is your chance," she said, kissing his shoulders. "The last time until after the baby is born. Then we'll make up for it. Most men never get to bed a pregnant woman on a train."

They slid together carefully and afterward rested in his bed with the lights out and the shade up to reveal profound darkness across the prairies.

"Rattling along," Eliza said, "looking out for lights and wondering who's out there, what they think. That's the best part. For years I did this, going to and from school, back and forth, mostly by myself. I loved school but gave it up. Charlie Cooper rubbed my neck and said he would be my teacher. Alberta would be my college."

"I knew a girl," Rossie said, "who claimed she was going down to Reno and up the hill to college. But there's lots beside colleges."

"They had a camp down by the river, him and Chevrolet. They set me up to knock on the banker's door on a Sunday afternoon, put a pistol in his face, and walk him up the street to the bank. I'd leave him locked in his vault and make off with the money, then give it to them. They said I was crazy enough to do it. I liked that talk, and they were right, I would have done it. You won't want to hear this, but I'm telling you. I kept going down to the river. I was from Pliny School in Chicago, and I'd been taught to love Indians. Pliny was a Greek who wrote about man and nature. Think of it as man and woman, cunt and cock. It's nature.

That's what I learned to think. Charlie carried his blanket out in the woods and we fucked all the way to Alberta, where I got pregnant. I would have burned down my father's house for Charlie. All he had to do was ask." She almost shone in the nighttime Pullman. "That is who I am, a girl from Pliny School. But Indians aren't an idea."

This sounded like craziness. Or lying. Why would she tell him such things? "Sounds like you're selling me something," he said.

Eliza hesitated, looking uncertain. "I'm trying to impress you," she said. "If you thought I was crazy over you, only you, and I'd let you do anything, what would happen to me? Sooner or later you'd know about me and Charlie. You'd give me the runaround like I was a Chinese whore. So, I've got you on a train. You can't ride away."

"A Chinese whore? You're knocked up. I don't need the details."

A great fall rain fell and the train swayed across a long, steel trestle over the Missouri River. "Soon there'll be nothing but cornfields," Lemma said to Rossie. "The great nation."

In Chicago, the night of September 26, they were greeted by Lemma's dark-suited twin brother, Howard, the long-faced banker who was, according to Lemma, "between wives."

"Wives are Howard's weakness. He's an utter romantic, helpless before certain women."

Howard was carrying clusters of hothouse flowers, one for Lemma, and another for Eliza. He was thrown near to helpless tears at the sight of his sister, who pushed away the flowers and held him at arm's length.

"You bozo," she said. "You," she said again. "Bozo."

Rossie wondered how his mother would act if he showed up in Reno bearing flowers.

Howard tried to smile after shaking Rossie's hand. "The cowboy. A welcome development."

With their luggage loaded into two taxicabs, the flowers riding in the front seats alongside the drivers, they headed for the Drake Hotel through a chaos of lights and traffic.

"You'll be walking around like a native," Eliza said, her hand on Rossie's thigh. "It's only a town. You'll get used to it."

Rossie kept his white hat in his lap as they plunged along. "I'll be hiding my head under a pillow."

"In the Drake," she said, "you'll have

feather-filled pillows." The taxicab driver snorted.

The Drake, with its array of public rooms adorned with marble and chains made of gold brocade, was a step beyond anything in Reno. Bernard passed folded greenbacks to bellmen taking the luggage away and made sure vases for the flowers, along with Scotch and house gin, would be sent directly up to their rooms. Ice and five dozen oysters on the half shell would follow.

"Breads and sweet butter," Lemma said. "Cheeses, brie and sharp cheddar, grapes, a selection of apples. Please."

Bernard and Lemma had a suite on the seventh floor, where the clusters of flowers were set up in tall crystal vases. Eliza and Rossie were in rooms of their own down the hall. When drinks had been poured — seltzer water for Eliza — Howard lifted his Scotch on ice and proposed a toast. "To these children," he said. "All of us."

Bernard eased his money clip from his pocket. "Rossie," he said, "this might as well be settled. What do you have for cash? You'll need to carry cash."

"One hundred and eleven dollars," Rossie said. It was all his money. So far he'd spent six dollars. "Everything in the hotel should be charged to this room," Bernard said.

"From drinks to room service."

"And oysters," Lemma said. "Where are they?"

"What if my pocket gets picked?" Rossie asked.

"Then we will get hold of more cash," Bernard said. "I go onto the streets with greenbacks hidden in my stockings. That way you cannot be robbed without violence."

"You figure there's a chance of that?"

"There are beggars, men capable of anything."

Just then the oysters arrived, five platters on a wheeled cart, a dozen for each of them, and the breads and cheeses, grapes and apples.

"Have you been to the ocean?" Bernard asked Rossie. "If not, these oysters, due to the miracles of refrigerated transportation, will be your introduction."

"Smell them," Lemma said. "Inhale. Squeeze the lemon, take one, dip it into vinegar, then the horseradish, and touch it into the red sauce." She took up a tiny fork and demonstrated, chewing slowly. "Savor, chew faintly, allow yourself to taste before swallowing."

"All my life I been eating brains and calf nuts and such shit," Rossie said. "Never found any I didn't like. But I never ate anything raw. Looks like eating eyeballs." He went with the lemon, then the vinegar and horseradish, chewed and swallowed, and made a face. Lemma and Bernard were watching intently. "So that," Rossie said, "is how the ocean tastes."

"What do you think?" Lemma said.

"Way better than I guessed," Rossie said, starting through the ritual another time. "I got a marble bathroom." He grinned. "I can order up oysters from downstairs. What the hell?"

Howard proposed another toast. "To romance."

"You," Lemma said. "Have you settled down? New Zealand? At least you spoke the language. Howard," she explained to Rossie, "is a wanderer."

Bernard rapped on Rossie's door the next morning. It was to be shopping at Marshall Field's for the women and baseball at Wrigley Field — the Chicago Cubs in a last series against Pittsburgh — for the men. "Today," Bernard said, "leave your straw fedora at home. In this town, it's a hat for the night. We go bareheaded."

Downstairs in a barbershop hung with crystal mirrors taller than a man, the air

322

was sweet with bay rum and lime and the murmur of barbers in immaculate white shirts and aprons and their soft-talking customers. Rossie was shaved by a man three times his age. His hair was trimmed, the back of his neck cool and tingling. He watched Bernard lay out silver dollars and examine his smooth face in one of the mirrors, then hold out his right hand before him to study as if looking for signs of trembling.

"If you ever think about baseball," Bernard told him as they made their way to Wrigley in a taxicab, "you will recall this as a stunning day. All forces are in conjunction."

"Can't say I'd know," Rossie said. "I wasn't one of those baseball boys."

"Cowboys wouldn't be. But you'll be sorry not to be a baseball boy now, I assure you. Lou Gehrig has just completed fifteen hundred consecutive games, a record, and this season he's got forty-eight home runs. Babe Ruth just played his final game for the Yankees three days ago, the same day Detroit clinched the pennant. Dizzy Dean is pitching this very afternoon on two days of rest and St. Louis might well win their pennant, too. And yesterday, in Yankee Stadium, before thirty thousand fans, the master unseen by white men, Satchel Paige, struck out twelve in a Negro exhibition. These are vast times. We have Wrigley, the shrine. My father brought me. I've been thinking about this for weeks."

The taxi driver let them off on Addison, two blocks from the ballpark. As they walked toward the stadium Rossie imagined Bernard sipping the wine he'd had shipped in to Montana and dreaming of days like this one, and what could be if he could go on being alive in the world.

Bernard had box-seat tickets, behind home plate on the third base line. "I love the sliding in at third and home. Others insist on first base, the hitters, but I love dustups. Lemma says it's my version of romance. What do women know?"

The reason for going bareheaded among so many men in fedoras was revealed. Bernard bought blue Cubs caps embroidered with a red C inside a white circle. They shaped the long brims, and Rossie realized that all morning he'd been watching Bernard for signs of how to conduct himself. "Does this make us fans?"

"Fanatics," Bernard said, gripping Rossie's shoulder.

As they edged down crowded steps toward their seats, Rossie felt enclosed not so much by people as by pleasures. The marked field, the wheeling sweep of ivy-covered wall, fans thronged in the windows of the apartments beyond the outfield, ballplayers carelessly rifling balls back and forth, this could be a thing to love.

"Wrigley Field, seasons end," Bernard said. "St. Patrick's Day is the model. Bless the faithful and fuck a Depression."

They were surrounded by redheaded Irish and black Irish, and Italians and Jewish fathers with sleeves rolled up to their elbows, some in business suits, others already boisterous with drink, smoking cigars and talking softly in the way of bosses. Cups of Schlitz on the railing, salted-peanut shells on the floor, hot dogs oozing Polish mustard, sharply hit infield outs, the sliding in at third, the Cubs taking Pittsburgh by a score of four to two — in all this Rossie was content. "What it was," he said as they filed slowly out in the midst of the crowd, "was dandy."

"It's catching," Bernard said.

At the Drake, Lemma and Eliza were drinking tea and eating sandwiches and lemon cakes off a table wheeled in by room service. Scatters of tissue paper and purple sacks from Marshall Field's surrounded them. They'd bought dark leather shoes with thin straps over the instep. There was a twenty-dollar bottle of Chanel No. 5 for Lemma, and Je Reviens for Eliza. " 'Je Reviens' means 'I'll return' in French," Eliza said. "To make your wait on my baby all the sweeter."

Lemma laid out a moss-green cashmere sweater for herself and a long, finely woven, off-white shawl of Scottish wool for Eliza. "We were practical," Lemma explained. "Winter is coming and we bought for Montana. Not that these are things to wear in Montana. But things to think about wearing." She went on, suddenly dismayed. "Women with those children, begging with filthy pillows and blankets at their feet? I'd forgotten."

Bernard shook his head.

"We were as flagrant as courtesans," Eliza said, "ignoring the poor, spending money given us by men."

"Given freely and happily," Bernard said.

"No money of mine," Rossie asserted. "None to give."

Lemma shook her head. "Yours is a temporary condition. For some it can become a state of being. But not you."

"In the meantime, there are gifts for you," Eliza said, bringing forth three Brooks Brothers shirts — one white, one in dark blue, another striped red and white — a blue-and-red-striped necktie and a blue blazer with brass buttons. "On trial," she said, "to see if it fits."

And it did. "This is too goddamned many clothes."

"But elegant," Lemma said.

The women posed in their shoes with the elaborate straps, Lemma in her sweater and Eliza in her shawl, then Rossie donned his new attire and posed with Bernard, both in Cubs caps, to laughter and applause.

"We did one other thing," Eliza said, studying her hands. "We looked at baby clothes, handwoven items."

"We'll see all that," Bernard said. "But I'm exhausted."

"If we aspire to live late, like Spaniards, he'll need a nap," Lemma said. "We'll gather at nine for cocktails. Howard is bringing a date. I can't wait to see this one."

Rossie went alone to his room and ordered up a gin and tonic on the telephone from room service just to see if it would come. After sleeping and showering, he got into the striped shirt and the new Brooks Brothers jacket but failed at tying the necktie.

"Look at you," Lemma said when Rossie knocked at their door. "Let me deal with that." She ducked her chin and looked up to him as if a question might be floating between them and touched the knot a final time. "Tending to you, young man, makes me feel weak and wicked." Then she frowned as if at herself, shook her head, and turned away. "Bernard isn't feeling right, and has gone to bed. We're staying in, but you and Eliza, the two of you, have dinner reservations."

"Where is she?" Rossie asked.

"Wasn't she with you?"

"You mean in my room? There's times when we go to our own rooms."

"I suppose there must be."

Bernard came wandering out in rumpled white pajamas. "Sorry about the evening," he said. "Howard has canceled on us, and there is only so much excitement I can stand. Tomorrow night we'll be ringside with Earl Hines."

The Steakhouse at Norton's Park was very much a Chicago affair: waiters in tuxedos, a flaming grill, and racks of beef on display in the cool room where Rossie went to pick his porterhouse. Eliza's steak tartare was prepared by the waiter alongside the table, its minced, raw sirloin mixed with capers and egg yolk.

"That's a new one on me," Rossie said.

Eliza smiled. "I don't think so," she said.

"I'm thinking nothing is a new one to you, you've seen it all. Women are envying me, all around the room, wondering why you came after me."

He accepted a forkful of her tartare. "Not oysters, but it's close."

Back at the Drake, Rossie unbuttoned his striped shirt and Eliza hung his new coat in the closet, then turned her back to him so he could help with the snaps on her dress. She asked if he felt properly kept.

"I'm a volunteer," he said. "Don't worry about me."

She lay back to display herself, swollen with her pregnancy, waiting for him on his bed. "Fondle me. Kiss me and caress me. That's all we'll need."

But it wasn't.

"This has got to stop," she said.

But not that night.

They toured north to Evanston and showed Rossie a tree-lined street and a pillared, white house nestled beyond a deep lawn amid Colorado blue spruce. It was where Bernard and Lemma and Eliza had lived. "There it is," Bernard said. "Lost years."

"Not so bad," Lemma said. "But you were ruthless."

In the silence that followed Rossie wondered to what degree Lemma had ever come to a truce with Bernard.

"Neither of you," Eliza said, "ever says what you mean."

"Nonsense. We say anything we mean."

"You're a nice woman," Rossie said, listening to his voice like it was someone else talking. "But Eliza is right. You don't either of you much say what you mean."

"Rossie," Bernard said. "Perhaps that's where we should leave it."

"What don't I say, for instance? What about this?" Lemma went on, focused on Rossie. "Why was Eliza alone in San Francisco? Why did she go at all? Are those unanswered questions?"

"Because I insisted," Eliza said.

"Ah," Bernard mused, "the prodigious truth."

"I ask," Lemma said. "No one answers."

Bernard turned to Rossie, signaling a new topic. "Tonight, the Panama hat."

They gathered in a dark hotel barroom, where Bernard toasted "this chance at life."

Lemma studied herself in a mirror. She was clad in a midlength, gray gown, with her hair in a high French bun. "Smiling through sadness," she said, then went on to describe another quarrel she'd had with Howard on the telephone. "Those women he thinks he picks. They pick him. They bleed him."

By ten-thirty they were in a taxicab heading down to Thirty-ninth Street and Southern Parkway. "The jive joints are deeper to the south," Bernard said. "It's another world. We want this to be glamorous."

The Earl Hines Band played a new music, called swing, in the Grand Terrace Ballroom. Locals boasted that it was the Cotton Club of Chicago. "They have an hour on NBC radio," Bernard said. "Every night, going out to all of America. I've caught it in Montana, radio from over the mountains, from Spokane. They advertise him as 'Fatha' Hines — an adman's moniker so I never say it." He explained that musicians like Earl Hines, who'd returned year after year to the same mob-run establishment since opening night in 1931, were said to be "owned." It was dangerous for them to talk of quitting, while others, like Louis Armstrong, had the power to work where they pleased. "Things around Chicago are commonly known. We'll be in God's hands, safe as sweet potatoes. This is Mafia land, pleasure for profit. Part of the pleasure lies in understanding the corruptions."

Storefronts along Southern Parkway were decorated by neon signs advertising rundown taverns and small groceries. The Grand Terrace itself was low and undistinguished. A little crowd, mostly black, had gathered on the sidewalk. Women cut dance steps as syncopated music came flooding out from the spangled doors, and stylish men snapped their fingers, admiring the women. "Hey, cowboy," one said to Rossie. "Five dollars for the hat."

"Can't do it," Rossie said. "It was a present."

The man smiled and gave him a thumbs up.

The space inside was brilliant under a dazzling, mirror-covered ball spinning over the bandstand. Earl Hines, a slim master of quickness, gleaming with perspiration beneath the lights, was got up in formal white, as was his band, to match the ivory-colored piano. Bernard passed a fold of money to a black man in a tuxedo.

During a break in the music the usher led them to a table at the edge of the dance floor that Bernard had reserved. Two young men were already there, one lean and pale-white with eyes quick as a bird, the other with skin a deep, almost bluish ebony.

"What if we don't fucking move?" the white fellow said. A battered trombone case lay across the second man's lap.

"Then, gentlemen, you'll embarrass the Grand Terrace Ballroom. I think you'll agree that's a very bad idea."

The men eyed one another.

"My friend here is a musician. Who are these assholes? They're bozos. Somebody should kick their asses."

"Are you threatening customers? I hope not. Surely you're not challenging our authority."

The black man with trombone case was already standing as his friend slowly pushed back from the little table.

"She sold me this fucking drink," the white fellow said. "What am I supposed to do with this fucking drink?"

"I'd carry it to the bar. I'd carry it carefully, I wouldn't spill, and I'd see if I was happy at the bar. If I weren't, I'd get out of here. Quickly."

The two men made their way slowly across the empty dance floor toward the dimly lit bar in the back of the room.

"Thank you," Bernard said. "Could we have a bottle of champagne?"

Lemma opened the tiny blue purse, took out a pack of Lucky Strike cigarettes, and waited as Bernard struck a match.

Eliza watched, eyes gleaming, as her mother blew smoke from her nostrils.

Rossie had started to take off his hat, and Lemma told him to leave it on.

"Don't," she said. "Never give up your style."

"Never saw you light up before," Rossie said.

"It's a filthy trick, but we love them." She blew another stream of smoke.

A woman in fishnet hosiery brought the champagne as Earl Hines and his men moved back to the bandstand. Hines was off into an intricate beginning on the piano.

Eliza held out her hand to Rossie. "Slowly," she said. "I want a man in a white summer hat. For you, once around the floor with a pregnant woman."

As the band swung into a flare of horns, Rossie led Eliza through an improvising waltz, jostling along as the dancers spun around him but happy because she was smiling and throwing her dark hair as she leaned back to study him. She moved forward and kissed him on the neck. Spinning slowly, with Eliza perspiring in his arms and Earl Hines touching that piano with careless intimacy, Rossie studied the mirrored ball above them and felt suddenly weightless, not so much dizzied as floating.

"There," Eliza said when they were seated with glasses of champagne before them.

"You've done it once and you can do it again."

"I can."

Eliza shook her head, gazing at him in an archly mystified way. She placed her hand on his knee. "Who are you?" she whispered.

"Your cowboy," Lemma said, over the music. "Mr. Buckaroo." Leaning in to Rossie, she said, "Now I'm going to drag my own prince onto the floor."

Bernard tipped his glass back to empty it and joined her with a sliding grace Rossie had not suspected, spinning with Lemma until the midnight show commenced with a blare of horns and a swirl of beauties who didn't so much dance as pose on the stage. Small girls — women, really — pranced around the floor, occasionally pausing to strike a few notes in time with Earl Hines on four white grand pianos that had been rolled out among the dancers. "Those little girls," Bernard said, returning to his seat. "They call them ponies."

A taxi delivered them back to the Drake at four-thirty in the morning. Rossie woke alone at nine to sunlight in on him through the window. He drank water, took four aspirin, got out of his clothes, and slept again. Much later, Eliza was at the door.

"Dinnertime," she said once he'd gotten

the lock to work. "Oysters are calling. You can hear their little voices echoing in the hallways."

The next afternoon, while Bernard stayed and Lemma was settled down to rereading Stendhal's *The Red and the Black,* Eliza and Rossie ventured out to see *Metropolis* at a movie house decorated in an ancient-Egyptian style.

Rossie hated it. "Nothing was ever like that." He was dismayed at the robotic people who labored in dark catacombs, operating steam-run power plants beneath gardens where the rich played tennis. "That was idiotic." He hesitated. "I don't know I ever said that word before. *Idiotic.* I'm learning, saying words I never said because you say them wrong and people laugh. Now, I might say words like *ridiculous.* I'm getting educated."

"You are," Eliza said. "But ridiculous?" Her smile was tentative and anxious for a hesitant second before she launched into her own tirade. "You can't mean it. Fascism isn't ridiculous. It's evil. Try thinking. What you're saying is ridiculous. You ought to be ashamed."

"What I think about ashamed, is fuck you."

Eliza flagged down a taxicab. "This was a mistake."

Near Lake Michigan, north of the Loop, she kept the taxi parked before a row of four-story, brickwork buildings and a reconstructed mansion connected to the coach house by covered walkways. A sign inside a white picket fence read Pliny School.

"We never came in this way," Eliza said. "We came through the back, across the tennis courts. There was a whole life. Boys and girls lived in the school. We wore Greek masks and staged Sophocles, and some of us played in string quartets. I spent my third winter memorizing Whitman. 'Free and make free.' That's Emerson. Whitman heard him say that in a lecture and was inspired."

"Where'd you live memorizing this Whitman?"

"Up there on the third floor. But we can't go in. I'm pregnant and unmarried. Louise Bryce, if you were one of her prize girls, would hate it if you showed up pregnant and unmarried. She doesn't want to see me right now. She wrote a letter, said I had ruined myself unless I came back to sanity. Next year we'll invite her to come west. She could bring a summer tour of students to the ranch. She'll see sanity. She was the first one to encourage me toward Alberta, in her way, and she knows it. She took me to Hull House, and said I could be just like Jane Addams. We'll show her."

Later, they walked streets lined with dirty buildings, where men rested their backs against rock walls and the windows were open in the overcast September heat. Soon it would rain. Eliza dropped a quarter into a cup held by a woman with long fingernails curled into claws, who sat with her back against a fire hydrant.

"You figure that's help?" Rossie said. "Two bits?"

Eliza's eyes went flat and shadowed as she studied him.

"You know what I'm thinking?" he said, still feeling insulted. "I'm thinking about hitching my way back to Montana, catching my horses. I'm thinking this party is over."

"Party?" Eliza shook her head. A drizzle of misting rain began, tapping the awning above them, and she led him off into the drizzle to walk through what she claimed was a famous public market, where men and women shouted and haggled over skinned lambs and pickled pig's feet, bundles of spinach, prayer shawls, dolls without arms. "It's been going on since before history, buying and trading. Do you think it's a party? Miss Bryce showed us photographs of festivals that have endured for centuries, people surviving because they could laugh at the joke of life. This is what's left."

"Which joke?"

"All of us." She led Rossie out of the rain, into a doorway across the street from a nondescript brick building.

"You and me?" Rossie's grin was bitter. "Our mommas and daddies? We're the joke, folks?"

"There, over there, Hull House. It's a refuge. Jane Addams won the Nobel Prize. She's ancient but alive, and I plan on being like her. The long-time thing, like Jane Addams. Who is entirely to admire."

"Sweet dreams," Rossie said. "I got no idea but that I'm tired of pissant hobby-farm cowboys and Indians. You got me walking down these streets a thousand miles from anywhere, and you're telling me I don't know anything."

"Nobody cares what you're tired of. What I'm saying is grow up and see what we could be."

"Yeah, we could be Jane whoever she is."

"You son of a bitch." For the second time in Rossie's nineteenth year, a young woman slugged him, this time an utterly unsuspected sucker punch in the gut. He took to his knees, gasping.

Once he caught his breath, he saw that his flannel pants were ripped, his right kneecap faintly abraded beneath. He wetted a fingertip, touched it and tasted the finger, looked up to find her turning to the street and waving down another taxi.

"The Drake," she told the driver. "Get in," she told Rossie, when the door was open and she was inside.

"Fuck off." He walked away, and when he looked back, she was gone. In filmy light, the sidewalk at his feet seemed far below as he dodged in the light traffic and crossed unfamiliar streets. He touched the wallet in his hip pocket and stopped on an empty run of the sidewalk to count his money, twenty in the billfold and add that to the thirty in a stocking. But there were no taxicabs on this block and half and the people around him were talking in languages he didn't know. He pushed into a tavern where three aged black men sat at the rail, idly talking with a white-shirted, deeply black bartender who looked to be Rossie's age.

"You lost?"

Rossie grinned, the old trick. "Lost my girlfriend," he said. "She rode off in a taxicab."

"Fucked up! You want a drink?"

Rossie eased onto a stool. "A martini."

"That's something, a martini. Don't see too many martini drinkers around here."

One of the old men turned to Rossie. "Now, you know, you could buy everybody a martini."

"Sure as hell. Martinis for everybody."

The bartender got started with his martini shaking. "You know what I'm going to say? I'm going to ask any asshole who comes in tomorrow if he was here when the white fellow stopped by and started buying martinis all around. I'm going to raise prices and tell people we're a white-man martini joint."

Rossie took his down in three swallows. "One more all around," the bartender said. "Then we got to get you out of here. Where do you go?"

"I'm home," Rossie said.

"No," the bartender said, "you are not home. Right now you're walking on water. Somebody is going to knock your head off. I'll telephone a cab. Where do you go?"

"The Drake Hotel."

"See what I say? Couple of hours it'll be dark, and you'll be on your knees. Come midnight you might be dead."

Rossie's taxicab pulled up to the Drake as darkness feathered down over Chicago. There was a note at the desk, in Eliza's quick script: "We were going to be each other's child." He went down a long hallway and banged on the door to her room. She faced him, cool-eyed in her nightdress, and said, "What? Drunk? At least you aren't dead."

"Could have been. They said I could have been."

She stepped back, relenting that bit. "You better feed yourself. Then you won't be so crazy." Rossie didn't respond. "Am I your mother? Eat whatever you eat. From downstairs, a big old, fat rib steak with chanterelle mushrooms. They could bring ice cream, scoops and scoops of vanilla ice cream. We're getting up early."

"Me, I'm going home."

"One step at a time. I'll order the food. Go take a bath. The food will come. Eat it and sleep. They're calling us at four-thirty. Bring your gloves. It's going to be cold. I'll meet you at the taxi stand. Your telephone will ring. Now, get out of here."

Inside his room, Rossie studied her note again. "Each other's child." Or, he thought, be your own daddy. By the time he was out of the bath, a waiter had arrived with the rib steak and ice dream on a wheeled cart. A single rose in a crystal vase adorned the setting. Rossie ate, thinking somebody had to be right. After the vanilla ice cream he curled up into sleep.

The next morning, after a long taxicab ride at the edge of daylight, Eliza led Rossie out onto a slatted walkway overlooking the killing floor of a slaughterhouse. Men moved clumsily across slippery concrete, their feet bound in bloody rags, as steam clouded the building and froze into blackish ice on the walls. Fat steers were goaded one by one into chutes and met their end with the knocker, a man so pale he looked albino, who swung a steel-headed sledge and struck blows to the center forehead — a dull thump and instant collapse, a dead creature every minute. Rossie heard the clank of chains as a gate tripped. Undone animals tumbled sideways onto the concrete floor, where a chain was fastened around their twitching hind legs and wound onto a metal drum to hoist the bodies aloft one at a time. The bleeder, first of the butchers, sliced into the jugular with his long slippery knife. Blood blossomed, then flowed along gutters in a clotting stream that was kept in motion by a man with a square-toed shovel. The carcasses drained while butchers whetted their knives on sharpening steels that dangled from their belts. Heavy bleeding done, the carcass was lowered, and another man severed the head, cracking apart the vertebra, while another man undid the chain at the feet. Skinning began with the draw of a blade down the belly, through the bag between the teats and around the pricks to end at the anus. The hide was attached to another chain and torn from the flesh with a great sucking noise as the fats separated. Split, gutted, and washed, the glistening bodies were dragged by yet another chain down a metal-topped table and sectioned into quarters and cut into back-strap steaks and the like.

"Pliny School was worth something," Eliza said. "Miss Bryce brought me here. She knew about this, and so did Henry Ford. He reinvented this for his automotive assembly lines."

"Sure as hell this isn't church." They climbed into the back of the taxi that, in exchange for five dollars, had waited for them. "What I want," Rossie said, "is you and horses and nobody ordering me around. That's all."

"You don't have to believe what I believe. But don't laugh at me."

"So that's the deal? My mother told me it was a chance I might not amount to anything. She said you could break your heart on it. I run away from Mattie Flynn and you got some Indian baby on the way but I don't run."

"Boy," the driver said, "your momma had it right."

Eliza ignored him. "His baby." She gazed out the window. "Is it going to be the killer with us?"

"Don't think so. How am I going to think when I see it? The worst that could happen is I'll be back where I am anyway."

Bernard was on the couch in late afternoon, still in his pajamas, watching as a gray-faced Howard, having shown up with another armload of flowers, shook martinis. Or, rather, a martini for himself.

Eliza announced that she and Rossie had solved their equation.

"What does this mean?" Lemma asked. "Marriage? Or further disgrace?"

"Thought your equation had long since been solved," Howard said. This was not his first martini of the afternoon. "Let's see if we can solve mine." He explained that his latest love affair was kaput. "So I'm here with these understanding people, picking up the pieces, being careful. Things can go ridiculously wrong."

"Why not marriage?" Bernard said, ignoring Howard. "It could work out." He gestured to Lemma. "Until I found this woman I was frantic. My parents were dead. I was increasingly disoriented. I credit myself with the wit to acknowledge it."

Bernard went into the bedroom and returned with a snub-nosed revolver, the sight of which made Rossie wonder what this marriage talk had become.

"I carried this weapon. Like a fool, I brought it on this trip. Terrible things do happen." He was talking directly and earnestly to Rossie. "Living here in the old days I imagined someone picking at the lock to my door. I lay in the dark and thought of a man silhouetted by the light from the hallway, and his surprise when he was shot, the flare of gunfire. I dreamed of shooting without hesitation. There is a Balzac novel in which a lawyer, frightened by the violence of Paris, moves to the country. Chicago frightened me, and Lemma was willing to humor me."

"You took us away," Lemma said, affecting surprise. "Eliza's childhood, my life." Then she smiled. "You bad old man. You stole us."

"My friends thought going to Montana was an insane thing," Bernard said. "Even more dangerous than Chicago. But I dreamed about killing a man, so I went west in self-defense. I've always thought of that move as having saved me. What you need, Rossie, is a plan, a scenario leading to long-term results, where the other shoe drops. I can help you. Natural progression is my agenda. You could do any number of things. You could go to law school."

"School?" Rossie walked to a dark window looking out to a scatter of lighted windows across the street.

"Take my word for it," Bernard said. "You'll want more than horses. You'll want to be taken seriously." He waited, fondling the pistol, but Rossie didn't turn away from the window. "Can you tell me which women, do you think, turn out smart? I'll tell you. Women like Eliza, who taste tragedy and understand balance."

"On the teeter-totter," Lemma said. Bernard joined Rossie at the window. "You and Eliza, we're thinking about your lives. Lemma and I never imagined you'd give up horses. We'd be saddened if you did. We'll pay your way forward. If you aren't in luck, who is?"

Howard was shaking himself another martini. "Where I'd go is to Spain, for the bullfights. We could go together. Ronda. Andalusia on the cliffs. Great bullfight town."

"Howard," Lemma said. "Shut up."

"Horses, and good work yet to be defined," Bernard said. "There you have it. We honor your ambitions and ours."

"Rossie," Lemma said. "You picked us."

In 1956, running for county commissioner in the Bitterroot, Rossie would tell the story of that evening in the Drake Hotel. "Nineteen thirty-four, in Chicago," he'd say. "Those people, they turned me."

The buzz among the men and women at the Elks Club in Hamilton would drop to quiet. They knew Rossie Benasco: he trained horses used by calf ropers and bulldoggers in the National Finals Rodeo in Denver. He was known as a talker, and this would be one of his stories about ironies.

"That Bernard, he let me convince myself — nineteen, no education, listening to talk about 'scenarios,' whatever that was — and all the while he was holding a short-barreled pistol. He should have been the politician. A toast to Bernard."

BLUE MOON

The larch turned. Golden needles showered over the mountain trails. Snow fell in the night and melted by noon. Eliza grew thicker, sleepy, and slower in the late days of pregnancy.

"Good food, clear air, and sleep," Lemma said. "That's the routine. Hot rooms and excitement of all kinds are to be strictly avoided." She frowned at Rossie. "So you, I hope there's been an end to you in the midnight hours."

Arnold Meisner and Leonard returned from the tribes in the north with crates of undeveloped glass negatives, and Leonard went off to Missoula for classes at the university. Life settled toward winter, the days bright and quiet, until Arnold declared that he wanted a chance at the female grizzly and twin cubs that had been seen feeding on fallen apples sixty miles to the north at the foot of the Mission Mountains.

"Carnivores," he said over coffee, "grazing on fruit like horses. No one has photographed them from near proximity. I have ambitions. Static images of the disenfranchised begin to seem like foolishness. What's real are energies. Theorists like Ezra Pound say that verbs and not nouns are real. Sounds like the theory of a man too long cooped up in England, but nevertheless . . . I want to photograph the bears as they act."

"Do you believe that, really?" Lemma said. "Photographs incite the imagination, which operates entirely in terms of energies."

"The bears may in any event photograph as energies." No one answered so he turned the subject. "Grizzlies are insanely dangerous. One hundred yards in three and a half seconds. Once they start after you, it's too late to run. Vivid energies. Verbs."

"I've no idea what you're trying to talk about." Something angry tinged Lemma's voice. "Your affliction sounds physical rather than philosophic. You've overtired yourself."

"No, I haven't." In the Flathead Valley he'd heard of a rancher who'd constructed a bunker specifically for viewing the grizzlies that came down in fall to feed on apples. It was constructed of discarded railroad ties, with viewing ports at eye level. Orchard trees were strung with lights that operated off a power plant. "The creatures are used to the lights and go on feeding," he explained. "The haven stinks of creosote but it's indestructible and utterly safe. Once there, with the creatures prowling, we're in for the night. There's no safe way out."

"You can bring your rifle," Bernard said to Rossie. "You might want to think about slaying one of the monsters."

"Don't sound like the point."

"You could at least sight them in," Lemma said, "and see them as something you might assassinate. Isn't that part of it?" She studied him a long moment, then dropped the matter. "So," she said. "Away we go."

Late on the sunny, windless afternoon of their excursion, the orchard in the Flathead Valley was littered with the husks of rotting apples abuzz with yellow jackets and huge black flies. A tattered buffalo robe lay across the floor of the bunker, which was otherwise furnished with army cots covered by Hudson Bay blankets, three cracked leather chairs that looked as if they had been rescued from the lobby of a defunct hotel, and a battered hardwood table, along with two crystal ashtrays from the Ritz Hotel in Paris, and German binoculars. There was even a home-built stove and dry, split larch stacked along the back wall.

Betty had provisioned them with roasted chickens, European cheeses, salad, hard-boiled eggs, coffee to heat, cube ice in a burlap-wrapped chest, gallons of spring water, bottles of French wine, and a quart of single-malt Scotch.

"We can't go dry into a thing like this," Bernard said as Lemma and Eliza set out the food and drink. Arnold aligned his camera with one of the observation slots. Rossie strained to close the heavy door built of six-by-twelve planking. He dropped two steel bars into place.

"Bulletproof," Bernard said. "I wonder what willingness to kill would be like. I wondered in Chicago. I wonder now. What it would be like to emulate Teddy Roosevelt and love vigorous reaping and killing. An ultimate capitalism."

Arnold shook his head. "Ultimate?"

The day was falling to twilight in reefs of clouds swirling violet and amber. Once Rossie got the generator going and lights blazed in the trees, Bernard claimed grizzlies were coming.

"It's something you know," he whispered. "Sit quiet, they'll smell our food and be on us, trying to batter down the doors."

"The outdoorsman," Arnold said, smiling for Rossie.

But Bernard was right. An acrid stench floated in to accompany the sounds of its breathing, and a great male grizzly humped and rippling and silvery, came to them silently. Arnold was under the hood of his camera, reaching to turn and adjust his lenses.

"We're secure," Bernard said. "Close enough. But secure."

"Close enough for what?" Lemma asked.

"Mr. Bear," Eliza whispered. "What do you think, Mr. Bear?"

Lemma tore a drumstick from one of Betty's baked chickens and tossed it out. The creature caught it in flight, crunched it away bone and all, then lifted onto its hind legs, poised there, reared with jaws chomping, settled, and reared again, and this time struck a shuddering blow against the door, which held.

"The rifle," Bernard whispered.

Arnold remained under his camera hood and muttered in a language Rossie took to be French while Lemma hovered close beside him.

Just as the bear turned and carelessly drifted off to feed on the apples, another grizzly appeared in the shadows, a female followed by twin cubs. "We waste our days," Lemma whispered. "It's her, with her babies."

The grizzly rose onto its hind legs again, eyeing the sow and cubs, then dropped, turned away, and was gone.

"What we want is a wedding photo," Lemma whispered. "Eliza and Rossie with the bears. Creatures lying down with one another. Fertility everywhere, Eliza swollen, there in the orchard with a mother bear and her babies."

"What I'm thinking about," Eliza said, "is walking out there. It's an idea that won't go away."

"Lying down with one another?" Rossie said.

"She can answer for herself," Lemma said.

"Sure," Rossie said. "So can I."

Arnold stepped away from the hood of his camera. "What you're talking is craziness. Our bride will be eaten like an apple."

"What would you do if she went out there?" Lemma asked Rossie. "Some cowboy trick?" She handed him a corkscrew. "In the meantime, a bottle of red and one of white."

Rossie thought of telling her to jam the corkscrew up her ass but instead opened the wine and carefully put together a fire in the home-built stove.

As Eliza and Lemma conspired to warm the chicken, each moving delicately in the ensuing silence, Arnold continued sliding glass plates into and out of the camera until finally he turned, hands trembling as he sipped a glass of the wine. "It worked," he said. "I think. We'll see."

After the food, the men sat in the leather chairs while Lemma and Eliza whispered and, laughing privately, tucked themselves in on the cots. The little enclosure remained lit by candles, and Bernard drank until he was asleep.

Arnold began whispering to Rossie. "These are not silly people. They're willing to be foolish. I hope you don't lose patience." He nodded toward Bernard. "He's facing a cruel time. She was selfish and hot. But she supports him in what he's got left. I envy him."

Rossie wondered if Arnold was confessing a connection to Lemma and if the others were listening and why Arnold would broadcast old news and if airing it could be cruelty. Looking around at Bernard in his chair and Arnold drifting off and the women already sleeping, Rossie thought not one of them knew how to mean anything they said. He was trapped in this barricade and despised himself for being here. Thoughts of the red-faced man he imagined as Bobby Cahill and stone buildings at Shoshone Meadows and riding at sunrise on a quick, three-year-old mare eventually drew him toward sleep — and toward the end of being their fool.

By noon the next day they were back in the Bitterroot and, with no word of goodbye, Rossie slipped off on the pretext of napping, loaded his bedroll and pack on Rock, saddled Pinky, and was down the road in a chill of wind. He closed the shutters on Eliza in his mind and rode on toward Hamilton until he heard her dusting up behind him in the Model A. Huge in pregnancy, she stepped from the car and stood before him. She was hard to make out in the cold sunlight of that late October. "You." Her pale eyes were huge in her white face. "You asshole. What? Look at yourself." Then her fury collapsed and her eyes went swollen.

"You all right?" He suddenly thought she wasn't.

"Fine." She was almost to weeping. "It'll snow tonight. You'll be in snow before you get to Idaho."

"Damned if I know."

"Where will you be?"

"Nevada."

"This is the last time I come after you." She bit her lip. "Never again. You should know that. You were the one. Right when I saw you, and then you smelled like it. You were the one even after that morning in Alberta. That was it. Then you came to find me, and I thought, 'What's this? I'm not wrecked?' "

"You want to walk in there with the grizzly bears like nothing could happen and everything is a joke. People would say you're the joke. You goddamned people."

She gazed away, her eyelids nearly swollen closed with her weeping. "This is the last time. You think about that."

"Go on back to the house," Rossie said.

"You know what they think? They think we're children." Then she was gone on the dusty road.

Rossie was alone for a bit, then nudged his Pinky horse and followed her back. That night, he went to the cookhouse too late for dinner, and Albert laughed and said he thought Rossie had been chased off for good. "But," he said, "I kept you a steak."

In the morning Rossie headed up to the house, let himself in, and found Bernard and Lemma over pancakes at the kitchen table.

"You're learning," Bernard said. "Keep the women stirred up."

Lemma touched Rossie's hand. "I was rude. Bernard told me last afternoon, when you were gone. He told me severely and for some time. We had a serious moment. I apologize."

Distended in a yellow brocade dressing gown, Eliza came into the kitchen, and Rossie was entirely given to watching her pale lips, slightly parted as she studied him.

"There you are," he said and he stood and pulled out a chair for her and she touched his hand and nodded and thanked him.

"Isn't that sweet," Lemma said. "Like a lady."

When Arnold came in to breakfast he announced that he would photograph Eliza with Rossie the next morning. Once he was back in his developing room in Chicago he would print an image with them alongside the bears. "Very uptown, very magic." He said this as if it was a photographer's joke.

At sunup the following day, he perched his wooden box of a camera up in another apple orchard and photographed them as they were after awakening, Eliza swollen and gravid in a bluish linen gown. "Actual lovers," he said. "I will bring the photograph

358

when I return for Christmas, for the wedding."

"The wedding?" Rossie said, looking across to Eliza who was looking to the ground.

"Didn't you know?" Arnold said, smiling.

"For that matter," Bernard said, "neither did I."

"Now you do," Arnold said. "I've sold a photo essay about an elegant western wedding in snowy distances to a notable fashion magazine. It will be called 'Beloved Turmoil.' "

"There it is," Lemma said. "Announced."

Eliza lifted her eyes and gave Rossie a sardonic smile, shaking her head slightly as she did but also watching to see how he was taking this.

"Guess it is," Rossie said.

Low clouds had begun to scatter rain and snow, bringing winter seriously down upon them, when Rossie found Larry in a pissed-off uproar at dinner. "You got it," he said to Rossie.

"That so? What's that?"

"My job. Didn't take too long."

Bernard had visited the cowhand only a couple of hours earlier to tell him he was to be out of the bunkhouse by December twenty-first. "I'm planning to issue you a check for three months' wages," he said. "Cause trouble about this and the sheriff from Hamilton will escort you from the property. Trouble for the sheriff means jail."

"Wintertime and out of work," Larry shouted.

"Shit," Albert said, "you never had no work. Nothing a man would call work."

"You better watch your little ass."

"If you plan on eating down here," Albert said, "you better watch yours."

The next afternoon, Bernard came to find Rossie. "You and I should go for a drive." He was dressed in a green fedora and Harris Tweed jacket.

"This will be more winter than you're used to," he said, once they were in the Buick. "I imagine it will be difficult. Eliza and some other man's child."

"Don't seem so far that it matters."

"I think it will. Do you continually consider going back to Nevada? Even when the women aren't driving you crazy?"

"Not right off."

Bernard bit at his lower lip. "It's in my interest to forestall such ideas." He pulled in before the empty cork-floored horse barn. "This will look different."

"Looks the same as any time I seen it."

"There's a difference. Now, since right now, it's yours. Eliza has her property on the cliff. I'm giving this barn to you. Consider it a premature wedding gift, an attempt to ensure that the birth of this baby doesn't incite you to spook again." Bernard smiled in mock conspiracy. "The barn, along with sixty acres, should be initially sufficient. You'll build your own corrals here in what we call the Tailfeather Field. Eliza lost a horse named Daisy to wire in this field. So it should carry weight in your burgeoning family. She'll make sure you keep the wire up."

"Two horses," Rossie said. "That's what I got."

"There'll be more. That's one major point in this. Leonard tells Lemma that you've talked about the horse business."

"Talked about it, him and me, one time. People where I come from would say that owning horses was the point. They'd say owning a barn was jumping the gun."

"What do you think?"

"I'm wondering what kind of horses."

"That, of course, is up to you."

"Quick fellows," Rossie said. "Smart and stout." Out of the Buick, he walked a slow route over to the barn and knocked his knuckles on the varnished, hardwood double doors before sliding one open to step inside into the dimness, which reeked faintly of timothy hay in the loft. Shuffling along on the soft cork flooring, he opened the immaculately clean stalls, climbed the ladder up to the loft, and flopped over backwards into the dry timothy to lie watching dust float in the faint light. Close to perfect, except it was too quiet and didn't stink of horseshit.

Bernard was still standing by the Buick. "Well?" he said.

"I'm learning to say what I'm thinking," Rossie replied. "You fired that cowboy, his job is open, and you're giving me this barn like it's not much. And to you it isn't. At the same time I can buy my ass back any time I want by riding away. So there's no use worrying. Eliza is what I want, and you got me. I should say thanks."

"Enough," Bernard said, eyes gleaming. "There will be papers." He gazed away toward the valley. "Signatures. In a few days we'll visit my Mr. Henry, the lawyer in Hamilton."

"My daddy would love this. He'd tell me to watch out for the next card, saying, 'You can't gamble an empty hand into anything more than once or twice.' "

"You didn't start empty. Lemma and I

regard you with considerable affection. Lemma has been on the telephone with your mother, and plans are in motion. I've negotiated a rate from the railroad. We don't want you to run off and leave all of us stranded. You own this barn and the acreage surrounding it. That should hold you." He laid a hand on Rossie's shoulder. "Enough with running for cover. Your friends will be coming, one of them a man named Flynn."

"Slivers? He was my boss in Nevada. He was the father of my girlfriend. The girl before Eliza."

"Betrayal?" Bernard was beaming. "Jealousy and discontent? A man of experience."

"Anyhow, man with a barn, who'd be a fool to run off?"

"Exactly. Your horses, if you have the will, someday might run at Santa Anita."

In his bunkhouse room, Rossie commenced the braiding of an intricate horsehair rope called a martingale, quickly settling down to what he thought of as winter work.

"That cowboy got his check," Albert said over pork chops and green beans drenched in hot bacon fat. "He rides off in the snow. Be a handsome boy in Hamilton with that wintertime paycheck. So your hired men are me and Nelson."

"Sounds right." Rossie smiled. "I'm sitting in my room, braiding and thinking like a boss."

"Careful with that. It's a malady."

Lemma and Bernard had wanted to take Eliza to the hospital in Missoula, or even into Hamilton, but she insisted on the midwife, a heavy-shouldered woman named Peters from down the valley. She brought blankets and her own pillow and moved in to share Eliza's rooms, proclaiming that they should call her the missus or Mrs. Peters, and declaring that Eliza was healthy as a barnyard animal. No one should even consider being worried about the birth.

"But if something went wrong," Lemma said, "we're helpless."

"Mam," the missus said, "things can go wrong, but not often by surprise. You sense if things might go wrong. There's not a thing in the world the matter with that girl. There's the doctor in Hamilton, but we won't need him. She's strong and her baby is in position to come." She spread a cloth on the chest of drawers in Eliza's room and laid out the steel forceps, a scalpel, scissors, a catheter, thermometers, linen cord, rolls of cotton, and a stethoscope. "This is normal," she told Eliza, smiling as she set out bottles of rubbing alcohol and disinfectant along with a vial of silver nitrate for the baby's eyes. "Tools of the trade."

Betty led Mrs. Peters to the kitchen and Lemma joined in to help with the stacks of white linen sheets the midwife kept in an old suitcase, which were to be steamed, ironed, and scorched dry, thus sterilized.

"It's man and woman," she said at dinner. "The babies come right out, the woman is happy with her love, the man loves her happiness." She spooned up a third helping of chicken soup.

"Everything is for the good?" Lemma asked.

"Part of happiness."

Eliza's contractions began at four in the morning two nights later, snow burying the roads, valley schools closed since midafternoon the day before.

Bernard came to breakfast in the bunkhouse with this news. "There is nobody cooking up there," he said. He dumped a half pint of brandy into the coffee and poured a cup for himself. "Just to take the edge off things." Albert smiled his toothless smile and helped himself to a cup. "After we eat," Bernard said to Rossie, "Eliza wants you scrubbed up and in the room with her."

Rossie waited out the minutes in one of the big chairs in her sitting room, the contractions getting serious after eight hours. He held Eliza's hands while Mrs. Peters said, "Cry out, loud as you please." But not one sound, nothing but the breathing and grunting, even during the quick cutting, when the odor of blood came over the room and blood dripped onto the floor. Rossie held Eliza's sweaty hand as she squeezed, until the crowning of the newborn and the ultimate putting on of pressure brought on the slippery birth, the baby boy appearing just after midnight. Seventeen hours after her labor had begun, Eliza lay back, her thighs smeared with blood, and avidly eyed the baby — with fright, Rossie thought — until the infant wailed and was then cleaned with a soft cloth and given to her.

Once the cord was tied and the afterbirth expelled, Mrs. Peters severed the cord with scissors. "No mystery. You feel the mother's pulse in the cord. It stops, you tie the cord off, and cut it. The child is on its own, in its life." She spoke calmly, quietly excited and damp with perspiration, but Eliza wasn't listening. "Good girl," Mrs. Peters said. "You didn't flinch."

By now Lemma was in the room, pretending that she wasn't weeping, and Rossie was sent to summon Bernard, who'd been asleep on the couch in his study.

"We're cleaned up spick-and-span," Mrs. Peters told Bernard when he came stocking-footed down the stairs. "No more bloodiness. The mother is sitting up with her child. Three stitches. A complete success."

Eliza was propped up by fresh pillows at her back, her pale eyes vivid as she looked up from the child, which was hidden from the rest of them by the folds of a cotton blanket.

"They told me in Hamilton, when I was packing to come up here," Mrs. Peters said, "that this baby would be a part Indian. I don't see it."

"Who told you that?" Lemma asked.

"Women told me." She gave them a reassuring smile. "I've seen surprises. Nobody cares what tribe if it's a live child."

"Little squatty face, like a baby," Rossie said. "You could tell me boy or girl or Indian. I wouldn't know."

Eliza's voice was barely audible. "Here, you have him," she said to Rossie. She tried a smile. "Nothing to it."

"It was a tough time," Rossie said.

Mrs. Peters took the child from her and

turned the blanket away from its tiny red-dish features. "Little squatty face," she said, moving to hand the child over to Rossie, who backed away.

"Don't know about that."

Mrs. Peters paid him no attention. Rossie took the fold of blankets with the child inside, a tiny boy sleeping, breathing, almost weightless, and not at all inert. "This is something," he said.

"He won't break," Mrs. Peters said, following him. "If you're going to be the man who's around, he better get used to your smell right away. You better start getting used to him."

"What're you calling him?" Rossie asked.

"That's up to us, you and me," Eliza said, her voice still a whisper. Then her tone sharpened. "His last name is Stevenson."

Rossie grinned, thinking he would try a joke. "How about Bucky Stevenson?"

"No," she said. "No to Bucky."

"Your folks ought to be in on it."

"He's not their boy. He's ours."

The baby began to whimper. "Now you rock him. You owe him that much."

"Never thought about this as owing any-thing."

"That's another idea you better get used to," Mrs. Peters said.

"What color are his eyes?"

"They'll turn blue," Eliza said. "Like mine. Or they won't."

"Well," Rossie said. "Blue. That's what I'd call him."

"You can't call a baby boy by the name of Blue," Mrs. Peters said.

"Sure can. I went to grade school with a fellow named Blue."

Bernard brightened. "There's Teddy Blue," he said, recalling a legendary cowhand who came to Montana from Texas with the trail herds. Teddy Blue Abbott had been a drinking buddy with Calamity Jane. "Those people knew about names," Bernard said. "Teddy Blue. His story begins with the name."

"This is not a cowboy story," Lemma said.

"It could be," Bernard said.

"Blue is not fair. Think of this boy in school." Lemma studied Rossie. "Are you serious?"

"Not much."

"It's fine," Eliza said, and she was smiling. "For anyway the time being. We'll call him Teddy Blue. Teddy for sure."

"Time being? That name is going to be hard to shake," Mrs. Peters warned.

"No need for any shaking," Rossie said, "once you're used to it."

"Teddy Blue," Eliza said. "Bring me my baby. I need to sleep with him."

Lemma finally smiled. "Here I am consorting with lunatics."

"This crazy boy is going back to sleep," Bernard said as Mrs. Peters ushered them out of the room.

"Wish I was named Blue," Rossie said. "Always did, sort of."

After wandering in the house wishing he'd feel sleepy, Rossie sat behind a worktable on the kitchen porch to watch the snowfall in the dim rising light. Lemma was there behind him. She struck a wooden match and lit one of her Lucky Strike cigarettes.

"They've got that house too hot," she said, blowing smoke. "All I can think of is holding a baby of my own, before my life is gone entirely. It's on me like a sickness."

Rossie sensed that she wasn't exactly talking to him.

After dragging on the cigarette, she went on. "You should know the truth. Bernard is experiencing pain. The dark part of his going may be starting, and then you'll be the man around here. For all of us." She stood and went across the porch to flick her cigarette away into the snow. "What's happening with me is I can't stop dreaming about men, night after night. Some of them

370

are you." Her voice turned to whispering. "Would you like me to ask for it? Isn't that what men like — women wanting it, giving in, asking for it, insisting?" She was quiet a long moment. "I see you seeing me. You don't have to be careful. I don't have any stitches."

Rossie understood where she was taking this talk and could hardly catch his breath. "Whatever you're doing, it's working, but I better get some sleep."

"So you won't have it in me on the couch in the living room where nobody would ever know but you and me."

"I'm thinking," Rossie said.

Lemma touched her cool fingertips to his cheek and blew him a kiss. Later, in the bunkhouse, he jacked off all over his belly and fell asleep without moving to wipe it up.

The next afternoon, alone with Eliza as she nursed her new boy under the folds of a lilac-colored goose-down quilt from Labrador, he recounted the previous night's encounter with Lemma. "She started telling me things, about fucking. I was wondering, why me?"

Eliza smiled down at her child. "Think of yourself as any port in the storm."

"You listen a minute. She was after me."

Eliza looked up from her suckling baby to the ceiling. "Did you want to get at her?"

"Thought about it."

"But you never did it? You never lifted a hand. Or did you?"

"I was sitting there with a hard-on and not much brain."

"But you didn't touch her?" She watched carefully as Rossie shook his head no. "Horny." She smiled. "I think we'll call it horny. I'd be worried if something didn't get you hot."

"Once it was over I felt like I'd got away but not from her — from me. I had the idea to put my hand on her bare arm and see how far that went, if she'd stop me once she felt how I was. I was surprised I didn't."

"Why do you tell me things like this? Do you want me to mother you? We don't momma and daddy one another, not in this life. Try to think about her. Her husband is dying, he won't talk about it, and she's frantic. But she wasn't after you. She loves you. You're her cowboy. She wanted you to understand. We don't want to ruin you. Nobody does."

TYING THE KNOT

Bernard and Lemma announced that Howard would not be coming to Montana for the wedding, Howard having gone deep into Mexico.

"Our boy is sipping fruit drinks on beaches under palm trees," Bernard said. "Bless him. Perhaps this will be his real life, in contact with primitive gods." He smiled like an angel. "If he's not careful, he'll end up in our bunkhouse. Eliza might be the sole support of her uncle Howard. That may be his real life."

"Nonsense," Lemma laughed, waving this talk away. "This one has her own money."

There had been endless telephone calls back and forth to Nevada, as they figured and retallied the costs, until Bernard finally blew the whistle on quibbling over money. "He just threw his hands in the air," Lemma said. "He considers this a time for inventing family, and so we'll forget expense." She explained that Katrina and Nito, Slivers Flynn and Mattie, would travel on the railroad from Reno.

"Mattie?" Rossie asked.

"Her romance with your friend Oscar apparently existed only in your daydreams," Eliza said. "She's coming, her idea. I didn't want her, but why not confront the thing? Let's see what she is."

"I know what she is."

"You? I'm certain you do — or think you do. Hot pussy."

The travelers were to change trains in Sacramento, sleep in Pullman berths, and sightsee through a day in Seattle, spend a night on the Great Northern, and arrive in Missoula midmorning on the twenty-first of December. Bernard and Rossie would greet them in the Buick while Lemma and Eliza waited at the ranch.

Arnold Meisner would arrive later, on a train from Chicago, and be met by Leonard in the Model A. His luggage was to include the enlarged, framed photograph of Eliza and Rossie taken in the orchard for which Lemma had cleared a place of honor on the living room wall.

There would be a reception on the night of December twenty-second, after the travelers had rested for a day. Guests from Missoula and the valley would join them if the roads were passable. Through all this Betty would have three women from Hamilton to help with the cooking and cleaning. Finally, the wedding itself would take place in the living room the afternoon of December twenty-fourth with family and close friends. Christmas Day would be celebrated with a tree and small gifts.

At the breakfast table over pancakes the day before the guests arrived, Eliza proposed that the marriage ceremony begin with a walk out into the snow. They would hold hands before the All Frogs Pole as Leonard said a Blackfeet prayer.

"Wouldn't it be better luck," Bernard asked, "if that pole heard things that might have been said on the Queen Charlotte Islands, where it was made?"

"Absolutely," Eliza said. "But no one knows Haida."

"Your guests from Nevada may think you're excessively interested in Indians and their mysteries," Lemma said. "Sacred prayers are seldom orchestrated to the howls of a freezing child."

Eliza, with the baby in her arms, went still and white. "Mother, that's nonsense. There are freezing children on the Northern Plains as we speak — many have frozen to death and people are praying in circumstances you can't imagine."

"Well, you would know."

"Mother, your sadness is not my fault. Not to speak of your jealousy."

"Jealousy? In what way? Of what, may I ask?"

Rossie held his breath, having learned long ago to ignore the women in his mother's house when they came to breakfast weeping. Even Betty kept silent, tending the stove with a spatula in her hand as eggs splattered and hissed.

"Jesus!" Lemma said. She dropped her napkin over her breakfast plate. "Jealous!" They heard her bedroom door slam.

Bernard, smiling, continued to discuss railroad connections. Rossie pondered the quicksand they had stepped around. By dinner, however, Lemma was back among them, the brittleness dissolved into laughter about the baby's doings. Bernard offered a final reconciliation with a round of whiskey after the meal.

Dry snow fell the next morning as Bernard and Rossie got into their coats and went to chain up the Buick for the drive to Missoula. Even with the heater turned on high and Rossie climbing out every few miles to clear ice from the windshield wipers, their progress was deliberate and slow along a highway and streets empty of traffic.

"You and I," Bernard said. "Going to the train is becoming a tradition."

The locomotive steamed and screeched into the Great Northern station just as Rossie and Bernard were parking the Buick in front of the old brick depot. Mattie appeared at the head of the stairway. Her red hair was twisted up under her stained hat, and she wore horseback Levi's and a coat sewn out of a Hudson Bay blanket. As she surveyed Missoula, her lips trembled so that Rossie thought she might be talking to herself.

"Hey, good looking," he said. "You come to see somebody married?"

She ignored him as Slivers, in a slicker made of canvas tenting, stepped out of the Pullman carrying a worn leather satchel.

"You better climb down," he told her. "There's people behind you."

He shook Rossie's hand as Mattie went on staring off to the mountains. "Redheaded and freckled like she always was. Your folks, they're getting their baggage." Then he reached down and packed a snowball with his raw hands. "Winter in this old Bitterroot is what I wanted to see," he said, pitching his snowball to bang against the side of the Pullman car.

"This here," Rossie said to Slivers, "is Bernard Stevenson. He's the father-in-law."

"Heard there was a baby kid involved," Slivers said.

"But this isn't the kid's father," Rossie explained. "This is Eliza's father. She's the mother of the baby kid, she's the woman I'm marrying, with the kid."

"Sounds like you need name tags."

"So, the horseman, named Slivers," Bernard said. "Quite utterly unique."

Slivers eyed him. "Born to the name of Everett," he said. "I had a granddad, dim old man, said he was tired of names he couldn't remember, so he called me Slivers. I got on the voting rolls in Battle Mountain with the name of Slivers Flynn. Had to go through a judge, but lawyers say that's enough to make it your name."

"Remarkable," Bernard replied.

Slivers hadn't smiled and Rossie wondered if Bernard would have caught a slap alongside the head if Katrina hadn't come down off the railway car at that moment, her hair tucked under a gray woolen beret. She stood close and Rossie looked away like a child but felt her watching, as she would through all these doings.

"You," Katrina said, reaching to Rossie as if no one else was there. Her grip was sure and fierce. "You," she said again. "Put your arms around me." Her perfume was lilac and citrus, and her softening features were not girlish anymore but broad and snowy pale. "On the cheek, there, like my child." Rossie was abruptly engulfed, eyes tearing, until she pushed him back and whispered, "Fine." She smiled. "You look healthy." Then she was taking Mattie by the hand and pulling her forward. "Her," she said. "You remember her."

"Hard to forget," Rossie said.

Mattie gave him a quick, big-toothed smile before pulling her hand away from Katrina. Nito had emerged from the Pullman bareheaded but wrapped in a long, black coat in which he posed, turning to show off. "Alpaca from Peru. I won it, jacks high, just for this trip. Cards can be a solution." His thin hands were strong as ever when he shook with Rossie, who noticed him eyeing the white, straw Panama hat that he had worn, despite the snow, to honor his father. "Kiss me on each cheek," Nito said, laughing. "Twice, like the European you turned out to be."

Bernard took Katrina's hand and raised it to kiss but not quite, then turned to grasp

Nito's while Slivers rested one of his huge hands on Rossie's shoulder. "If we don't land on our feet like a pack of cats," he said. "My father's older brother, Little Jamison they called him, come up here hunting gold before nineteen hundred. He said this Bitterroot Valley was the best horse country he'd ever seen."

The snowfall persisted, dry flakes drifting in the stillness.

Katrina and Nito were traveling in the Buick with Rossie and Bernard.

Slivers and Mattie, who would ride with Leonard Three Boy and Arnold when the Chicago train arrived, waved farewell to the Benascos once they had loaded their luggage into the Buick. "I got dealings in this town," Slivers said. "There's a man might show me a horse. I might rent a tuxedo."

On the highway, Nito reared around in his seat and spoke to Rossie, who was in back with Katrina. "This Bernard," he said, speaking as if Bernard were not beside him. "He's a man for horses, is he?"

"Race horses." This was maybe the first joke Rossie had ever shared with his father. "He tells me about going down to the Kentucky Derby but he never owned purebreds. That Bernard says he likes the idea of owning one."

"Or two," Bernard said.

"Seeing them run," Nito said, "would do us good."

Katrina had been crouched forward, looking out to the snowy world, but now she sighed and sat back. "You," she said to Rossie. "Look to me. This is all right, I see it. You're with good people and you'll amount to something."

"You told me — I was listening — not to break my heart. You said amounting up was a worry that could break your heart."

"That was for then. You're going to be a man with a wife."

"Anyhow, Eliza does the worrying."

"Nevada, the way you were going, amounted to idiocy."

"Horses is no idiocy," he said, and wished he'd let it go.

"Idiocy. For a boy without schooling."

"At least he made his way to us," Bernard said after a long moment.

At the house, Betty came out with a tray of steaming whiskey drinks. The adults gathered around Lemma, just in from a walk in the snowy meadows and got up in a canvas coat, a man's brown fedora, and black, buckled galoshes. Her eyes shone. "Good fortune," she said, "on our doorstep."

Bernard had Rossie's parents in his study looking at *Krazy Kat* when the other travelers arrived in the Model A. They went down to gather in the snow again, and this time it was Arnold who produced a flask of brandy. "Bless Leonard," he said. "He wouldn't take a sip. So now there's enough to pass around."

Slivers said, after his pull on the flask, "This much snow is an excuse for anything."

Arnold handed the brandy to Rossie. "Slivers tells me he's to blame for you."

"Not entirely," Katrina said.

Eliza appeared with the baby fresh from a nap, and held him so his face could be seen amid the flannel blankets. "Teddy," she said, after he'd been inspected. "Teddy Blue. He's named for a trail-herding cowboy."

"You don't know how lucky you was," Slivers said to Rossie. "Trail driving is at its end. You caught the last. It's gone to railroads."

"The young men might trail drive our boxes and suitcases down the hall to our rooms," Arnold said. "They could get on with that while Mr. Flynn and I get inside and warm up."

When Rossie and Leonard finished their muscling, they found the others around the table in the dining room, helping themselves to a late-lunch spread of lamb stew and bowls of chopped condiments — a Basque recipe Betty had prepared in Nito's honor.

"Arnold kissed me," Lemma said to Rossie. "Do you think he's softening?"

"Could be he's in love."

"Ought to be," Bernard said. "Considering the way he's treated around here."

Mattie finished up eating and went outside to roll a cigarette.

"Did you talk to her?" Eliza asked Rossie, who rolled his eyes. "You go do it. I mean you."

Rossie shuffled out to stand in the snow behind Mattie, who was staring away toward gray light in the timber. She was bareheaded, and snow had already nestled into little piles among the pinned-up redness of her hair. "They smoke in that house," he said.

"There's a baby," she said. She didn't look at him.

"What do you think of this country?" Rossie said.

"Too soon to tell."

Eliza had come out, closing the door behind her. "So Mattie," she said. "This thing in my arms is Teddy Blue."

Mattie flipped her cigarette into the snow and stepped forward. Her eyes, to Rossie's

383

surprise, had gone wide.

"We call him Teddy," Eliza said. "Rossie wanted to call him Blue but we put a stop to that. Take him." Eliza held the bundled-up baby out to Mattie.

"Wish he was mine,' Mattie said.

Eliza turned the blanket over the baby's face to keep away the snow. "You'll have yours. While you're here, we can play like he's yours."

"You might never lose me," Mattie whispered.

Nito and Katrina — Lemma called them "the family" — were in a bedroom suite off the back hallway, sharing a blue-tiled bathroom with Mattie. Slivers and Leonard would sleep in the bunkhouse, and Arnold had the bedroom where he'd lived during the summer — "with private facilities," he attested, "as older men require them."

"I'll be down in the bunkhouse with you," Rossie told Slivers.

"Not for long," Lemma said. "Not that you've ever been, really?" She smiled to clear away any misapprehension. "Another drink for everyone," she said to the silence that followed. "Then we take a rest. There will be chaos soon enough."

"When we're done with resting, dinner at

eight," Bernard said. "Promptly," Lemma added, "or Betty will kill us."

"What I'm looking for is my bed," Slivers said. "Spent my night looking out the window on that train."

Katrina caught Rossie by the arm. "Before you lead Mr. Flynn away, your father and I want to see you for a moment. Privately." She didn't smile.

"You and us," Nito said.

Rossie led them to the bedroom that was to be theirs, and Katrina took a tiny box from her purse. "The ring," she said. "Gertrude's, your great-grandmother's wedding ring, from Sweden."

Katrina had always kept it in a box in her bedroom, one of her treasures, plain gold, his great-grandmother's worn name etched inside.

"You sure about this?" Rossie asked. They had talked about the ring on the telephone.

"You're the only child we'll have," she said. "What do you mean, are we sure? Of course we're sure." She studied him, eyes glowing, then opened the tiny box, and held it out to him. "It's yours," she said, blinking away tears, "for ever, for Eliza."

Rossie had to look away. This was so important to her and meant so little to him. "Let's hope for sweet, holy times." Nito, too, was looking away.

Back in the living room, Slivers had a tall drink in his hand. "You want to finish that?" Rossie asked.

"The world's made of drinks," Slivers said. "Let's find that bunkhouse."

"There was a fellow called himself a cowhand but he's gone," Rossie explained as they walked down through the snow. "An Irish gardener they've got cleaning stalls in the milking barns this winter, and a cook, sorry old bastard, and me. Crowd of pensioners, nobody you'd hire."

"Never know who you'll hire," Slivers said. "I hired you. Get me up for dinner."

When Rossie knocked, he found Slivers sharpening a long-bladed cowman knife in the light of a kerosene lantern. "Staying quiet." He pocketed the knife and his whetstone. "They got hot water? I got to shave." He hung his shirt on the back of a battered ladder-back chair and carried his worn leather pouch of gear to the washroom. Rossie sat on the edge of the bathtub and watched him lather up before the only mirror and strop his straight razor on the leather strap that hung there. His body was knobby, with knots of muscle and bone under the milk-white flesh.

"I got a knife that belongs to you," Rossie

said. "Mattie stole it and give it to me when I was leaving."

"She told me that, said it was foolishness. But it was fine so far as I was concerned, if somebody would want an old knife of mine."

"I still got it, if you ever want it back."

"Don't think so," Slivers said, and he got down to his shaving.

For dinner there were the linen napkins in silver rings; fluted crystal glasses; white candles; heavy plain china; and two kinds of chicken, baked and southern fried; an oyster soufflé; wine from bottles with French labels; canned spinach with shredded almonds; Italian pasta salad; hearty bread; bowls of mashed yellow potatoes; and a sauce of morel mushrooms that had been gathered from the creek banks in late spring and dried.

"Betty, you're our genius," Arnold said, confronted with huckleberry and strawberry-rhubarb pies and vanilla ice cream with various sauces. When the sweets were gone, as they sat over cups of European coffee, Mattie tilted her head to the side to study Rossie from across the table. "So, Mr. Buckaroo," she said in a voice that was abruptly loud and outgoing, "what did you learn with your horse chasing? I'd like to try it myself."

Rossie sipped his coffee. "She's a big country," he said, trying a grin before looking up directly at her. "Thought you was never going to need another pair of gloves."

Mattie regarded him with long hesitation. "I got over that idea. Guess I'll always be a big old woman with gloves."

Nito, posed at the far end of the table from Bernard, tapped his wine glass with a spoon. "There was more to it than country," he said.

"I met people who show up in my dreams," Rossie said. "Fellow named Bob Waters got me to buy the rifle. Clear as hell, I see him gutting a mule deer, in a deer I shot, teaching me to butcher. He baked meat pie in a Dutch oven, though he never showed me how to do that. I dream about a fellow name of Bill Sweet, who busted his leg bone out through the skin trying to ride a bucking horse. White bone showing in the blood. It's like dreaming right now, getting married, sitting around with you, here at this table in Montana."

"No more martinis," Arnold said.

"See there," Mattie said, looking down the table to Slivers. "If he can make it, I could move to Reno, or come to Montana, or do anything he can do."

"You dream about people and they know tricks," Rossie said. "Like Nito."

His father lifted his hands in a protest of innocence.

"And now," Arnold said, "we'll move to the ridiculous. I'll take over as the fool. Rossie and Leonard could bring my crates to the living room. I'll need a claw hammer."

Bernard produced the hammer and Arnold began taking apart his home-built wooden boxes, each of which held framed photographs wrapped in newspaper.

"But first," he said, "where's Eliza?"

"She'll be along when the baby is down," Lemma said just as Eliza came from the back of the house in a dark-reddish dress, her hair up to show the back of her neck. "Eliza, milky and maternal, wishing she felt handsome."

Arnold began stripping the newsprint from around his "very magic" photograph of Eliza and Rossie in sharp focus and the sow grizzly with her cubs superimposed dimly behind them. She was rearing, her jaws open like the mouth of a phantom before a feather of forest in the distance.

"Spectacular," Lemma said.

"About to get ate up," Rossie said.

"Dazzling," Lemma cooed.

"Arnold?" Bernard finally asked. "The other crate?"

"This is for Lemma." Arnold peeled back newsprint to reveal a framed photo of Bernard sleeping on his leather couch — in his study — an aging man curled like a baby and a book splayed open on the floor.

"And this," Arnold said, tearing newsprint from another photograph, "is for Eliza."

Lemma coughed when it was entirely there before them. "Do you despise us so entirely?" she said softly. "But never mind. Keep quiet. I understand but nevertheless feel betrayed. Bernard will oversee the rest of your evening." She turned to leave, pausing in front of Arnold. "Don't you say a thing."

"Well," Bernard said, smiling when she was gone. "Our hostess has retired. Isn't this the real item?"

The photograph was framed in scratched, rusting steel. It was Charlie Cooper with long hair woven into a braid that hung over his shoulder. His powerful hands grasped at the black prison bars and his features stood sharp and hard in silvery light. He was looking beyond the camera, half-smiling.

"How did you get him to pose?" Bernard asked.

"I got off the train on my way to Chicago

and went to Deer Lodge Prison. He said he'd let me take his picture if I cut off a finger. I told him no, I won't cut off a finger, it's for Eliza. He laughed and asked for thirty dollars. It seemed a reasonable fee."

"He's like a ghost," Eliza said.

"For those who don't understand Lemma's consternation, this man is the father of Eliza's child. He's in Deer Lodge Penitentiary. He didn't," Bernard said, sighing, playing at regret, "go by the rules."

Slivers Flynn eased away from the table and was shrugging into his coat, getting ready to make the walk down to the bunkhouse. "What I forgot," he said, "is a night's sleep."

"One more drink?" Arnold offered.

"Feel like I'm drunk already," Slivers said.

When Rossie carried the steel-framed photo to Eliza's room, she lifted her sleeping baby from the crib. "There, Mister Teddy," she whispered. "The man in that picture is your father. Don't you forget."

"You're early," Betty said when Rossie, Leonard, and Slivers trooped up from the bunkhouse for breakfast. The snowfall had blown by and the morning sky shone with thin, frigid brightness. The kitchen table was set, and Betty was pouring pancake batter on the hot grill, cracking eggs by the time they were out of their coats.

"We're not going to eat that bunkhouse cooking," Slivers said. "Not if you're feeding us up here."

Mattie came out in woolly sheepskin slippers and a rose-colored housedress, her red hair in a swirling knot at the back of her head.

"Damn," Slivers said. "You're a beauty for breakfast."

"Eliza loaned me this dress and did my hair for me, just now." She smiled in her old green-eyed, unclouded way, and shrugged. "You and me," she said to Rossie, "we might as well make it up. That's why I come, to swallow my pride. But I don't eat any shit."

"Tell you what, kid," Slivers said to Rossie. "Might as well give up. They got you surrounded."

"There, that's settled," Betty said after a moment, splattering more eggs on the grill. "While you're waiting on me, have a look at Arnold's photograph of Eliza and Rossie in its place on the living room wall. After midnight I could hear them, Bernard and Arnold and Lemma. They were laughing and drunk."

"You know everything that goes on in this

house?" Slivers asked. "Most of it," she said, leaving Rossie to wonder how often she'd heard him making his midnight way to Eliza's rooms from the bunkhouse.

They stood before the lighted photograph. Slivers put a hand on Rossie's shoulder as he always had. "The bear buckaroo. Wonder where they hung up that other fellow?"

"In Eliza's room, under the bed."

Mattie studied Rossie with distant good humor. "Isn't that something? Your rival's under your own bed."

As if a signal had passed, and it had, Slivers turned back to the kitchen, leaving Mattie and Rossie with the picture.

"You wait a minute," Mattie said. "I won't bite."

"You might knock me out," Rossie said. "You done being pissed off?"

"Heart broke, not all the way healed but curing. No use staying heartbroke. Slivers told me that when my mother died. Oscar was trying to get under my bed, you know. He come home saying you were took up with Bobby Cahill's wife. Who'd believe that crock of shit from Oscar?"

"Malinda? What do you call it? We was friends. That's what you'd call it." Rossie shrugged as Mattie rolled her eyes. "But Oscar, he's working for Slivers?"

"He sold that Packard and might be drunk in town right now," Mattie said. "That's part of why I come up here, to get away from him."

"What's the other part?"

"See you walk the plank, selling your ass. That girl is going to eat you alive, balls and all."

"I saw some things, I paid attention to what it means to be your own man with nobody around but other men. It feels like living in a cardboard box with no way out until a woman shows up. There was my mother and there was you and now there's Eliza and even her mother."

"Sweet thing for you. So long as you got a woman waiting someplace, you can just ride away. But it can work the other way, too. Wouldn't a woman feel happy on the road if some man was waiting? Women can ride. And her mother? She's hot for you. She'll be humped up under you in some hiding-hole if you don't watch out."

"Shit," Rossie said. "Cut it out." He glared at her, took a long breath, and licked his lips. "What I want is not fighting you before it gets started. These people like to have their own way. They're spoiled by being rich, but I won't ride away. There's damned few people trying to be bad. Don't know I ever saw one. Did you ever think you were trying to be bad?"

"You're believing your own bullshit. But you're right. Most people just want somebody to kiss their ass. That's your job."

"Goddammit, why don't you kiss my ass?"

Mattie smiled. "I had enough of that. So you might as well get off your high horse."

"The two of you," Betty called from the kitchen, "get in here or forget breakfast." Slivers was finished with his easy-over eggs on top of pancakes with maple syrup but had stayed on to talk cow prices with Bernard, who himself looked the worse for wear and hungover as he waited for his own breakfast.

"Jap Hardy said you could work for him anywhere," Slivers said to Rossie. "Tarz spent three months in San Francisco, trying to get work on the docks to earn pocket money for moving to Australia. Don't know where them boys get their ideas." This was Slivers, gossiping to Rossie like he was a man.

"Tarz is another one I dream about," Rossie said. "Hear you had Oscar working."

"Oscar can't stop talking some bullshit or another. Makes you want to skip dinner if he's going to be there." He changed the topic to Dufferena. "Did you get paid up?"

"Right in Calgary."

"Lucky thing. The old man died in September. Hotel outside Sacramento. His relatives never yet found where he kept most of his money. One too many secrets." Slivers smiled as Betty refilled his coffee cup and set poached eggs on toast in front of Bernard. "But Bernard, here, is going to show us dairy-cow secrets. Nito and me and you are going to take a ride with him. We're going to walk through cow barns."

Eventually the men piled into the Buick, and Bernard negotiated the roads. Unlike the dry cold outside, the milking barns were warm and rank as they walked the long cement aisles.

"It's like the crap tables at the Riverside," Nito said. "Cows in their stalls."

"Them fellows come down here every morning?" Slivers asked, gesturing at one of the men sweeping up. "Before daylight? For milking?" He shook his head as if there was no explaining the docility of some men.

Back in the Buick, a half mile up the road, they came up on horseback travelers, a man and woman with ice hanging from their eyebrows despite silk stockings tied over their ears and towels wrapped around their chins for warmth. They were breathing out clouds like spooks, and Rossie nearly missed seeing who it was as Bernard eased the Buick past them. "Christ almighty," he said. "Hold it." He lurched out of the Buick to stand in the snow, and shouted to them, "Where are you going? You come down off that horse!"

The man swung his right leg high, spun out of his saddle and landed running and staggering. He dived and tackled Rossie like some raggedy football player, and both of them tumbled down in the snow, wrestling before escaping each other to sit there grinning.

"Should have bit your nose off," Rossie said.

"Why not?" the other fellow said. "You been in that Buick, warm as toast. We been out here toughing the cold."

When the two of them were on their feet, Rossie hobbled over to the men in the Buick. "This here is trouble."

It was Bill Sweet and Margie. They'd been three days coming south from Charlo, melting snow for drinking water, eating alongside campfires and sleeping in the bedroll strapped to the back of Bill Sweet's saddle. "Talk in the Flathead," he said, "is that you're marrying a rich girl. Didn't figure you'd want us to miss out."

"Couldn't stand it if you missed anything," Rossie said. "Keep on up the road, I'll be waiting for you. Plenty of room in the bunkhouse. The old man there can cook you some food. Big table up the hill for dinner tonight."

"We'll eat," Bill Sweet said, "and thaw out. You come get us up for that dinner."

"There's more for supper," Rossie said when he was back in the Buick.

"Quite startling," Bernard said. "This fellow, how do you explain him?"

"Don't think I have to explain him. He just came riding in. He's got his girlfriend with him. Can't run them off in this snow. They're wandering Arkies out of the Ozarks. She's a fine girl, that's what she is." He tried a grin on Bernard. "See what you got yourself into with me. Running with riff-raff."

"Bernard, they sound like renegade Scots," Lemma said, after finding there would be two more for dinner. "Your people."

"Not quite the right tribe," Bernard said. "But close. Lowland Scots, the Lord's fearless avengers."

The outdoor temperature was near zero and falling in the twilight, sending Lemma into a fuss over icy roads that could foil the night's dress-up dinner party. But her special guests, a banker driving up from Hamilton and Bernard's urologist coming all the way from Missoula, arrived on time with their wives. The smooth-faced banker introduced himself as Lefty, and his wife, whose steel-colored hair was cut short as a man's, went by Quint. As Bernard introduced his doctor, Steven Fullerman, and his lean, quiet wife, Sara, to the other guests, Rossie led Bill Sweet and Margie in from the bunkhouse, both of them raggedy but scrubbed.

"You mean sweetheart?" Nito said when Bill Sweet referred to Margie as his pal. "She's your sweetheart?" He was dressed in a double-breasted black jacket with brass buttons, and had commenced demonstrating trick shuffles for Bernard and a bearded, shockingly blue-eyed fellow named Mr. Davidson, the manager of Bernard's milking barns. "Pick a card, any card," he commanded Bill Sweet. "Put it in the deck, cut the deck." After riffling the deck twice in a careless way, he cut it himself. "Is this your card, buried between two aces?"

"Shit," Bill Sweet said. "I'll be fucked."

The banker's wife, Quint, snorted and rolled her eyes. "No doubt," she said.

Nito smiled at Margie. "He will be indeed

fucked if he plays cards with people like me. Entirely fucked."

"By God, I'll shake your hand," Bill Sweet said to Nito, "if old Rossie comes out of your house."

"Gamblers never shake hands. But just now, for Rossie's sake."

"Here's the man who owns the place," Rossie told Bill Sweet once that ritual was done with. "This is Mr. Bernard Stevenson. And Mr. Davidson, who runs the dairy barns."

"You a ranch hand?" Davidson asked Bill Sweet.

"Not any sort of working hand. Just a buckaroo."

As Davidson frowned at this, Lemma and Katrina entered the room, both in high-shouldered gray dresses of almost identical make, but Katrina wore a single string of pearls. "The women," Bernard said.

"With Rossie's compadres from Charlo we had thirteen," Lemma said, once the introductions had been run. "So Mr. Davidson was a fortunate addition."

"Do you believe in that?" Mattie asked her. "Thirteen?"

"Not for a minute, but there's Bernard to think about."

"I'm scientific," Bernard explained. "But

why tempt demons?"

"You could tempt me," Arnold said, "with a drink."

"Compadres? What do you think of that?" Bill Sweet patted Rossie's back.

Bernard had crossed the room toward the bottles. "Your people are Scotch?"

"Way back, seventy, eighty years ago they come to Carolina."

"I saw it in you. So the first toast is to you. My grandfather came to Carolina in those years."

"Runaways," Bill Sweet said. "Runaways for hundreds of years. That's where I get it. They run to Arkansas, and here I am in Montana."

"The Scottish soul loves independence. Scots flock to Montana because they despise restriction."

"They don't listen to nobody's sheriff," Bill Sweet said. Arnold interrupted this exchange to announce that he was going back to Europe, "where they're listening to too many sheriffs." Italy had been fascist for more than a decade, and in Spain the liberal government was in collapse. "Mr. Hitler plays on fury like a violin. He's backed with cash from Krupp and Ford and has convinced the Germans that his leadership is the solution to their problems. A European war is inevitable."

Resting back on the couch, Mr. Davidson cleared his throat. "Good, clean work," he said, "that's the solution." He folded his huge hands and smiled.

"You think it's that serious?" the banker asked Arnold. "I'm a city man," Arnold replied, "off to photograph the end of cities."

"How to help anyone?" the banker muttered.

"Trainload of canned goods?" Slivers offered. "Or cashier's checks?"

Quint gave off a laugh that echoed like a bark. "Lemma," she said, "I like your people."

Slivers ignored that. "You think it's war?"

Arnold nodded. "To end wars."

"Last war," Slivers said, "there was men like me thought they were pissing their lives away. Lot of us boys in France."

"Would you say," Bernard asked of Slivers, "that it's never simply a matter of honor?"

"That's talk for the newspapers. The real thing is staying upright. I was one of them boys in France. We knew who'd been tricked. It was us. We were scared shitless."

"Do you worry that American politics are so countrified and isolated?" Arnold asked incredulously. "Six months ago Hitler assassinated his opposition and established himself as dictator. And here we are, in this forgotten valley, walled in by mountains. This house is a castle. It seems to be in the world, but it's not. Bernard must feel like an anthropologist at the edge of things."

"Basques are going back to Spain," Nito said. "Men who have never seen Spain. They say war is coming, for Basque independence. I say I'm no warrior, and they say what of pride? I say forget pride. I'm too old."

"In San Francisco," Eliza said, "I thought pride might kill me."

Margie interrupted, loud and flushed. "People saying somebody like me shouldn't have babies."

"You should have all the babies you can cook up," Slivers said.

"Malinda Cahill told me to be my own daddy," Rossie said, looking across to Slivers. "Bobby Cahill's wife."

"Malinda." Slivers chuckled. "Around Malinda, in my day, you would sure as hell want to be your own daddy."

"So much for the topic of international power," Lemma observed. "Women's work lies in making men behave."

Quint snorted again.

"It's true," Bernard said. "A man with a good, hardheaded woman lives longer."

"If she don't always piss him off," Slivers said. "I might of married Malinda if she wasn't running the bars. But you couldn't get me back to war with a shotgun at my head, and Malinda looked like war." He shook his head as if he'd been transported elsewhere. "You sit in one of their trenches trying to eat what they give you, and there's a hand with maggots buried in the mud next to where you're sitting. That's what breakfast you get. War is tricking yourself." He turned to Arnold. "That Indian fellow over in the penitentiary has tricked himself."

"We don't want to be criminals," the banker said. "We want to be successful. There's not much difference, but there's some."

"Once they got you, they sure as hell got you." Slivers looked at Rossie. "There's a hard time coming home from mistreatment like that fellow will see in prison."

"Mistreatment," Rossie repeated. It wasn't the kind of word Slivers ever said.

" 'Never glad confident morning again,' " Lemma said. "That's Browning. Robert Browning."

"Robert Browning, lost in Montana," Arnold said.

Margie had her own take. "Niceness won't get nobody across the street."

"All this deploring, while we wait to have our dinner served by hired ladies in this house in Montana." Lemma shook her head as if to accept defeat, while the urologist and his wife went on smiling and smiling.

Nito lifted his drink. "A toast to facing up. To my son Rossie and Eliza and her new boy, Mr. Teddy Blue, and to good fortune for everyone of us here, forever."

After dinner, Bernard played slow jazz and they all but Mr. Davidson danced. As the guests were gathering their coats and buckling their galoshes, preparing to leave, the telephone rang and Lemma called them upstairs to crowd transfixed before Bernard's great expanse of window overlooking the valley. Far off in the darkness out there, on other properties, a barn was burning, the brief, enormous torch of it reflecting off the snow and lighting the undersides of clouds.

"Worst thing there is," Slivers said.

"For our party," Lemma said. "Melodrama." Already those flames were dying.

"Jesus, Lady!"

"What?" she said. "Jesus what?"

"Jesus or somebody," Slivers said, "should light your ass afire if you thinks that's make-believe." Then he smiled like what he'd said might be a joke, like it might have been the whiskey talking, it could be taken that way, and they all, exclaiming and semidrunk, trooped back downstairs to their leavetaking.

At breakfast Betty announced that six horses in that barn had died screaming, and that the blaze was rumored to be arson.

The Presbyterian minister from Missoula, the good Scottish Dr. MacLean, called to say he was in bed with influenza and could not perform the wedding on the day before Christmas.

"Very sad," Bernard said. "A defeat. But you'll meet him next summer. His eldest son stands fire lookout out of Missoula. They're legendary walkers and fishermen, two brothers and the father."

"Fishers of souls," Arnold said.

"Never mind the scoffing, I'm talking about American Scots, extraordinary individuals. But in any event we've found another Presbyterian, this one from Hamilton."

Hothouse flowers arrived from Missoula just after a late breakfast, among them white chrysanthemums bundled with green ferns for the living room and corsages of orchids for the women, each to wear a color that matched her dress. Once these had been distributed and arranged, Rossie and Bill Sweet, who was to be the best man, were sent off to the bunkhouse.

"Your father will come for you," Katrina said. "He will knot your necktie. Mr. Sweet will keep you company."

When Nito came, Rossie was in his Brooks Brothers coat from Chicago. Nito expertly flipped through the perfect tying of his necktie. "The final mile," he said. "Look around." He led Rossie and Bill Sweet up through the snow toward the big house. "Your last sight of the free world."

Bill Sweet was smirking. "You could make a break for it. We could say you got away in the timber."

Slivers Flynn and Arnold, both in brown tweed jackets, were lurking in the depths of the living room, amid the flowers. "Wore this when I got married," Slivers said to Rossie. "Hope it brings you more luck than it did me." Pastor Durant, a small man with octagonal eyeglasses, arrived precisely at noon. Nito opened the door and stood back.

"Mr. Benison?" the minister said.

"He means you," Nito said to Rossie. "Tell him your name is Benasco. Shake his hand."

Wooden folding chairs were arranged in a

semicircle, and Lemma swept in wearing a dark-velvet dress cut on the bias, followed by Katrina in crimson brocade. Talking, laughing, they ignored the men. Mattie, in a rose dress with a slit up one side that showed her legs, looked at no one and sat at the end of the row with the older women. Once everyone was present, the minister summoned Rossie and Bill Sweet, who was carrying Great-Grandmother Gertrude's ring. Eliza appeared at the far end of the room, her black hair stacked on her head and held in place by pins that matched her silvery dress. Betty, in her blue suit and a white blouse with a man's necktie, played a recording of "The Wedding March" on Bernard's Victrola.

Eliza took Bernard's arm, and on they came. The minister smiled and said words about Christian charity that Rossie, then Eliza, repeated after him. Bill Sweet passed Rossie the ring, which he slipped onto Eliza's slim finger.

"Children," the minister said. "You are man and wife. God cherish you."

Eliza's lips were cold, and Rossie wondered if she could be frightened. He felt Nito grip his shoulder. He kissed his weeping mother's cheek and ducked his eyes away from Mattie, who watched from across the room. Margie offered her cheek but not Betty. She stood back, eyes alert as if daring him.

As the skies lowered to a late, cloudy afternoon, Lemma called for attention. "We're adjourning to the Tailfeather Field," she announced, and she sent Bernard and Leonard to warm up the Buick and the Model A. "Get into your boots," she said. "Attendance is mandatory." They made the trip easy enough with women sitting on laps and hooting with laughter. Mattie had gone down ahead of them to swing open the hardwood doors to the brickwork barn.

"Inside," she said, "we got a surprise present."

Sure enough, in the first cork-floored stall stood a four-year-old bay mare, one of those strong-necked Morgan crossbreds with delicate legs and a diamond-shaped splash of white on her forehead. She eyed Rossie and Eliza in an appraising way as they moved into the stall to touch her.

"Got a horse," Rossie said. "If that ain't something."

"And a wife," Katrina said, "and a child."

"I come down just to sit with her," Mattie said.

Slivers had gone to Bobby Cahill, picked the mare, negotiated the purchase price, and arranged railroad transportation to Montana.

"She's quick as a big cat," he said. "I rode her into that herd of steers Bobby keeps. Cut 'em apart like hot butter. She's the real thing."

"We brought her down from Missoula in a padded trailer towed by a creamery truck," Bernard explained.

Slivers brushed his hard right hand on the mare's withers. "Malinda wanted to know if you'd been up to the old Railroad Tavern. She's dead sure that she can get Bobby up here for a visit, now that you got one of his mares in the Bitterroot."

"Why not?" Bernard said. "Railroads run."

"That's more horse than I ever owned," Slivers said.

Bill Sweet was standing back between Margie and Mattie. "You going to breed her?" he asked. "You going to be selling horses?"

"Sure am," Rossie said.

"I'm wide-eyed," Sweet said. "You need a man, you call on me." Mattie faked a little punch at Bill Sweet's shoulder. "You and me."

"Don't you touch him," Margie said, but she was smiling.

Rossie led the mare out into the snow,

improvised a set of reins with a halter rope, and swung up to ride her bareback. She stood for it until Rossie nudged her with his heels, then stepped off into a canter, throwing dry snow behind her as he took her through a long figure eight across the meadow, turning her with a touch on the neck. Back to the barn, he slid down to stand with his hand on her withers.

"Horses," Slivers said, "they like doing things, learning a trick like those loops in the snow. Go to horses with no rush but no fucking around, that's the deal."

"Sanity in motion," Bernard said. "What will you name her?"

"Well," Rossie said, "I can't call her Bernard. What I need to do is say thanks." Rossie had the urge to stay with that mare until she got used to him and he said so. "I feel like moving in with her and seeing her sleep."

"Never mind," Eliza said. "You can watch me sleep."

"She's probably got a name, but I'm going to call her Katrina." He'd surprised himself for ancient and unknown reasons. He lifted his hand. "This makes me think to cry. So that's thank you. These horses, them and Eliza are my hill to climb. There it is."

"You take care of this luck," Slivers said.

"It would make us feel good to see it."

Up in the big house, Nito proposed the first toast. "My son and our new daughter, enjoy what you are, not what you ought to be."

Bernard put a jazzy drift of Beiderbecke on his Victrola, and Rossie danced two-step with Eliza until Bernard cut in. Lemma brought Rossie a martini mixed by Nito, who in turn asked Mattie to dance. Bill Sweet and Margie awkwardly tried it while Slivers looped in waltzing circles with Katrina. Lemma announced she was jealous, that she'd had her eye on Slivers, and asked Rossie to dance. Nito led Mattie to them, laid his hands on their shoulders, and all together they swept around the room in long turns.

Rossie offered a toast to the country girl beside the Snake River and her uncle Jamsie playing "The Cowboy's Lament" on his banjo, and to the blind Hawaiian guitarist who had shut up the raggedy men idling away beside the Clark Fork River. "Such musics," he said. Eliza said this was the start of an answer, though she didn't know what the question was, and Nito said they should get back to dancing.

In Eliza's room, on a bedside table at his side of the bed, Rossie found two new books inscribed to "My Husband": Walter Prescott Webb's *The Great Plains* and a trail drive book about going to Montana called *Log of a Cowboy,* by a man named Andy Adams. His wife looked up from the baby, whom she was tucking away. "These will start your schooling."

"I can think of something else."

"We got away with it, didn't we?"

Eventually Rossie lay back on his side of the bed and peered out the windows. His bedroll, brought all this way from Nevada, was rolled up and stored, his shirts were hung on a special pole in her closet, his underclothes folded into one of her dresser drawers. "Guess you got me," he said.

"You got yourself. You did the getting."

Mattie was there before him, up bareback on the mare with a snaffle-bit bridle, easing off into the snowy Tailfeather Field. Daylight came bluish and faint in the shadows of willow and cottonwood beyond the far fence. When she saw Rossie coming, Mattie nudged the mare with her heels and they were gone, her brush of red braid flying out in tandem with a haze of snow behind hooves as they plunged off into another galloping circumference. Rossie stood a long moment, watching, then walked slowly out toward the snowy center of the field and stood quiet until Mattie, laughing and crazy-eyed, slid the mare up to an icy stop.

"Me and her," she said, sliding down, "we're pals. We know the score on you."

"Give me them bridle reins." Rossie's voice was level, like he was speaking to a child.

"Sure, any time. She's yours. But I can still get your goat and I'll stick with Nevada. These people got you bought. You'll get enough and you'll come home. See you there."

After dinner, Lemma insisted on sharing a passage with them. *There is a coherence in things,* she said, reading from a book, *a stability; something is immune from change, and shines out. Of such moments the thing is made that endures.* She looked up from the page. "Virginia Woolf." She had been re-reading *To the Lighthouse* after being re-minded of it when she saw their party reflected in windows while dancing the night before. So she claimed.

"The lighthouse," Bernard said, "was built by the Stevenson family."

"Reflected in our windows, the thing that endures."

Leonard Three Boy told a story of a wife vanishing from an encampment on the grassland Plains only to be found years later running with a herd of wild horses led by a black stallion. Captured, the woman said the stallion was her husband, that she was a horse, and her children horses. After they were released, the wild horses ran to freedom in a dust cloud of their own making, with the woman in the lead. "Eliza, running with horses."

"Aristophanes," Arnold said. "The women run away."

Lemma hooted. "Aristophanes?" She pointed a finger at Arnold like a pistol and pulled a make-believe trigger. "Bang."

Arnold turned to Rossie. "You could come away with me. Long ago, the French siege at Saragossa failed and they went for home. The Basque ambushed them in a pass through the Pyrenees. So began the *Song of Roland,* the song of great deeds." He went on about traditions of heroism that began with the tale of that battle. "Basques! *The Chanson de Rossie.*"

"He might come home unmarried," Eliza said.

"Or dead," Nito said, careful to speak slowly and precisely. "Pride, I'm thinking, is another thing from war and revenge. My wife takes pride in gardening and her house. I cheat no one at cards although I could.

415

That's my pride."

"When word comes," Lemma said to Arnold, "that you died in Spain, I'll walk out in the garden and moan, and think I should cut off a finger. In Paris, after your war, in the Brasserie Lipp with French cigarettes, I'll eat Bélon oysters and toast your memory with wines that cost fifty dollars a bottle. Maybe you'll be there."

"Everyone is failing her," Eliza said afterward, in their bedroom. "Arnold is leaving, forever. Bernard's preoccupied with dying. There's just you and me. She may turn cruel as a cat."

Bernard collapsed at breakfast. Nito and Katrina and Slivers and Mattie were packed up, getting ready for the drive to the Northern Pacific Railway in Missoula, when Bernard moaned and slipped from his chair. His plate rattled onto the floor, splattering pancakes and maple syrup. Rossie got him under the arms and dragged him down the hall to the bedroom where Lemma was still curled under a down comforter.

She sat up in a plain, flannel gown, vividly alert as Rossie eased Bernard onto the bed beside her. "He's dead," she said. "Is he dead?"

"He's breathing. He's just out." As Bernard stirred and muttered, Lemma scurried into the bathroom and emerged prying at the top of a small, rattling vial of pills. Bernard shook his head, his eyes frantic. Sweating and slick-faced, he kept his lips clamped shut when Lemma brought a glass of water.

"Open up," she said. When he refused, she turned to Rossie. "Blood-pressure pills. He must have forgotten."

"What do you think?" Rossie said to him. "Those pills cause the fainting?"

Bernard nodded. "Fainting, utterly," he murmured.

Slivers came into the doorway. "Mop off his face," he said, bending over Bernard. "Any pain?"

"Nothing," Bernard muttered. His color was coming back. "Too much Scotch whiskey, and them pills," Slivers said. "I never did get much help from pills. But we're staying on. That train runs every day or so."

Steven Fullerman drove down from Missoula that afternoon, unshaved and exhausted, and spent a half hour in the bedroom where Bernard lay quiet and stunned. "The damage report is nil," he said, when he came out. "Signs are vital. He'll survive, unless the depression persists."

"Crazy!" Lemma asked. "He's not crazy?"

"Some give up. Fold their hands and quit.

417

People do."

"Jesus Christ," Rossie said. "He's not crazy. He's tired."

"He needs rest," the doctor said, turning to Betty. "You tend to him and keep them out of that bedroom." When Lemma thanked him for coming so far, the doctor waved her away. "It's my duty."

The rest of the day was leftover lamb stew for lunch and a walk in the snow organized by Arnold in early afternoon. Lemma begged off, saying she had to watch over Bernard. Eliza, Mattie, and Margie drifted off on their own along a trail above Kanaka Creek with the baby while the remaining men — Rossie, Bill Sweet, Nito, Slivers, Leonard, and Arnold, the six of them in coats and gloves, watch caps and rubber galoshes — straggled up the snowy road in a shuffling pack. "Well, young fellows, if it's not Spain, what will it be?" Arnold asked. "Mares and stallions?"

After a moment of no answering, Leonard said he was going back to Alberta. "Accounting work for the reservations."

Slivers rolled and lit a cigarette, looking away as if he wasn't talking to any of them. "Tell you something," he said, then embarked on a life story of gathering cattle off the Nevada deserts in the fall; herding them onto frozen meadows where crews fed them from the haystacks through February; doctoring heifers through a cold, bloody cycle of first births and cutting out two-year-old steers and cull heifers to be shipped on the railroad from Winnemucca to the feed lots in the rice country north of Sacramento; driving dry cows and heifers and the cows with spring-born calves to the deserts in April, followed by purebred bulls to ensure another run of calves the next spring; going out with the wagon to brand on the desert in June and moving the damnable creatures to water when the country dried up in the fall; and, when the snow was about to blow again, gathering off the deserts for another year. "Point is, enough years, and it runs out on you. Same damned things, too many times."

"That's the personal news," Arnold said, "behind my leaving for Europe."

"Keep it in mind," Slivers said, his eyes on Rossie. "Horses is one thing. Tending other people's property is another."

The next morning Bernard was dressed and back into himself, so he claimed, insisting on driving them to the train in Missoula the next day.

"Bernard, for God's sake!" Lemma said.

"Last afternoon I thought about us, and I was sick of your risking yourself."

Slivers clapped a hand on Bernard's shoulder, smiling. "I'm not riding with the likes of you at the wheel."

"You let me do the driving," Bill Sweet said.

"Like hell, I seen you drive," Margie said. "Me, I'll drive."

"Shit, I never seen you drive."

She smiled. "There's plenty you never seen. I was driving my boyfriend's Ford around Riverside when I was fifteen, all over the place since he was a drunk and couldn't be trusted. Not that you are altogether a drunk. But you can't be trusted."

As Rossie gathered Nito and Katrina's suitcases to load for the trip to the railroad, Katrina shut the door to their bedroom. "You wait a minute," she said. "You have to tell me something. This girl, do you love her enough to put up with all this?"

"Suppose so."

"Don't tell me you suppose so. I'm your mother and I'll tell you something. There'll be bad times and there's one solution. You take her into the bedroom and you come out the bedroom door on the other side of what the trouble was. That's how it has to work." Rossie tried ducking away but she wouldn't allow it. "You look at me," she said, "and you look at this bed where your father and I were sleeping."

"Sure deal. You told me, in that letter you sent to Calgary."

"Don't you laugh me off. You remember."

Rossie wondered if his mother truly believed it was possible to fuck your way to happiness, or if she was driven to giving him such opinions in order to explain away the life she had. There was no asking, and he put it from his mind.

Betty came out to see them off. "Spain," she said to Arnold. "I might want to go with you."

Arnold nodded like this was not altogether unexpected news. "You and I, we'll stay in touch."

Whatever mysterious deal they were negotiating lay in the cold air, silencing the others as they finished loading up. Leonard and Margie drove them to Missoula while Bill Sweet stayed behind and did patch-up carpentry on horse stalls in the old barn. Bernard had hired the two of them to live out the winter in the bunkhouse and work for their keep. "Rossie will find your work," he'd said. "You will be his first hired hands."

On the railroad platform, Rossie went over to Slivers. "Mattie and me," he said, "we knew the same things but that was all we knew."

"Shit," Slivers said, and he laid one of those hands on Rossie's shoulder. "Wasn't your fault I run you off. Good thing, anyhow. Cowherding don't go anywhere in the long run."

Katrina took Rossie's hand. "You look at me," she said, "and you remember."

The locomotive engineer blew his steam whistle and the drive wheels ground into motion. "It's over," Lemma said. She was looking off toward the sky over Missoula, smudged by dark smoke from the lumber mills.

"We built a contraption," Eliza said as she and Rossie made ready for bed. "Pulleys and whistles." She offered her irony-will-see-us-through smile.

Rossie knew she was talking about the collection of family. "Your mother, she was fixed on Slivers."

"Her life is her own fault. She went for it."

"That's the way you talk about your mother?"

"Sometimes," Eliza said, staring at herself in the bathroom mirror.

A week later they made a trip to Hamilton

to visit the lawyer and sign the papers deeding the brick barn to Rossie. "A family partnership," Bernard explained to Rossie at breakfast. "It will exist equal in status, if not in the extent of your holdings, with the agreement owned by Lemma and myself."

Ned Henry, a calm, gray-headed man, sat behind a clean desk in an office with hardwood paneling. Once the introductions were over, Eliza and Bernard sat down with her baby beside her in his portable bassinette, and Rossie remained standing with hands on the backs of their chairs.

"If you think of selling this property, if a thing went wrong . . ." Ned Henry bridged his fingers. "If Eliza left for New Zealand, and Mr. Benasco elected to go with her, Bernard and Lemma would have first refusal. They could match any reasonable price if you wanted to sell."

"Don't think it'll be New Zealand," Rossie said. "Anybody, if he was leaving, would just give it back."

"I'm used to Scots," Bernard said. "They're inclined to give nothing back."

"It comes around to what you'd expect. I might ask," Ned Henry said, "how do you see your future in the Bitterroot?"

"Eliza and horses, no milking."

"Horses equal freedom? Eliza means family. Does that add up?"

"Never did the arithmetic," Rossie said.

"Aren't you young to give up so much of your freedom? I was three years in the Far East, Hong Kong and the like, with the merchant marine. I sometimes wonder who I'd be if I'd stayed there, then I wave that thought away. But it isn't nonsense. I sold my life for this law office, the love of my wife and my children, and this community, my work. Without work, we're nothing."

"Rossie's had his runaway," Bernard said. "But that time is over."

"For Rossie, all this may be premature," Ned Henry said.

Bernard stared away at the window and shook his head.

"Rossie is married with a child and responsibilities," Ned Henry said. "He could someday wonder if he was tricked, if he had tricked himself, and think of escaping to a life of his own choosing. So we're simply attempting to get ahead of that idea." He spread his hands on the desk. "Which gets us around to work. You could work afternoons for me. See if the law takes with you. To begin with, errands and filing. Boring at the start, I'll admit. That said, let's finish the paperwork. See what you think." Not in this lifetime, Rossie thought, would he work in this office.

The secretary brought a folder containing the stacked deeds. Once the signing was done, the papers swept away, Ned Henry sat back and smiled at Rossie. "You're a man with property. But you have no high school diploma, as I understand it. That can be arranged. You're three years behind your peers. But you've seen something of the world. It might be time to embrace an idea of who you want to be."

"Dumb is no way to go," Rossie said. "I know that much."

"Ambitions are important," Ned Henry said. "You could start coming to the office at the beginning of February. But be careful. We come to recall the days of youth as the legendary time when we chose our life. An office like this can become everything you know."

"No shit. Don't doubt it."

"Perhaps you don't have a lawyer's mind."

DEER LODGE

In the quiet house, after dinner, Lemma read more Virginia Woolf aloud. "For you," she said to Bernard. *She began to smile for though she had not said a word, he knew, of course he knew, that she loved him. He could not deny it. And smiling she looked out of the window and thought, Nothing on earth can equal this happiness.*

The next afternoon, Eliza extracted the little photograph of Charlie Cooper from beneath the bed. She wandered the house with it late in the night after fussing over the baby and appeared at breakfast still carrying it, shards of broken glass clinging in the frame.

"Berserk and crazy," Lemma said. "Angry enough to be evil. He hones in on wreckage, and will bring you down with it if it can."

"Berserk isn't crazy," Eliza said. "Or evil. Berserk is overwhelmed by fury or sorrow."

She turned to Rossie. "This is nothing about you, but you're coming with me. You, you're my husband."

"Where you going?"

"To see him." She looked away from Rossie like he was not so much dense as beside the point.

Three mornings later, Leonard drove Rossie and Eliza and the baby to catch the eastbound train from Missoula, which they would ride to Deer Lodge. Eliza would show her baby to his blood father. Arrangements had been made.

The prison resembled a stone castle, with crenellated rock walls and guard towers three stories above the main street of what otherwise looked to be a Montana rancher's town, with a scattering of black automobiles parked diagonally to the concrete curbs and women idling at their shopping in a food market but almost no men on this working day.

"You and me," Rossie said, holding Eliza by the elbow and shuffling the icy sidewalk in black rubber galoshes, "you carrying that baby, we could be just about anybody."

"We are," Eliza said.

Inside the first gate, they were shown into separate rooms and searched. A tall, gray-faced guard with watery, brown-flecked eyes

427

grew suspicious when Rossie fished up his knife. The man snapped the main blade open and tested it with his thumb.

"That's an implement you don't take with you," the guard said. "Blades like that have sliced jugulars in here. We'll hold it."

"You keep an eye on it," Rossie said.

"I'll try."

"You better. Otherwise there's me."

"What's that to mean?"

"Same thing it always means."

"Are you threatening me?"

Rossie looked away. He had meant to threaten the man. "Sorry," he said. "This place gives me the skitters."

"Worse than that, if you get caught threatening officials. But no mind. It happens with you fellows, they lose their balance."

Escorted through a series of clanging gates that the guards opened with antique keys, Rossie followed Eliza down echoing corridors to more gates and eventually into Charlie Cooper's presence. They were directed to sit on a bare bench in a cramped chamber, facing a portal blocked by steel bars that separated them from a rock-walled room. Charlie Cooper sat well back from them, in the isolated center of the holding cell. A uniformed guard with smooth jowls, absorbed in a pulp magazine called *Western*

Action, sat looking down onto Charlie from a third chamber. "Do not pass anything back and forth," he said in a quiet voice, then turned back to his raggedy magazine.

Charlie Cooper was indeed the man in those photographs, except that his head had been shaved. On the side of his skull, a tiny swirl of tattoo depicted a dark-feathered bird spreading its wings above his left ear.

"Here he is," Eliza said, displaying the baby. "Your son. His name is Teddy Blue."

Charlie Cooper shook his head. "Black and Blue? He's not mine, he's yours. A quarter-breed who'll wish he was pure. You see me? You see my eyes are open? You see I'm past hating. I'll be out. I'll want to be dealt a hand."

"Pure?" Eliza asked.

"Pure white, that's what he'll want. Unless he's crazy."

"Would you like to kiss him?" Eliza offered. "I imagine you kissing him."

The guard looked up from his reading. "Not allowed."

"They think I might bite him," Charlie Cooper said. "They think I'm a wolf." He smiled as if this was something he had been waiting to announce. "My son someday will love me and kiss me. You'll see it. Under these floors they lock me in alone. I tell myself stories about fishing with my mother and my grandfather, Kicking Goose, and cooking trout with onions and spuds. I wash the frying pan. The story lasts all night." Charlie's eyes flashed with amusement. "Dog time. Everybody does dog time." He looked to Rossie. "You got her, and I got dreams about onions and spuds. But you're the same as me."

"Trying to be our own luck," Rossie said because he needed to say something. "Most things don't amount to shit. We know that. They don't amount to a goddamn."

"You want to be my friend," Charlie Cooper said, "but you don't know anything. How could you? You don't see anybody who don't love you." He spread his hands. "One day I'll be out. You'll see me."

"What's that bird mean?" Rossie asked. "On your skull."

"It means I'm not like you."

"You're just like us," Eliza said.

"Nope. In here, we're junkyard people, dead if we do and dead if we don't."

"I brought money," Eliza said.

"Thought you would. That's your job. We're not stupid. Some of us, we been counting on your money, soon as I heard you were coming. I told people she's money in the bank. How much?"

Eliza folded three ten-dollar bills together and tossed them inside the bars, where they floated onto the concrete floor.

"That's handsome." Charlie stood and bowed. "That's it? Enough."

"Sit," the guard said.

Abruptly, Charlie crouched on his knees, head down, as if he might be ill.

The guard laid down his reading. "Back on the bench," he said. "Sit." Charlie looked up. "I'm praying."

"Sit."

"I'm praying that you can swallow shit." Charlie came to his feet, poised there a moment with hands down in his trousers, then growled and charged toward the guard in his barred window. He had fished a toilet-paper roll filled with shit out of his pants as he crouched, and it was shit he was hurling, shit splattering on the walls and even on the guard.

A clanging bell was ringing and Baby Teddy began to shriek. Three men in yellow shirts banged the door open and rushed in, cautious for a moment as they eyed Charlie before one of them circled around to tackle him on the slick concrete floor, and the others batted at him with lead-weighted saps until he went quiet and Rossie thought he was dead. Blood streamed from his shaved head as they dragged him, his skull just bouncing on the floor, trailing blood. When the steel door slammed behind them Rossie found himself standing, grasping the bars, while Eliza clutched her wailing baby and the guard mopped at his own long face.

A stocky man sporting a dark, buttoned-up suit and a thin necktie had come into the room behind them. "Out of here," he said. His hand felt hard as iron when he took hold of Rossie's arm and they went out before him, as Eliza said later, "Like lambs."

The warden escorted them along the echoing, concrete hallways. "Don't come back," he told them.

"They got to get my knife," Rossie said.

At the entrance, a different guard handed the knife to the warden, who leered at Rossie.

"This it?" Rossie nodded, but when he reached for his knife, the warden opened the long blade and tested it on his thumb, then moved to a doorway, slipped the blade into the crack between the door and the jamb and snapped it off.

"Illegal weapon," he said, offering Rossie the ruined bone handle that remained. "What do you think of that?"

"Shit," Rossie said. There was not a thing

to do but throw a fit and then he'd be in there with Charlie. "You taught me a lesson," he said finally. "Never trust no jailer."

"I do anything necessary," the man said. "You keep that in mind. But you're a civilized man."

"What does civilized mean? Chickenshit?"

The jailer smiled. "It means you're too sensible to cut your own throat when you'd like to be cutting mine."

"Chickenshit."

"Me," Eliza said, as they paused on the icy snow outside Deer Lodge Prison, "I'm going to be ready when Charlie comes." Her face was pale in the snowy, gray light. "We'll be barricaded." After they'd walked a block toward the railroad station, she stopped again. "Our hearts ought to be broken. You've seen a man who's been overwhelmed, where it gets him."

"Them walls," Rossie said. "Jailers, they lead shithead lives." He knew this sounded pathetic and insufficient.

They waited three hours in the Deer Lodge station in silence broken only when the baby whimpered and Eliza gave comfort. On the clacking ride home Rossie dreamed of horses running under a flashing storm, and awoke as the train began clattering beside the Clark Fork, approaching Missoula. "I was dreaming about horses," he told Eliza. "Horses going batshit."

"You sound like you lost something."

"Boy on a train."

"We saw something awful," she said.

And we don't know the cure, Rossie thought. Or how much we should give a shit.

Before midnight they were off the train and checked into a room in the Florence Hotel, a room overlooking Higgins Avenue and the frozen Clark Fork River. Toward daybreak, while Eliza and the baby were sleeping, Rossie stood looking out at to snow blowing along the cold streets and down the icy river in waves and tried to recall exactly how stocking-footed bays and the blacks and sorrels and blue roans looked on a dew-heavy morning, grazing in the willow fields outside Eagleville.

When Eliza awoke and rolled onto her side, Rossie turned to face her. "What if I went to Spain?"

Eliza rolled her eyes, then went attentive, like a bird he was to think, and he would remark on this likeness time and again during those years as the war came toward them.

"I'd be hell on wheels," he whispered.

"You're with me," she said.

"Monkey in a cage," he answered. But Eliza was looking past him. "I'm a little bit serious," he went on whispering. "Men like Charlie and that prison warden will run you down if you don't let things go their way. They'd kill you and me if it came to that. There's people who would. Makes me think I ought to do something."

"Try to get some sleep. Let's act like we don't know what all that implies," Eliza said. "There won't be any answer in Spain, not for a boy like you. Not for you and me."

"Probably not, I guess, for anybody."

■ ■ ■ ■

PART THREE
A MAN WITH HORSES

■ ■ ■ ■

LEARNING TO PLOW

After Deer Lodge, Rossie valued even more than before his time with his Bobby Cahill mare named Katrina. "We're a secret story," he told Eliza, "me and her."

Eliza made a clown's face. "Isn't that the problem? Secret stories?"

"Does everything need to be a problem? What if my secret is about an afternoon without bullshit."

She looked genuinely surprised. "Who are you? Can you tell me?" Rossie forced a grinning, boyish, mock lewdness. "You," he said. "You're my secret."

"See there. Maybe all your secrets are fuck-me jokes."

"Don't count it out." He quit grinning. "I go down to the Tailfeather Field and lope along on with Katrina. It's my idea of fancy. I got secrets. When I'm out with that little horse I don't want nothing to do with a lawyer's office in Hamilton. But I don't tell you and I don't tell Bernard. That's another secret."

"I'm glad to know. It's news Bernard can swallow, too. Holding secrets is like poison. Get them out of your system or end up like Charlie."

"Missus preacher is telling me to puke up," Rossie said. "So fine."

Over dinner he blurted out the news that he didn't think he was up for shuffling papers in a lawyer's office. Bernard sat poised with a dab of spinach on his fork. He seemed curious.

"Is your willingness to say no a thing you learned at Deer Lodge Prison?" he asked, finishing the bite of spinach. "If so, your trip was worth it."

"Partway," Rossie said. "Partways got from a woman."

Bernard smiled. "I congratulate you. Learning from women is not easy." This was clearly meant to be a man-to-man joke, and Bernard was beaming at his own humor. "I, too, have my own announcement. Persuaded by a woman, I've scheduled my prostate operation for Groundhog Day. I'll hope to see my own shadow."

By late March Bernard had suffered through. He'd gone into St. Patrick's Hospital in Missoula with depressed determination and five days later emerged in jaunty spirits. "Alive and kicking," he said, as Rossie wheeled him out to the Buick. "Don't have to spread my legs to piss."

"Bernard," Lemma said, "you are indeed such a sweet asshole."

"They haven't," Bernard said, "gotten rid of me. It must be spring fever. My fleas are jumping."

Lawyers came to the house, and he closed a deal on a hundred acres of plow ground on Fever Creek, half a mile south from the big house.

"Water rights and a homesteader orchard, level land, garden plots. An answer to Eliza's fever for good works."

By mid-April Rossie was out on that land, plowing with a platter-footed team of yellow Belgians. Leonard had put the word around in Canada, and Blood Indians were said to be coming. "Native farmers," Bernard said at dinner. "We'll hope there are such a people."

"A year ago I was horseback, going to Canada. Now I'm plowing hobby farms," Rossie mused. "Don't know if that's forwards or backwards."

Eliza told him to pull up his socks, but his weather didn't turn until a May morning when he was nailing together tent house frames alongside the garden plots and spotted a hawk-faced man, three old women, and a half dozen kids watching him from a mule-drawn wagon. They'd come from Browning and within a day were raking the fine Bitterroot loam and planting carrots and beets in long, meandering rows. A cook fire smoldered for the cutthroat trout the runny-nosed kids were hooking out of Fever Creek. "That Lester Ben," Rossie said of the hawk-faced man that night. "Lester's like me except he don't get a shot of single malt at sundown."

"Do you think that's a joke?" Eliza scolded. "His life is infinitely more difficult than yours."

"Yes, Mrs. Mammy, I thought it was a joke." It was true, he had.

Another wagonload of people arrived, having traveled hundreds of miles from the Blood Reserve in Alberta. "Teddy, my boy," Rossie whispered to the baby, "we got our work cut out for us."

Then after four families they stopped coming. "Not many Indians are interested in farming," Leonard wrote. "The anthropologists say farming for Indians is a trick, by what Marx called the ruling class, to corral them into menial labor, a form of imprisonment once they've been done out of their homelands. They know it, and know they'd rather be running horses. So would anyone. I've had to stop recommending your 'farm.' "

"Not so many of anybody is interested in farming anyway," Rossie said.

Eliza answered defeat by searching out Piegan grandmothers, bundling up Baby Teddy, and traveling in the Model A to the east side of the Rockies.

"We visit and talk and I listen" she said. "They tell me I'm a patronizing do-gooder, and I ask them, 'Who else do you have?' and we laugh." Eventually she persuaded Bernard to buy a former bunkhouse in Browning, which she then turned over to those grandmothers, who in turn converted it into a home for young women with pregnancies and no tribal location to harbor them or any man to stand up for them. Eliza called it a place to practice "jointedness and connection." The tribes since "time immemorial" had done so, as well as European generations who had labored for centuries building cathedrals and caring for the mad and the dispossessed. She bought other houses in Missoula and Great Falls and Billings. Raising money to support them became, Eliza said, her "business life."

"You and me, Mr. Teddy Blue," Rossie

said. "Maybe, we get a hustle on, we could be her real business."

But Rossie's initial inclination toward the horses soon turned to what Bernard called "the checkbook work." With his father-in-law's blessing and access to his funds, along with a strict accounting, Rossie was sent on trips to public and private sales in the Bitterroot, then throughout western Montana and over east on the prairies, to old cow towns like Miles City. His major responsibility in all this, according to Bernard, was "to observe and learn to evade the hustlers, to tell a genuine enthusiasm from nonsense among horse traders and hobby riders." This travel culminated in a week-long trip to the Sand Hill country of Nebraska, followed by another to the Tulare Basin in the central valley of California, where Rossie bought two three-year-old geldings and had them shipped home to the Bitterroot for him and Bill Sweet to work with the next spring.

Bill Sweet and Margie were established in a small house next to the highway and went out each morning to tend whatever work there was, mending the fences and caring for the young horses in the Tailfeather Field. One evening in early autumn, Bill Sweet put on a clean shirt and knocked at the door of the main house. What he was after, Bill Sweet said, was business talk.

"You and me good enough friends for this?" he said to Rossie, then went on without waiting for an answer. "Margie and me talked. Looks like you're skipping the main thing. You got us a couple of horses. But you and me, we don't know what we're doing. You better ought to see this Bobby Cahill, if he'll teach you, and you can educate me. That's what I got to say."

That talk was irrefutable. Rossie called Nevada and talked to Malinda and caught up with her legendary husband a week later.

"Malinda tells me you're trying to be a man who makes sense," Bobby Cahill shouted into the phone. "I'm taking her word. What I got is a three-year-old gelding — big hot-blooded, quarter-horse kid with quick enough moves, colored red. I can sell him to you, and you can come down here and learn to get him started. You want to come down here, you got to buy this horse. That way, you fuck him up, you don't leave me with a crazy red horse."

"Red?" Rossie asked.

"What the fuck does red have to do with anything? You superstitious?"

Rossie got right off that topic. "Thought you was breeding Morgans to long-jointed

445

traveling mares."

"Them was remuda horses, for the ranches," Cahill said. "These days it's roping horses. Thought it was roping horses you were after."

By early October, Rossie had traveled to Nevada, where he found Bobby Cahill batching it in a thick-walled stone house that was cool and dark as a cavern. The faded linoleum was worn through at the kitchen sink and the cast-iron wood stove — all of it similarly old and used — but every lick of it, each spoon and cup, was immaculately clean.

"You got to spend a half hour every day mopping and cleaning," Bobby Cahill said. "Or you won't amount to shit."

There was no sign of Malinda. Bobby shrugged and said she was bound to show up at some point.

"You won't be missing her," Bobby said. "You're going to have enough to think about with that horse."

And it was true. Rossie was watching and listening daybreak-to-dark in the willow-walled corrals, wondering if he really could learn to think like a horse as it tried to make sense of what a slow-spoken man might possibly want.

"Man has a contract," Bobby told him,

dumping catsup over fried-ham-and-egg sandwiches the first morning. "Contract with his horse. You can't *force* him to do anything worth a damn. A horse has got to think that you are with him in playing the game together." He tapped his knife on the faded, blue-pattern oilcloth.

"That mare of mine you got locked up in a barn, there in Montana. That's pure foolishness. Horses don't like it all the time alone any better than you do. She isn't going to be worth a shit if you're not careful. You know why? Because she's going to think you're the jailer, the man with the key. Horse don't work for some jailer, he works *with* you or you got nothing. Horses and women, if they're not ruined by mistreatment, they love good work. Nobody picks on a woman or a horse if I'm around. Man who beats on one of my horses is beating on me. I find out, I'll kick his ass. If I'm old and can't get the job done, I'll hire somebody who can. I make it clear when I sell a horse: You don't own my Bobby Cahill horses. You work with them like they's your partner and going to be all your life. You study them like they might be your wife. Each horse has got his own ways. Take your time and study each one like you're studying a woman. That's the deal. Rest of the shit will take care of itself."

Rossie devoted those bright October days to reading the look in his gelding's eyes, the implications of the way he set his ears.

"Horses are like ballplayers," Bobby Cahill said. "Some of them got more spring than others, some are smarter. You're always hoping to find one who can do anything. But mostly you don't." He lifted his big hands and studied them, then looked up to Rossie with a vivid, off-center light in his eyes. "One-of-a-kind is what we want. Springy and well-knit, with pretty actions. Ordinary horses, they can be sweethearts and you love 'em, but they can't get the job done. Swaybacks and high withers or them stick-necked boys, they can't do it. Simple enough, they don't have the right muscles. They know they won't do any good at roping, so you got to treat them right or they can sulk up and act like assholes, same as you and me." Rossie was wondering how his red gelding stacked up in this game.

"Piggy eyes and Roman noses was born stupid and stubborn. Your fine horse is smart enough to be interested in what you're showing him. He trusts you and stays so busy studying what you're doing that he can't be bothered with any meanness — unless you fuck him up, which is a criminal shame. Putting your claim on a horse is like hiring and firing. You always want to hire men who can build better fence corners than you ever could, fellows who understood the work before you was born even though they may drink too much. But they also got to be smart enough to know who is the boss and that you'll fire 'em before breakfast if they start trying to take over. Six parts of training horses is finding the good ones to start with."

"What's the other parts?"

"There's only one. Letting your horses figure out that you want them to be having a good time. You learn to talk so they know clear-through what you mean and that you mean it. They don't understand, it's your fault. You got to stay ahead and wait for 'em. Come trouble, you got to know what they're thinking and why they back off from whatever it is you've got them doing. If you're too dumb to figure it out, you ought to enlist in the Army. If one set of thinking don't sell, you got to stop and turn it around and try getting to the same place from another direction."

The days were repetitive and sometimes boring. On Bobby's instruction Rossie sat in the barn watching a black, three-year-old mare with the habit of squalling back and snapping halter ropes. "You're going to be friends with this lady," Bobby said, as he tied her into an empty stall with a single strand of baler twine. Rossie waited until she jerked back and snapped the baler twine, then gave her ten or so minutes to think over the idea that she was still alone in that empty stall before going in and retying her with more baler twine. On the afternoon of the second day, she stopped breaking twine, and Rossie returned every hour to feed her carrots for being good.

"She's getting it," Bobby said. "Or maybe not. Anyhow, this is how we get the work done. One clear thing at a time, day after day."

After a week, and running a few dozen calves through the roping arena, with Rossie missing the catch more times than not, Bobby called a halt.

"This party is over," Bobby said. "Beats me how you can go out buying horses if you don't know none of what I been telling you."

"I got a couple of decent ones," Rossie said. "Beginner's luck."

"Must have been," Bobby said. "Trouble is you, throwing a piss-poor loop. Your horse has got to see you do the catching, they got to feel the loop in the air. A calf on the line is like a trout. The horse loves it like you do. If they bust a gut and get you into position, you got to make the catch most every time, or the horse will get disgusted. Just like if you throw me the baseball and I don't catch it, game goes to hell in a hurry. What you got to do is buy a half dozen of those Mexican roping steers out of Sonora, and have them shipped up to you on the railroad early next spring by the time the mud goes dry. You turn 'em out of a roping chute all summer and learn to rope so you never miss. If you can catch them little rabbit bastards you can catch anything. Then you come back down here in the fall and we'll talk horses. I'll keep that red horse through the winter."

"You think so? Mexican steers?"

"I damned well know so. You've got to learn to rope. It ain't some mystery, just takes work. But you can't teach a horse how to set up with the loop in the air and just about to catch something when you can't catch nothing."

This was inarguable. Rossie was already getting set to approach Bernard on the subject of buying Mexican steers.

Cahill cadences echoed in Rossie's head on the long drive back to Montana as he thought about teaching Bill Sweet to forget the roughhouse bronco busting. The day

451

after his return home he laid out the deal to Bill Sweet in what he thought of as Cahill terms. "What if you beat on Margie?"

"She'd stab me while I was sleeping."

"You rough up our horses I'll kick your ass while you're wide awake."

Rossie ordered a half dozen many-colored Mexican calves from Sonora. By the time winter had set in he and Bill Sweet had built a stout, round corral at the edge of the Tailfeather Field, and constructed a roping chute with used railroad ties. The Mexican steers came off a railroad car in Hamilton in late March, and Rossie and Bill Sweet started burning their hands with seagrass ropes, learning to sling loops with a rolling wrist and to set back in the stirrups anticipating that the catch was a dead-on sure thing, every time after every time. In August Rossie returned to Nevada and found that roping horses were less of a mystery if you got them into the game.

"Couple of more years," Bobby Cahill said, "and you might know something." Rossie heard that as high praise, and as soon as he was back in Montana he told Eliza that Bobby Cahill had showed him where his life had always been aimed, in the direction of smart horses and her.

"You always knew that kind of talk. It's a

function of not fucked in a couple of weeks."
He smiled. "So?"

On a rainy May morning in 1939, a man named Eldon Bermuda loaded a .44 pistol, walked a mile and a half of muddy road to the eastern outskirts of Hamilton, entered a tavern called The Mint, took dead aim, and shot his nineteen-year-old wife off the bar-stool, where she had been sitting with another man's hand up under her skirt. Bermuda then took the .44 into his mouth and without hesitation destroyed his own brains. "Blood on the walls," the Hamilton newspaper wrote.

Home from a week of looking at horses in Wyoming, Rossie banged his way into the house around midnight and found Eliza on the leather couch in their rooms with a skinny, startlingly blue-eyed two-year-old blond girl on her lap. The girl was wearing new, pink button-up pajamas. She gave him only darting looks.

"This is Corrie," Eliza said. "Corrie couldn't sleep so I was telling her a story. Corrie lives here now. Her name was Bermuda. It's going to be Stevenson. I was telling her about you and horses, how you'd be home and how she could have a horse." Eliza spoke quietly, and the message for

Rossie, as he stood there with his hat in his hand, was clear. "What you should do," Eliza said to him, "is tell us about your horse, your Katrina."

Rossie sat at the far end of the couch while the girl stared at her knees. "Well, Katrina and Eliza are my sweethearts."

"Corrie," Eliza said, "will be another of your sweethearts."

Rossie nodded. "Corrie, did you ever ride a horse?" The girl shook her head. "Corrie, what if I picked you up and you and me trotted around this room like I was a horse?"

"Why don't you?" Eliza said. "Why don't you let him pick you up and trot you around?"

There it began, the dancing that was Rossie and Eliza and Teddy and the blue-eyed girl named Corrie, child of a marriage that ended on the bloody floor of The Mint, whom Eliza had rescued from huddling in her dead father's barnyard. Those years before the war the dark boy and the pale girl were to Rossie like sides of the coin called childhood, and he would call them by nicknames, Teddy being "Fine" and Corrie "Bright."

HONOLULU

After Betty had gone off on the railroad in the direction of Spain by way of New York, Eliza insisted on doing the cooking. "I don't want anybody serving me," she said. "Nobody in this house except for us."

Bernard shook his head. "You are out of luck. We're overrun with ghosts."

His pronouncement was felt most heavily in the early winter of 1939, when word came from Arnold that Betty had died of pneumonia on the rainy northwest coast of Spain. Just that, a card signed, "Heartbroken, as you may also be, Arnold."

This was only a beginning. A global war was tearing across three continents, already the primary divide in the lives of their generation. After long nights of unresolved debate with Eliza, Rossie joined the frenzy of patriotism that followed the attack on Pearl Harbor and enlisted in the Marine Corps just before Christmas in 1941. Bill

455

Sweet, with an agricultural deferment of the sort Rossie had refused, was left with Margie and the task of selling off the horses except for Katrina. From then on he was in charge of holding Bernard's home-place properties together, which wasn't much of a chore since there were no plans for going forward. "Holding the line on this end," Bernard said. "That's us."

By New Year's Day Rossie was sleeping in the aisle of a passenger train that was taking him along with hundreds of other recruits east across the nation to South Carolina for nine weeks of boot camp at Parris Island. "We're learning basics," he wrote Eliza. "Don't quit and marksmanship. They've nicknamed me 'Cowboy.' "

But shooting to kill didn't loom in his future. For reasons he wouldn't soon discover, Rossie was irrevocably assigned to supply. "You don't need no training for supply," he was told. "Any dumb shit can hand out blankets."

Six weeks out of Parris Island, he came off a transport docked in sight of the wreckage at Pearl Harbor. The beach at Waikiki was strung with barbed wire, but somewhere beyond it he would find Eliza. A young Hamilton hotshot who worked for a senator from Billings had arranged a Red Cross job for her, keeping records of durable foods stockpiled for "native relief" on islands eventually to be reconquered. She settled with the children in a tin-roofed mountainside house with a view across canyons of jungle to the glistening sea. Geckos ran the walls, pursuing insects.

Eliza took a bus to a downtown office. Rossie bought a secondhand Chevrolet and drove to a warehouse at Pearl Harbor. Teddy and Corrie were picked up by a stern Chinese woman with a British accent, Lydia Lee, and taken daily to the private advantages of Punahou School, for classes in European art, piano, and French. Teddy kept track of the war day by day, marking boyish notes on the maps he had up on the walls of his room and pasting war stories from the newspapers into big scrapbooks. Corrie ran in the brush with a throng of Hawaiian girls and occasional boys and came home scratched and speaking the island patois. But Eliza and Rossie often forgot them, ignored them in the rush of other urgencies. "We were children raising children," Eliza would say years later.

Eventually they hired a live-in nanny, a young mixed-blood widow, Shirley Vesper, so they could take the Chevy on the twisting road through jungles over the stunningly precipitous Koʻolau Range — fluted heights like nothing in the Rockies — to sundowner parties on pavilions beside the Lanikai beaches.

Purple and orange orchids on strings around their necks they danced to Glenn Miller recordings and on the way home they stood in the moonlight at the Nuʻuanu Pali Lookout where they wrapped their arms around each other, still feeling the vodka, and gazed out at the shimmering seas. On Hotel Street in downtown Honolulu where beleaguered prostitutes lived in cribs above taverns thick with enlisted men, Rossie and Eliza danced and drank among them. They traveled in a pack with friends, joking and flirting to armor their souls against thoughts of being called up for invasions and the chance of instant dismemberment. No one spoke of fate or death until the late hours, when drunken, sweaty men cursed and broke bottles and stared out at the darkness while women wept over them.

At work, Rossie talked his way onto transport aircraft that made island-hopping sweeps all the way to Fiji. He came to love the long hours of flying over the featureless Pacific to minuscule destinations, atolls with tiny lights amid the black immensity of water.

"If this is war, I'm dreaming," he told Eliza.

"Better than that," she said. "You're alive."

A turning came on Christmas Day, 1943, when the Great Falls newspaper broke the story that Charlie Cooper, who'd enlisted in the Marines with false documents after release from Deer Lodge Prison, lost an arm during the invasion of Tarawa. Lemma sent a copy of the newspaper, which displayed a front-page picture of Charlie, hard-eyed in hospital whites, and labeled him "a genuine American hero."

Rossie found Eliza in the kitchen with a glass of bourbon over ice. "Hell of a thing," he said, reading from the news report. "Bleeding in the salt flats, arm shot off, knowing he was dying. Blue and yellow fish all around, ready to feed on him."

"Hero!" Eliza cried. "Charlie's a one-armed ex-con who is going to talk about being a hero until he's dead. What Charlie found out there is blood, and shit in the water. Little fish, eating dead flesh and shit."

Rossie poured himself some bourbon. "Little fish and shit." He tossed it back, poured another inch, and they were quiet, looking away from each other until Rossie tossed back his second hit of bourbon.

"All you can do is drink?"

"Seems like it sometimes. Tell you what, I run away from school and my mother's house and I run away from Mattie and I been raising horses with your money and now I'm handing out blankets in Hawaii. There's got to be an end to ducking out or I'm going to be the sorry son of a bitch who got out of everything. Charlie's done a hell of a lot more than me. Slivers told us he'd never go back but he went once. If Slivers hadn't gone once then he couldn't say anything. I'm going to be the man who can't look anybody in the eye if I'm not careful."

"What heroes are for," Eliza said, "is getting killed so life can go on. You go be a hero. Corrie and Teddy and I will run horses while your bones rot into the coral. We'll drink to your memory. Dead is dead. War isn't a horseback trip to Canada." She explained that his assignment to base supply in Honolulu had been managed by the same Harvard-pedigreed Hamilton lawyer who'd arranged her Red Cross assignment. "Anybody but a fool would be grateful."

"Too late for grateful," Rossie said.

He called the lawyer and talked his way into reassignment onto a ship headed for New Caledonia, where he would be issued combat gear and join the Third Marine Corps Division, survivors of the miseries

460

involved in the conquest of the Solomon Islands.

Upon awakening the last morning together Eliza nudged his shoulder. "You must be the man who wants to be dead." When he finished shaving she didn't get out of bed or say anything but, "Goddamn you."

While training on Eniwetok atoll Rossie learned of the Allied landing in Normandy on the same day he read a brief, precise note from Eliza. *This is to reassure you that I understand your need to be what you think you are. I await your homecoming with prayer. Imagine it, even me, praying.* All those thousands of miles away from her, dripping sweat and aching and stunned with such fatigue that he could barely fight off the black flies swarming around him, Rossie persuaded himself to smile.

In first light on July 21, 1944, he climbed down a net of rope hung over the barnacled side of the troop ship to a landing boat. He had lived below deck in steamy, reeking intimacy with hundreds of other men, and now he was confined only by his gear — his rifle and a long, black-bladed knife, two canteens, a rain poncho, a shovel and gloves, K rations, waterproofed cigarettes, matches, candy bars, and oranges. He wasn't the supply sergeant anymore.

They were carried toward a coral reef just off the high, green shore of Guam. Mortar and artillery shells exploded in flowering bursts of seawater as a pitched howl rang out through the ongoing incandescence. In the warm, waist-deep seawater colored by blood, as Rossie stumbled across the sharp coral offshore from the beach, he saw a man fall screaming, but no one could hear him over the amphibious tractors churning and wallowing and the constant explosions. Machine gun fire from concrete bunkers on the bluff above the beach came sweeping along, kicking up little splashes, and felling other men.

"Numb," Rossie would say, telling the story years later. "They said to leave the wounded and keep going. The medics would get them. A lot of them drowned and there was nothing to do but keep going. I had no idea what dying meant. I thought about it at night in my hammock and I guessed you'd never know. Of thirty men in our landing craft, nineteen went down on the reef. By the time I got to the beach I wasn't scared, I was alive, and I'd quit thinking."

Rossie found shelter at the bottom of the cliffs and dug in behind a fallen palm, throwing sand to make himself a hole while the Japanese machine guns were firing off over his head, up the cliff, fifty or sixty feet above him.

A young Marine hunkered close to dig in beside him, and they remained there all night, until the cliffs were cleared. This new companion looked not a day over eighteen. He called himself Vernon and curled up in the dark and talked about his mother in Missouri and drinking water in the Ozarks. "Pure water and a good woman. She's doing prayers for me."

"Shut up if you don't want to get us killed," Rossie said.

They had heard stories about enormous rats in the dark so he and Vernon stayed awake and smoked their cigarettes and ate their candy bars and peeled their oranges. Rossie managed to imagine morning sun on the Bitterroot peaks, then slept and dreamed about frogs croaking until gray light slipped in over Guam and he was still there in the sand-sided hole. He suddenly thought of killing Vernon if he talked any more but knew that was crazy.

Then they were told to advance. Rossie and Vernon O'Hearn and a row of other men straggled up sandy trails through blasted vegetation to the bluffs. There was dried blood on the floor of the pillbox bunkers and bodies covered with flies and already turning green in the heat. An Arabian-looking fellow remarked on the dead Japanese soldiers, how they were just like the Americans, all of them stupid shooters. "This isn't anything we earned," he said. "Not any of us deserves it, not the Japs or us." He was talking fast and going on crazy until a sniper got him and half his face blew off, his blood splattering through the air like he'd exploded.

A slight, half-naked Japanese soldier was found hiding empty-handed in a rat hole under the trunk of a fallen palm. The hole crawled with coconut crabs, and Rossie, though he'd been warned about going pure batshit in war, felt helpless against the urge to shoot him. He wanted the prisoner to crawl and kept jabbing away with his rifle at the man's neck.

Then Vernon O'Hearn shot his rifle and Rossie was flat on his back, with a bone-shattering wound in his shoulder. Vernon stood above him, weeping and protesting. "Ross, it weren't Christian."

Thirteen weeks later, Rossie disembarked from a transport ship in Honolulu. Surgeons had sewn up his left shoulder, which was bandaged and healing, and he had ridden topside while Vernon O'Hearn was kept in a steel lockup six decks below. Eliza was at the dock swishing her blue, polka-dot, silk dress around her legs, and they fixed their gaze on each other like radar as Rossie marched down the swaying gangplank.

"Now, look at you," she said. "The sergeant survives."

"You've been thinking about saying that, haven't you?"

Other wounded men, without women to greet them, were watching.

"Are you checked out?" she said. "Can you come with me?"

She lifted her hands, swayed toward him, and touched his cheek with her cool fingers. She shut her eyes, and he rested his hands on her hips and kissed her. Men around them cheered.

Rossie was quiet as she drove up mountain roads to the house in Honolulu, where she led him right off to the bedroom with gaudy Hawaiian flowers in vases, and linen sheets and goose-down pillows on the bed.

"Now," she said, undoing his necktie, "the children will be coming home, so no talking just yet."

Rossie slept away the days. Eliza brought him marmalade as he breakfasted with the children — breakfasts of cantaloupe and mango and heavy bacon and poached eggs.

He went back to bed and woke with rain splattering on the metal roof and told Eliza that she'd been right about wars, that wars were "the most dipshit insanities of mankind."

Eliza touched his shoulder. "If I'd killed that man my life would have been done. I'd lay awake in the dark for all my life, ruined and a killer, a man who'd murdered."

She went on touching him, unabashed, eager to bestow herself and receive him. One night she said maybe the yearning she felt in her depths was something complex beyond fucking. Years later she said she'd loved taking him inside her those first weeks, unlike anything before or since, and that she used to think about it all day long.

The Marines had shipped Rossie to Honolulu because of Vernon. Other men healed up in hospitals on Guam and made it back to duty in time to die on Okinawa.

"Vernon saved me. I like as not would have killed that Japanese fellow," he told Eliza. "The military would have shot me for killing a prisoner of war. And if I'd gotten away with it, I'd still have myself to deal with, night after night. So I have to save Vernon. Otherwise, who knows what they might do to him."

Vernon O'Hearn was accused of deliber-

466

ately wounding a fellow combat marine. "It was an accident," Rossie said to the officers overseeing the hearing. "Vernon stumbled. I saw it. Everything in the war caused it."

The colonel in charge frowned. "Sergeant Benasco, the war is only the most remote cause of this incident. You're contradicting the reports of other men, but your testimony, claiming to have seen yourself shot, outweighs all the rest. In my opinion, Sergeant Benasco, you're not fit to be a combat marine. You are a natural supply sergeant, and you're going back to it before you get some good men killed."

Inside a week, Vernon was pulling ninety days in the brig for "careless conduct in the field," and Rossie was handing out transient barracks pillows and brown GI blankets to marines processing through Pearl Harbor. On Honolulu nights, in bed and on wooden decks beside the sea and in taverns on Hotel Street, he talked out theories. "I was trying to keep up with Charlie Cooper. That's nuts."

"Let's forget Charlie," Eliza said. "Forever."

"When they carried me off that bluff and the machine guns were rattling away, I thought about Slivers. They'll never get to me again." Into his latest scrapbook Teddy pasted photographs of gray-faced Rossie with his shoulder in bandages alongside newspaper clippings of one-armed Charlie Cooper. Then, a note from Nito: *I deal cards like I thought I wanted to do, but my job is looking for cheats and I sure as hell wouldn't recommend a steady diet of that. Stay with what you care for.*

"He couldn't get himself to write about love," Eliza said.

Along with recurring dreams of fleeing and being unable to escape, Rossie was inflicted with a sense of having been eager and more than willing to murder — he killed men in dreams that were impossible to recall at daybreak, when nothing remained but a guilt that felt true and earned.

Eliza said the dreams were an infection and would cure naturally, but on the lanai at three in the morning, breathing the cool night air and eyeing the black infinities of ocean beyond the lights of Honolulu, Rossie told her that the dreams were coming to him from another life.

"Somebody's memories crossed up with mine."

"That's crazy."

CURES

In the fall of 1946, mustered out of the marines and heading home to the Bitterroot on railway trains from southern California, Rossie felt the idea of admitting his state of mind was as frightening as his dreams. Label yourself a misfit and there you were, a misfit staring out a Pullman window to the harvested farmlands north of Eugene.

"Shuffle the deck," Eliza said, "and draw another card."

Bernard and Lemma greeted them at the station. After Bernard's handshake and the hugging and tears, they rode down the Bitterroot Valley in a brand-new, yellow Buick convertible, and shared the evening meal of osso bucco. The day seemed to Rossie a distant enactment of a movie.

When Bernard finally said, "Now, tell us in detail about your war," Rossie shook his head and went off as if bound for the bathroom. He ducked into Eliza's apartment, pulled off his boots, tucked himself away into their bed, and was happy to awaken far after midnight with Eliza breathing softly beside him. He hadn't dreamed of anything he could recall.

Bill Sweet and Margie were married. She spent her mornings sorting post office mail in Hamilton, and Bill was a changed creature, a hardhanded country man who had gotten used to seeing that Bernard's work was done. "You got it back," he said. "The whole show."

Rossie took a deep breath and thought what to answer. Bill Sweet with good reason had to hate the fact that Rossie was automatically taking back his job. Bill had to hate the fact that his work through the war had earned him nothing permanent. "We'll bring in some young horses," Rossie said. "Two for each one of us. We been friends since Eagleville, nineteen thirty-four."

Bill Sweet didn't answer.

Down in the corrals beside his brickwork barn, Rossie touched at his Cahill mare, thankful for this remnant of life. It was evidence like this that saved him in the months to come. Things began to solidify, and he escaped his quaking fearfulness.

Then, in the spring, a pencil-written letter from Vernon O'Hearn made its way to

Rossie's hand though it was simply addressed to Ross Benasco, Hamilton, Montana. *Ross, if I had let you shoot then I'd have as much to live down as you do. This is to let you know I'm praying.*

Weeks later, into a third shot of Scotch with Bernard in his study, Rossie said, "You know about me."

Bernard said that indeed he did and reminded Rossie that he had suffered a collapse of his own in Chicago. "Staying busy is central in any cure. Focus on accomplishments. Maintain objectivity."

Rossie took Bill Sweet on a driving trip to the Sacramento Valley, where they brought four warm-blooded colts. With Bill loaded on the train with the horses, to feed and mind them during the trip to Montana, Rossie thought maybe he'd be lulled into peace by driving back alone.

But it wasn't roads or horses or any abstract idea like trust which got Rossie moving toward the restoration of his nerves. It was sitting up late in motel rooms on the trip and by Eliza's side after he got home, reading about the Montana fur trade of the 1830s in a novel called *The Big Sky*. The writer was A. B. Guthrie, a middle-aged fellow from Choteau whom Rossie had seen sitting alone in the Florence Hotel barroom in Missoula. As he suffered through Guthrie's book and wondered how much time a man had to spend paying attention in the country where he lived to know such detail, Rossie began understanding who he himself had become. The men in the novel — in their confusions in that wilderness they were like Bob Waters in the mountains beyond Banff, and like anybody. Rossie wondered if Bob Waters still regretted the loss of the woman who had been his wife and if that kind of thing was something you were bound never to get over. Women and horses, he thought, were sides of the same coin, cures for desolation.

Eliza hooted when he tried the idea on her. "Women? Who need to be placated with babies and diamond earrings. It's a pleasure, watching you try to think."

On the advice of Bernard, who told him he needed to focus on "rationality," Rossie in early 1947 read of commercial speculators trying to take over the federal lands across the west, including the national parks. A man named Bernard De Voto wrote in *Harper's* magazine that an economy in the West would have to be based on *the natural resources of the West, developed and integrated to produce a steady, sustained, permanent yield.* The region, De Voto wrote, was *moving to destroy the natural resources forever. The future of the West hinges on whether it can defend itself against itself.* This was an idea that resonated with Rossie. Dam the rivers, strip-mine the hills, clear-cut the forests, wreck the beauties, and they'll never come back.

"Not in a lifetime," Rossie would say. He read De Voto aloud at the breakfast table. "Defend what you love," Eliza said. "That's what he's saying."

"Simple as that," Bernard said. "There you'll find your intentions."

"Your true story," Eliza added, and it sounded like she meant it.

"At the moment I'm paying attention to this man Marshall," Bernard said in June, talking with a New York newspaper in his hands. Outdated by a week upon its arrival by train, the paper reported on a speech that Secretary of State George C. Marshall had given at Harvard, advocating a plan to restore "the confidence of the European people in the economic future of their own countries." Secretary Marshall proposed giving billions of dollars in aid to European nations, thus, Bernard said, "reinventing generosity. Restoring trust to the world."

Bernard theatrically drummed his fingers, in his pose of the rational man considering.

"We, all of us, should be thinking of how to reinvent trust. Without trust we're hopeless. That's my experience. Trust. There's your cure."

It was an intimation of purpose. Rossie woke one August morning to realize he hadn't dreamed in weeks, or wasn't remembering. He moved slowly through that day and the days after, as if hurrying might bring back his dread. Years later, he'd sit up entangled in sheets and shrug dreams away, still tempted to think that these terrors came to him from some other ruined life. The dreams, he'd say, laughing to cover his uneasiness, were "someone else's bad movie."

In early September Bill Sweet announced that he and Margie had been asking around for months and had found a job managing the horseback work on the old Battle Creek, a historic ranch out on the eastern Montana prairies beyond the Little Rockies. "This Bitterroot is gone to pony farms," Bill Sweet said. "But come the end of September I'm going to be my own boy over in that big country. They do it the old way. That's the idea, isn't it? Be your own boy."

"You're kind gimpy for a boy," Rossie said.

"You and me can visit back and forth.

That's my idea."

It was an idea that sounded like it might keep them healed. There was nothing to argue about. "Bernard could put up some money. You could run brood mares," Rossie said. "That way we could have excuses to visit."

But they didn't, not for most of two decades.

By October Rossie had sold four of what he called "gentle-broke" horses, animals he'd picked up around in the Bitterroot just that spring and worked with for only four months, three to women who just loved to ride and one to a realtor from Hamilton who made a hobby of competing in small-town roping events in Montana. "Good idea to show some income," he told Eliza, "or Bernard might be shutting me down at the money tree."

"Did you ask Bernard about that? He's not going to shut you down, and you know it. You didn't do it for Bernard. You did it for yourself, so you could be your own man, selling horses like Bobby."

Which was true when he gave it serious thought, and a surprise. Man ought to grow up eventually and trade with other men. He'd been building his horse deal and sometimes the going was slow, he had to admit it. With nothing else to do throughout the short, overcast afternoons of that winter he drew sketches of a barn that would enclose a circular corral where he and the horses could stay in out of the snow while he worked. While he felt lucky each day as his craziness slept, he knew that merely biding time was no way to go. He needed full-time work year-round and to work with others — Bobby Cahill was a loner but Rossie wasn't, he needed companions in the work, somebody to talk to in the barn and corrals. So he listened to Eliza and in April brought in two wild-haired young men from the Crow Reservation over southeast of Billings, paying them little but promising to educate them in Bobby Cahill's art of gentling horses, skills that would find them work wherever they might settle. It became a tradition, and such men would come and go, year after year, summering in tents by the creek and putting up through the winter in the old cookhouse. "I got my degree from Bobby Cahill," he'd tell them. "Good as college. I pay for the food, you do your own cooking, and don't do no drinking. You boys will get your degree from me."

But in the waning days of the next summer Rossie's sense of trust — if that was what he was relearning — was severely tested. A former communist named Whittaker Chambers had testified before the House Committee on Un-American Activities that Alger Hiss, president of the Carnegie Endowment for International Peace, was a spy for the Stalinist communists. News of this sent Bernard into a tirade.

"Turncoats and informers," Bernard said as he and Lemma were heading out on a walk. "We're turning Nazi." Stomping along beside an irrigation ditch between chest-high rows of flowers in the garden, he lifted his arms and shouted, with what seemed to be mock anger. "Un-American activities? There can be no un-American activities. This is a democracy."

He then convulsed and grimaced, took two stumbling steps, and tumbled sidelong into a flowing ditch.

Rossie heard the keening cries, the wailing, and found Lemma herself down in the ditch in her yellow dress, muddy and soaking, with Bernard's head in her lap. "So heavy," she gasped after Rossie got her out of the muck and piled the slippery and ungainly deadness of the thing that had been Bernard into a wheelbarrow. "His head," she whispered. She was panting like an animal, hovering as Rossie maneuvered the wheelbarrow along paths between banks of red and yellow roses.

Only days after Bernard was buried at the foot of the All Frogs Pole, Eliza reached to Rossie in their bed, murmuring and consenting, and eight weeks later he wasn't surprised when she announced at breakfast that she was pregnant. The fucking cure, he thought, which leads to the child — that cure. But he never said such things to Eliza.

On a chilly, clear, bluebird afternoon in October, while he was currying a new bay mare brought in from Nebraska, Rossie was surprised by Lemma in the open doorway of the barn, her back to the sun. The light shone through a gauzy black dress, silhouetting her long legs.

"I had to get out," she said. "I came to find someone who smells like a man." Her smile was not in the least uncertain. "Once you did us both a favor. You didn't go after me when I asked for it. But Eliza's pregnant again and even widows get horny."

Rossie lifted the curry comb between them, but she came in under his arm.

"Right now," she said. "Can you smell my horniness?"

Rossie took her by the shoulders and held her away. "Sure can," he said. "I can smell. Not now."

"Not ever. You're afraid to sink your

princely ship. You always have been."

He was indeed the one who was afraid.

She studied him, then pulled away. "Who could blame you? This is what you've got. It's all you're going to get. Why risk it? But you should know that marriage is a mirage, a movie. You should have got me but now I don't want it."

"The last time this happened — you should know this — I jerked off thinking about you. All over my belly, more than once."

"Now you'll do it again."

Over breakfast at a table set up outdoors beside the All Frogs Pole, he tried recounting this to Eliza. "Your mother, she's suffering. She tells me marriage is a mirage. Like the whole world is a ghost to her."

Eliza was looking past him at a tiny, dark-headed hummingbird, and Rossie sat regarding her silence, remembering that time years before when Lemma had propositioned him. Eliza had shrugged it away after asking if he'd complied, as if the chance that her husband was enjoying her mother might be a practical problem, perhaps permissible once in a while if they kept it quiet but not as a regular thing. As if only when such a thing became regular would it have to be dealt with. He was beginning to suspect that women and men together, families, were always a conspiracy. It was a thought he hated and put from his mind until that night in bed.

Eliza came to him breathless and began stroking at him. "There'll always be secrets," she whispered, "but we can have this. If we're careful, if you ease it into me, we can do it — even while this baby grows in my belly." As they progressed, Rossie managed to turn his mind from imagining Lemma.

In late May 1949, fifteen years after the agonies of Teddy's debut into the world, Eliza gave birth to a gray-eyed girl they named Veronica in a moment of frivolity, after the actress Veronica Lake. Rossie held the baby and said she smelled like flowers although she didn't. He said miracle cures might not be necessary if distractions like this one came along.

"Cures?" Eliza snorted. "I've been run over by a train."

Rossie tried his big grin. "Baby," he said, "you've been long-cocked."

She regarded him solemnly for a moment, shook her head, and turned back to her newborn. "Your own blood child," she murmured.

"The blood of your passing goes through you into your child," Rossie said, smiling like this was a joke. "That's how Bernard would say you stay in the world. Always sounded like bullshit to me. I'm just going to keep an eye on this girl and see how she's going to be."

Eliza looked up, finally smiling. "That can be one of your jobs."

Rossie hadn't finished high school, but he'd been entirely convinced by Bernard's claim that a useful person "necessarily" operated on the basis of knowledge. Rossie had counted on another twenty years of learning from those evenings over Scotch and despised his own ignorance, which seemed a perpetual impediment to the assiduous urge to be more than he was.

At the poker game in the back room of a dance hall just north of Hamilton, Rossie chanced to be seated beside a university professor named Otto Nelson, who was locally famous for huge lecture classes in Montana history at the university. Balding and blade-thin, he was renowned for going out each day, into every Montana environment, dressed in a pinstriped suit from New York.

"Bernard Stevenson's son-in-law, that's who you are," Nelson said through the smoke hanging in the glare of the low-hanging light over the table. "Bernard was a beauty. If Montana had any sense, Bernard would have been governor. Think of the governor asking us to Helena for evenings in his mansion. French food and 'le jazz hot' and talk of the Scottish renaissance? Let's have a drink to Bernard." Otto smiled. "Then, perhaps, another one after that."

Two weeks later they spent an evening in Missoula over dinner, during which Otto Nelson quizzed Rossie on whether "authentic Spanish horsemanship" was displayed by Nevada and California vaqueros. They drifted into friendship, and by fall Rossie was driving to Missoula two afternoons a week to sit in on Nelson's lectures.

With ironic humor and smiling distaste, the historian dissected mindless conquest and colonization — the lurid injustices brought onto the native peoples and then the settlers — first by the ruthless, racist military and then by the rampant, oligarchic powers of mining and logging corporations. He would smirk in his practiced way, then go on to evoke the details of this corruption — "yellow arsenic fogs hang in the air over Butte, children struggle for life while the air they breathe goes on killing them, wealthy men gaze over the heads of snot-nosed children at play in the muddy streets."

After lecturing, Otto led Rossie off to martinis in the art deco confines of the old Florence Hotel lobby — where Rossie had once spotted the writer A. B. Guthrie sitting alone over his own martini. It was now redecorated with brass and hardwoods and renamed The Clark Fork: A Tavern. Rossie told him of Eliza with the Blood Indians along the Bow River, and this talk led Otto to musing on the Spanish mustangs drifting north across the interior in the 1700s and native men on the Plains who then enjoyed a glorious century, chasing horseback after buffalo and one another until the buffalo vanished.

William Hornaday's expedition from the Smithsonian in 1886 had killed the last wild bison, Otto explained. They sent heads and hides and bones to the museum, in order *to save the bison.*

That remark generated another round of martinis.

When Rossie recounted Bernard's fatal fury after Whittaker Chambers's performance before the House Committee, Otto shook his head. " 'Un-American.' That's nonsense. But it's a long way from Montana. I don't care anymore." Obviously, he did care. "I've escaped, and prize nothing but friendship." He looked up and smiled in his thin way. "If that isn't fucked."

But the semester was ending. Rossie wondered if their meetings would continue. Then, after dinner one evening shortly before Christmas, the telephone rang.

"It's your friend Professor Nelson," Eliza said.

"Indeed," Otto Nelson said, " 'your friend.' " He was calling to invite Rossie and Eliza to his annual New Year's Day party. "You will be fresh blood," he said. "We're killing the fatted calf in honor of 1950."

Otto's parties were understood in Missoula to be resplendent events, so Eliza bought a new dress, dark purple with silver stripes, and Rossie wore a necktie. Three blocks from the oval brickwork entrance to the university, Otto lived in what passed for an old-money mansion, the historic, three-story Buckingham House, built in the 1880s. Otto greeted them at the door and kissed Eliza's hand. "High time," he said, ignoring Rossie. "A beauty arrives."

"This, isn't it the famous house?" Eliza asked.

"It's true. A governor shot himself here. Bad drugs. But we have good booze. And the will to consume. Get on to the bar, and introduce yourselves to the citizens."

The atmosphere of the huge room was that of a public museum, with great, dark oil paintings of western vistas, buffalo and steer heads mounted on pale-yellow walls, hardwood floors beneath Turkish carpets, ancient chairs and sofas covered in tanned zebra and spotted-leopard skins, a grizzly's hide with head attached and fangs exposed, and buffalo robes bought long ago from the remnant tribes. A bartender in a white coat was telling a run of Okie and Arkie jokes to fellows with full, graying beards down over their vests, and to students, at least two of whom were in possession of marijuana, the odor of which eventually drifted up from the basement.

Remarkably, after their decades in Montana, Rossie and Eliza found that the "citizens" were mostly strangers. They were rescued by Otto's wife, Marion Overlook, who had kept her maiden name into this third marriage. Tall and pale-eyed, she wore great diamonds on her lean, dark fingers. "You two," she said, coming through the crowd at the bar, "must be Benascos. I'm the slave Otto calls Maid Marion." She gave Rossie an ironic look. "Otto tells me you have a history with martinis." She ordered their drinks accordingly, winking as she handed them the conical glasses.

"It's a mistake to throw a party and know everybody. You two are my saving grace." Then she was gone, supervising the placement of baked cheeses and smoked turkeys, hams spiral-sliced on the bone, and steaming mounds of asparagus.

Hours had gone by when Otto whispered to Rossie. "Nobody will be left but for kids smoking dope in the basement with Marion. Stick around."

The three of them, Rossie and Eliza and Otto, settled in a room walled by glass-faced cases of books while the hired help went on with cleaning up in the public rooms. "Here we have it," Otto said. "The scholar, his wife's money, the brick house on the best street in a backwoods town full of third-rate university intellectuals blabbing away. The rewards of choosing a minor field."

"Minor?" Eliza asked.

Otto swirled his brandy. "The famous West." Marion appeared. "I've come to think of our romance as a cowboy drama. I let him bring me out to Missoula in the summer for a look around, and said yes. There was enough I wanted to get away from and this was a place for escaping. Why couldn't it have been a man who loved Tuscany?"

Weeks later, Eliza asked about Marion's

money. "First husband," Otto said. "Petroleum in the early days. Pennsylvania."

In February 1950 Senator Joseph R. McCarthy gave a speech in Wheeling, West Virginia, in which he asserted he knew of more than two hundred communists in the State Department. Otto claimed to have privileged information from friends in government that made it obvious McCarthy was lying. But nothing was to be done.

"Know history and the more you know the more cynical you become. But pay me no attention, inside each cynic there's a frantic, disillusioned, crybaby idealist."

Shooting began in Korea in June. By winter, after American success with the amphibious assault at Inchon, Chinese communists had intervened. When advance and retreat stalled along the thirty-eighth parallel in April, political discussions at home focused on failures, the "fall of China" to the reds, and supposed communist infiltration in U.S. policy making.

Truman's presidency, Otto said, was ruined. "All of it idiotic, stunning," he told his classes. "Do people in their right mind actually think the communists are about to take over the United States government? Do they imagine Russians are going to invade? There are oceans out there." He ragged at Rossie on the topic of Nevada and its corruptions. "Your Senator McCarran," he said, "is simultaneously hideous and unthinkable." To temper his own disgust, he echoed Bernard on the Marshall Plan. "Trust, trust one another. There's no other way. Wars and these witch-hunting denunciations will otherwise go on forever as they always have in history. Which is most likely."

The fall of 1952, Illinois governor Adlai Stevenson was defeated in his attempt at the presidency by General of the Army Dwight Eisenhower. Richard Nixon, who'd come to prominence prosecuting Alger Hiss, was vice president. Together they carried the Republicans to control of Congress.

"The rains came," Otto Nelson said, lifting a glass in toast to Stevenson. "We've lost the last decent man who will ever run for the presidency."

In the fall of 1953, after the Korean armistice had eased the nation's nerves, Eliza bought and refurbished a three-bedroom apartment on the sixth floor of the Hudson Building in downtown Missoula. Veronica was four and old enough to be left with a sitter, so Rossie and Eliza began staying in town overnight. The apartment looked down on Higgins Avenue and the bridge across the Clark Fork River, inspiring Rossie to invest in a high-end set of binoculars. He flaunted these as his personal spy gear when people — mostly university poets and historians they'd met through Otto — came for drinks.

Eliza had a television installed, and from April to June in 1954 guests came to huddle with the shades drawn in the afternoon, watching the thirty-six-day drama of the Army-McCarthy hearings, which came to a head when McCarthy attempted to destroy a younger lawyer's career by saying, without proof, that the man was a communist sympathizer, and the Army attorney faced him down.

"Until this moment, Senator," the avuncular Boston attorney representing the Army, Joseph N. Welch, said, "I think I never really gauged your cruelty or your recklessness." Eliza turned up the sound over the satisfied murmur that had erupted in her living room. "If it were in my power to forgive you for your reckless cruelty, I would do so. I like to think I'm a gentle man, but your forgiveness will have to come from someone other than me." At this Rossie clinked glasses with Eliza and others joined in. But Welch wasn't finished. "Have you no sense of decency, sir, at long last? Have you left no sense of decency?"

"There," Otto Nelson said. "At last. Civilization."

"You're topping off my education," Rossie said.

"You, my friend, have cultivated your own understanding in the art of tranquilizing an afternoon."

At night Eliza and Rossie sat with Otto at oilcloth-covered tables in Mollie's Place, a beatnik bar that became their club. Named for a bordello that had thrived in that same location until after the end of the war, the bar was now populated by pool-shooting hippie girls on scholarship and sad, bearded painters from the university art department, as well as firefighters who split cedar shakes to make a living through the snowy months, drug-dealing semi-poets, and Stalinist biochemists, all of them served by a tattooed, single-mother barmaid who owned the place and swore at her bartenders in Russian while Hank Williams and Ray Charles moaned, "Why don't you love me like you used to do?" and "I can't stop loving you."

Eliza said they were wasting the vitality of their finest years. "Drunk forever, every waking hour. That's where we're heading." Then she tasted the salt on the back of her hand and tossed back her tequila and smiled with sweet romantic bitterness, like a fall in that direction might be a fine idea for another night even if the years were getting away. Who knew what the children were thinking?

HOUSEHOLD MYSTERIES

Home from the bar, Eliza paid off Veronica's sitter and fussed about Corrie, now grown into a tall, blond, volleyball star who led the honor roll in science and math. She came and went so quietly, always smiling, that Eliza worried she was actually frantic, just keeping the lid on.

"Wouldn't you be frightened," she said to Rossie, "if your father shot your mother in a tavern and then himself? And your next family turned out to be alcoholics?"

"For Christ's sake," Rossie said, "nobody is drunks and she's seventeen years old." But Eliza insisted, so he tried a talk with Corrie.

She splayed her fingers and peeked at him between them, almost flirting. "Daddy, I don't need reassurance. Each morning, I'm all right." She spoke as if Rossie was the child. From nowhere, for the first time, she'd said, "Daddy."

Teddy at twenty was dark-eyed, stocky, heavy-shouldered, and a head shorter than Rossie. He was gone the other way, the antithesis of Corrie. "A perfectly predictable skunk," Eliza called him. "Does blood actually tell?"

Fights in the Hamilton High locker room with farm boys who called him a monkey-fucker brought him to the edge of being kicked out of school, which only compounded the fact that he was two years behind in his studies. Eliza accused him of acting out fantasies. "You're only a quarter-blood! And an entirely rotten apple." At night she wept.

Rossie eventually got Teddy down to the corrals to help with the colts, while Veronica, five that autumn, sat on a fence and watched. "Stands to reason you'd be smart-assed," Rossie said. "Charlie and your mother are old-fashioned pissers. But you ought to think about it. There's all ways of beating your head. Don't fall for the dumb ones."

Through this talk, Veronica was quiet and listening. "All ears," as Eliza said when Rossie told her about it, "a little girl gathering steam." What, Rossie wondered, for what? In time he would learn.

Meanwhile, the talk with Teddy seemed to

work until the cold February of 1955 when, age twenty-one and finally out of high school, he vanished off the midnight streets of Hamilton. There had been no warning. Rossie said leave it alone, but Eliza talked of hiring detectives. "He could be in the river," she said.

"Well, then, it's too late," Rossie said. "And he ain't in the river. He's seeing for himself. What can you do? Arrest him for ignoring you? He's a grown man and he's as all right as he's going to be."

"You don't know," Eliza said. "There's that river."

But Teddy, it turned out, was trying his hand at rough-stock, the bulls and bareback horses across New Mexico and Arizona, embracing the notion of conquering animals Rossie had taught him to despise. And he was having no luck. A red-freckled bull had stepped on his left ankle in Las Cruces, and he was reduced to clumping along in a hard cast and bumming his way through beer joints around Flagstaff, Arizona. Then he encountered a girl, Wilma Duckfinder, who said she was escaping from the Crow Agency in eastern Montana. That's why she was a barmaid in Foster's Tavern. She touched Teddy's bare forearm and asked what he needed. When he answered that he needed a line of credit, Wilma brought him a Miller High Life and ignored his wrinkled dollar. He couldn't stop watching as she waltzed away, switching that long black ponytail.

In late August, two days after Eliza got home from driving Corrie back to the University of Washington, Teddy called and stammered out his story. "This girl, we went and got married in Las Vegas. We're on our way home."

Teddy hung up without saying how they'd get there, but on a hot evening two days later he called from Hamilton and asked if Rossie could come give them a ride. Sure enough, they were standing on a street corner, Teddy and his sharp-featured little woman, when Rossie pulled the car into town.

Eliza had brought a handful of pink-and-white gladiolas from her garden but then wouldn't get out of the Buick. "I can't," she said. "Leave me. Let me look at them."

Rossie didn't hide his pleasure. "You find anybody better than her," he said, reaching for Teddy's hand but eyeing Wilma, "you cut me a share."

Wilma was staring off toward the mountains.

"Well," Teddy said, his clenched, boyish

sternness falling away, "she's a deal all right."

Eliza at last materialized out of the Buick and held forth the gladiolas. "Glories," she said to Wilma. "For you, now that you're here."

"What I really want," Wilma said, turning and softening, "is a shower."

When they got back to the house Veronica was out front to greet them, a serious girl in the twilight. "Brother," she said, after Teddy had picked her up, "I love you." She was cutting her eyes sideways toward Wilma. "Her too."

"Miss Big-Eyes," Eliza said. "She sees everything."

Deep in the night, after Veronica had been put to bed, they called Corrie on the telephone in Seattle.

"I'm jealous," she said to Teddy. "You know what you want."

Teddy tried joking. "Wilma and me, you got it right, we're going to be somebody. We don't know who it is, but it's going to be somebody who don't shit in their own nest."

"See?" Corrie said. "I'm going to college. You've got a real life."

"A real life," Teddy said, after he'd hung up. "She said I've got a real life."

"Maybe so," Eliza said, "if you study

curiosity. Find out which somebody to be. Both of you."

When Teddy rolled his eyes, Rossie patted her back. "There it is, these women. They got plans under way."

Wilma was soon pregnant. In the icy winter of 1956, she bore twins named Max and Leo. Rossie would soon be calling them Wrack and Ruin, as they rolled through the house like bear cubs, upsetting chairs and babbling a semiprivate patois, absorbed in their games.

Lemma had moved to Chicago several years earlier to share an apartment with Howard, asserting that Bernard wouldn't have wanted her to live there in Montana without him. She'd cultivated new friends, accompanying women and their elderly husbands to chamber concerts and operas. Then, late spring of 1956, Lemma began her "extreme forgetting," a result of what her doctor said was a long series of accumulating strokes. In the fall, after failing rapidly, she died with Eliza at her bedside.

"She wouldn't let go of that photo of Teddy's boys. It was like her ticket to someplace," Eliza told Rossie on the telephone. "She was lost and laughing and happy to be on her way."

Larch needles were turning and falling as Rossie walked out into the dry fields where Lemma had come to find him that long-ago afternoon. All their summers were ending. "They're gone," Eliza said when she got home. "We're on our own. There's nobody else."

Arnold Meisner, after so many years, flew to Chicago from Berlin and traveled west on the railroad with Lemma's zinc-lined casket. He'd been in Europe throughout the last decade, photographing portraits of "ancient Nazis" as they contemplated the end of their regime. "It's vengeance," he said. "My way of getting even."

On a rainy Bitterroot afternoon, Lemma's casket was lowered into its grave alongside Bernard's at the foot of the All Frogs Pole. She had willed her properties to Eliza, writing that the future generations were on their own so far as she and Bernard were concerned. "We've gone to the frogs."

Arnold spoke before Lemma's remains were lowered. "Lemma and Bernard Stevenson were people I cherished. I admired their wit and will, and I was jealous of their support for one another. On sleepless nights, as bombs fell in Spain, I thought of my old friends in this valley with their tranquilities. I cursed myself because I hadn't the sense to be here with them. Now they're gone and we've lost another foundation from under our reasons to continue. I weep for them and for myself." Arnold grimaced, looking around as if he had just realized that he might in actual fact weep.

Later, he chastised Eliza. "Look around. Where are your lives?" he demanded. "What do you see? Children's treasures, volleyball trophies, and silver-mounted saddles. Anything of significance came from Lemma and Bernard. Not one stick of their furniture has been replaced. What do you have that's only yours?" It was true, the flooring and the redwood walls and the river-stone fireplaces and *Krazy Kat* and the photograph of Eliza and Rossie with the bears, all had been laid down or put up and cherished by Lemma and Bernard.

"Scaly handed little shit," Eliza said, once Arnold was on his flight back to Berlin. "This house is inhabited by breathing memories." At that time she was given to reading aloud from Proust on the death of his grandmother, a dead-on connection with sadness, Rossie thought, and contrary to her insistence that the atmosphere in their house resonated with the living essence of her parents. This continued for months until she finally gave it up and admitted that Arnold was correct.

"You think they'll live forever," she said. "It's entirely our house now." In the spring she ordered bedding and drapes and kitchenware in Seattle. "A beginning," she said.

It had come clear to Rossie that Eliza's determined ambitions had in some part been a rebuttal to Lemma's steadfast willingness to accede to Bernard's whims. In girlhood, as he saw it, Eliza had learned to insist on having life her own way. But that, he thought, could be a recipe for another kind of ruthlessness.

He wondered if she might even have condoned his fucking with Lemma once in a while if it had actually happened. Fondling his cock in the bed, with Eliza sleeping there beside him, he sorrowed again for Lemma and found himself recalling her long, white legs and wondering whatever she had been offering, if it had been more than simply a fuck on the side.

That summer Rossie found his twenty-six-year-old mare, Katrina, in the Tailfeather Field, dead of aging after a venerable duration for a horse. There was nothing to be done. That which couldn't be cured had to be suffered, though he found solace in watching Veronica, his scrappy child, gallop bareback across the meadows on an old gelding named Snip. "I wanted a buckaroo like you," he told her. "That's secret. Don't tell your mother."

Years later, as Veronica grew, Rossie watched her turn away from Eliza and her manipulations to focus her own efforts toward acquiescence and "true womanliness," as she called it, though it turned out to mean nothing more than caring for her man. But not until Veronica was a woman with children of her own, and it was too late in the game, did he try to understand the stop-loss reasons why she'd felt moved to perfect the art of relinquishing.

Rossie eventually came to feel he had failed her, his blood-related horseback girl and only progeny, in some minutely incremental but vastly consequential degree. It came down, he thought, to the fact that there hadn't been enough bottom or foundation to their lives, his and Eliza's — that was how he understood it: failure learned at home, by example.

While Teddy plugged along, in and out of school at the university in Missoula, Corrie had finished up at the University of Washington and announced her intention to spend a summer at an archeological dig in southern Chile. "Hearths, like ours," she said. "They were cooking stew twelve thousand years ago."

As Rossie opened the second bottle of pinot noir at the dinner table, Eliza started again on her lamentation about "these numbing years." Rossie said it was her way of tricking herself into sadness.

"Why not?" she said. "Without sadness, we forget."

"You just want somebody to stir your pot."

"What you ought to try is fucking yourself."

"I've tried it. It's pointless."

Eliza looked to be amused perhaps by the notion that they understood each other on a level that was not numbing but always their contest. "That's what I'm sad about," she said. "Pointlessness."

Veronica, half hidden in the hallway, watched them and listened.

"Things got scattered," Rossie said. "Hell to tomorrow."

Awake at daybreak he lay beside her and wondered if it was grief that had soured her or if she was really just bored and not soured at all. The years had got away after Honolulu. Teddy and Corrie slammed through high school, volleyball girls slept over, Teddy stayed out all night in Hamilton, and telephone cords reached under closed doors into closets where some friend from school was weeping over love. In summer break, Teddy and Corrie worked the hay fields and came home sunburned, sweaty, and proud as they headed for their showers. They would all of them ride out for evening meals on Hudson Bay blankets by the creek and fish for rainbow trout that Eliza fried up in cast-iron skillets as soon as they were caught and gutted. So fresh, nerves still active if not alive, the trout would sometimes writhe in the pan as they cooked. Flowing water, dark mountains above them, the family noisy and bright riding home after dark, it should have been enough. But another fall: Bernard and Lemma in the ground beside the All Frogs Pole and Teddy and Corrie gone off. The house undeniably had emptied out.

"This July," he told Eliza, "I'm renting a house on Flathead, a dock, the speed boat, the works. The kids can speed around and swim or sleep on the lawn or read a book or anything they can think of. But they're going to sit down with us at supper every night. You and me will be old folks."

In July they convened their first summer encampment on Flathead Lake. Rossie got them into life jackets, even Wilma's babies, and into the wooden speedboat. After roaring across the open water they watched sunset from among the spruce-crowned Bird Islands as an osprey folded and plummeted into the water like a thrown stone to emerge with a flopping kokanee in its talons. They feasted on cold roasted chicken, spiral-sliced ham, and slices of Walla Walla sweet onions, wedges of cheese, plums, and Flathead cherries picked that day, iced Anchor Steam Beer from San Francisco, and Vernors ginger ale for Veronica.

Corrie had called from Seattle and persuaded Rossie to bring six pounds of venison steak for a *mole de venado.* Coming off the plane she lugged a duffle loaded with items from a Mexican market on the south side of Tacoma, jalapeños, serrano chilies, costeno and guajillo chilies, sprigs of espazote and avocado leaves, heads of garlic for the soup. She spent a day chopping and simmering, toasting chilies and roasting unpeeled garlic cloves, to assemble a dinner with corn tamales and quarts of Pacífico beer.

"She brought it off," Eliza whispered that night.

"For our children," Rossie said. Not exactly his children or grandchildren, in terms of blood, except for Veronica. "One of them, anyway, is mine."

"Every one of them," she murmured, shaking her head, turning away.

The last night, Eliza sat them down before a fire. "Think," she told them, in her lecturing mode. "To be happy we have to be smart." She said it would take "relentless concentration and smartness" if they were to realize their ambitions.

"I'm working on mine," Teddy said. "No luck yet." He was amused.

Eliza was not. "You have ambitions," she said. "Or you'll be a wandering soul. We couldn't stand that. You owe us more than that."

In bed she read Rossie a passage about Levin laboring in the fields from *Anna Karenina.* "We'll do this every summer." And they did. By the time Teddy and Wilma's children could manage horses, the encampments involved weeklong horse packing trips to tent camps on the shores of tiny lakes high in the Idaho wilderness.

Having found her passion in the excavations in Chile, Corrie returned to the University of Washington to begin graduate work in archeology, and after years of on-and-off attendance, Teddy, at twenty-six, finished at the university in Missoula. Veronica rode a yellow bus to her last year of grade school in Hamilton.

"You," Rossie said to Eliza. "You've got everybody on the job, everybody but you."

This resumed an old argument about Rossie's intentions, and hers, their chances of having what Eliza had taken to calling a "positive effect" on the world.

"You go through the motions, year after year," she said. "Those men come from California to buy horses, you go buy theirs. What are we doing?"

It was true. Without admitting it to Eliza, Rossie recollected that snowy day down by the creek, just after they were married, when Slivers Flynn talked about doing the same work all your life, over and over. He tried to think of where he could go beyond horses.

Finally, the summer of 1962, Rossie declared for a seat on the county commission in the Bitterroot and embarked on a campaign going horseback up and down roads across the valley to demonstrate neighborliness, stammering speeches in support of agricultural communities and good schools and flexible conservation rules for public lands, and telling his stories of having come home from Guam "wounded and scatter-headed." After all this, along with hand-shaking and joking at the livestock auction yards and interviews at school board meetings, Rossie, much to his surprise, won.

"Of course," Eliza said. "You're the good, prosperous man."

He went on running every two years, winning and going out to meetings in Hamilton Courthouse on Monday nights.

"A smiling public man," Eliza said, paraphrasing William Butler Yeats's comment on his own political career in the country W. H. Auden, one of her other favorites, had called Mad Ireland in his eulogy to Yeats.

Deep in the small hours of November 23, 1963, a heavy-shouldered man with a black patch over his left eye, the cuffs of his Levi's jacket worn to threads no doubt by bucking hay bales in some field, spat on the tavern floor and scowled at Otto Nelson. Three teeth were missing. "Candy-asses," he said.

It was four in the morning but the bars wouldn't be closing. All bets were off. It was homecoming weekend but the Missoula-Bozeman football game was canceled. President Kennedy was dead and the drinking had begun in the afternoon. Downtown taverns were awash with clamor and the unfocused confusion and grief that the one-eyed man seemed to reflect as he spat.

"Grieving in truth for themselves," Otto said. "What everyone wants, this night, is fucking. Make-believe perpetuating. It's a good night to get laid."

"Or beat up," Rossie said. "There are boys out here who think they can set things straight."

"Lone Rangers." Otto eyed the one-eyed man. "Cowboys thrashing candy-asses, and the candy-asses outwitting cowboys, a cyclical intimacy."

"Tell you, Mister," the one-eyed man said, turning to Otto. "Go piss in your pocket."

Rossie felt a half-drunken flare of anger. "You sound like you want to get your ass kicked."

The one-eyed man turned on his stool and grinned. "You're pretty old for that kind of roostering."

"Don't worry about me. You want your ass kicked, I can find friends. I can hire them. They'll do it."

The man shook his head, picked up his beer glass, eased off his stool, and walked away.

Otto Nelson was chuckling. "Roostering! The colonialist tableaux. They yearn to kill us, we mention hiring violence, and it's over, they have the wisdom to melt. Power. It worked for Hitler, why not us?"

But Rossie was watching the one-eyed man hunch his way onto another stool.

"Otto, you must think you're walking on water. One of these boys is going to knock your teeth out."

"It's only bar talk, Ross."

But it wasn't, not only. Rossie realized that he was far across the boundary that separated the one-eyed man from Otto. He'd found his way over onto Otto's side of the street, and he wasn't sure that was where he wanted to be. He considered walking down the bar to buy the one-eyed man a beer and a shot, but the scab-handed Basque boy who had ridden out of Nevada wouldn't have liked the one-eyed man or Otto Nelson, not either one of them. So he ordered a fifty-dollar round of drinks, a beer and a shot for "every swinging dick up and down the bar," including the one-eyed man, all the while watching himself in the mirror behind the bartender. Rossie told the man he saw there to forget it, live with it.

At daybreak, they stepped into the Buckingham House room with glass-fronted bookcases. Rossie was falling-down tired but unwilling to think of sleeping. The day before he'd been driving Eliza to Missoula, heading for the homecoming party at Otto's house, when they'd heard the news on the radio in the Buick. By that time John Kennedy was dead. They detoured to their apartment in the Hudson Building and were watching the chaos on television when Otto called. "Get over here," he said. "We need company." By twilight they had gone out to join the mob rolling all over town, spilling from the taverns into the streets. "The last time I saw this," Otto said, "was VJ day." Then their women went home, but Otto said they had to see it through.

So there they were in the half-light of Otto's study, with Rossie babbling about that movie, *Metropolis,* that Eliza had taken him to see in Chicago all those decades in the past.

"Eliza and I fought like dogs about that one, right in the street. She said it could come true. I had to think she was preaching horseshit. But maybe she was right. Maybe the shooting match could come unglued and fall through the cracks like a house of cards."

"You," Otto said, "are a master of metaphor."

"That's what everyone's afraid of, what we're afraid of," Otto went on. "So they're out there fucking with their eyes shut." He pretended to croon an old song lyric: *They can't take that away from me.* "But we won't come unglued. Not so long as the people believe in American royalty, princes like

Citizen Kane and Gatsby and Jack Kennedy. We forgive them their cruelty and all the injustice they stir up so long as we get to believe in them and their fine fresh shirts." Otto was lecturing. "Equality is our prime theoretical value. We dump slavery, champion civil rights, labor rights, ethnic rights, voting rights, women's rights. But we're afraid to face down the injustice and corruption which is the water we swim in. We can't stand the idea that our political and economic masters are indifferent to the suffering they cause, so we imagine them to be wounded princes, driven by memories of a childhood love, boys seeking approval, and thus forgivable."

"Lemma, years ago" — in a drunk-man way, Rossie understood that saying this indicated how profoundly he trusted Otto — "she asked me to fuck her and I wouldn't. She said she didn't blame me if I was afraid it might jeopardize my chickenshit princedom. Maybe she didn't say chickenshit but she said we'd be friends the next day and we were. All was forgotten."

"She asked? Bless her," Otto said. "Should have given me a call." He poured himself another shot of the bourbon. "But she wanted a cowboy. Women are more like us than we want to think, but disciplined because they have to be. There's no one harder than a woman who won't let compassion get in her way. You have your marching orders, Captain. Use your powers for the good of all. Roostering. It's our mission."

In late spring, just before Teddy's graduation from business school at the university, Eliza sat him down and asked what he expected. "You must have something on your mind."

"Wilma," Teddy said. "No more school." He grinned at Rossie. "The corrals been good to you. You got away with it."

Eliza's eyes glazed, like she couldn't stand looking at either of them. "No doubt you'll think of something."

The day Teddy was to wear his black gown for his university graduation, the family gathered in a Missoula restaurant for breakfast — Rossie and Eliza, Teddy and Wilma and their boys, Max and Leo, and Veronica and Corrie. After Swedish pancakes, Eliza slid a heavy ring of keys across the table to Teddy. These were keys to the old Wilson Brothers hardware store in Hamilton.

"The deed is in your name," Rossie said, following her instructions. "It's your ship. Go down there and start sailing. Piss it away, and you're on your own."

"Huh!" Teddy said. "Hardware?"

But Wilma wasn't hesitant. "Not too hard to think about," she said. "Thank you."

Teddy came around rather quickly. He borrowed money and bought a fixer-up house under cottonwoods beside the river south of Hamilton and put up a neon sign over the store: Blue Hardware. "Sounds mystical," he said, "like it might be an Indian store." He gave wheezing, corpulent Lon Winston, who had varying uses and dimensions of the thousands of hardware items catalogued in his memory, a raise of ten dollars a week. "So he never quits," Teddy explained, since without Lon, at least until Teddy learned the trade, there was effectively no store.

He set up a ring of captain's chairs around a woodstove back by the office. Coffee went free. Men carrying half-pint bottles of whiskey, country wives, and women used to loud talk and making themselves heard got into the habit of visiting like the store was a club. In addition to bins of galvanized nails and one-ton rolls of logging cable stored in a lot on the alley, Teddy ordered whatever Lon Winston told him to order or anything anybody could draw him a picture of or describe in a sensible way. His evenings were spent memorizing the stock items in the store. It was its own language: carriage bolts, Jennings double-twist auger bits, jay rollers used by the men putting down veneer and laminates, radiator air-bleeder valves, tack hammers, spring-loaded brad drivers to set small finishing nails without a hammer, cat's-paw pry bars, and on and on, the apparatus of a civilization.

Teddy also spent time at a rolltop desk in the store, writing in buckram-bound journals he'd ordered from an art supply house in Chicago. He noted down scraps of talk and pasted in newspaper stories about Native affairs, birthday cards, and photographs people brought him. That habit, writing and pasting, learned as a boy in his room in Honolulu, had become a lifetime routine.

"So you see," Eliza said. "Everything can come out all right."

Wait a while, just wait, Rossie thought.

On a July morning, a red-bearded fellow from Santa Cruz, California, ambled into Teddy's store. "They tell me you are simpatico to wanderers," he said. "You might know of work for a good man who's relocating. This is the valley I'm looking for. I'm changing my name to Mr. Bitterroot, a man who's not hunting handouts. Gardening and carpentering is my talents. You and me can be friends and allies. You and Mr. Bitterroot."

"We could be friends and allies?" Teddy said. "Who told you I'm simpatico to wanderers? That's a thing you made up, or I'd be wall to wall with tramps and hippies."

"They say you're simpatico to everybody. Why not wanderers?"

"You hitchhiking? On the run? You a miscreant, a badlands killer?"

But Teddy was smiling and the red-bearded fellow turned out to be looking for actual work. He was thirty-seven dollars from broke but driving a red 1954 GMC pickup he'd brought north from Santa Cruz. "All-day work," he said. "Paying debts to the Lord." The fellow's hands were hard with calluses, and that GMC was a working man's pickup.

"Which variety of carpentering?" Teddy asked.

"My finish work is rough but I'm learning."

"Well, you're in luck. Rough might be good enough. My mother is hiring. Talking to her, I'd shitcan that talk of the Lord. She has her own ideas."

"She a freethinker? That's good. Freethinkers are into strength of soul and mind."

After lunch, Teddy took him to meet Eliza.

She'd been talking of hiring a carpenter to rebuild the old Cliff House above Kanaka Creek. It was Teddy's idea that "Mr. Bitterroot" might live up there for free in return for carpenter work.

"Got here with nearly no money," the fellow told Eliza. "Give me use of the buildings and garden land down here, and I'll fix it up cheap. Next year I'll provide vegetables. I'll split a profit with you on what produce I can sell in the valley."

"I was bored," Eliza told Rossie over dinner that night. "He was cute. I went for it."

After the first weeks, when the fellow was joked about as "Eliza's hippie," locals shifted to muted respect, saying Mr. Bitterroot was loon-crazy but a hell of a worker.

"It's a deal for Eliza," Rossie said, getting his trim in the Hamilton barbershop. "Everybody is doing fine." He looked as if he might expect argument. "Anyway, his real name is Lionel. We won't hear any more of that 'Mr. Bitterroot.' "

To bring in cash that first summer, Lionel worked around in the valley for day wages, cleaning up trash dumped along the banks of sloughs and out behind barns, using his GMC pickup to haul off rusted-out fuel barrels and rotted mattresses to the landfill east of Victor. When people asked what he was up to, he replied, "Looking skyward to the turnings of evolution. No revolutions but in the sky."

"That boy may be onto something," a grinning Hamilton car dealer told Rossie. "We could stand evolutions around here."

Come winter, when the road up the mountain was blocked by drifted snow and sheeted with ice, Lionel lived in the old bunkhouse room where Rossie had slept when he was courting Eliza. "Rather be up there on the mountain," he said, "hearing the snow fall, flake by flake."

In the spring, Eliza hired a Caterpillar road grader to cut an irrigation ditch to her onetime Indian farm. Apple and pear and cherry trees in the old homesteader's orchard hadn't seen irrigation in decades and were mostly dead. Lionel dragged them from the soft loamy ground with a borrowed Fordson tractor, stacking the trunks to be cut into firewood in the fall. He plowed under reefs of decaying sweet clover. "This is the only time we'll use a tractor on this land," he said. "Can't stand compaction."

Two young men and a young woman from California arrived. Each of them, Lionel said, he'd vouch for, each was a "vitalist primo horticulturist" from the "primo garden systems" at the college on the hill above Santa Cruz. "They came up here," Lionel said, "to put their education to work."

"They let you graduate in gardening?" Rossie said.

"It's called horticulture," Lionel said.

"Looks like you'd have stayed in a place like that," Rossie said.

But Lionel's friends worked from sunup into darkness, raking, planting, building little garden-ditch headgates. A blond Vermont woman with hair in braids to her waist showed up with a child in arms and a toddler, two pale creatures. Bitterroot people wondered how long it would be until one of those children fell from the cliff. But she hauled those kids up the mountain and down as she worked the garden like the rest of them.

"How far," Rossie asked Eliza, "are you going with this hippie farming?"

"It's under control," Eliza said.

He left it at that. In their division of powers, Eliza ran her properties, the creamery and dairies, and the acreages that she'd inherited. Rossie had his barn at the edge of the Tailfeather Field and his horses and occasional young men who worked with him, as well as his arcane network of horse people, livestock merchants and trainers and veterinarians and rodeo ropers who would sometimes call at night and want to spend an hour or so talking over what had happened that week at the cutting show in Lubbock, or at the million-dollar quarter-horse race in Ruidoso.

"What I'm doing about those garden kids," Rossie said in the barbershop, "is looking the other way."

"Hard to tell them apart," people said. But come daybreak those kids were down in the garden, bare-legged and barefoot, muddy to their knees.

The garden was brilliant with vegetables — sixteen varieties of hot pepper, cantaloupe by the pickup load, corn and cabbage and sweet yellowish Siberian tomatoes. In the evenings they hauled two-by-fours and sheetrock up from Teddy's store in Hamilton and hammered away at the Cliff House. A preacher from the Mormon community sent a letter to the Hamilton newspaper calling them "communists" and asking, "Who invited them? What are their purposes?"

Eliza held her silence. Rossie, in the barbershop, said he guessed they were doing "just fine enough." But rumors of drugs and free love and perversities drifted across the valley. Another letter to the editor questioned if those "ninnies on the hill" intended to stay in the valley and "start families and send their children to the local schools. Corrupt ideas and heedlessness could infect the younger generation. What if a child came down with disease? What about doctors?"

This line of reasoning collapsed when Teresa Robertson, a retired medical doctor, moved in and said she was offering free care to "my kids." Public service and challenge, she said, were just what she was looking for. She had come west to give something back.

"At last," Eliza said, "educated company." Overhearing a woman in the Hamilton Bi-Lo grocery store speculating if Teresa Robertson was sleeping with "the boys or the girls," Eliza announced aloud in the woman's presence that such talk was "common, sluttish, indecent bitchery."

Teresa contracted to have a tight shingle-sided house built on a former homestead site beside the next creek south from Kanaka, and when the work was finished, brought her eighty-six-year-old mother from Boston to share it with her.

Eliza said that should put a stop to talk about Teresa's motives. "What she's on the lookout for is clear sailing. People who say what they mean." Then she smiled. "Whatever that is."

Rossie kept his head down, intent every morning on breaking in a pair of brothers from the Crow Reservation to his version of the horse world and getting another set of three-year-old geldings settled for the summer. Teddy ran his hardware store and Corrie was in Seattle, deep into the writing of her scientific thesis about archeological developments in Chile. Veronica thrived in her senior year at the high school in Hamilton, a strapping girl and an utterly whirlwind softball pitcher. Breakfast after breakfast, after the winter snows and into spring and summer, Rossie read the day-old sports page out of the Missoula newspaper he'd saved from the afternoon before, and went out to his horses, leaving domesticities to go their own way.

"Evolutions," Eliza said after an evening telephone talk with Teresa Robertson. "Don't you love it?" When Rossie didn't answer, she smiled in a cold way and accused him of having turned into "one petrified buckaroo, not so interesting anymore."

"Get you into the bedroom," he said, "and we'll see what's interesting."

But she only shook her head. "Don't you wish," she said, and she started washing the dishes.

FAR POINT

In May of 1966, there came a scribbled note from Bill Sweet, mailed from the eastern Montana town of Malta: *Time you got off the rocking chair and drove over to see the real thing. Come late June, over a Sunday. We'll brand calves and show you country roping. Call on the telephone.*

This was after nineteen years of silence punctuated only by Christmas cards. When he called on the telephone Margie answered and Bill Sweet never did come on the line, but Rossie could hear him shouting in the background, telling Margie what to say.

"We're getting along in years," Margie said. "That's why. You ought to see this country before we all die. That's what Bill says. Blow off the old stick-in-the-mud Bitterroot stink."

"Certainly, go," Eliza said. "It would be a vast relief to both of us. Maybe you're one of nature's on-the-road men."

On a late June evening, after a long day of traveling up the Blackfoot River and over the Continental Divide to the Montana high-line, Rossie turned off a two-lane highway about thirty miles south of Malta and followed a dirt road out onto the infinite run of rolling grasslands. The headquarters building at Battle Creek Ranch was a slumping but freshly painted white house surrounded by a patchy lawn and suckerwood remnants of hundred-year-old cottonwood and locust trees planted by the first generation of cattlemen from Texas. The yard was boxed by a hog-wire fence that was thick with wild roses.

Bill Sweet — it was clearly him, the same towheaded fellow after all the years — was out at the gate, darker at first sight, heavier through the shoulders but otherwise the same skinny piece of work. "Heard you coming," he said after Rossie stepped out of his Ford. "Heard you half a mile away. Can't get away with making a sound in this country."

Before Rossie could answer, Margie came from the house. She was meatier but solid, looking strong rather than at all fatty. "Christ in heaven," she shouted, wiping her hands on her apron. "Kiss my cheeks."

So Rossie did it, both cheeks.

"Kiss mine," Sweet said, and he bent over, sticking out his butt.

"You boys," Margie said. "What a welcome. Me and Jack Sprat, living on the lean and fat of the land. What we got tonight is rib steaks, ice cream, and whiskey. Peach ice cream Mr. Sweet churned himself and a half gallon of Jack Daniel's."

Rossie and Bill Sweet sipped bourbon and water over ice while Margie went to the cooking.

"You'll be on my blue mare," she told Rossie as she stirred up a salad. "You can rope off her. She'll drag a calf. Less you don't want a mare. In which case I'll be insulted. Piss on them that don't want a mare."

Bill Sweet broke from his brooding quiet and grinned. "Them women."

"This woman," she said to Rossie, "is going to be trucking your bedrolls and your dinner down to the river tomorrow. Same old delivery service. Isn't got no kids but I got you boys."

It was planned that Rossie and Bill Sweet would ride off south the next morning across the folds of prairie to the remains of a defunct town called Far Point, down on the banks of the Missouri River. They'd camp amid the abandoned storefront buildings for a night and the next day help out at a branding. Margie would spend an afternoon quilting in Malta and be along in the late afternoon.

"God knows . . ." Rossie didn't know what to say beyond that.

"Yes sir," Margie said. "And he don't give a shit."

Horseback in ninety-degree heat the next afternoon, Rossie and Bill Sweet gazed down from high, chalky cliffs above the sand-bar undulations of the Missouri River. They'd crossed dry creek beds and rode through a dozen hundred-acre prairie dog towns but seen no fences and only a lone sod-walled schoolhouse. "This here was the Exeter School," Sweet said. "Kids all came in on horseback. It was still going when we first come out. But too much of this rangeland went back to the federals during the Depression. All along the river it's a federal preserve. Off limits to hunting down by the river. A lot of the early settlers are gone. Fucking federals. How would they know anything?" He took off his hat and mopped his forehead. "Seen it when there was a breeze up on these cliffs."

But this day it was dead still. They made their way down a long, brushy ravine to the river, where a hundred and thirty-some-odd mother cows and their unbranded spring calves grazed a roughly fenced, thousand-acre field.

This was Far Point, an occasional cow camp set up amid the saw-lumber buildings that remained from what eighty years ago had been a steamboat stop and then a renowned Montana wolf-hunter town. With their horses turned loose to roll in the dust of a pasture, they found their bedrolls where Margie had left them, in a cabin sealed against vermin with flattened tin cans nailed over the knot and rat holes. She'd provided them with canned peaches and fresh tomatoes, which they rustled from the cool water of a spring bubbling up inside a cavern in the white cliffs.

"Them wolfers killed each other and every other damned thing," Bill Sweet said. "Held up trains, stole horses, and rustled calves. Ranchers hanged them off cottonwoods. Don't think we miss those times, though I'd take the music and dancing that came with the steamboats tied up here for putting on wood for the boilers. You recall the Snake River and that Gypsy girl? You was a fearless dancer."

They were salting the fresh tomatoes, biting in and letting the juice run down their chins, and spooning peaches out of the cans.

"You could buy into this country."

"You selling me something?"

Bill Sweet turned serious. "I'm offering a present. This life out here is a Christmas present. I think about you once in a while. Too many corrals, you end up taming yourself."

"You always was a philosopher."

The evening cooled as Bill Sweet led Rossie up into an erosion canyon in the white cliffs. "They's been a lot of this forgot," he said showing Rossie an enormous thigh bone, six or eight feet long, embedded in a chalky wall above their heads. "Dinosaurs. Professors come looking for bones, but so far they don't know about these. I got a feeling that someday they'll be out here in Jeeps."

"What I got," Rossie said, "is a feeling we could eat them hamhock beans cold and unplug that whiskey."

So they sat on logs and spooned beans from the pot Margie had left, wiping their fingers on their pants and sipping from the bottle as they watched young, limber-legged elk graze and dance at one another across the river.

A Labrador retriever came dripping from the water, a huge, brown fellow.

"Bruno," Bill Sweet said, as the dog

bounded toward him. "You're far from home."

The dog stared off into the canyon behind them, where Rossie saw a man on a gray horse, a slow ghost in the shadows.

"Mr. Frakes," Bill Sweet shouted without looking around. "Your dog is running loose. You been shooting coyotes?"

Standing before them, the man was tiny and ancient. "Poisoning prairie dogs. Heard you'd be down here tonight. Thought I'd get some company and a drink of whiskey."

"You bring your bedroll? Turn your horse loose in the catch pasture. You ain't going home. Can't have you wandering around drunk in the dark." Bill Sweet held up the bottle. "Then you can start drinking whiskey."

"Afraid I started seventy years ago, in Wales, where you never been." He looked to Rossie. "I was bumming the world, then ended up here and never left."

"Mr. Frakes has been in these badlands since you and me were born. He keeps track for us. He's had cows in these breaks since the First World War."

"Keeping track of more than you," Mr. Frakes said. "There's plenty to keep track of, plenty." He was at the whiskey bottle. "What do you think of Mr. Sweet?" he asked Rossie. "He spends all his life running other people's cows. *Somebody* has got to keep track of him if he's going with that much foolishness." He pushed the bottle toward Rossie. "Don't let me near that whiskey again. Another shot and I'll be asleep."

But Mr. Frakes didn't make a pass at sleep until the moon was clear and high overhead. He told the tale of the first Texas trail drive in 1866, when Nelson Story and his hands brought six hundred head of longhorn cattle north to Montana. By 1883, some six hundred thousand had been turned loose on the eastern ranges only to perish in the blizzard winters by the hundreds of thousands.

"Texas cowboys was bullshit. They didn't own none of the land. This is the people's land. We got some history too. Crazy, snoose-eating fuckers robbing trains and the ranchers hanging them. Habitual killers." Mr. Frakes grinned, his false teeth huge and white in the moonlight. Blasphemous talk about the old, heroic, nineteenthcentury killing spree was clearly his forte. When it was done, he worked his way to his feet and wandered into the shadows, hunting his bedroll.

Bill Sweet caught a nightcap hit on the

whiskey. "Other people's cows. I've thought about your Slivers Flynn. The work runs out on you was what he said. Branding and fixing fence, seeing after the cows, which is the stupidest animal you can find. Partway he was right. Trailing cows, you can feel like you ought to be ashamed of yourself that you didn't do more with your life. But it's work that comes with horses attached, so I take it. I think of riding out here alone for a few days, and I do it. Margie, she don't mind. She likes this country with me or without me, she says."

At dawn a rattling old blue Dodge pickup truck came down a rutted, two-track road through the breaks. It was driven by a suntanned woman with a yellow dog in the seat beside her. Three shaggy-headed boys, brothers by their looks, rode in back, wedged between juniper firewood, camp coolers, and crates of oranges and boxed raspberries. She pulled up beside the fire where Rossie and Bill Sweet were back into the ham-hock and beans and sipping coffee from tin cups.

"Mrs. Bart," Bill Sweet said. "You're early." The woman was slight and pretty even if worn beyond her years. Her husband was Wilson Bart, who owned the calves they'd be branding.

"This is our day to put on the party," she said. "The boys, they wouldn't sleep."

"Them boys are thinking about eating calves' nuts off the branding fire," Bill Sweet said.

But the boys, eyeing the men with solemnity, would not give away a smile.

"It's going to be a fine day," she said. "People can load their plates off the tailgate."

"There's plenty of time for setting up. You better have a cup of coffee with me and Rossie. This fellow is Ross Benasco, come over from the Bitterroot to see how the good people are doing." He turned to Rossie. "This is Mrs. Bart, name of Gert."

Gertrude Bart colored slightly as she met Rossie's gaze. "Pleased," she said. "Which is true. Pleased."

When Mr. Frakes emerged from the weeds where he'd rolled out his bed, Bill Sweet tossed the dregs of his coffee, poured the cup full again, and gave it to the old man, who in turn wiped his mouth with his sleeve.

"Wilson tells me they's a hundred and thirty-six spring calves and a sprinkle of two-year-olds we missed last year. Three, maybe four of those two-year-olds."

Gertrude Bart turned away from him and smiled out over her shaggy boys. "This is one year we'll have a Christmas."

"Too much for an old man," Mr. Frakes said. "Better off I saddle up and go home soon as I finish this coffee."

"You got steaks in them coolers?" Bill Sweet asked. Gertrude Bart nodded. "But don't you think about it. Those boys will get the coolers up into the spring. We'll fill the water bags."

As Mr. Frakes rode away into the luminous morning, the smiling, mustachioed owner, Wilson Bart, turned up on a gray roper he called Bermuda, along with five other men who'd saddled up miles away in dark corrals before daybreak. Stirring a dust, they drove the lowing cows and dithering calves before them,

A fire was built inside the log-fended corral. Wilson Bart claimed his three Circle T branding irons from the Dodge pickup driven by his wife and put them on the fire, where they were heated red. Then he and Bill Sweet caught their horses while Rossie stayed to work on the ground. Newcomers roped only when invited. The ropers rode quietly into the herd as the men at the fire sharpened knives. Bawling calves were dragged by their hind legs to the branders, who seared a black Circle T onto their left ribs while men with knives notched ears and went through the quick motions of castration before tossing the testicles, to be cooked later, into a clean gallon can.

After most of an hour, Rossie pulled the hobbles off Margie's blue mare, tightened his cinch, shook down his riata, and went out to rope, and Bill Sweet and Wilson Bart got down to take their turn at wrestling the calves amid the pungent smoke, bloodying their hands. Dusty and sweaty in the heat, they drank from burlap water bags brought by Gertrude Bart and sharpened their own knives. The little crew was at it in such shifts until the last snot-slinging, young heifer was dragged to the fire, wrestled there, and branded, and the herd was turned loose to drift into the hills beyond the fenced pasture.

As the men opened bottles of home-brewed beer, and the Barts set up to grill steaks over the remnants of the branding fire, Margie came rattling and jostling down the road in an Army surplus Jeep. Another woman was with her.

"You drink up that first bottle of whiskey?" Margie called to Rossie, then she turned without waiting for an answer and shouted to the other woman in a voice loud enough for Rossie to hear, "Sister Hutchison, here's a fellow who's sure hoping I brought another bottle."

When they climbed out of the Jeep, Rossie saw that Sister Hutchison was tall and lank, with eyes so dark as to be ebony. She wore jagged-off trousers that just reached the top of her lace-up boots, and her black-and-gray hair was swirled into a French coil at the back of her head.

Margie marched off to help setting up the food, and Rossie was left with Sister Hutchison.

"Sister, you some kind of Catholic?"

"Some kind of twin. My brother died in Paris. He was Brother and I was Sister, growing up in Malta. Can you and I eat together?"

So she and Rossie sat alongside each other on a punky cottonwood log. They sipped at the whiskey bottle when it came passing and cut at steaks and spooned up beans.

"I've been on these prairies since I was twenty-three," she said. "There's no other place for me."

Her husband had died amid hedgerows in the French countryside just a few days after the Allied invasion. Staying on, she managed the grazing properties they had bought together, and she'd made ends meet teaching lower grades in a schoolhouse like the Exeter School, winter after winter, until the nearby children left and her one-room schoolhouse was closed.

"I never remarried because frankly I never encountered a man I'd want to wake up alongside of on a regular basis. That's what I say. Truth is, a lot of the mornings, I'd take anybody who had anything to say."

Rossie wondered why she had picked him to eat with and where this was going. "And Brother?" he asked.

"Oh, poor Brother."

He had been a schoolboy legend with his singing voice, and gone from Malta to New York with a scholarship at the Juilliard School and then chased his love of Baroque music to France in the late 1940s, where he'd died of whiskey and narcotics. "Nobody ever thought it would come to that. We never do. For years I didn't want to think about what I missed by not going to find my brother. In this country a girl wants to escape. But a woman finds herself located. I was a very young woman but I was located. Maybe, over much."

At that she stood, wiping her mouth on a white handkerchief. "Good talking with you," she said. "I wanted to talk to you about traveling. Margie told me you've traveled. I might have gone to Paris and saved Brother, but I didn't, I stayed here."

"Well, neither one of us has been to Paris."

She turned back to him. "We could have some drinks on your way home. Tomorrow or the next night. You could stay over at the ranch. That would cause a scandal but it wouldn't be like we were losing our heads and going to the Mint Motel in Malta." She held his eyes, unflinching.

Quick as that, the ranch or the Mint Motel. "I someways hope you won't," she said. "Our lives are quiet out here."

"I figured it out," Rossie said. "You remind me of my mother."

Sister's features lit up, abruptly amused. "There you are. The perfect getaway line. Do I sound like I'm talking mother to you?"

"It's the hair. My mother used to coil her hair just like you got it."

"Floats down to my waist. I brush it and see myself in the mirror and coil it up again. Aren't we the beauties?"

In twilight, the men caught their horses and rode off toward evening dusk. They would get home under moonlight. After Margie and Sister Hutchison drove off in the Jeep, Rossie and Bill Sweet were left with their bourbon by their fire. "You going to visit with Sister?"

"You mean shacking up? How'd you get that idea?"

"You see it. Anybody out here is bound to be curious about people from your end of the world. They wonder what they're missing."

"Don't think I'm going to be visiting Sister," Rossie said.

But in the night he imagined a dark, simple motel room in Malta and thought of Sister Hutchison naked, her breasts floating as she lifted her arms to brush at her hair. Ever so quietly he pulled at his cock and came onto his belly and thought that's that, one more time he'd been true to Eliza in fact if not in spirit. He again wondered if trueness mattered or if it was just a habit he'd taught himself so as to not, as Lemma had said those years go, fuck up his deal.

Driving home, he detoured over to Choteau country along the Rockies Front, for a look at the cliffs of the Chinese Wall up in the mountains.

"You were right, getting on the road was good for me," he told Eliza when he got home. "People over there don't like to think about living anywhere else. Makes you realize the sun don't set in your ass. I wondered what if you and me walked into the high country and stayed for a summer of grizzlies and shitting in the woods and eating nothing but trout and berries?"

"At our age," Eliza said, "people get tired and think new country is an answer." She sounded worn out rather than amused by his notion.

THE PUBLIC MAN

In June of the next year, Eliza asked Rossie if he'd noticed that Veronica was in love. Just out of high school, his daughter had transmuted into a lean, suntanned creature with contours of the kind men joked about in the barbershop. While the physical changes were obvious, Rossie had missed the signs, whatever they were, of love.

"Not much," he said.

"Your daughter, you should have. Don't be surprised if Lionel shows up this evening."

The once-upon-a-time Mr. Bitterroot indeed came knocking, wearing a sweat-stained denim shirt with the sleeves torn off to show his thick arms with their veins.

"It's about Ronnie," Lionel said.

Rossie didn't follow.

"Veronica."

"You caught up with her?" Rossie said.

"It was me," Lionel said.

Veronica's dark eyes were guarded when she came in from the pickup. "Lionel has a master's degree. I get to sink my own ship, and nobody can stop me. That's how it is with daughters." She smiled.

"This Bitterroot is just right," Lionel said, as if that remark might heal the moment. "All the stars at night, with the lights off."

"Sounds like it worked for *you,*" Rossie said.

He didn't come off his high horse until days later when Eliza pointed out that he, Rossie, had in true fact located himself in the world in exactly the same way.

"You caught up with a girl," she said, "and here you are, years later, puffed up like Daddy Warbucks."

"Veronica is the one who's puffed up."

Eliza smiled into her knitting. "They'll be married. Remember? I was pumped up. That didn't bother you. Congratulate your daughter and shut your mouth."

He hadn't bothered to look at Veronica, except with the attentiveness he ordinarily devoted to horses, as a form of solace. It hadn't crossed his thoughts that his blood girl might be lusting for the touch and stink of a man. He had never been jealous of Eliza and Charlie Cooper, and he had thought, for reasons he didn't understand, that covetousness wasn't a bone that had mattered in him. But the idea of Veronica bedding that boy sat like a twittering bird in his mind.

"She was yours," Eliza said. "Now, she's not. You act like you've lost a possession. You'll want to cure that inclination. You're disappointed with her when it's you that caused the trouble. Learn to be happy for her." She smiled. "It might take a while."

After the wedding in the Hamilton courthouse, Eliza gave Veronica title to the garden acreage and the orchard and lent Lionel the money to buy a double-wide, New Moon trailer house that he had set up on a concrete foundation at the high end of that property. He worked at developing his roadside nursery business and specialized in barnyard construction and European, raised-bed gardening for the cold climate.

At the Cliff House that autumn, the organic gardeners were swamped by a massive harvest and sold pumpkins and squash around the valley by the pickup load. Teddy called them "Lionel and the Lord's enthusiasts." Eliza wouldn't hear such talk.

"Who would have guessed that you and Rossie would make a pair, with your sarcasm? The place is flowering. Look to the sweetness in your sister's life. We should bless them."

"God save the gardener's wife," Rossie said.

Eliza looked away, trying cold-eyed anger but failing, smiling. "It's her life," she said.

From the pastoral island of Chiloé in southern Chile, the fields fenced by ten-foot hedges and wooden Catholic churches built tight as ships in the small towns, Corrie called and said she'd pledged to marry Benny Waxman, the archeologist who headed her research party.

But marriage between Corrie and Benny Waxman didn't seem to be an issue when they flew north from Puerto Montt for Christmas in the Bitterroot. With eyelashes almost white against his tanned skin and a flippant way of tossing his hair, this Benny Waxman was a matched set with Corrie.

Eliza shook her head. "They're not getting married. It's sport fucking all the way. They think nobody's looking."

Rossie asked Eliza if she was envious. "If you are," he said, "I've got a cure."

At Christmas dinner with all the children present, he offered what would become his traditional toast "to our little circus." But in secret he felt the show was Eliza's — a pissant notion, he knew.

"He acts," Teddy wrote in his journal that

evening, "like a fat-assed worm in Eliza's bright apple."

By New Year's Day Teddy and Veronica were off again to lives with children of their own, and Corrie had gone back to Chile, following her archeologist.

"What do you want next?" Rossie asked, after Eliza complained about what she called their "drooling aimlessness."

Eliza smiled. "Coming to terms with privilege. That's next." She insisted that service was necessary and essential to long-term sanity, soothing and vital as breathing. "We fall to sleep breathing one another's odors and we're tranquil — like that."

This was pure Eliza, Lemma's girl paying heed to the notion that anxiety could be alleviated by chasing significance. She'd long ago told him that girls who rebel against dominating mothers end up mirroring them.

Rossie wondered who Veronica, with her determined passivity, was mirroring. But he kept his tongue quiet and there evolved a standoff that lasted a week, until a former governor — a long-jawed, slick-skinned old man reputed to be dying — called and announced that he was coming over from Helena to "confab." He was going to ask Rossie to run for governor of Montana.

That, Eliza said, was "common knowledge among Democrats."

"Just keeping yourself entertained, aren't you?"

"Always have," she said. "Give us a smile."

"What a tin bitch you are."

"Damned right I am, little tin Jesus all the way. And I mean to call in my chips."

They slept that night in separate rooms, but in the morning she found Rossie reading the letters to the editor in the day-old Missoula newspaper.

"You owe me," she said.

This was a rancorous beginning, so she shut up and began breaking eggs for omelets — three for him, two for her — mixing in a chopped handful of chanterelle mushrooms and spinach from their dinner the night before along with chopped ham.

"You," she said, tending the omelet pan. "You owe me and I owe you. We owe each other."

Rossie held his silence as she set his meal before him.

"We'll do what we do," she said. "Eat."

She should have shut herself up, and she knew it. Rossie was not evading responsibilities. He trained his horses to be confident and sensible. Rodeo ropers from California and Texas paid thousands to truck his animals off to Cheyenne and Pendleton. Multiple winners rode Benasco horses in calf-roping and bulldogging and steer-stopping events across America. Not to mention the succession of young men from the Indian settlements over the years who lived in the bunkhouse or camped in tepees among the aspen along Kanaka Creek. Those men had quieted their angers and gentled themselves while calming the horses that drifted through the willow fields.

Nevertheless, she felt justified in thinking it wasn't enough to gentle horses in the morning and spend afternoons down at the county courthouse arguing over taxation and water rights with the other county commissioners. Horses were a sport, and though she'd never quite said such a thing to Rossie, she felt it was deadly ever to mistake games for a purpose. This was about more than Rossie. It was about her and her intentions, nurtured since her girlhood in Chicago.

The ex-governor came. Over coffee, after the veal chops, he asked Rossie to think about running for office.

"Let's be candid," the old man said. "Your wife can afford it and working people trust you. You do fine work with horses. People this side of the mountains are confident you'd take care of jobs. We've had boys out asking questions. People would vote for you. In the party we're certain we can trust you. We need fresh blood. We think you're part of our future."

"Who ever claimed his wife could afford anything?" Eliza protested, smiling.

"Dear, sweet Eliza," the ex-governor said, "we're all liberals but not indecently naive. I know damned well this idea doesn't offend you."

"Proud you thought of me," Rossie said, "but this hits me as a deal you boys and Eliza cooked up without asking me. A commissioner in the Bitterroot is one thing. Governor is another. I don't know a thing about the budgets or the national government except that I know we're pissing in the wind in Vietnam. Lyndon Johnson would think I was a joke in a big, white Stetson, doing a Tom Mix act and spreading bullshit. Besides, it's hard to think working people would vote for a man who got what he has from his wife."

"Sounds like Lyndon would love you, Ross. You won't lose, don't worry. There are plenty of people who know about issues. Governors hire them by the dozens. After the briefings, you'll know what they know."

"I never even graduated from high

school."

The old man smiled. "You rose from the corrals, and voters will respond to that. Think it over. There's time. It's something you owe Montana."

"And me," Eliza said. "Both of us, actually — me and Montana."

Days later, as Eliza gathered their breakfast plates, Rossie was still at his thinking.

"You were proud to be asked," she said, trying her old peacemaking smile. "I'm asking again, why not?"

"There's nothing wrong with how things are, that's why not."

"There's a few things wrong. It used to be we fucked. It was you and me fucking like skunks."

"Skunks?"

"Any time we got the idea. But that seems to be over. It's time for something else."

"Any time, like right now?" he said, grinning.

Eliza shook her head. "No chance with this girl."

After he was gone off, Eliza thought of following him along the icy road to the barn but instead bathed and lay warmed and naked on their bed, lifted her knees and stroked at herself. Nearing her ecstasy she remembered the stars, each alone and individual, hundreds of stars above the sodded banks of the Bow River south of Calgary and Rossie coming into her and her excitement on a summer morning when she went with Rossie to watch a blooded mare called Louise stand for a stud named Vernon. There was the squealing and rearing and futile kicking and heedless penetration followed by repose, horses quiet, neck to neck, before wandering away from each other as if stunned, and she and Rossie had without thought of anyone seeing coupled with each other on a ledge above the creek and then slept.

When she was done, her thoughts drifted to wondering how long it would take for Rossie to comprehend what was being offered by those old men from Helena. He would come around or not. But then what? How to be old? What if she forgot about him down there in his corrals, if in her preoccupation with this question she left him behind?

The bone-chilling and discontented weeks didn't offer much in the way of fresh snowfall. Day after day Eliza and Rossie retreated and came together as the early darkness began, sharing drinks and the television news in the kitchen while Eliza clattered around preparing their nightly sit-down dinner.

At half past midnight on January 31, the North Vietnamese launched a sixty-seven-thousand-man offensive against the Da Nang air base and thirty-six cities, taking the war from the jungle to urban areas. At a quarter to three on that morning the American embassy in Saigon was invaded by a suicide squad. Despite the fact that the Vietcong couldn't hold a single city, the Tet Offensive was a public relations nightmare. Seeing their troops confused, retreating, and dying on television, Americans began intuiting that chances of success in Vietnam might be misrepresented by Dean Rusk and Robert McNamara. When Eddie Adams witnessed the South Vietnamese national police chief firing a bullet into the head of a prisoner with bound hands, *The New York Times* ran the photo front page. Walter Cronkite returned from Vietnam to tell the nation that their leaders were lying. *We are mired in a stalemate . . . The only rational way out will be to negotiate, not as victors, but as an honorable people who lived up to their pledge to defend democracy and did the best they could.*

Rossie shut off the television. "What I'm really wondering is what in the fuck our politicians think they're doing."

Eliza shrugged. "We're powerless, and anyway I can't stand that kind of thinking. So I'll fry my other fish." Her smile was brittle.

For years she had insisted that the 1964 Civil Rights Act was evidence of an inevitable progress toward justice, and she wouldn't hear any other opinion. Through days of violence in Selma and riots in Harlem and Watts and Newark and Detroit, she had kept on with that insistence. But now she was ducking away from the evidence that progress was not, in fact, inevitable.

"We're dying on the vine, and right now I hate this country," Eliza said. "I've got tickets to Paris." She wondered if Rossie would go with her or if she should invite Teresa Robertson, the doctor from Boston.

"I'm with you, breathing hard," he said.

By March they were strolling on what Eliza called her Hadley Hemingway and Zelda Fitzgerald memorial walks. Rossie renewed a habit, begun with Otto Nelson years earlier in Missoula, of sitting at an outdoor, streetside table in the evening to smoke a Cuban cigar. They feasted on platters of Bélon oysters in the Brasserie Lipp, where the maître d' took to calling him Le Cowboy. Walking the narrow alleyways in snakeskin boots, Rossie eyed the Parisian girls in their silk, see-through skirts and high, Italian heels but more closely watched Eliza move through her sadness.

Then word came that Otto Nelson had tumbled over before a classroom with students seated even in the aisles. He'd been lecturing on the ruinous working conditions in a narrow mine shaft some seven thousand feet down through "fundamental stone" beneath Butte, and he was dead when he hit the floor, absolutely gone. Teddy read the Missoula newspaper obituary aloud over the long-distance telephone.

"So, here we are," Rossie said. "On foreign shores."

They talked of flying home, but didn't, since Otto would have laughed off the gesture as ridiculous. Instead they sent telegrams, wired flowers, and toasted Otto with a hundred-franc bottle of wine at dinner. The next day, restless in their grief, they undertook a journey and strolled along the river and the Quay Voltaire to the Musée d'Orsay, where Renoir's *Dancing at the Moulin de la Galette* — its lovers at a pavilion with yellow-green light bobbing on the heads of couples and children clamoring around them — struck them as a ghost of years and lives long gone. They took a taxi to the Cimetière du Montparnasse and walked the perimeter, then followed along the Boulevard Raspail to its intersection with the Boulevard du Montparnasse and stood before Rodin's enormous greenish bronze likeness of Balzac, a favorite of Otto's. They'd had enough walking and crossed the street to end their journey at the Dôme, with a stacked platter of snails and langostina, before taking a taxi back to the hotel for a nap.

"Sadness," Eliza said, "has to be walked to death."

That evening, on their way to watch children sail toy boats across the great circular pond in the Luxembourg Gardens, Rossie bought a bouquet of purple violets.

"Guess what?" he said. "You win."

Eliza looked up from the blossoms, her face alight with surprise. "Which game?"

"Governor."

She eyed him like he might be lying.

"Really?" Finally, tentatively, she smiled.

"It was Paris," he explained, over lamb shank at the ancient Restaurant Benoît, "and Otto." He marked lines on the tablecloth with a butter knife as he talked. "Over here, they eat better than we can dream of and they've got Renoir and Rodin and string trios playing Bach in the cathedral by the river, but still they move to Montana. It's open country that draws them. Even our share of hardheaded nitwits in the Bitterroot aren't banded up so tight as the people in these European towns, who've lived side by side for ten or fifteen generations. The wild ones run to America or Australia like Nevada boys running to Montana."

"Not so often," Eliza said, but he shrugged and went on.

"Montana is settled all it can stand," he said, "and the damage is just beginning. Anybody knows it, if they've got eyes to see. Bernard said that you and me would have to take responsibility for keeping the roof from caving in."

"He never said any such thing."

"It's what he meant," Rossie said. "What we want from France is traditions and talents, not the people themselves, in person, not many of them, anyway. We need cooks and artists." He continued inscribing the tablecloth with the butter knife, talking about outside money that could be lured to Montana and invested in high school teachers and summer festivals, rich-man money that could be poured into Yellowstone and Glacier lodges, and dude ranches and backpacking trails and Indian powwows, and old time-fiddling contests. Attractions, he called these.

"Hippies, drawing in chalk on the sidewalks, four or five colors, like they do," Eliza cracked.

But Rossie went on about pioneer reenactments, men sharpening Bowie knives and shooting flintlock rifles, casinos on the shores of Flathead Lake, full-scale operas brought in from the East Coast to Missoula and Billings, and cowhands reading their poems in Glendive and Big Timber. Montana could rework the laws that allowed mining and timbering corporations to ransack the pretty country and abandon it. "Here's our motto," he said. "Give Montana back to the independent people. Take it back."

Eliza was stirring cold coffee, eyeing him like an unexpected problem. "Baby, that's all sort of batshit."

"I'm talking about people with patient money, interested in hooking up to the future. Money from people in those apartments down by the river."

Walking the Île St-Louis, they had gazed up through second-story windows to lighted rooms where Parisian wealth lived, ceilings painted with angels.

"Open land will be worth as much as gas and oil. That's where the real millions will be. This isn't crazy. We'll have French restaurants in Miles City and Chinese merchants from India partnered up with ranchers on the Musselshell. Everybody stands to win."

"Auction us off to Chinamen? Don't think I'd try selling that one in the Bitterroot. Outside money won't cure everything. Maybe not even anything." But clearly she was taking him seriously, if not his ideas.

"Montana is nothing but outsiders all along, except for Indians," he said. "All Montana ever had was outside money. Bernard was outside money."

"You mean this, don't you?"

"All my life I've followed my nose. This is the next thing. It might keep us from altogether dying on the vine."

"We've kicked and battled," she said, "but we'll be all the way together in this. This could be our reward."

Ignoring this implication of mutual emptiness, he smiled.

Two days later, on March 13, the *International Herald Tribune* reported that Eugene McCarthy came within 230 votes of defeating Lyndon Johnson in the New Hampshire primary. On March 31, Johnson shocked the world by announcing that he was withdrawing from the Presidential election, and the next day an acquaintance from the U.S. embassy in Paris sent word to their hotel that Rossie and Eliza should get on a flight to New York. The note read, *On April Fool's Day Paris is going to turn unpleasant and dangerous for U.S. citizens. Chaos on the streets.* Then, as they packed, word came that Martin Luther King Jr. had been killed in Memphis. On April 5, as they flew from the night into sunlight over the towers of New York, they saw that Harlem was afire, sending vast plumes of smoke into the fresh sky.

"The house is burning down," Eliza said.

A month later, they heard that Paris had come unglued. Who knew where the trouble started — students throwing stones at the police or the police going after students without provocation — but when the students set barricades, the police attacked them with gas grenades. By May 13, protesters, students and teachers, and unionist workers numbering more than eight hundred thousand were on the streets, preaching revolution and freedom. By May 22, nine million workers were on strike across France.

■ ■ ■ ■

Even as the European and American mood soured, working people in Montana were enjoying a positive turn in their fortunes. The huge and plutocratic corporations that had dominated Montana's economy for more than a century were in decline. The nation might be sliding into chaotic sadness, but people in Montana felt they finally had a chance to build a society of their own choosing. They took pride in overcoming a century of robber-baron exploitation and loved their prairies and wheat fields and mountains.

"The roads end above our house," Rossie said, talking of the wilderness that ran along the spine of the Bitterroot Mountains and deep into Idaho. "Up there you're into the real world."

"The real world?" Eliza said. "You sound like the chamber of commerce."

But Rossie never wavered and was soon out on the road, traveling town-to-town and talking to Democrats. On May 30, 1968, at an anti–Vietnam War gathering on the lawns at old Fort Missoula, Rossie was introduced as "our natural candidate for Governor." He stood, removed his hat, and looked out on college students dressed up in clownish U.S. Army costumes and Frisbees flying across the lawns as the odor of marijuana wafted toward him in the twilight. Perched on a temporary stage wrapped in Montana flags, he began his speech. "Years ago I come to Montana with nothing but two horses and a passion for Eliza Stevenson. I owe her and her parents a considerable debt for educating me in the importance of freedom and justice and every possible reward for all the hardworking enterprise we can muster. And I owe a debt to Montana, a debt I'd enjoy the paying back. So I'm going to run for governor even if I can't stand wearing neckties."

When this joke didn't seem to be appreciated, Rossie tried a more direct tack. "Helping people make a living with their work in a way that doesn't tear down the house is my idea. The thing that most impressed me when I rode into Montana was the rivers and how far you could see, and the run of mountains and the way big territories encourage people to try seeking what they want. Those things still impress me. Corporations like the Anaconda Company and Montana Power ran Montana. They owned the newspapers and a lot of the politicians. They ran Montana like a fiefdom, and that wasn't good for anybody but them. But *our* independent people can take their state back. I'll support the workers and their towns. I'll take care of rivers and fields and forests. We'll have something left in the long run to be proud of."

Rossie recited Lyndon Johnson's words upon his signing of the Wilderness Act of 1964: *If future generations are to remember us with gratitude rather than contempt, then we must leave them with something more than the miracles of technology. We must leave them a glimpse of the world as it was in the beginning.*

"Lyndon Johnson was right on that one, even if he's dead-on wrong on Vietnam. We've got to preserve our forests, where the elk can bugle and the bears can hide."

Rossie lifted his hands. "You, you folks, tell me what you think. This is your state."

After a long rustling, an elderly man stood. "Some of us up in Lincoln been working on that proposition quite a while," he said.

"And you deserve success," Rossie said. "I'm proud to acknowledge the work of citizens in Lincoln like Cecil Garland, who owns the hardware store. Cecil and his friends are working to save the wild country outside their back doors, by the Bob Marshall Wilderness. The Forest Service and their timber company cronies see it as just more land to be logged, but some folks in Lincoln are determined to create a people's wilderness. Generations will walk the forests north of Lincoln and bless them. They'll bless Lyndon Johnson for the Wilderness Act."

Rossie reached down, shook the old man's hand, and then stood to face his audience. "Makes me proud to be here. We can make a good living without cutting every stick of timber, without clear-cuts and roads in the wilderness. Locals should be logging with horses, not tearing up the woods with D-Eights. We should be investing in furniture factories, door and window factories. They're doing it in Oregon, and they're on their way to getting rich. Meanwhile, we've polluted rivers with hard metals and poisons from the mines and chemical pesticides and fertilizers. We should cut it out. What do we want with more gold and silver? There's enough gold in Fort Knox to hold the dentists and precision tool makers for centuries. Has anybody read *Silent Spring* by Rachael Carson? You ought to. They got copies in the libraries. Nobody likes to watch the world die. I realize there are Montana citizens who are leery of change.

They think changes equal the failure of our proven ways, but change is how the world works. We've *got* to change in order to take care of ourselves. We have no choice. The great world out there is a goddamned mess. We see it on the news every night. There's not much we can do about that. But we can hold the line on this end. Here, in Montana."

Rossie gestured to the students in mock army uniforms, some of whom were responding with their signature, two-fingered peace sign. "I believe in taking care of our own but I despise this war in Vietnam. It kills people and erodes belief in America as a force for justice. Since John Kennedy was shot people have been trying to rebuild belief in America. Lyndon Johnson rode that impulse. But he ought to be ashamed of this bombing. Maybe he is, maybe that's his trouble, too much shame to swallow. The war I believed in was against the Nazis and Japanese. I've got a gunshot hole in my shoulder to prove it. But most of anything I believe in Eliza. She's my luck. Eliza tells me to believe in no chickenshit cynicism of any stripe whatsoever. I've had years working as a commissioner in the Bitterroot and that experience has trained me on the practicalities. I've learned enough about politicking to do this job. You'll see me. I'll be marching around, asking for your vote."

Oliver Wardell, the sweating former P-38 pilot who was running the program, came to the microphone in the quiet after Rossie sat down.

"Damn you, Ross," he said. "I'll buy you a drink on that one. That's the first time I ever heard somebody say 'chickenshit cynicism' in a political speech. We know what you stand for, and we sure as hell ought to vote for you."

"That wasn't exactly the story about the Chinaman from Bombay," Eliza whispered, after Rossie kissed her cheek.

"One thing at a time."

Rossie said he was "riding my horse down the street at the right moment," advocating a program he called "good people taking charge, playing a smart hand." Montana couldn't go on supporting itself through mining and logging and farming. The state needed to cultivate tourism and develop "a phalanx of value-added buisnesses to export our beauties to the world."

"Phalanx?" Eliza gasped.

The week after Memorial Day, Rossie was out on horseback, wearing a new, white Stetson hat and riding the back roads, climbing down and shaking hands outside country stores, talking, listening, laying a hand on some husband's shoulder, asking if hard thinking wasn't one of the good things, like everyday work. "People want decent jobs, and corporations off their backs," he announced. "They want their hunting and fishing preserved, they want to take pride in the place where they live. We'll have town meetings and pull in ideas from all over Montana."

Walking the hillside streets of downtown Butte, Montana's ruined empire city and the radical, working-class heart of his Democratic constituency, Rossie talked and laughed with a newspaper reporter who accompanied him as he shook hands. They met with a huge, shaven-headed man named Truman, a shift boss in one of the only remaining deep-shaft mines — the very one Otto had been lecturing about before his fatal collapse. When they entered the battered old M&M tavern an ancient humpbacked man, seated at the bar with two equally ruined women, turned on his stool.

"Here's the pretty boy," he cackled when he was introduced to Rossie. "Tell you what, good-looking, buy us a drink."

Rossie paid for boilermakers all around, even for the newspaper reporter. "There's spirit," the old man said, coming down off his stool. "A toast," he cried, radiating happiness, "to the Anaconda Company."

Shot glasses clinked.

"Fuck the company," he screeched. "Another round on the pretty boy."

The story of that toast to the company, under the headline "A Real Montana Candidate," made newspapers all over the state, only to be eclipsed the following day by headlines announcing that Robert Kennedy, having won the presidential primary in both California and South Dakota, had been shot dead in the Ambassador Hotel in San Francisco shortly after midnight. The psychic chaos had gathered momentum. America was increasingly numbed.

Eliza stayed in her bed for two days. "He wasn't anybody you could like," she said, "but I thought he was going to win. He'd have stopped the war. He believed in justice. Now we're hopeless. The motherfuckers have fucked all the mothers."

Rossie kept his feelings out of public statements. He hadn't liked the look of Kennedy, but he'd believed in his chances against Nixon. "There's not much we can do about the craziness out there," he told people. "We have to hold the line on this end and take care of things here in Montana. America is going to have to heal herself."

His Missoula campaign office distributed letters and flyers headed with a quotation from H. L. Mencken: *For every complex problem there's an answer which is clear, simple, and wrong.* "Simplicities won't do us any good," Rossie explained. "We need real solutions."

His horseback tour of western Montana accumulated an entourage which included a hawk-faced Vietnam vet from Browning, a Blackfeet man who rode his pinto horse bareback like the old warriors, three Irish miners' wives from Butte in an eight-year-old, rusty Ford pickup and Flathead farmers in wagons pulled by Farmall tractors, and horseback ranch boys sent out by their fathers. "We're running for governor," Rossie would say at a gathering in Plains or Polson. "Drawing a crowd, talking about the idea of a new Montana. Come join us."

A Bitterroot Valley rancher was quoted in the Missoula newspaper: "I've dealt with Ross Benasco for twenty years. You can trust that man to think his way past the idiots and foolishness."

Eliza was impressed. "Who would have thought?"

When the western tour finished after three weeks on the road, the Butte miners' wives led a caravan of ranchers hauling horses on parades through the towns on the eastern side of the state. Hard-eyed ranch widows and a variety of preachers and Chicano sugar beet farmers from south of Billings and city council members from Livingston and Miles City and Glendive and Circle and Plentywood came and gave their endorsement. Crowds got bigger and downright massive by the time Bill Sweet and Margie came to see him in Malta. Sister Hutchison was with them, her hair done up in that French bun.

"We could turn this into a circus act," Rossie said to the cluster of people in a meat market parking lot. "But let's forget the clowning and do the good work together."

"Paris," Sister Hutchison said when she and Bill Sweet and Margie got together with a bottle of bourbon in Rossie's motel room. She sat on the edge of the bed and shook out her French bun, letting her graying hair cascade down around her. "You're our ambassador from Paris."

"You got me there," Rossie told her.

"Sister," Margie asked. "You staying in town or riding home with us?"

Rossie was careful not to catch her eye.

"Riding home," she said.

His tour looped back through high-line

towns like Harlem and Havre and Great Falls, where the newspaper said the talk in the Bitterroot was that Rossie had been *a first-rate county commissioner. He's a public officer in touch with the people's needs. His secret is on-the-ground friendships with ranchers and schoolteachers, gyppo loggers and preachers, building contractors and plow-ground farmers.* The article went on to say he was a fellow who listened, had great foresight, and would be an ideal governor. When a national newsmagazine called him *a quintessential Montana man* he and Eliza allowed themselves to fantasize about a triumphant election-night ride on the streets of Missoula in the back of a red fire truck, the sirens wailing. She'd redo the governor's mansion in Helena, adding white wicker furniture to the patio for fine days and a felt-topped table to the den for the winter evenings and poker games. Over in the capital building Rossie would decorate his office with a silver-mounted saddle, photographs of miners in narrow shafts through rocky depths below long-ago Butte, nineteenth-century Blackfeet shields and beaded Gros Ventre moccasins, a Remington bronze of cowboys lassoing mustangs, and a print of Margaret Bourke-White's cover for the initial *Life* magazine depicting the vast concrete spillway at the Fort Peck Dam on the Missouri in 1936.

Back in Missoula at a Union Club fundraiser, Rossie smiled out over high school teachers, small-engine mechanics, framing carpenters, mothers who made their living sanding floors and painting trim, and hippies of various stripes. Behind him on the stage was the evening's entertainment: a sweating band, Janine and the Chile Teppines, which featured a bangled Missoula girl given to shouting lyrics in imitation of Janis Joplin. He'd been handed a bourbon-ditch.

"Proud to be here," he said. "Running for office is a pleasure, like eating hotcakes. As a man who loves horses, there's one thing I've learned: the horsemen I admire and the working people and hippies I admire are the same breed of cat." He raised the bourbon. "Let's drink to the future. Now you all ought to go dance holes in your socks."

Janine grabbed the microphone. "Come on, Governor. Let's you and me get sweaty."

Careful not to flinch, Rossie waved goodbye. "Got to be over to the Am Vets in a half hour."

As he went, a reporter asked if he regretted leaving the ranch.

"First place, I don't have any ranch. My wife owns dairy cows. Second place, sure, I have regrets. That Bitterroot is hard to beat."

Rossie had been ignoring his Republican opponent, a balding, dark-suited car dealer from Bozeman, name of Lincoln Hutter, who was known to turn from a podium and spit on the floor. At the rate things were going, it was working. Rossie was going to be governor, and the Missoula office became clogged with hundreds of calls from people who wanted to prove they were pals with the would-be Governor Benasco.

"There's so much a man can do," Rossie said on a call-in radio show. "Only so much telephone you can answer. There's not much I can do for people who are upset about things I didn't start, not at this stage in the game. Men from Billings want me to set up a golf weekend in Virginia with the federal money men. 'Hey, old buddy,' they say, 'how about setting us up?' They ought to be ashamed. We can make our own way here in Montana. We don't need to suck around."

Ashamed and *suck around* didn't play well in the newspapers. A druggist in the high-line town of Harlem was reported as saying, "This big man ought to come out here and try to make a living." Rossie was told that druggists in eastern Montana were his natural constituency — men and women who'd been to college — and that he'd damned well better start courting them. Towns on the high-line were dying, the economy drying up across the thousands of miles of the short-grass prairie running from Texas to the Golden Triangle wheat lands north of Great Falls. Reservation towns everywhere were even worse off.

Waiting for a statehouse elevator in Helena, the ex-governor laid a hand on Rossie's shoulder. "Ross," he said, in his hard, old voice, "it's time to shut entirely up. This election is in your pocket."

Rossie had been walking the marble-floored hallways in the company of oil industry lawyers from Billings and an economist from Bozeman — midcareer men with Ph.D.s from Pomona and Stanford and the University of Virginia — who were paying close attention to what he thought. Embarrassed in their presence, he brushed aside the ex-governor.

"Can't say I agree. We're into a high gear. It's time to get specific."

The old man nodded and walked away, a bridge burned but Rossie didn't pay it much attention.

With an eye to educating Montana, he took up reading from Adam Smith on what he called "the innate goodness in man" to honor students in Missoula. When he finished, a young university woman shouted, "Sir, do you understand that you are nonsensical? Don't you know that this world is rampant with evil?"

A New York newspaper surveying elections in the "square-state hinterlands" wrote, *Ross Benasco is a country intellectual in love with the sound of his own voice.* Rossie began saying that New York was "New Pork" until told that this wasn't universally amusing.

"You fellows," Rossie told a delegation of ranchers and mayors from eastern Montana, each wearing his own name and the name of his community on a tag around his neck, "you feel like you're out of the loop. And you are. We all are. On our side of the state we've mined and logged unto death but not quite, and now people want to subdivide the Bitterroot. Sure, I tell 'em: pony farms and Quonset huts and plywood subdivision houses from one end to the other. Good idea. Wake up. And over in the east, your buffalo are killed and speculators are still plowing thousands of acres that'll get the rain to support a crop about one year in twenty. The corporations and the railroads feed off you, and your family farms and ranches are going. We all know of towns with nothing in income but Social Security checks, nobody but old people and ghosts walking the streets. The boys with money keep you poor so they can call the shots, and you let them. People want to pity themselves and hate the government which is their only hope for relief, while the railroads plan to haul garbage from Minneapolis to dumping grounds in eastern Montana. There's people think that might be a good idea. Such ideas are a set of goddamned travesties. They are sins against Montana, you know it and I know it. Your living and way of life are on the line. You're bringing tragedies down on your own heads. Don't blame me for your troubles. I'm not the source of your defeats. Here in Montana we've been doing everything we were supposed to do in this nation. As a result we lose everything? We've lost all sense of how to control our fate and our lives, and with good reason we feel betrayed. It's hard to keep from souring on the vine."

By this time those men had gone wooden in their anger. A lawyer from Glendive called out, "Ross, we're dying and came to see if you offered any help. We didn't come for a lecture." The ranchers were putting on their hats.

A red-faced man named Bert Swan according to his name tag, who came from the Rosebud country in southeastern Montana, lifted his hands. "Ross, we got to sell something for money if we want to support ourselves. That's real simple, we understand. But the only thing we got is our prairies. You got a better idea than to sell the use of that space? Otherwise, it's sell the land altogether and go off someplace to town."

"You're right," Rossie said. "We've got to make a living without trashing what we've got, and I won't talk a straight-line tourist deal. We've got our pride, but territory is our one sure commodity. Ruining the country with mines and clear-cuts and polluting rivers and plowing up the prairies and, to top off the dumbness, cutting back on money for education — those are sure ways to lose track of the future. But if we preserve our beauties and educate our kids, people from around the world will be eager to pay their way into our economy. There's lots of folk who want to walk in the woods and jump up a mule deer. They like to eat good and sleep to the sounds of running water. Give them those kind of things, and we can call our shots. It's true, you watch. We can use our space to sell ourselves."

Bert Swan was putting on his Stockman's town hat. "Yeah," he said. "Singing cowboys on the streets of Miles City. 'Ring Dang Do, all covered with hair like a pussy cat.' Pimping for tourists."

"You think so?" Rossie was smiling like he'd got the joke.

"You're full of horseshit so far as I can tell," Bert Swan said. His pale eyes were bright and hard.

"Don't remember anybody ever telling me I was entirely full of shit before," Rossie said.

"You keep talking whorehouse ideas, you better get used to it."

Rossie had the sense to stay quiet while the men turned away from him.

That same month, a youngster named Abbie Hoffman published an essay called "The Yippies Are Going to Chicago" in a magazine called *The Realist.* He called attention to a movement that was committed to displays of disorder, like disrupting trading on the floor of the Stock Exchange and destroying clocks in New York's Grand Central Terminal. On August 8, the Republican National Convention nominated Richard Nixon for president. On August 20, a full-scale Russian army moved into Czechoslovakia with tanks and two hundred thousand men, demanding that the Czech leaders pledge allegiance to international communism. Thus ended the Prague Spring, during which Alexander DubcŠek had instituted liberal reforms he'd called "socialism with a human face."

Amid assassinations, burning ghettos, French riots, a profound sense of national futility in Vietnam, stoned and tattooed hippies reputedly wandering the streets of San Francisco and fucking whenever the mood struck, and Nixon's RNC nomination in Miami, this Czechoslovakian affair became the prime metaphor for failures everywhere. The American mood was divisive and rancorous as Democratic politicians readied for their own national convention in Chicago, to be convened August 26 in an amphitheater near the Union Stockyards. The issues were clear: racial, ethnic, religious, and women's equality; and what to do about the war in Vietnam. Eliza insisted that "rampant brainlessness" be included as she and Rossie prepared for their trip as unofficial delegates from Montana.

It was predicted that a million militant protesters would come to Chicago for a Yippie Festival of Life. But the Yippies and hippies, combined with the SDS and Black

575

Power adherents, numbered only a few thousand, and many of them were Chicago locals. It was rumored that they meant to close down the city, inject LSD into the water system, and send Chicago on a trip. But they seemed more intent on sport, dressing up in quasi-Vietcong outfits and handing out rice to citizens on the streets, floating naked in Lake Michigan, and nominating a pig for president. Nonetheless, Mayor Daley mobilized six thousand National Guardsmen to control the expected chaos. *Never before,* Mike Royko wrote in the *Chicago Sun-Times, had so many feared so much from so few.*

Rossie and Eliza arrived at the Conrad Hilton Hotel the Saturday before official events began. Demonstrators were chanting, "Revolution now!" The police were about to drive them out when Allen Ginsberg, ceaselessly humming "Ommmm," led them from the park.

But Rossie and Eliza didn't know of that. They'd spent the evening with Montana delegates, toasting one another at a famous steakhouse in the Loop, and only learned of the showdown in the park from newspapers over breakfast the next day. The conflict seemed like a joke, a comedy act.

On Sunday Vice President Hubert Humphrey arrived. A clowning and opportunistic figure, Humphrey shared Johnson's position on Vietnam and liked to be known as the Happy Warrior. Demonstrators moved to Grant Park and set up barricades of trash baskets and picnic tables. They flew Vietcong flags and the black flag of anarchy and the red flag of revolutionary communism, while calling out, "pigs, pigs" and "oink, oink" as the police moved in on them.

Swinging their clubs, the police shouted, "Kill the motherfuckers." They followed the demonstrators into the streets and took to clubbing bystanders, beating journalists, breaking cameras, and slashing the tires of every car in the Lincoln Park lot with a Eugene McCarthy campaign sticker. In the morning, violence in Chicago shared national headlines with updates on the Soviet invasion of Czechoslovakia. The festival of love was over, and brutal, blood-splattered mayhem would continue on the Chicago streets through three more nights.

In their room on the ninth floor of the hotel, Rossie gave up on the idea of seeking out jazz joints of the kind they visited with Bernard and Lemma in 1934.

"I learned civility in this town," Eliza agreed. "Now it's a shit house." Ordering room service and watching television, she sat there in her nightdress and refused to leave the room.

"We could go home," Rossie said.

"This hoopla is for you," she said. "Go see it."

On August 28, Rossie took a taxi out to the amphitheater, and stood in the back to watch as the Democratic party endorsed the Vietnam War and Hubert Humphrey, backed by Richard Daley, as their candidate for president. Thus they sanctioned repression. That was how Rossie read it.

Across from the Hilton in Grant Park, the demonstrators were exhausted, bloodied, and angry. A young man spoke and tried to calm them, inciting the police. He was beaten, then taken to a hospital as another night of clubbing commenced. Rossie watched from a window in the Hilton restaurant as the crowd surged into Grant Park, which stank and seethed with tear gas. Banks of blinding television lights illuminated the Chicago police and guardsmen battering away with clubs and rifle butts, beating on men who were bloodied and already fallen, dragging women across the asphalt, and in one case clobbering a child. The bloodied fell back against the windows of the hotel restaurant as they tried to escape. Glass shattered and they were inside, followed by police, who chased them into the lobby and beat them as they fled onto the streets again.

All this splattering of blood was on national television, seventeen minutes of unedited film. America saw the spill of its rationality and honor while a radical crowd in Chicago went on chanting, "The whole world is watching."

Rossie made his way through the abandoned kitchen, its floor slick with spilled grease, and up an interior stair to the ninth floor. He found Eliza with a glass of white wine, gazing into the Chicago night.

She studied the sprays of other people's blood on his face and his white shirt and poured him Scotch. "Snow on the moon. We could have gone home. I'm glad we didn't. Get out of that shirt. We'll have it framed and hang it on the wall, unwashed."

"Otto would have loved this one."

"Come here," she said when Rossie came from the shower. "You're shining like a boy. I want my hands on you, all over you." She threw the blankets back. "Come on," she whispered.

She was wet when he touched her and lay quiet as Rossie got above her and without particular gentleness lifted her knees over his shoulders and sank in her, rewarded by her breathlessness.

She awakened him in sunlight, crouching and sliding him in, her breasts swaying as she went off into whatever was happening inside her being until she collapsed, her warmth utterly soft. After a long moment she looked up, not quite tearful. "This," she whispered. "This is who we'll always be."

As they packed their suitcases, they watched Hubert Humphrey accept the nomination on television. Humphrey blamed the violence on the demonstrators' profanities: *An insult to every woman, every daughter, indeed every human being, the kind of language no human being would tolerate at all. Is it any wonder the police had to take action.*

"That rat-faced, tin-hearted, chickenshit son-of-a-bitch," Eliza said. "I'm a mother and a daughter and a woman. He'll never know anything about obscenities unless he looks in the mirror."

Back home in Montana, in an interview broadcast only on Montana television, Rossie gave his assessment of the ordeal. "Any fool there in Chicago, like me, would have been ashamed of his nation. Power makes men crazy. Lyndon Johnson helped the poor and blacks, but he thinks giving up in Vietnam is a personal insult. This fellow

Humphrey is lying and devious and sadly ambitious as man can be. He'll say anything he thinks people want to hear. Nixon is more of the same. The presidency seems to be a job only nut cases want. I wonder if we'll always have crazy presidents. Maybe that kind of work would make anybody crazy." As if he'd shared a fine truth, Rossie smiled, glassy-eyed, into the camera. "Voters want answers to questions which aren't answerable. They want daddies . . . Politicians who talk about complicated ideas are accused of equivocating, and, realizing this, they try to sound decisive while knowing there are no simple solutions. They talk complications in private and simplicities in public. It's a royal route to double-blind insanity."

Newspapers across Montana were horrified at Rossie's *schoolboy nonsense.* It was an insult to the traditions of American politics, an accusation Rossie tried to escape with talk about liberty.

"Freedom, racial and emotional freedom, cowboy freedom and women's freedom. They were taken to the junkyard in Chicago."

When a reporter asked if Rossie supported gun control, he smiled and shook his head. "You're not getting me on that one. We all know there are legitimate uses for guns, hunting and defending yourself and your liberties. But there is also drunks and crazy people killing each other. It would be good for everybody if we'd get the guns out of their hands. What we need is education. We've got to give up the idea of beating on people who don't agree with us. We've got to sit down and reason. That would have been a fine policy in Chicago."

The reporter smiled and asked if Rossie supported abortion rights.

"I support liberties so long as they don't hurt anybody."

"So you think killing a fetus isn't hurting anybody?"

"Everybody is hurt," Rossie said. "But I don't think you're talking about killing a human being. It might be saving a woman."

Eliza was furious when she saw in the newspaper headline, "Benasco Advocates Abortion." "This is suicidal!"

Rossie shrugged. "It's what I think. At least my horses will talk to me when I get home."

She mimicked him. "My horses will talk to me. You sound like a baby. Keep it to yourself."

Lincoln Hutter, the Republican candidate from Bozeman, went on the attack. "Benasco says America is crazy. But it's Benasco who is crazy. Benasco claims to be a man of the people, but he's an elitist, supported by a leftist wife, determined to destroy the corporations that have brought us a hundred years of prosperity. As a consequence of his policies we'd have no jobs and empty pockets. Benasco and his wife go to Paris in the spring. They consort with the Frenchmen in fancy restaurants. Montana citizens are left to feed on their country fellows like ravenous fishes in the sea. We have to take Montana back from schemers like Ross Benasco. He reeks of confusion. Voting for gun control could possibly be thought of as voting against death but advocating abortion rights is voting in favor of death. He should go back to his horses. Then his Indian name could be Runs Away with Horses."

"Ravenous fishes," Eliza said. "It's from Shakespeare. Maybe he's not as dumb as we thought."

The most legendary roping horse Rossie had ever trained was a roan gelding named Blue. "I keep track of that Blue horse," Rossie told a young woman from the Billings newspaper. "He dances like Fred Astaire, and he knows every second where momentum is taking him."

The reporter wrote: *Ross Benasco lights up when talking about a horse named Blue. Some think he should go back to his corrals.*

On an early October afternoon, Rossie was holed up in the Missoula apartment, looking down from a living room window on a cluster of high school children gathered under the approach ramp to the Higgins Avenue Bridge. A girl with hair in a bright-yellow braid licked the joint she'd rolled, dragged on it deeply, and turned to a gawky boy, digging her fingers into his neck, to pull him to her. She enclosed their mouths with her hands and blew smoke into him.

Hang on, boy, Rossie thought, hang tight. He held out his left hand against the sky, testing it for steadiness. He'd been enduring thoughts of his own mother sliding off, drugged against pain and willing to welcome the endless sleep. Evening dropped to darkness. The children under the bridge went on home, and recollections ran in shadows everywhere. He pulled the cork on twelve-year-old McCallum's Scotch and poured a shot over ice. After that taste of life, he would call Eliza to tell her it was too late for the highway. He'd say he'd dozed off, and no matter what her response he would catch the remedy of her voice.

On the third ring she answered. "You're

not coming," she said before he could speak.

No, he wasn't.

"That's not a surprise," she said, and hung up.

With another Scotch, this one lighter, Rossie accepted her anger and thought about going down to the Railroad Tavern, where he'd find men he'd known since the 1930s. They'd be in the back room at poker, smoking cigars, and would give him a smile when he bought a round of drinks and pulled up a chair. Then they'd be way down the road toward drunk by closing time and would want to come to the apartment and play on until sunrise. Rossie had been along that road and liked the idea that it was still paved, but not tonight. So he tried the cure that had worked for him the night before, punching the buttons on his tape deck until Bob Dylan and "It's All Over Now, Baby Blue" came up. There was an unforgiving quality in Dylan that Rossie liked, but he was sick of himself and of Dylan, and shut down the tape deck. Poor, old, sad-assed baby Blue. He'd go down to the Railroad Tavern and stay with it until daybreak.

But the telephone rang as he was getting into his windbreaker. "I caught you," Eliza said. She sounded faintly breathless. "I'm coming into town. Open two bottles of that

Heitz Cabernet. Stay out of them until I get there."

Surely what she hadn't liked the most, down there in that empty house in the Bitterroot, was the echoing of her own thoughts. She would be an hour on the road. He called down to the Delta restaurant and learned they had grass-range chickens raised by Hutterites. "Could you send one up?" he asked. "Tonight, I'm the cook." After opening the Heitz he stood in the pale-yellow light before the open door to the refrigerator, peeling the wrapping from a brick of butter for the chicken when it came. Finally he was smiling. His lifetime treasure was on her way to find him.

When the antique elevator bell clanged, Rossie pressed the little yellow button that would buzz the visitor onto the creaking car. He opened the door to the hallway and listened as the lift ascended, looking forward to the familiar exchange with a delivery kid who looked like Bill Sweet thirty-five years earlier. But the young, clean-shaven man who came from the elevator, wearing a gray stocking cap pulled down over his ears, was someone he had never seen before. The man's wide, blue eyes gleamed with what Rossie took for excitement.

"Behold," the stranger said, standing in

the elevator door to prevent it from closing. Then he lifted a small silvery pistol, took careful aim, and fired. The shock of the bullet into Rossie's left shoulder spun him sideways. He would recall only the man's eyes and the flash of light. Arriving minutes later by pure luck of the draw, Eliza found blood pooling on the imitation marble floor and Rossie on his knees. Amid his raking attempts to open the heavy apartment door, which had automatically swung shut and locked, he'd smeared blood across it and the walls.

After the frenzy of police and ambulance, their sirens howling through the darkness to St. Patrick's Hospital, where surgeons probed for the slug of lead and sewed up, Rossie muttered to the police captain that he had no idea who the assailant was. He had been drugged and put to bed when a nurse knocked on the door to the room where Eliza was sitting by his side. She was followed by Emerald Finnegan, a newspaper reporter who had learned her work covering the crime beat in Butte. Eliza had known her for years.

"We need *something*," Emerald Finnegan said. "We're holding papers all over the state."

Eliza shook her head. "We were very lucky.

Tell them that."

"Maybe not lucky at all. The shooter called the police. They were on the way before you arrived. This is just what he intended. Your husband would not have died."

"Would not have died?"

"Probably not."

"Possibly, probably, hell," Eliza said. "They shot him."

"Who's they? So far as is known, one man shot him."

Eliza rolled her eyes. "Tell them that we were very lucky. That's what I have to say."

The Missoula newspaper printed a confession received in the mail, postmarked locally before the shooting. Bearing no fingerprints, it was signed by Fenimore Blake, who identified himself as a resident of Plentywood, in northeastern Montana. No one in that faraway town acknowledged having heard of any such person. An official from Plentywood was quoted saying that "the shooter was likely some crazy, blaming Plentywood because of our sins." By sins he likely meant an election in the 1920s in which the county elected "an entirely communist slate of officials."

The confession began with, *Greetings from your future,* claimed credit for the shooting, then delivered an ultimatum: *Let this be a warning to you and your elitist kind. The consequences of scientific materialism and the leftist theft of inherent spiritual liberties have been devastating. We'll strike again, in more serious ways, unless you amend your irreligious federalism and consequent liberal social programs. We are determined to determine our own future. Benasco thinks he is a bridegroom but we will never be his bride. Darwinian fascisms will not be tolerated.*

"Whatever that means," Eliza said.

There were no more letters. The shooter and his phantom cohorts were never identified, and while initial reports in the national news described Rossie as a hero of suffering, within days his shooting was being discussed as a mere symbol of unrest in the heartland. Rossie's policies, it was written in a Chicago Op-Ed column, agitated the economic despair of the victimized poor, and violence was a logical consequence.

Rossie held a press conference billed as the termination of his campaign. "I'm ruined and out of this. I been shot twice, in the same shoulder each time, for pushing myself into places I didn't understand. It's too late for a Democrat in my place to have much chance. For which I'm sorry but there isn't much I can do about it. A lot of people don't want anything to change. I see how they think. Nineteen thirty-four, that was the great year of my life, should have gone on forever so far as I'm concerned. But anybody with eyes can see that standing still won't ever work. A sizeable number of Montana people don't believe in evolution even when their lives teach them to believe in survival of the fittest. I proposed changes, and that encouraged people to think I'm the devil's helper. Politics should be about finding agreement and justice. But it's more like football, banging heads. There's plenty about this country to be afraid of. I don't envy the man who takes my place. So, I'll finish with words spoken two years ago by Robert Kennedy, in South Africa."

Rossie cleared his throat, and read from a typescript, his cadences faintly but unconsciously echoing the Kennedy he'd seen on television. *First is the danger of futility; the belief there is nothing one man — or one woman — can do against the enormous array of the world's ills. Yet, each time a man stands up for an ideal, or acts to improve the lot of others, or strikes out against injustice, he sends forth a tiny ripple of hope, and crossing each other from a million different centers of energy and daring, those ripples build a current which can sweep down the mightiest walls of oppression and resistance.*

Eliza was smiling, almost tearful, but Rossie couldn't leave it.

"Otherwise, dreams of freedom turn into every bozo for himself."

After he sat down, she whispered, "You could have left out the part about bozos."

A university journalism student came up and asked if he'd been educated in the east like so many children of the Western rancher aristocracy.

"University of Neversweat," Rossie said, smiling.

At the breakfast table two days later, Eliza read from the Helena newspaper: *Ross Benasco, the martyred lion, wouldn't shut up and go with grace. He claims to have quit because of his injury but in truth he seems to be quitting in disgust, no doubt in part with himself.*

"I believed what I said," he told Eliza. "I was partway right and partway wrong." While in the hospital, he had lain awake before daylight and grappled with a mounting sense that his ideas about reinventing Montana were just another load of pointless nonsense. "Carloads of people have ideas of what's right to do, and most of them are cockeyed and trying to run the world. Drumming your ideas at people is bound to turn them away from you. I forgot all I learned from working with the horses."

Eliza drove him south in the Cadillac to California, where they rented a many-windowed house on a mountain overlooking the sea north of Santa Barbara. Together they walked the beaches and dined with the ranchers who raised quarter horses on the inland plains to the north — old Spanish, land-grant country turning green around Los Olivos. Maybe a dozen people would gather at a long table in one of the sprawling, Spanish-modern houses and talk of the stud horses and mares, their blood-lines and confirmation and whether these contributed to intelligence.

"Horse people, our kind," Eliza told friends when they got home to Montana. "Nobody mentioned the idea of extending intelligent breeding to politics. Not once."

BLUE

The summer of 1972, Teddy enticed Leonard Three Boy to come down from Edmonton and introduce them to the woman he planned to marry. Also, he'd noticed "a mystic and inexplicable demeanor has come over Rossie. You might help him make sense of it."

Leonard didn't make the drive until the bright, short days of late September. His new wife, when she stepped from their nine-year-old El Camino, lifted her arms to stretch while she looked around. Slender and graying-blond, she was got up in ballet slippers and a shirt embroidered with her name, Sylvie, and she was unadorned by jewelry — not a ring on her fingers — yet she shone.

Leonard was all leanness and eyeglasses and braids. "Here," he said, "we have my Sylvie Delmonico."

Sylvie smiled. "Not yet," she said, "nobody's got her."

Leonard lifted his hands. "I'm trying."

"We are," Sylvie said, "we're trying." She turned to Rossie. "We hope you can stand us. We're caught up in one another."

"You're looking pretty good. Think I might be able to stand it."

"You'll get used to this," Leonard said to her. "Rossie has an eye for horseflesh."

When they'd settled with the suitcases and were lunching on turkey soup and fried ham-and-egg sandwiches, redheaded Lionel appeared.

"Lionel," Eliza said to Leonard and Sylvie. "This fellow Lionel and our Veronica are wedded."

Lionel deposited a box of snap beans, beets, carrots, and kale on the kitchen floor. "Working," Lionel muttered, dangling his heavy arms and hands, no longer the blithe, chipper California boy. "Out in raspberry heaven." Lionel finally smiled. "The boys are boxing berries like they ought to be, even the youngest, just learning to walk. Winter's coming, the season is about over."

"Let it rest," Eliza said. "This is Leonard Three Boy, a friend from the old days. And his wife, Sylvie Delmonico."

"Raspberry heaven," Leonard said. "Sounds like a name some hippie Indian cooked up."

Lionel grinned. "Come down and we'll show you. Try some picking. But I got water running. It won't wait on me."

"Important and barefoot in his ditches," Rossie said when Lionel was gone. "Mud halfway to his knees."

"Veronica says he dreams about his gardens," Eliza said. "What if running water and raspberries materialized in your dreams. Rossie dreams of horses. He says they're as real as we are now."

Rossie rolled his eyes.

"Dreams could be as alive as anything," Leonard said. "I once met a Navajo medicine man in the northern Arizona outback who told me that each thing is part of a living whole, that the world is alive and everywhere holy. He said each name is the name of all things including the gods in the mountains. Which is where I climbed off the boat."

"That's where I would have gotten off," Eliza said.

"But I wonder. I was educated to believe that electricity is fundamental to the way nature behaves. So the flutter of electricity zapping around in our cortex is the essence of what's real. Seems like gods could live in the connections between our synapses.

Where else?"

"For Christ's sake," Rossie said. "Let's go down and look at the horses."

"You seem pretty sensible," Leonard said. "I got the idea you'd gone goofy."

"Oh, I'm good for picking a destination every morning and going a few miles horseback after my first coffee. There are times when I don't get to where I started for and end up sitting like a fool watching the eddies in the creek or find myself down in the weeds under an old railroad bridge on the logging line between Hamilton and Missoula, listening to the breathing and scratching of the short-term world."

"There it is," Leonard said. "Goofiness."

"I always thought it was a good idea to teach a horse to think. But too much figuring what you ought to be thinking, and you're in blinders. I'm out of plans beyond buying a couple of horses."

In the afternoon Leonard and Sylvie rode out with Rossie beyond the last field to a sandy-bottomed spring-fed pool called Fandango. The Salish had camped there for hundreds of years before they were driven off to the Flathead. Then the Bitterroot locals came in their place and left behind heaps of trash. Bernard locked the gates in the 1920s.

"This pool was forgotten," Rossie said. "There was bottles and rusted cans scattered everywhere when I found it. I hauled that shit out of here in gunnysacks."

They sat on a fallen aspen looking down into the clear water bubbling from under the mountains. Rossie told them he imagined people feasting on mule deer and fucking in the firelight. This, clearly, was a remark cooked up in advance.

"What I do," he said, "is study long-legged spiders walking on water. Stars or the sun, whatever it is, quit their whispering. Water bubbles up and I fall asleep. I come awake and the bats are out. Would you think a man like that was crazy?"

"Fucking in the firelight," Sylvie said. "The hippies said nineteen sixty-seven was the golden age of fucking. Doesn't sound goofy to me."

Rossie skipped a stone off the water. "If it was me," he said, "I would have picked nineteen thirty-four."

In October, Rossie and Eliza were off at the Montana Constitutional Convention in Helena when Corrie came home to visit, sad-eyed and lamenting her marriage to the archeologist. "I loved the look of his hands on me," she told Teddy. "He was so sun-

dark and I was white. I thought his hands
were what he was, that he was beautiful."
She smiled in a heartbroken way that
seemed learned. "But other women love
them, too."

After a dinner with Wilma, she wanted to
go walking in cottonwood leaves by the
river. Teddy saw what she really had in mind
when she began rolling yet another joint. "It
helps me," she said. She got it lighted and
offered it to him. "I smoke and remember
happiness."

"I remember," Teddy said, "but I don't
need your smoke."

She drew on it, deeply. "Daddy would
carry us on his shoulders," she said. "One
of us and then the other. Before Veronica
was born. I wonder about Daddy, don't you,
ever? What does he think of us? Do we make
him happy, or are we just things that happened?"

"Now we're on our own," Teddy said, "so
we don't happen so much anymore, I
guess."

"What was wrong with you and me?" she
said. "We were Eliza's projects. We were accomplishments." Corrie drew on the joint
again. "How about your real father, do you
wonder about him?"

These were things they'd never talked

about. "I don't know," Teddy said. She was staring at him. "How would I know?"

"You could know. You could be his child."

That night Benny Waxman called from Seattle, and early the next morning Teddy drove Corrie to the airport in Missoula.

"I'm a mess," she said, "but I'm going back." She kissed Teddy, close to tears.

It was curiosity that got Teddy to wondering about Charlie Cooper up in Edmonton, Alberta. What had Charlie turned out to be? What did he even look like? What did it mean to be his child? He kissed Wilma and their boys goodbye, left wheezing Lon Winston in charge of the store, and drove twelve long, highway hours into northern Alberta to visit Leonard Three Boy, who was managing an intertribal relief organization.

"What do you want with Charlie?" Leonard asked. They were sitting in his shabby offices on the outskirts of Edmonton, and Leonard was lean as ever, his braids flecked with gray.

"I got no idea," Teddy said. "He's somebody I don't know. That's my fault. He escaped or I did. Like he fell out of my pocket or I fell out of his."

Leonard told him that Charlie had three summers before gone to live with the Beaver

Indian hunters and trappers on a reserve three hundred miles northwest of Edmonton, thirty miles from what Leonard referred to as a rat town called Batch Camp. Population: eight thousand, composed of Canadian old-timers, cowboys, draft-evading peacenik hippies from the States, oil field roughnecks, and natives in a strip of Quonset huts and steel prefabs.

"He's up there on his trap lines. You could make the drive. You never know. Big spirits might be speaking." Again, the ironic smile. "Charlie and I both got where we thought we wanted to go when we were young. We got plenty of attention for it. But we stalled, we didn't know what next. Nowadays, I manage my accounts. Charlie runs his trap lines. We were boys with dreams, but our dreams only took us halfway. Eliza turned you into a white man in a hardware store. That's not the last step. Think about the next one."

"Maybe I don't want to take a step," Teddy said.

"Then why don't you go home?"

Teddy realized he didn't know the answer to that question, and spent the evening sorting out his thoughts in his journal. Sure, another two or three days would keep him away from the store too long. But he had long ago learned that excessive and endless efforts to order the world are evidence of excessive and endless fearfulness. And his worrying was a version of the same impulse. Had he missed the boat, making regret inevitable? Or was it that discovery and play unto themselves would equate with pleasure and happiness?

The next morning he called home and told Wilma he'd be one more week. By evening he was parking his pickup beside the Batch Camp Hotel and Lounge, a two-story, plywood building with peeling, white paint. He went inside seeking a man named Sammy Blacker, who Leonard had said would know where to find Charlie.

"Sure," Sammy Blacker boomed. He was a porky-looking fellow, his mouth flashing with gold inlays. "A hundred and fifty dollars. Take us two days. So buy me a beer."

"A hundred and fifty dollars is okay with me if you find him in two days or ten minutes."

Sammy Blacker ordered his drink. "A green bottle of that Dutch beer." It took several bottles and a case for the road to get going.

Thirty kilometers to the north, jolting on a rough track through a backland thick with ferns and second-growth timber, they wound down into a steep canyon until the road ended at the banks of a rocky creek.

"Not too much walking from here," Sammy Blacker said. "One more beer and we walk. No beer in there." After ceremoniously sharing another green bottle of the Heineken, Teddy and Sammy Blacker crossed the creek on the back of a fallen pine. They climbed rocky steps up out of the creek canyon and wound in and around the timber until Rossie spotted still water in a beaver pond gleaming through an aspen thicket. A string of smoke drifted above a steep-roofed log house with tufts of moss growing from the cedar shingles and chinking. Steel traps hung from wooden pegs.

"He's there," Sammy Blacker said. "There's smoke. We'll hang quiet. I got to call him out. We don't want some craziness."

"Cooper," Sammy Blacker called. "This here is Sammy. I come bringing you company."

Beyond the calling of a magpie there was silence.

"Son of a bitch," he said. "He's got a fire. But could be he ain't here. Could be the woman. Guess we got to ease on down."

They commenced moving carefully along the trail toward the cabin when a single shot from a small-gauge rifle twanged over their heads. In the silence, Teddy stood with one foot off the ground and Sammy Blacker crouched. The ravens had gone quiet.

"Cooper!" Sammy shouted. "This is friends. What the fuck is wrong with you?"

The answer came drifting from nowhere. "Just playing with you boys." The one-armed man in greasy leathers resting on a rotting stump off in the undergrowth was Charlie. His rifle was cracked open, lying across his knees. He snapped it shut. "Heard you coming a half mile away."

Sammy Blacker raised his hands, palms up. "This fellow says he saw you once before, when he was a baby but he don't remember."

"I don't either," Charlie said, slowly getting up off the stump.

"Me," Teddy said. "I'm Eliza's boy. You remember Eliza?"

"You're the boy called Teddy?"

"The same one."

This Charlie Cooper was not the man Teddy had expected. Later, in his journal, he would write: *One-armed, toothless. Mean if he wanted to be, a warrior in retirement, gone contemplative.*

"You and me got older," Charlie said, stepping closer to his son. He shook his head. "Hope you did better than me."

Inside the house, remnants of a fire smoldered in a cast-iron cookstove. Charlie looked into a simmering pot. "Mary made stew. She'll be coming back. Everything with her is pretty soon." He gestured toward the roll of tanned hides and greenish carpeting that lay on the plank flooring. "No chairs, but we'll have stew pretty quick."

"What got you coming here?" he asked Teddy.

"You," Teddy said.

The old man gazed toward one of the three dim windows. "Must have been. There's nobody else you know around here. What you wondering about?"

Teddy shook his head. "Wondering what you made of things. Who you are. Who you think I ought to be."

"What could anybody make of things? You been playing sweet little Teddy Bear? You got Teddy Bear buttons for eyes?" The old man grinned, holding it for what seemed an intentionally cruel amount of time. "What you can do," he said, after minutes of this, "is go cold and freeze and swell up like ice in the water and break out cracks in the rocks. Freeze up and break out. But way out here I don't think about being a shithead. I do the hunting, Mary cooks."

He gestured toward the gaunt woman easing in through the creaking back door. She was not old, her hair was clean and black, and she was silent while dishing steaming bowls of stew.

"Damn," Sammy Blacker said, holding out his bowl for another helping. "Charlie, you got the idea."

"High time," Charlie said. "Me and Mary struck a treaty." He placed his hand on Teddy's shoulder.

"Mary, this here is Teddy Bear. You know about Teddy Bear."

The woman smiled, her teeth rich with gold. "You come to see us," she said. "He knew you was coming to see us."

"What we're doing is settling before we die," Charlie answered. "Me and Mary give up on freezing the rock."

Mary was still smiling. "That's what he's doing. I don't expect dying for a long time."

"Teddy Bear, what I tell you?" Charlie said, and he was quiet for a moment. "There's not enough time. You got any cigarettes?"

Teddy didn't, but Sammy Blacker had a full pack of Chesterfields. "He always wants Chesterfields."

Faint, drifting flakes of snow flurried softly as they walked Charlie's trap lines along the creek. Charlie sniffed the air. "Be at it before long." As he showed them how he set and positioned the traps, he said that killing the animals he caught could get him to hating how he'd let himself get trapped. "Towns are the trap line."

Back at the cabin they ate another round of stew, and Teddy and Sammy, wrapped in the fur rugs, slept by the stove.

"Teddy Bear," Charlie said in the light of the morning, after he'd built a fire. "You don't want trap lines. Quick as you can, go out there and be sweet." He waved Teddy off, not offering to listen when his son stammered at an answer.

Teddy and Sammy Blacker walked out through four inches of snow, and after three long days of driving Teddy was home in Hamilton. He called Eliza and announced that he'd come back changed.

"Into what?" Eliza asked.

"Charlie walks his trap lines, and no matter what he says, I think he loves it. I take care of my hardware. Wilma takes care of me and the kids. She says it's what she wants. I'm lucky, so long as that lasts. But hardware, lately, is nothing but making a living. I mean I loved the store at first, the ten thousand specific things in their bins in the system of bins — each with a name. No mysteries. But I'm ready for the next stage.

Rossie did it and so can I. I've decided to try for Rossie's old job and run for county commissioner in the Bitterroot."

Eliza hooted with dismay. Indian bloodlines weren't often elected to office in Montana. "They'll laugh. They'll slap you on the shoulder and call you Chief. Behind your back they'll call you a quarter-blood bastard."

"Actually people might think a quarter-blood bastard is just the ticket. Without it I'd be considered an elitist with unearned privileges, but I've got the Blackfeet blood. People in Montana know what happened to the Indians, and they see that it's happening to them. Some of them will overcome their racism and think I'm okay because I'm an Indian and Indians are oppressed like they are. They might think I was a hell of a good idea." Then he hung up, tired of her apprehensions. *Trust Eliza,* he wrote in his journal. *She keeps the bees in our bonnets.*

Teddy started traveling the valley, imitating Rossie in his methods, up streets and down roads, knocking on doors, door to door, parking the big, three-quarter-ton pickup he used to haul logging cable out into the woods, and walking and talking. To the surprise of not many locals, he won, and

607

kept winning, year after year.

In Hawaii for the first time in nearly four decades, Eliza retreated to her rustic cabin after a daylong hike in the dry crater on Maui. She sat cross-legged on the floor and, sipping pinot noir from a plastic cup, wrote in her journal of the ideas she had been encountering in D. H. Lawrence for years. Until now, at sixty-nine, she had never considered them foremost in her mind.

The worth of marriage lies in disillusionment. Marriage confounds, and delivers us into the reality of solitude, natural separateness, to discover the true nature of intimacy.

The next day, when she read this aloud to the women she was hiking with, and a younger one asked if she ever said such things to Rossie, Eliza rolled her eyes. "Why? They said he was a failure at ideas so he went back to being a boy with horses. It's easy to say horses are a game, but for him it's life. He says it's his last turn at bat."

"They're all boys, aren't they," another woman said. They had stopped for a picnic on Waikamo Ridge, and Eliza — with good humor, even eagerness — poured herself another glass of wine and raised it to her companions. "We'll get our turns at bat, do you think?"

In the meantime, while Eliza traveled the islands, Rossie was towing an empty horse trailer behind his Cadillac on back roads across the San Joaquin Valley. He played the music of that countryside, a tape of Merle Haggard's lamentations he'd found in a truck stop before turning off the interstate south of Tracy. Bellowing along with "Tulare Dust" and "Shopping for Dresses" and "They're Tearing the Labor Camps Down," he made his way into the Tulare Basin, the dusty cotton field of what had been one of the largest lakes in the Far West before it was drained for agriculture — if you could call cotton a kind of agriculture, he thought.

He had driven south from Montana to pick up a quick little roping horse named Blue, a creature of twenty-one years and the best roping horse he'd ever bred and trained. Blue was old for a horse but still sound in the legs after all the cross-country travel to rodeos. The man who owned him and had retired him was a farmer and Saturday roper named Ben Ambler, and he'd told Rossie on the telephone that Blue wasn't for sale but Rossie could have him — he was the one man who could.

"I won't ride him," Rossie said. "I'm

heavy for that little old horse. But my wife might."

The price was one fresh-mint silver dollar. "I'd mount that shiny dollar in a plaque," Ben Ambler said. "Show up with a trailer, and that Blue horse is yours. I worry about him out in them empty fields. There's nothing to occupy the mind in cotton country if you don't have work. He's just out there thinking, remembering. Good horses don't forget anything."

The faint, snowy Sierras shone on the eastern horizon like spooks of mountains on the moon as Rossie drifted past great, empty, wintertime cotton fields and an endless scatter of rigs pumping oil. That night he put up in a plank-walled hotel in a field-worker's town. Across the broken highway in a tavern, he sat alone at a table, listening to the rhythms of Mexican talk from the bar as he ate the chicken-fried steak, drank cans of Blitz, and counted his blessings. But for the grace of Eliza he might have centered his life in this faraway, dusty, son-of-a-bitching flatland instead of Montana.

The roan, Blue, was abruptly alert when Rossie approached the next morning, recognizing maybe his odor or his demeanor. As Rossie stepped forward with a halter in his hand, Blue watched, twitching his ears forward but showing no sign of suspicion. "You're right," Rossie said. "They don't forget a goddamned thing."

"You got him," Ben Ambler croaked. He was a broken-fingered old fellow leaning on a steelwork fence.

Rossie handed over the single silver dollar.

"Too bad that horse can't talk," Ambler said. "We could run him for president."

"I tried that," Rossie said. "Made me crazy."

"Running for president? Was you already crazy?"

"Politics. I made a sorry show of it."

"Anybody would," Ben Ambler said. "What politics we got around here is the Boswell family, from mountain to mountain. The Boswells run politics. They showed up in the twenties and Old Man Boswell bought out the Portagee farmers along the Kern River during the Depression. Myself, I worked for Boswells for thirty years — hired and fired Mexicans and paid for this property." He shook his head. "There's no way of accounting for what's wrong with the rich boys. They set theyselves up like little kings. Boswells bought into the federal government and had them dam the Kern River and dry the lake for farming. It was a wall-

to-wall crime. Fields started blowing selenium. I'm pleased to see you take that horse
out of here. He don't deserve selenium.
That's best left for me and the Boswells and
the Mexicans. I could leave, but I won't.
Mexicans come up from down south and
don't find much rewards when they get
here. One of these days they're going to
come off those fields after us, me and the
Boswells."

"Selenium?"

"Poison, some kind of chemistry. This was
pretty a country as anybody ever saw, with
grasslands and flowers in the spring and that
big lake with the redhead ducks and can-
vasbacks. Don't see many of those anymore.
Blue herons and sandhill cranes, they're
gone. So you got out of politics?"

"Went sane," Rossie said. "But I kept
thinking that I should have gone back after
the bastards instead of quitting like a chickenshit."

"Stay at it long enough and you'll turn
into a pure-bred bastard," Ben Ambler said.
"That's what it looks like. The best ones go
sour or get out early. We better load up that
horse and send you on your way."

The road to Montana was four days on
interstate highways. Rossie had it timed so
Eliza would be home from Hawaii on the

same autumn afternoon as his return, and indeed she was down to greet him when he came driving in through the dusty twilight to pull up before his cork-floored barn in the Tailfeather Field. Without a word of hello, except for her look, she came to help him let down the tailgate.

"Anyway," Rossie said, "he's yours. For you to ride around on. Smartest horse you ever saw, he's yours and for nobody else."

Together they unloaded that Blue horse into a corral where he'd once upon a time been introduced to Rossie and roping.

"Horses," he said, grinning at Eliza, as if he was echoing some country song, "look good on you."

Her face lit up, and why not? He'd meant it, and saw she was pleased.

EPILOGUE: FANDANGO

In 1991 Teddy announced his retirement. He'd been county commissioner in the Bitterroot for seventeen years, running for reelection every other autumn, trekking out on winter nights to explain bond issues at school board meetings, then convening at breakfasts on winter mornings to discuss the funding for a sewage treatment plant. He'd listened to the endless tirades, semicoherent anger, and smooth-talking hustle and negotiated and renegotiated and called bluffs.

Bitterroot people filled the Elks Club ballroom in Hamilton for Teddy's farewell speech: "Bricks get laid one at a time. Each brick is part of getting the work done. Houses get built brick by brick, one at a time. I'd like to think I've helped build the house we have here in the Bitterroot. There's a story about a young girl skipping across the Red Wolf Crossing of the Snake River on the backs of the sockeye salmon. Which now, of course, are extinct in that river. My whole life I've wanted to dance with that girl and go to powwows and watch fancy dancers and drummers and hang around by the chutes at rodeos and join boys and girls down by the river while the fish jump. I've been playing white man. Now I'm going Indian. I'm giving up on what might have been or ought to be and living with what we've got."

That same spring, Eliza and Rossie received an invitation from Mattie, who was putting on a gathering out at the Neversweat on the Fourth of July, to celebrate Slivers "while he's still kicking." Eliza hadn't ever seen that country, and Rossie hadn't been back all those fifty-seven years. So sure as hell they were going.

Mattie had been married to a field geologist named Peter Gottaka. They'd lived twenty-eight years in Elko and raised six redheaded girls, five of them married and "off into California" and the other a single mother dealing blackjack in Las Vegas. When Peter Gottaka died from colon cancer, Mattie had gone back to the Neversweat, where she could keep an eye on Slivers.

"Thirteen grandchildren," she promised.

"They'll be here. Along with what's left of the old Nevada boys. Hope you and your kids can come. It would be a good thing."

Rossie held up a photograph Mattie had enclosed, displaying a life-sized horse sculpted of woven willow switches. "Damndest thing," he said. "You can see the horse in those willow sticks, like it was alive."

"I've seen them on lawns in Beverly Hills," Eliza said.

"There's no keeping up with California."

In June, before the trip to Nevada, Teddy inscribed in his journal a line from the letter Leonard Three Boy had sent from Edmonton. *This visit will be ancestor worship.* He wouldn't be coming. *Your people are no longer my life.* Leonard had written in what Teddy thought of as his Native vein. Leonard had also written that the journal in which Teddy recorded the trip might be titled *Cadillac Happiness.* Teddy smiled as he copied that down, then added his own two cents. *In the desert I will be the man upon whom nothing is lost.* He liked this, his own nonsense.

Long ago, when Lemma learned that he collected coils of psychological memory, which she called "archives," she told him that recording memories was a sacred duty, and she quoted a line from what he guessed was poetry. *The heart has reasons that reason knows nothing of.* Then she laughed about reasons the heart doesn't want to think about.

Veronica and Lionel and their girls and Corrie and her archeologist husband and Wilma and the boys were flying in to Reno and renting cars for the drive to the Neversweat on the morning of the Fourth of July. But Eliza and Rossie and Teddy were traveling the old horse-drive route from the Bitterroot, through the Oregon deserts to Eagleville and on south in the Cadillac. Teddy insisted on doing the driving, as Rossie and Eliza would beyond doubt fall into quarreling after days alone together on dusty roads, and besides, Teddy wanted to come along to see the territory he'd heard about so often, and anyway they were old.

On the first day of July he took them east on Interstate 90, then south from Butte on Interstate 15 into Idaho at Monida Pass, where the horse herd had stayed a night and Jap Hardy had said, "She's all of it grass from here to Calgary." They cut through the lava bed moonscape below Arco and detoured for a night in the Sun Valley Lodge, as Eliza wanted to try a sleep in room 333, where Hemingway had holed up to finish *For Whom the Bell Tolls.* Past Boise, they crossed over the Snake River, where traffic had been held up while the horses crossed a rickety, long since demolished bridge and a woman in a green dress had photographed Jap Hardy. Then they headed off across a hundred and fifty miles of undulating sage hills before turning south at Burns, toward the highlands of Steens Mountains and the wetlands of the Malheur Wildlife Refuge. At Peter French's barn, its conical, shingled roof still intact, Rossie broke out crystal glasses and uncorked a sixty-dollar bottle of Willamette Valley Pinot Noir. In a slant of sunlight falling across the red-juniper center post, Rossie proposed a toast. "Right here is where we stood," he said. "Drink to them boys heading out."

"How do you see them?" Eliza asked. "How do they look?"

"Just them boys," Rossie said. "Suppose they're dead." Bill Sweet, for sure, had been dead eleven years, of the liver cancer. At his funeral Rossie said he'd know him out in the far reaches. "Tarz and Jap Hardy and Dickie Wilson are anyway old as angels if they're still alive. Jap Hardy brought me in here, stood where we're standing, and told me the Peter French story about breaking horses indoors in the wintertime."

"The only one of them I knew was Bill Sweet," Eliza said. "How did he look, those first days?" She sipped at her wine.

"Looked same as he did when you saw him. Slick-haired blond fellow."

"There's more than that."

"Suppose there is," Rossie said. "But I can't recall it."

"Or won't."

"Goddamn it," Rossie said. "Leave it alone."

"Fine," Eliza said. "There you were, before a post."

Teddy wondered if he should say some stupid anything about distances accumulating but didn't. They were that night in the Frenchglen Hotel under its enclosure of Lombardy poplar and by sunrise had negotiated a dozen dusty miles of washboard gravel to the top of Steens Mountain, a ten-thousand-foot fault block sloping from the deserts to drop a precipitous mile down to the alkaline playa of the Alvord Desert on the east side. On the uppermost ridge they lifted their arms and cast feathering shadows over the deserts of Catlow Valley.

"Kings of the mountain," Eliza said.

"And the queen," Teddy said.

"Never saw this before," Rossie said. That was it from him.

At Roaring Springs, where Rossie and the others had tromped out barefoot and naked through skunk cabbage and bathed in the icy water of a sand-bottomed spring, they confronted a padlocked gate.

"Bill Sweet told us that water was cold and clean as heaven," Rossie said. "Tarz said he always thought heaven was slick and pink like a pussy. Something like that."

"There they were," Eliza said.

They dusted along the edge of Catlow Valley to Denio — its houses left from the early days, plus a service station and tavern combined, then west across the Sheldon Wildlife Refuge, on gravel roads built by the Civilian Conservation Corps during the Depression. On the bed of a dry wet-weather lake, they found antelope drifting in groups of two or eleven or in dozens. In Eagleville, the hotel had been torn down, and they traveled to Gerlach in silence, air conditioning turned up high in order to keep out the dust.

"Dust and lava rock," Eliza said. "But you're remembering what's gone. Is that why you won't say anything?"

"We're seeing plenty," Rossie said. "What about them antelope? When's the last time you saw so many antelope?"

How could they manage to stay so strange

to each other after five decades? But maybe this was just more of their ordinary struggling, dating back to the start of things.

The pitted highway across greasewood flats was paved all the way to the gates of the Neversweat. Poplar and silver cottonwood still boxed the yard. Russian olive and apple and peach trees were planted in a grove behind the whitewashed ranch house, which pitched east like a grounded ship on the edge of hayfields after years of winter winds. The bunkhouse where Rossie had first unloaded his saddle and bedroll, where Nito had shaken his hand and had said, "Loneliness cures," was sided with dusty white plastic shingles.

Mattie, barelegged in a pale-green dress, was holding the screen door open with her back and rocking a vividly redheaded baby in her arms as they drove up. She came to them carrying the baby, her own hair gone nearly white. "So you got here," she said. "Fifty years."

This was for Rossie. Teddy thought it was a thing she'd been waiting half a century to say.

"Sure did," Rossie said.

Mattie held up the big-eyed baby. "This is Lorene. Isn't she a beauty? I've had her two weeks. Her mother's coming from Las Vegas this weekend to take her home." She focused on Teddy. "You were the baby," she said. "You broke my heart."

Slivers waited in a rocking chair, so very old, waiting and shaved slick, with what remained of his hair sharply combed. His eyes were entirely on Rossie. "Thought you'd got away."

"Where the hell do you keep your horses?" Rossie asked.

Slivers grinned. "In the willows. All the horses worth a shit are the ones I remember."

Teddy boosted suitcases upstairs to the plain, board-walled bedrooms and returned to find them sitting in silence in a room with braided rugs over a linoleum floor, like they had forgotten language.

"You remind me," Teddy said, "of Buddhists in Missoula. They spend a lot of time thinking things over."

This didn't take well until Slivers said, "Better than most of them schoolhouse preachers."

"Let me show you *my* church," Mattie said, as if this had reminded her, and she gathered good-baby Lorene into her arms and led them past the old dining hall where the cowhand crew had eaten when they were around and through the kitchen into the addition where she lived. Its huge windows looked beyond yellowing hay meadows to the Bloody Run Mountains. On a plywood sheet in the middle of the floor there stood a half-built, life-size horse — haunches curving with muscle, its muzzle down as if to feed — constructed of willow switches but coming alive. "This is where I find my horses," Mattie said.

Alongside knives and a hatchet on a battered workbench lay sprays and tufts of multicolored feathers, vivid green and red, which had come from parrots in Mexico.

"I'm lighting my horses up with feathers. It's a new thing. So here you have me, every morning, my job. This last week, it's been with Lorene on the floor."

"Can't think what prices she gets," Slivers said.

Rossie touched at the half-built horse, and Mattie told them her husband had been a hunter, crazy about shooting ducks and geese off the marshes below the Ruby Mountains beyond Elko. He'd shown her duck decoys, preserved in desert caves, that had been woven from tule reeds by the ancient Shoshone.

"Poorest people in the world," Mattie said. "In terms of objects."

She'd made little animals out of tule reeds

— cats and dogs and chickens — and sold them at craft fairs. It was Slivers who had said she could make a horse out of willow switches.

"First horse took the winter. I'm faster now. They're my babies. I know who bought every one and where they are."

"Redheaded as she ever was," Silvers said. "Why don't we run that Cadillac? Won't hurt the son of a bitch. We could hunt up those horses."

All five of them — six, counting baby Lorene — went cruising over stubble fields to find a dozen geldings grazing among the willows.

"Pretty cute," Rossie said. "I was wondering what become of Tarz Witzell."

"Couldn't guess, haven't thought of Tarz in thirty years."

Upstairs in late afternoon, Eliza lay alone in her nightdress on a creaking, iron-framed double bed in the bare room she shared with Rossie. Partly unpacked suitcases lined the wall, and the shades were pulled against the brightness. Listening to feathered voices from downstairs, Eliza was dismayed by the feeling that Rossie was whole only in this backland.

Reno had certainly never been his home. Over the years he would stop and see Katrina and Nito on his way to and from California, and they had come to Montana every few years for Christmas or the Fourth of July, but Rossie had never talked of special trips to see them. Then on a September morning, he'd told her it was necessary that he fly down to Sacramento. It was, he said, "business." After three days of silence, he called to tell her, to Eliza's surprise and dismay — because he hadn't prepared her at all — that he'd really been in Reno, to witness Katrina's death, her final gasping as she slid out into depths caused by the drugs being used to mediate the agony of pancreatic cancer. He'd be home, he said, soon as he'd attended to her burial in the old pioneer cemetery in Carson City, and had "got Nito settled."

What could she say? When she stammered at him, he cut her off.

"Never mind. Stay where you are. This is mine to deal with."

As it worked out, he shipped home a walnut case containing Katrina's sixteen-place setting of table silver, signed some papers authorizing the sale of her house on the banks of the Truckee, left her scarves and dresses hanging in closets, and moved his father into a rest home in the care of a male nurse named Carlos. After two days back in Montana, during which he had been utterly unwilling to speak of those last days in Reno, word came that Nito had died, and finally Rossie broke silence.

"I should have been there," he said, and he told Eliza of telling Nito that Katrina was gone and how Nito had responded, sitting at the dining room table dealing hands of blackjack to no one and unable to recall even his own name. "Who would have thought he'd go so soon?"

Then Rossie had calmly telephoned a Basque club in Reno and persuaded those good men to go out at three in the morning, when the city police weren't looking, and cast Nito's ashes into the Truckee River as it flowed by the old Riverside Hotel.

Rossie had left his mother and father behind and embraced Eliza's family and life among northern rivers and mountains. Those were the bargains. Those deals, which had started as makeshift, she understood, were now their lives.

That night, after their gin, when the pot roast was sliced and eaten, Mattie poured them coffee with shots of bourbon alongside and then turned to Teddy. "Your natural father," she said. "I heard he froze to death?"

"Out by the highway, north of Edmonton.

Nobody knew for weeks. They found him frozen in a pile of snow thrown up by the plows. He went off drunk, hitchhiking, after Mary died. Anyway, he was freezing to death all his life, trying to crack rock. That's what he told me. Cracking rock. Most of us don't see everything as bullshit like he did. Or anyway we look away."

After a moment, Mattie asked Rossie about the man who had shot him. "Did they ever find him?"

"No, but he done his job. Shucked me out. I used to watch, day after day, for a man with a gun. But I've turned the game over. I pretend I'm invisible."

"Oh, hell," Mattie said, "somebody tell us a happy story." She went on herself, telling of magpies chattering in cottonwoods as she hiked across the meadows to the Hog House, which was still standing. "That's a story. I go walking and I pick flowers. I've swept out the ratshit and mopped the floors. Widow woman, mopping up in her memories."

"Well, then," Rossie said, and he lifted a toast to Mattie and little Lorene and to Slivers and Teddy and Eliza. "Not long after I left, up in the Canadian Rockies," he said, "a man named Bob Waters told me he thought maybe women and men were too strange for one another. But I've come to think maybe that's why they stick together, always trying to make sense of the other one. Here's to strangeness."

"Plumb drunk," Teddy said, grinning at Slivers.

But Rossie was started. He talked about the bay mare named Katrina, after his mother, and evenings of just him and the mare, dry snow lifting behind her hooves, before the war. He drifted on to talking about the shadows that ran everywhere, the dead walking and talking like they were real. He told of Eliza on her white horse beside the Bow River. "It was all pure luck. There's no getting back to it."

What did they see? Teddy Blue watched as Eliza touched Rossie's hand.

"You," she said. "Tomorrow's a big day. The kids are going to be here and everybody. That'll be a happy story. Time to get upstairs and out of those clothes."

Mattie went alert like a startled bird. So, it never ends. Teddy imagined watching a redheaded girl stride across the willow fields, her green dress luminous in the morning sunlight and flowers in her fists. What could heal the abrasions suffered and delivered while going off to be your own man with horses?

ACKNOWLEDGMENTS

This is to thank, first of all, my companion, Annick Smith, who talked me through it over the years, and read and reread the manuscript. And then, Amanda Urban, who offered her wise counsel over and over. And then, David James Duncan, who read the manuscript so carefully and offered crucial advice. And for certain, Gary Fisketjon, who took a chance on an aging first novelist, then helped develop the story, and finally cleaned it up with his legendary pencil. And Liz Van Hoose, whose patience and intelligent taste saw me through the countless revisions, and Kevin Bourke, whose copyediting was immaculate. All possible gratitude to all of you.

ABOUT THE AUTHOR

William Kittredge is the author, most recently, of *The Nature of Generosity,* and with Annick Smith he edited *The Last Best Place: A Montana Anthology.* He grew up in Oregon and now lives in Missoula, where for many years he taught at the University of Montana.

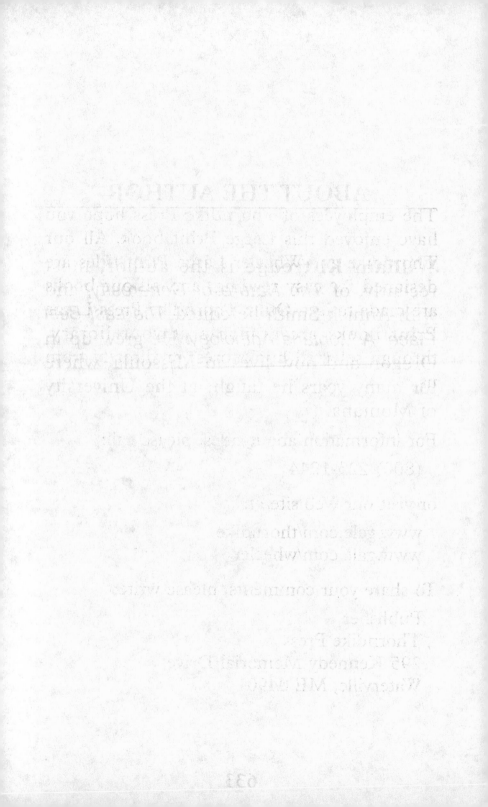

The employees of Thorndike Press hope you have enjoyed this Large Print book. All our Thorndike and Wheeler Large Print titles are designed for easy reading, and all our books are made to last. Other Thorndike Press Large Print books are available at your library, through selected bookstores, or directly from us.

For information about titles, please call:
(800) 223-1244

or visit our Web site at:
www.gale.com/thorndike
www.gale.com/wheeler

To share your comments, please write:
Publisher
Thorndike Press
295 Kennedy Memorial Drive
Waterville, ME 04901